Hi, it's Dianne from Star Talk magazine. Would you be available for an interview?

7:59AM

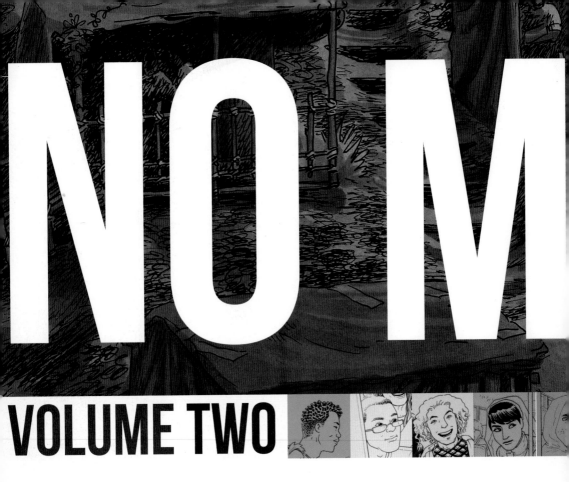

NO M

VOLUME TWO

NO MERCY, VOL 2. First Printing. JUNE 2016. Published by Image Comics, Inc. Office of publication: 2001 Center Street, 6th Floor, Berkeley, CA 94704. Copyright © 2016 Alex de Campi and Carla Speed McNeil. All rights reserved. Originally published in single magazine form as NO MERCY #5-9. NO MERCY™ (including all prominent characters featured herein), its logo and all character likenesses are trademarks of Alex de Campi and Carla Speed McNeil, unless otherwise noted. Image Comics® and its logos are registered trademarks of Image Comics, Inc. No part of this publication may be reproduced or transmitted, in any form or by any means (except for short excerpts for review purposes) without the express written permission of Image Comics, Inc. All names, characters, events and locales in this publication are entirely fictional. Any resemblance to actual persons (living or dead), events or places, without satiric intent, is coincidental. PRINTED IN THE U.S.A. For information regarding the CPSIA on this printed material call: 203-595-3636 and provide reference # RICH – 680780. For international rights, contact: foreignlicensing@imagecomics.com
ISBN: 978-1-63215-690-7

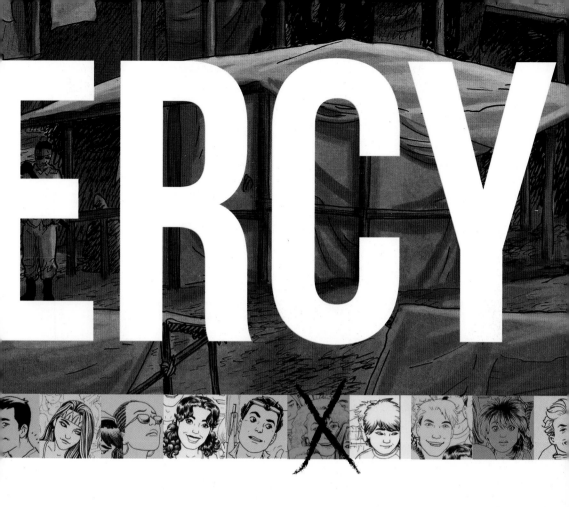

ERCY

ALEX DE CAMPI
CARLA SPEED MCNEIL
JENN MANLEY LEE
AND FELIPE SOBREIRO

WITH SUPPLEMENTAL DESIGN BY SASHA HEAD

CHAPTER FIVE

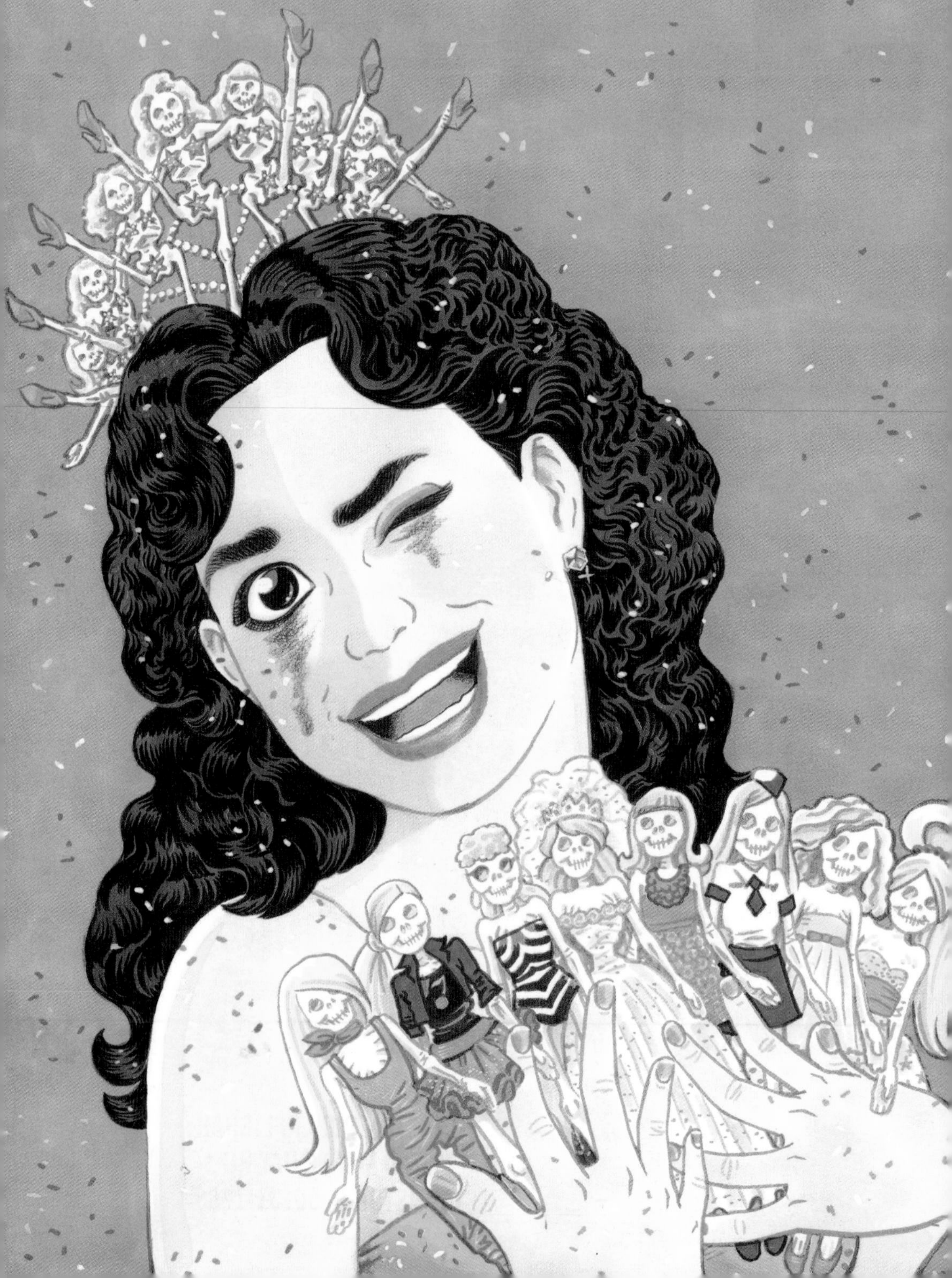

OHHH GOD DON'TLOOKUP DON'TLOOKUP I'MNOTUPHERE PLEAAASE

AAH!

WAIT!

NNUU

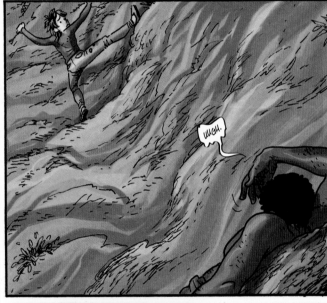

DESHAWN! DON'T MOVE! THEY'RE GONNA KILL EVERYONE!

UUGH.

BRRT BRRT

STOP! HER LEG--

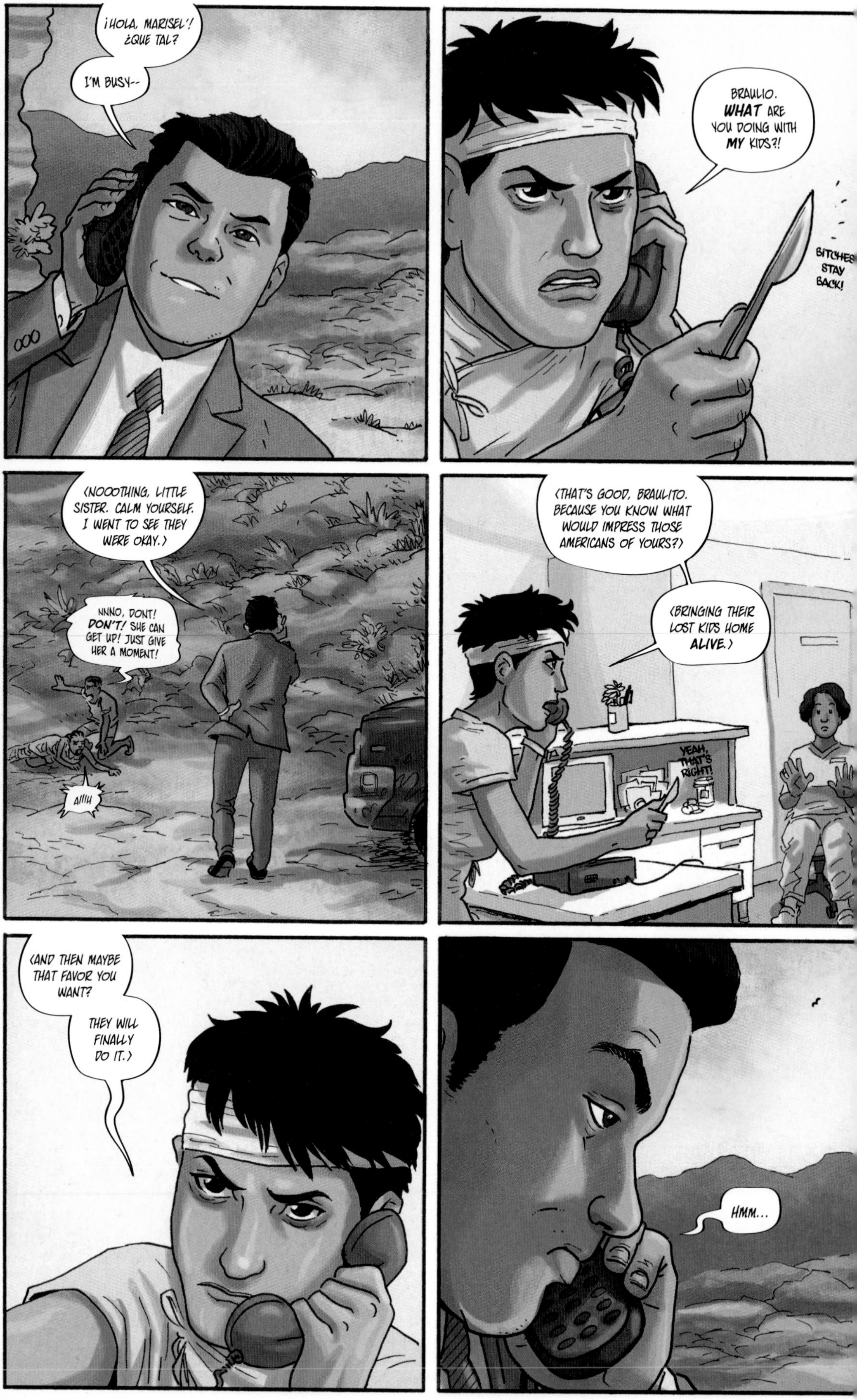
¡HOLA, MARISEL'! ¿QUE TAL?
I'M BUSY--
BRAULIO. **WHAT** ARE YOU DOING WITH **MY** KIDS?!
BITCHES STAY BACK!
‹NOOOTHING, LITTLE SISTER. CALM YOURSELF. I WENT TO SEE THEY WERE OKAY.›
NNNO, DONT! **DON'T!** SHE CAN GET UP! JUST GIVE HER A MOMENT!
AIIIH
‹THAT'S GOOD, BRAULITO. BECAUSE YOU KNOW WHAT WOULD IMPRESS THOSE AMERICANS OF YOURS?›
‹BRINGING THEIR LOST KIDS HOME **ALIVE.**›
YEAH, THAT'S RIGHT!
‹AND THEN MAYBE THAT FAVOR YOU WANT?
THEY WILL FINALLY DO IT.›
HMM...

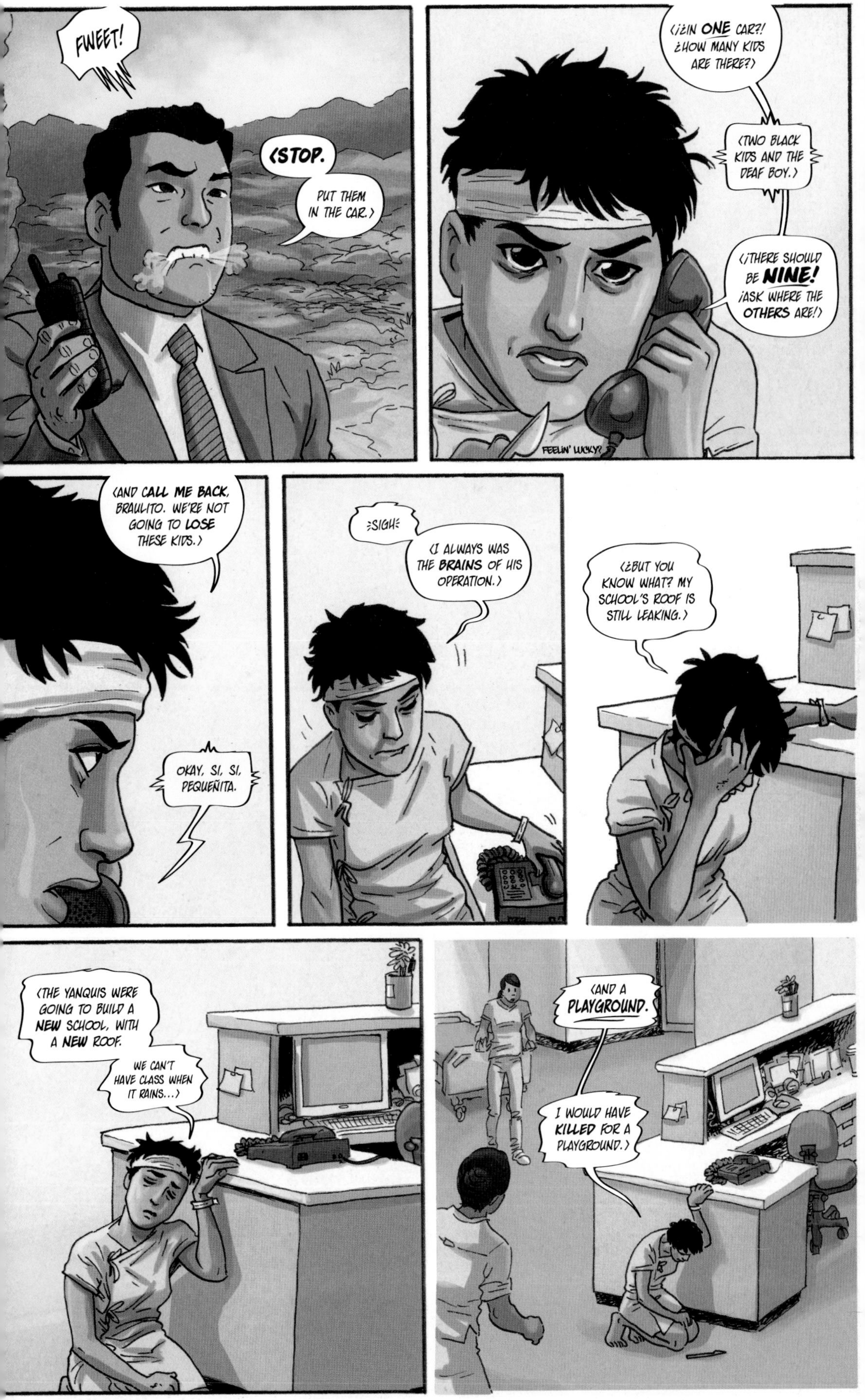

FWEET!
‹STOP.
PUT THEM IN THE CAR.›
‹¿¡IN ONE CAR?! ¿HOW MANY KIDS ARE THERE?›
‹TWO BLACK KIDS AND THE DEAF BOY.›
‹¡THERE SHOULD BE NINE! ¡ASK WHERE THE OTHERS ARE!›
FEELIN' LUCKY?
‹AND CALL ME BACK, BRAULITO. WE'RE NOT GOING TO LOSE THESE KIDS.›
OKAY, SI, SI, PEQUEÑITA.
SIGH
‹I ALWAYS WAS THE BRAINS OF HIS OPERATION.›
‹¿BUT YOU KNOW WHAT? MY SCHOOL'S ROOF IS STILL LEAKING.›
‹THE YANQUIS WERE GOING TO BUILD A NEW SCHOOL, WITH A NEW ROOF.
WE CAN'T HAVE CLASS WHEN IT RAINS...›
‹AND A PLAYGROUND.
I WOULD HAVE KILLED FOR A PLAYGROUND.›

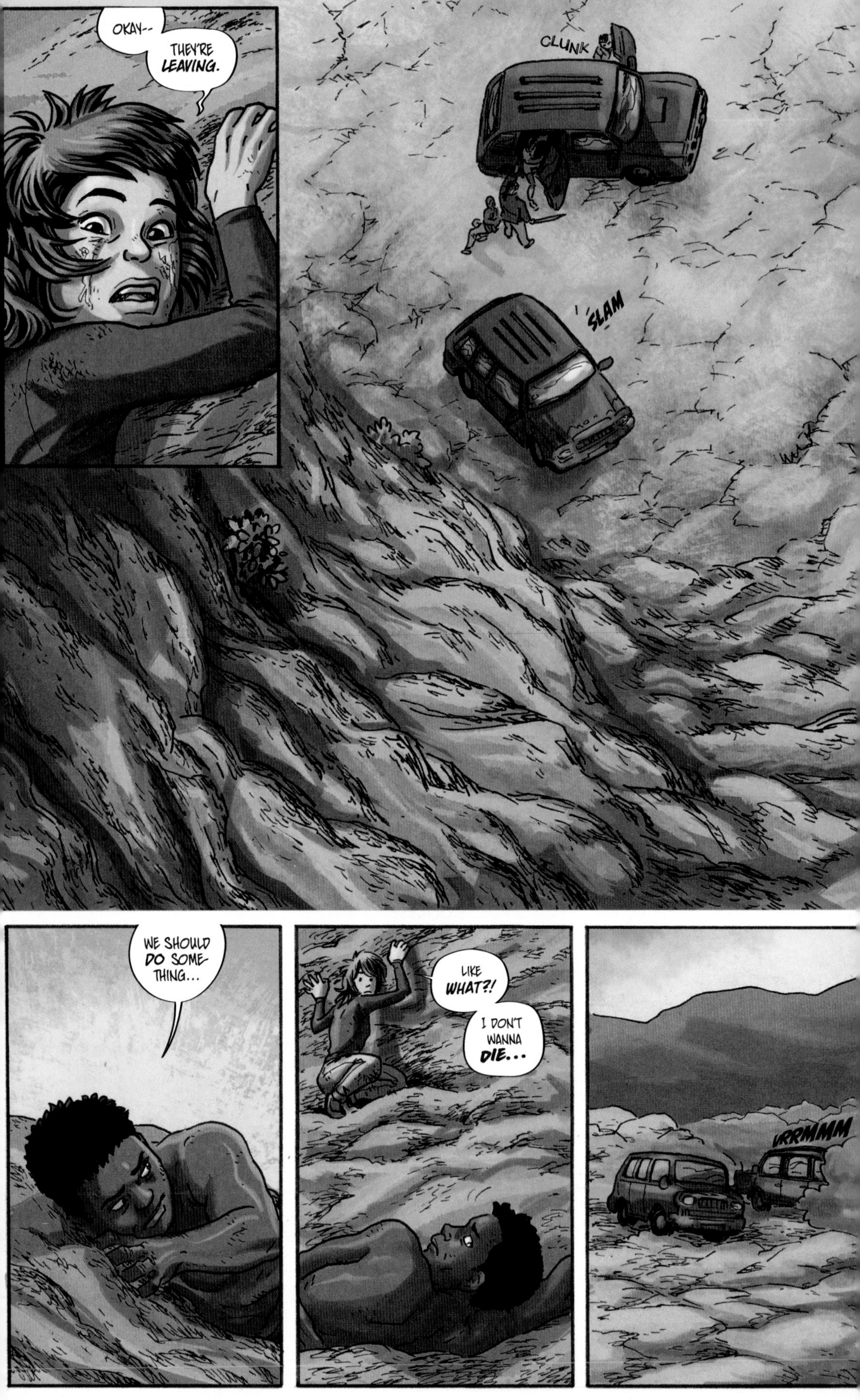
OKAY--
THEY'RE LEAVING.
CLUNK
SLAM
WE SHOULD DO SOME-THING...
LIKE WHAT?!
I DON'T WANNA DIE...
URRMMM

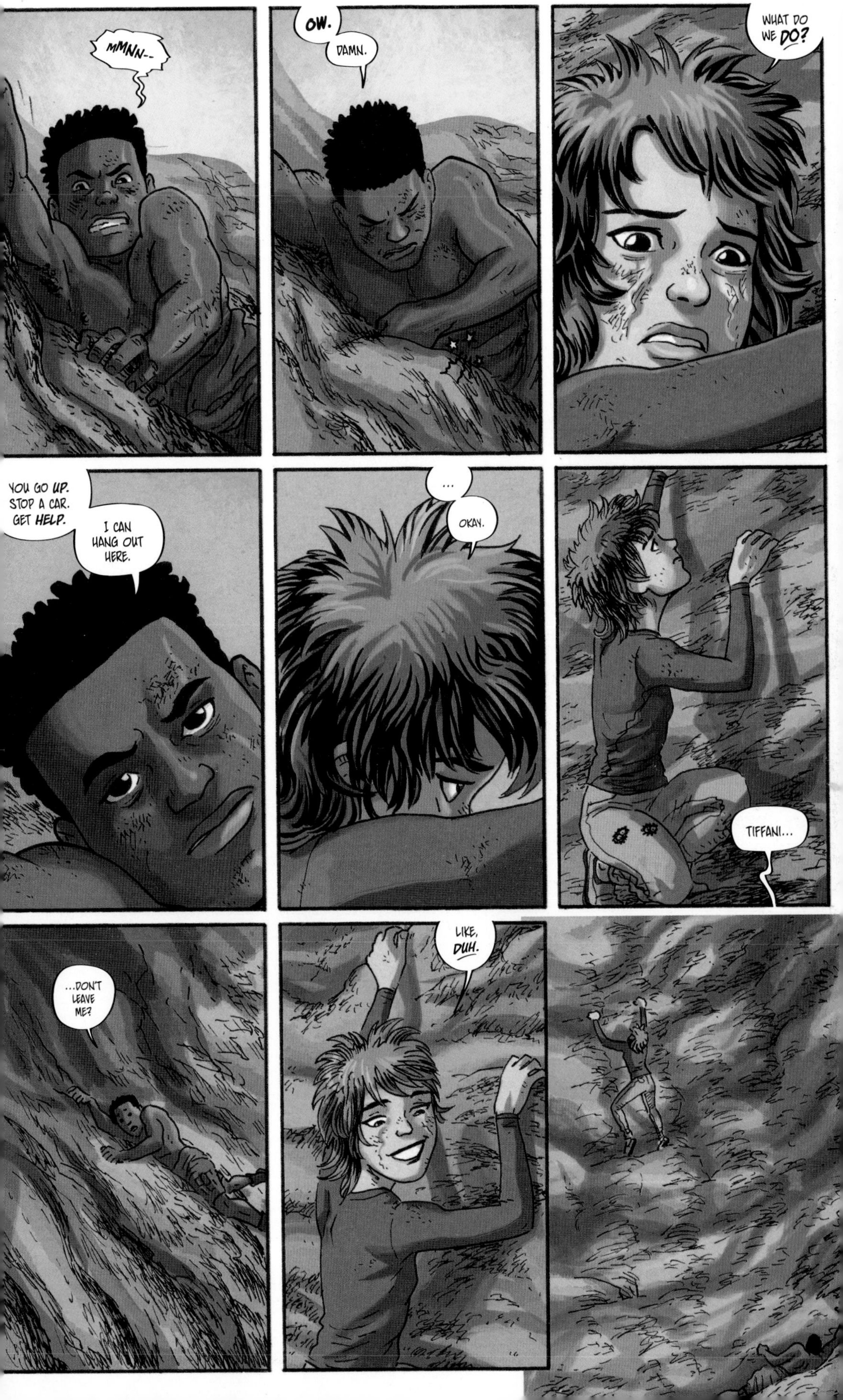
MMNN--
OW.
DAMN.
WHAT DO WE DO?
YOU GO UP. STOP A CAR. GET HELP.
I CAN HANG OUT HERE.
...
OKAY.
TIFFANI...
...DON'T LEAVE ME?
LIKE, DUH.

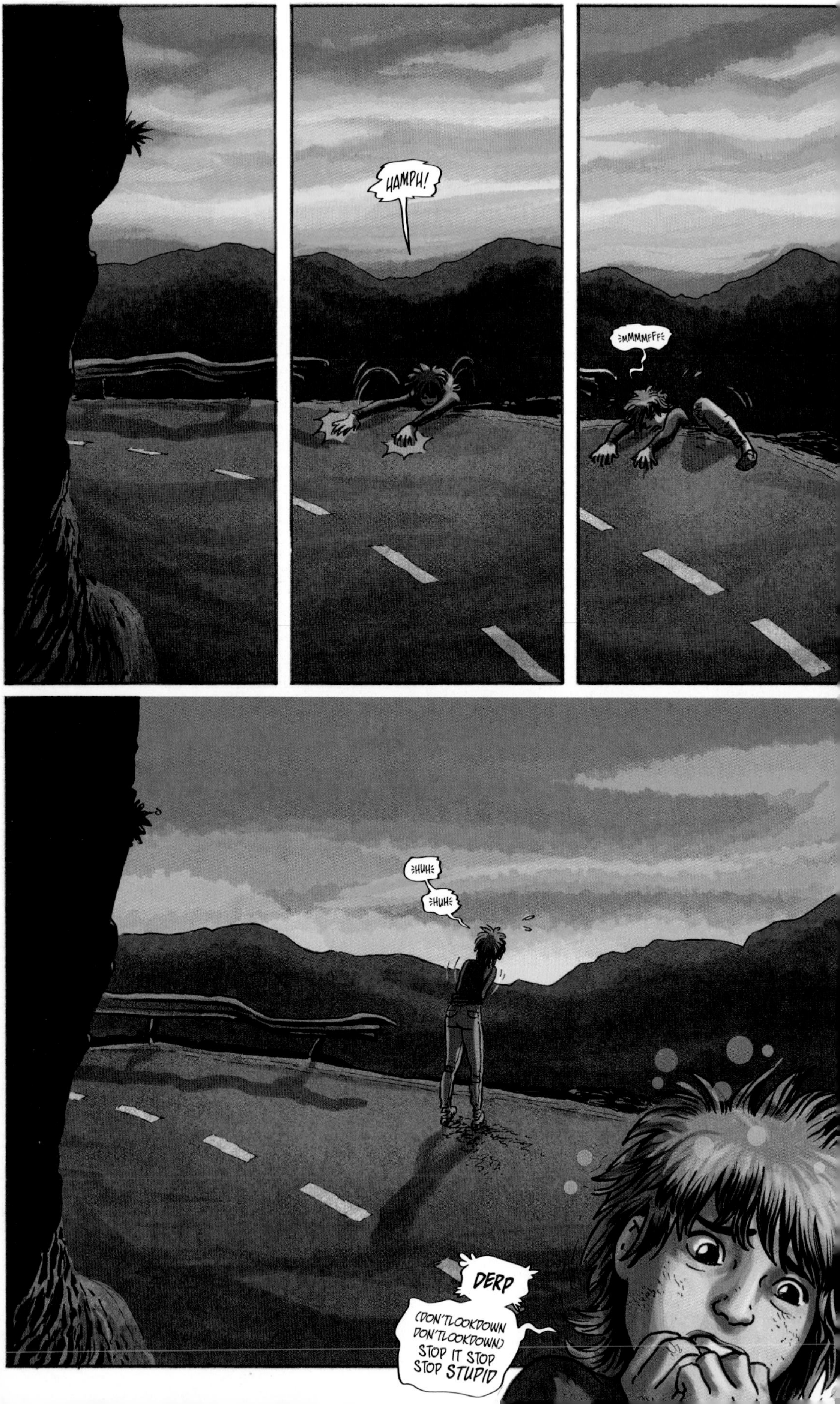
HAMPH!
MMMMFFF
HUH
HUH
DERP
(DON'TLOOKDOWN DON'TLOOKDOWN) STOP IT STOP STOP STUPID

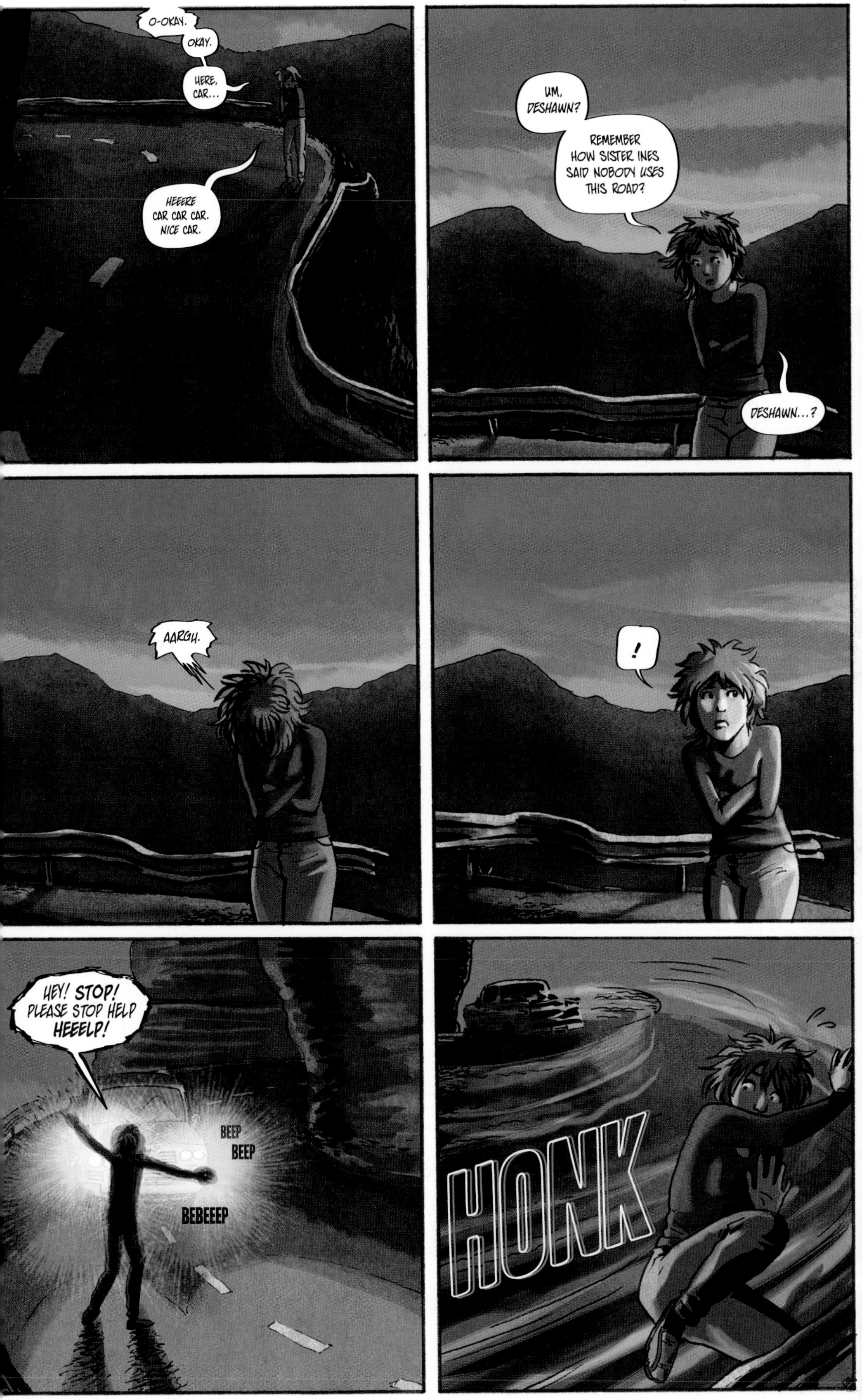
O-OKAY.
OKAY.
HERE, CAR...
HEEERE CAR CAR CAR. NICE CAR.
UM, DESHAWN?
REMEMBER HOW SISTER INES SAID NOBODY USES THIS ROAD?
DESHAWN...?
AARGH.
!
HEY! STOP! PLEASE STOP HELP HEEELP!
BEEP
BEEP
BEBEEEP
HONK

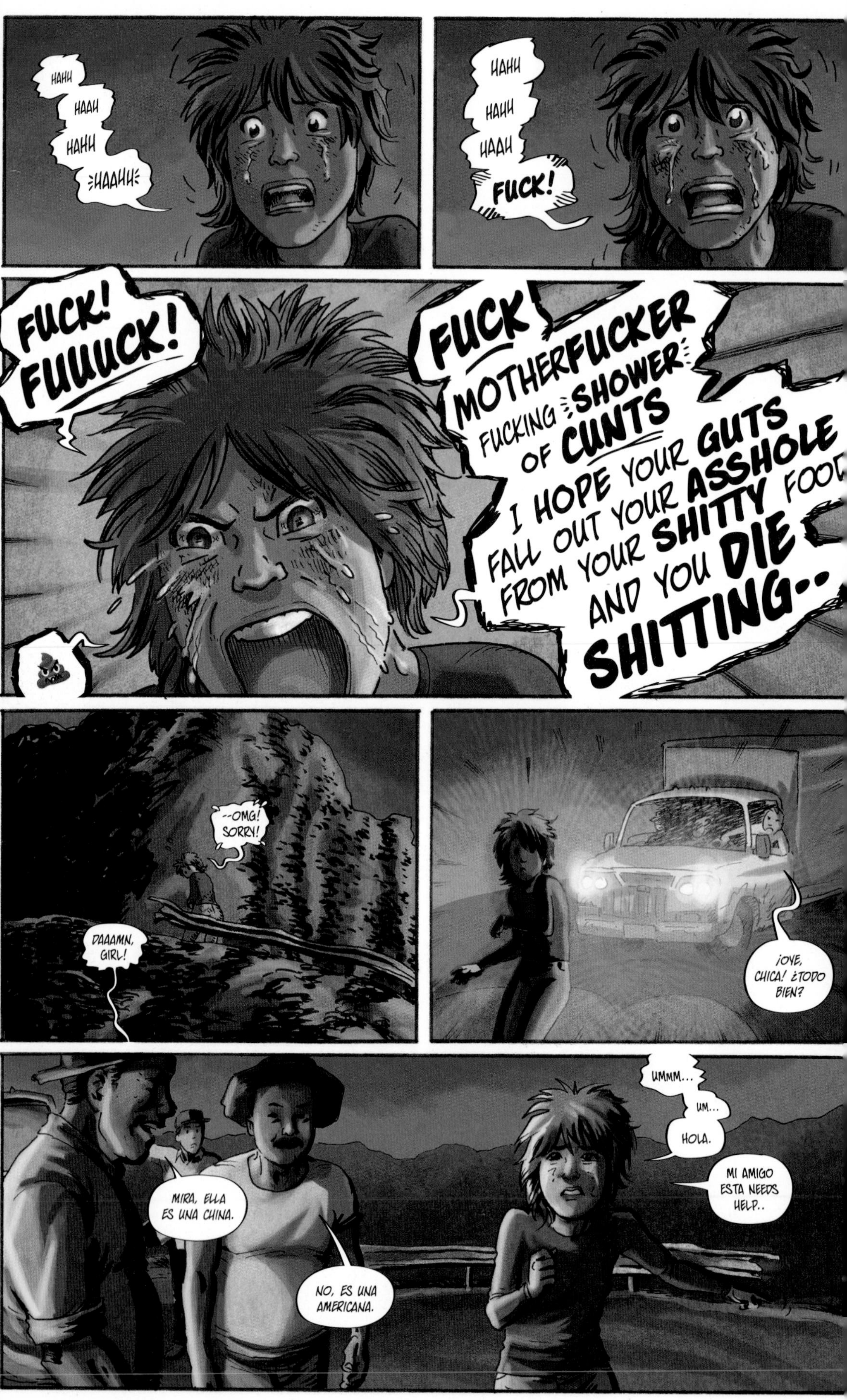
HAHH
HAAH
HAHH
HAAHH
HAHH
HAHH
HAAH
FUCK!
FUCK! FUUUCK!
FUCK MOTHERFUCKER FUCKING SHOWER OF CUNTS
I HOPE YOUR GUTS FALL OUT YOUR ASSHOLE FROM YOUR SHITTY FOOD AND YOU DIE SHITTING..
--OMG! SORRY!
DAAAMN, GIRL!
¡OYE, CHICA! ¿TODO BIEN?
UMMM...
UM...
HOLA.
MI AMIGO ESTA NEEDS HELP..
MIRA, ELLA ES UNA CHINA.
NO, ES UNA AMERICANA.

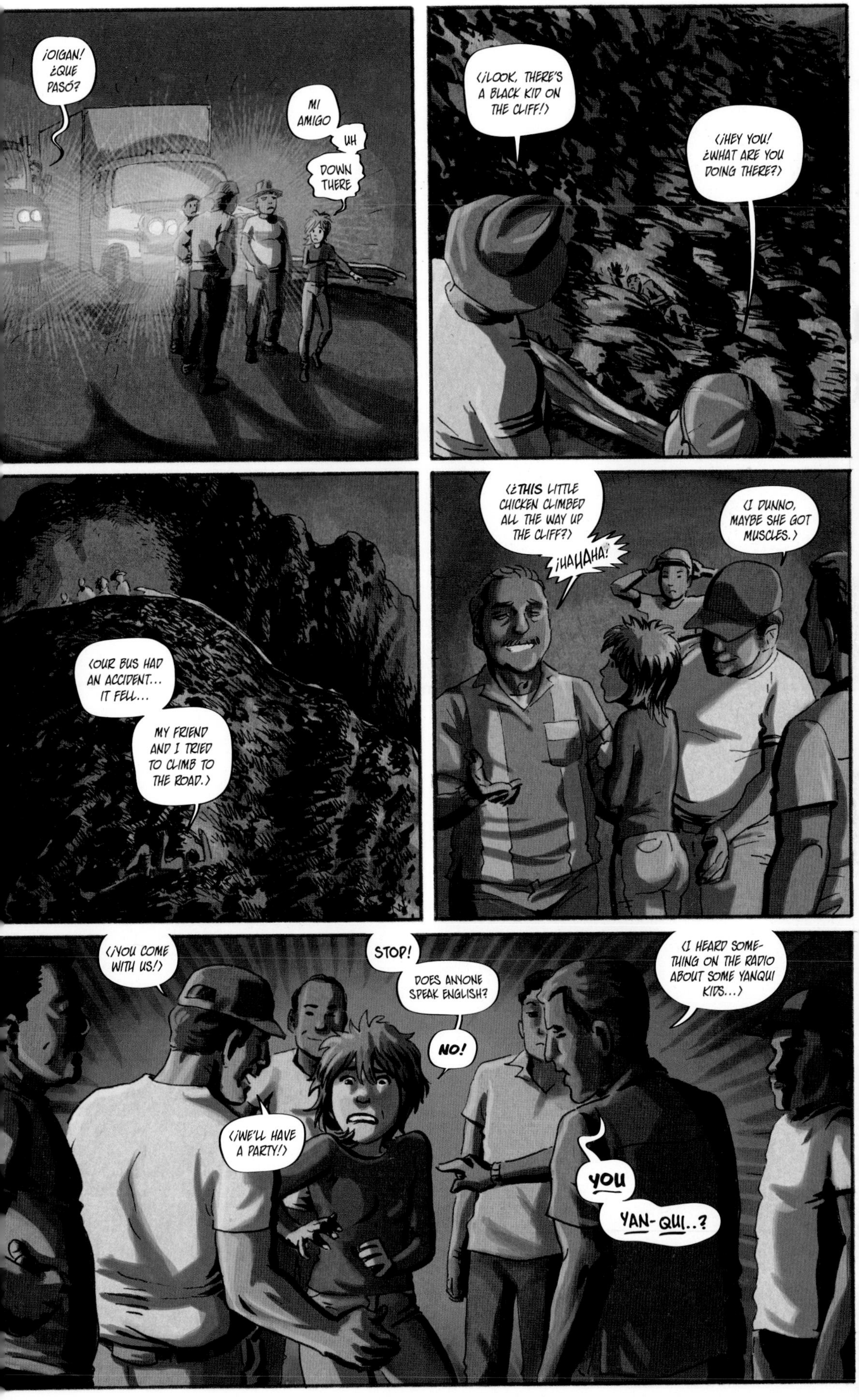
¡OIGAN! ¿QUE PASÓ?
MI AMIGO
UH
DOWN THERE
‹¡LOOK, THERE'S A BLACK KID ON THE CLIFF!›
‹¡HEY YOU! ¿WHAT ARE YOU DOING THERE?›
‹OUR BUS HAD AN ACCIDENT... IT FELL...
MY FRIEND AND I TRIED TO CLIMB TO THE ROAD.›
‹¿THIS LITTLE CHICKEN CLIMBED ALL THE WAY UP THE CLIFF?›
¡HAHAHA!
‹I DUNNO, MAYBE SHE GOT MUSCLES.›
‹¡YOU COME WITH US!›
STOP!
DOES ANYONE SPEAK ENGLISH?
NO!
‹I HEARD SOME-THING ON THE RADIO ABOUT SOME YANQUI KIDS...›
‹¡WE'LL HAVE A PARTY!›
YOU
YAN-QUI..?

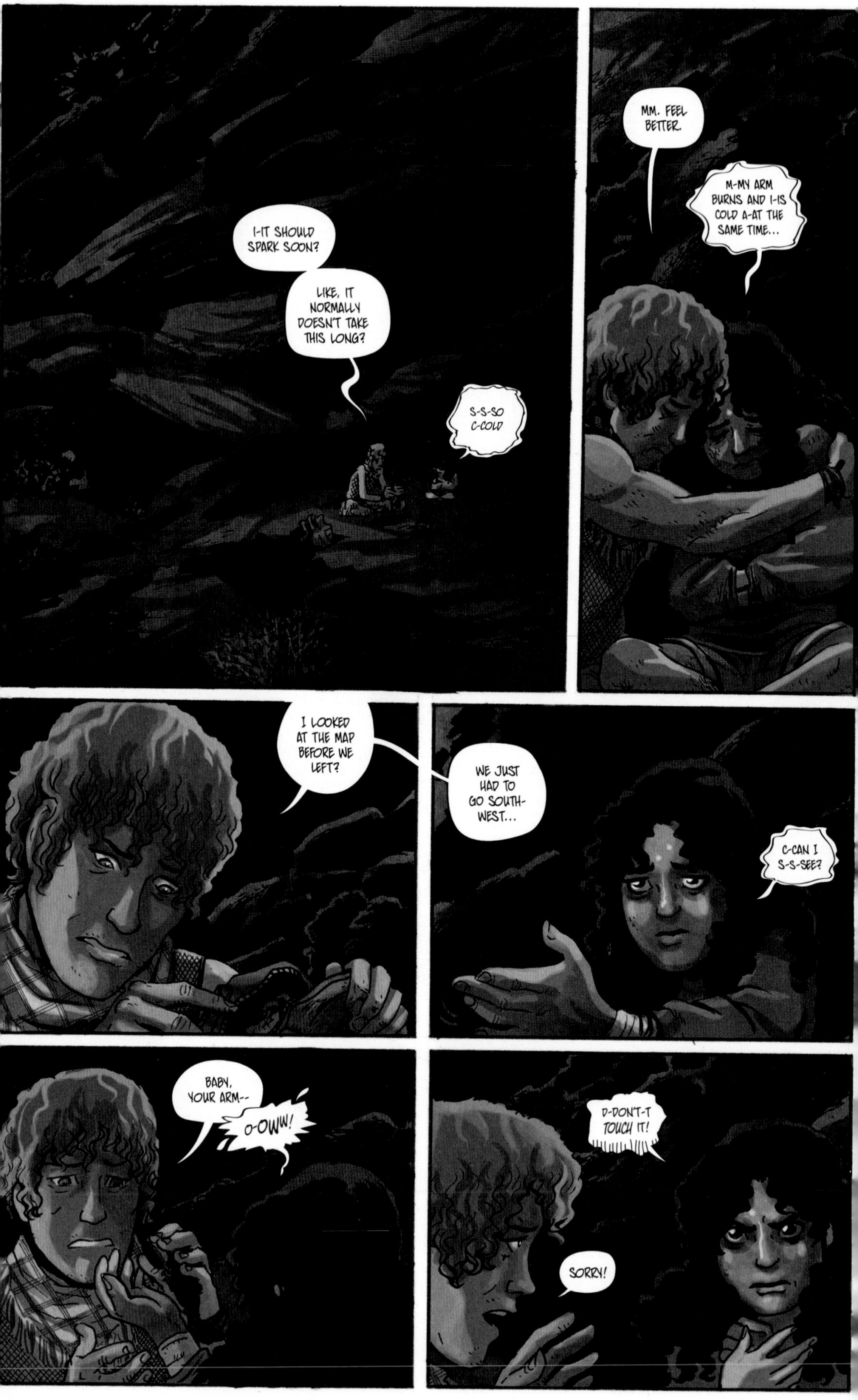
I-IT SHOULD SPARK SOON?
LIKE, IT NORMALLY DOESN'T TAKE THIS LONG?
S-S-SO C-COLD
MM. FEEL BETTER.
M-MY ARM BURNS AND I-IS COLD A-AT THE SAME TIME...
I LOOKED AT THE MAP BEFORE WE LEFT?
WE JUST HAD TO GO SOUTH-WEST...
C-CAN I S-S-SEE?
BABY, YOUR ARM--
O-OWW!
D-DON'T-T TOUCH IT!
SORRY!

HM.

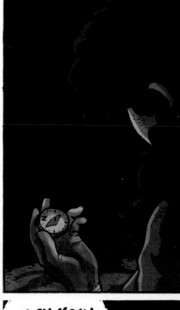

...

OHH TRAVIS...

FUCK YOU!

WHA-OW!

GINA, CHILL!

IT'S BROKEN!

IT'S STUCK!

YOU HAVE GOTTEN US TOTALLY LOST!

THAT'S WHAT YOU GET FOR PICKING STUFF OUT OF DUMPSTERS.

BABY, I--

I--

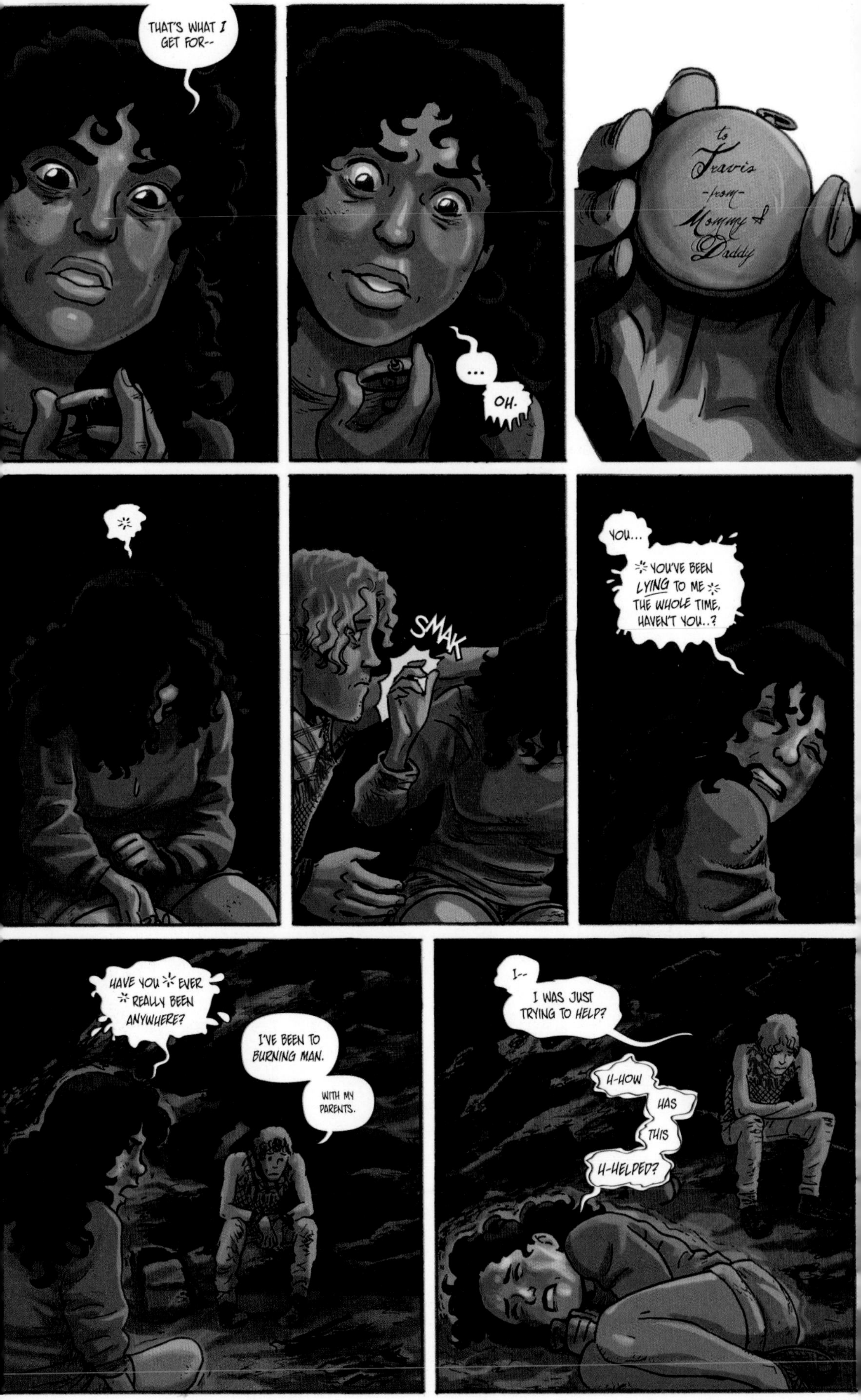
THAT'S WHAT I GET FOR--
...
OH.
to Travis -from- Mommy & Daddy
YOU...
YOU'VE BEEN LYING TO ME THE WHOLE TIME, HAVEN'T YOU..?
SMAK
HAVE YOU EVER REALLY BEEN ANYWHERE?
I'VE BEEN TO BURNING MAN.
WITH MY PARENTS.
I--
I WAS JUST TRYING TO HELP?
H-HOW HAS THIS H-HELPED?

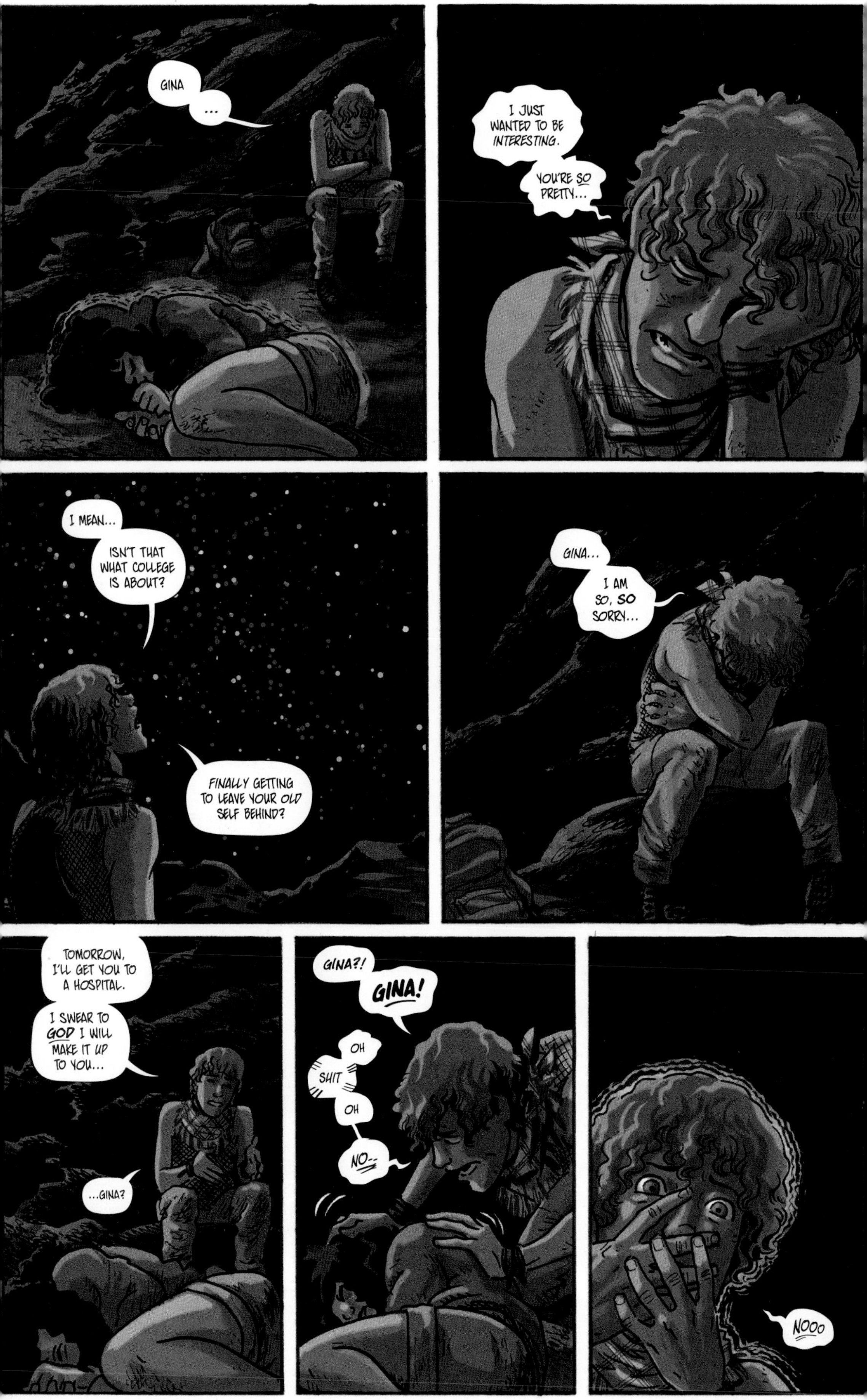
GINA
...
I JUST WANTED TO BE INTERESTING.
YOU'RE SO PRETTY...
I MEAN...
ISN'T THAT WHAT COLLEGE IS ABOUT?
FINALLY GETTING TO LEAVE YOUR OLD SELF BEHIND?
GINA...
I AM SO, SO SORRY...
TOMORROW, I'LL GET YOU TO A HOSPITAL.
I SWEAR TO GOD I WILL MAKE IT UP TO YOU...
...GINA?
GINA?!
GINA!
OH
SHIT
OH
NO--
NOOO

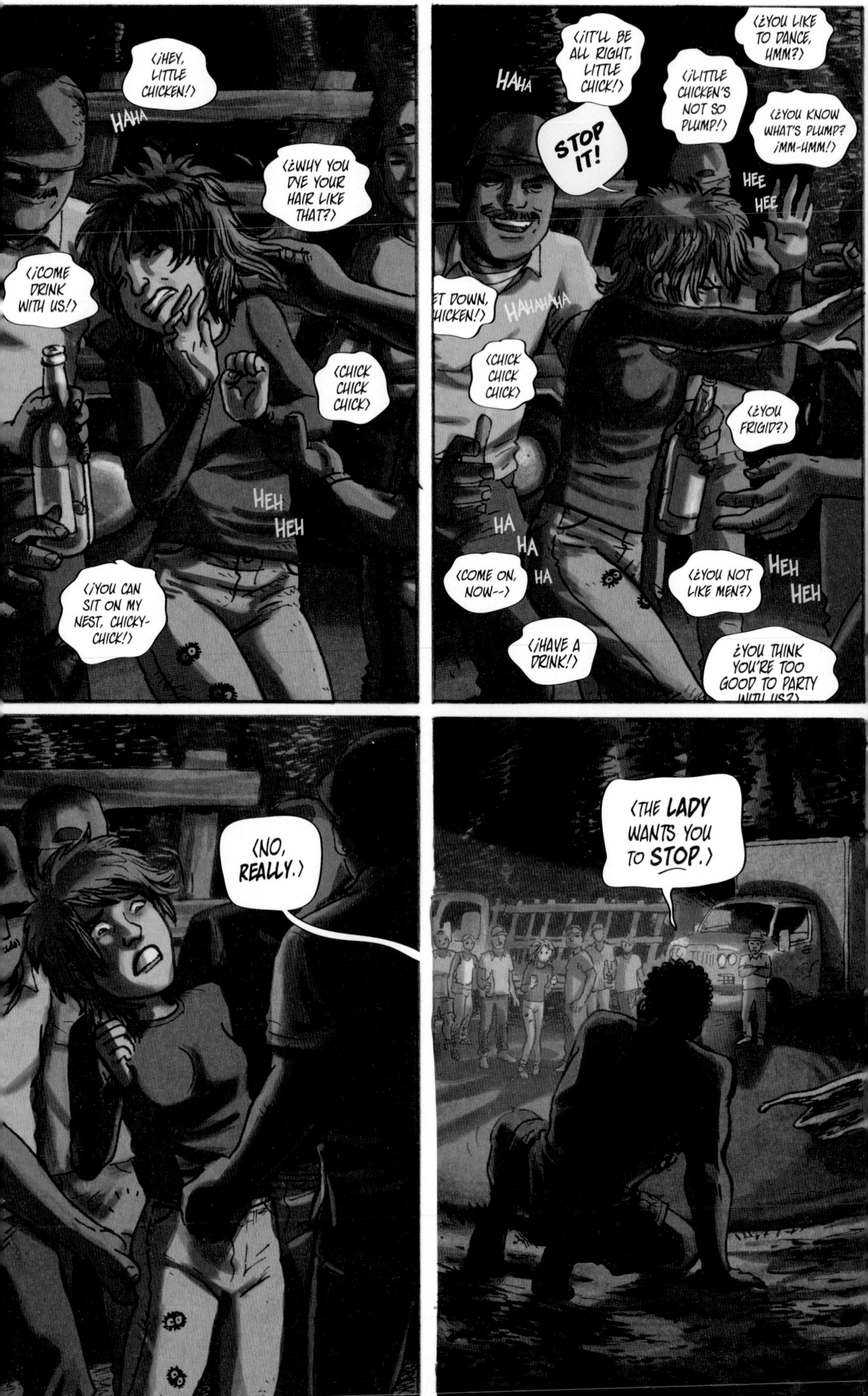
⟨¡HEY, LITTLE CHICKEN!⟩
HAHA
⟨¿WHY YOU DYE YOUR HAIR LIKE THAT?⟩
⟨¡COME DRINK WITH US!⟩
⟨CHICK CHICK CHICK⟩
HEH HEH
⟨¡YOU CAN SIT ON MY NEST, CHICKY-CHICK!⟩
HAHA
⟨¡IT'LL BE ALL RIGHT, LITTLE CHICK!⟩
STOP IT!
⟨¡LITTLE CHICKEN'S NOT SO PLUMP!⟩
⟨¿YOU LIKE TO DANCE, HMM?⟩
⟨¿YOU KNOW WHAT'S PLUMP? ¡MM-HMM!⟩
HEE HEE
ET DOWN, HICKEN!⟩
HAHAHAHA
⟨CHICK CHICK CHICK⟩
⟨¿YOU FRIGID?⟩
HA HA HA
⟨COME ON, NOW--⟩
⟨¿YOU NOT LIKE MEN?⟩
HEH HEH
⟨¡HAVE A DRINK!⟩
¿YOU THINK YOU'RE TOO GOOD TO PARTY
⟨NO, REALLY.⟩
⟨THE LADY WANTS YOU TO STOP.⟩

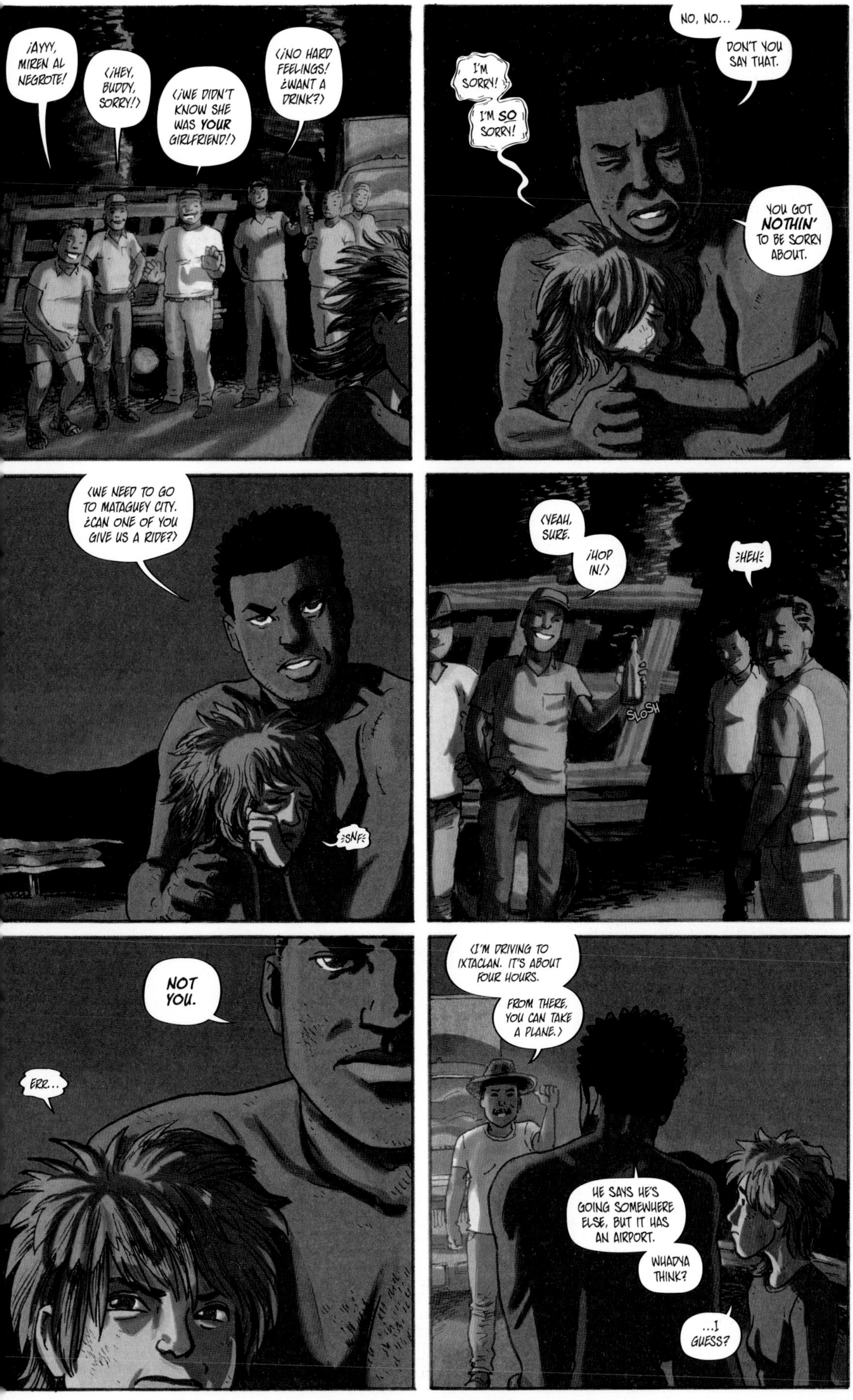
¡AYYY, MIREN AL NEGROTE!
‹¡HEY, BUDDY, SORRY!›
‹¡WE DIDN'T KNOW SHE WAS YOUR GIRLFRIEND!›
‹¡NO HARD FEELINGS! ¿WANT A DRINK?›
NO, NO...
I'M SORRY!
I'M SO SORRY!
DON'T YOU SAY THAT.
YOU GOT NOTHIN' TO BE SORRY ABOUT.
‹WE NEED TO GO TO MATAGUEY CITY. ¿CAN ONE OF YOU GIVE US A RIDE?›
SNF
‹YEAH, SURE.
¡HOP IN!›
HEH
SLOSH
NOT YOU.
ERR...
‹I'M DRIVING TO IXTACLAN. IT'S ABOUT FOUR HOURS.
FROM THERE, YOU CAN TAKE A PLANE.›
HE SAYS HE'S GOING SOMEWHERE ELSE, BUT IT HAS AN AIRPORT.
WHADYA THINK?
...I GUESS?

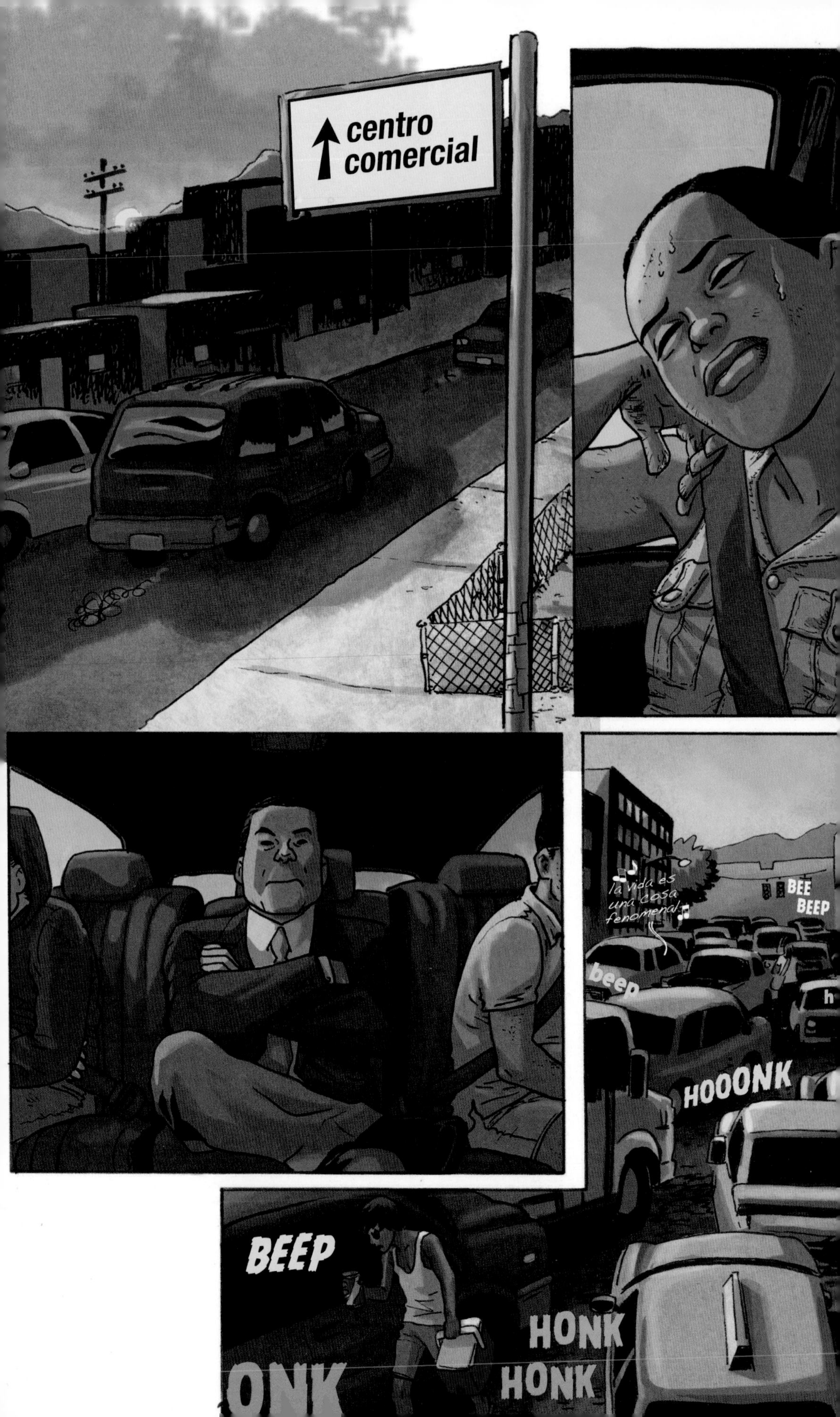
centro
comercial
la vida es
una cosa
fenomenal
BEE
BEEP
beep
h
HOOONK
BEEP
HONK
ONK
HONK

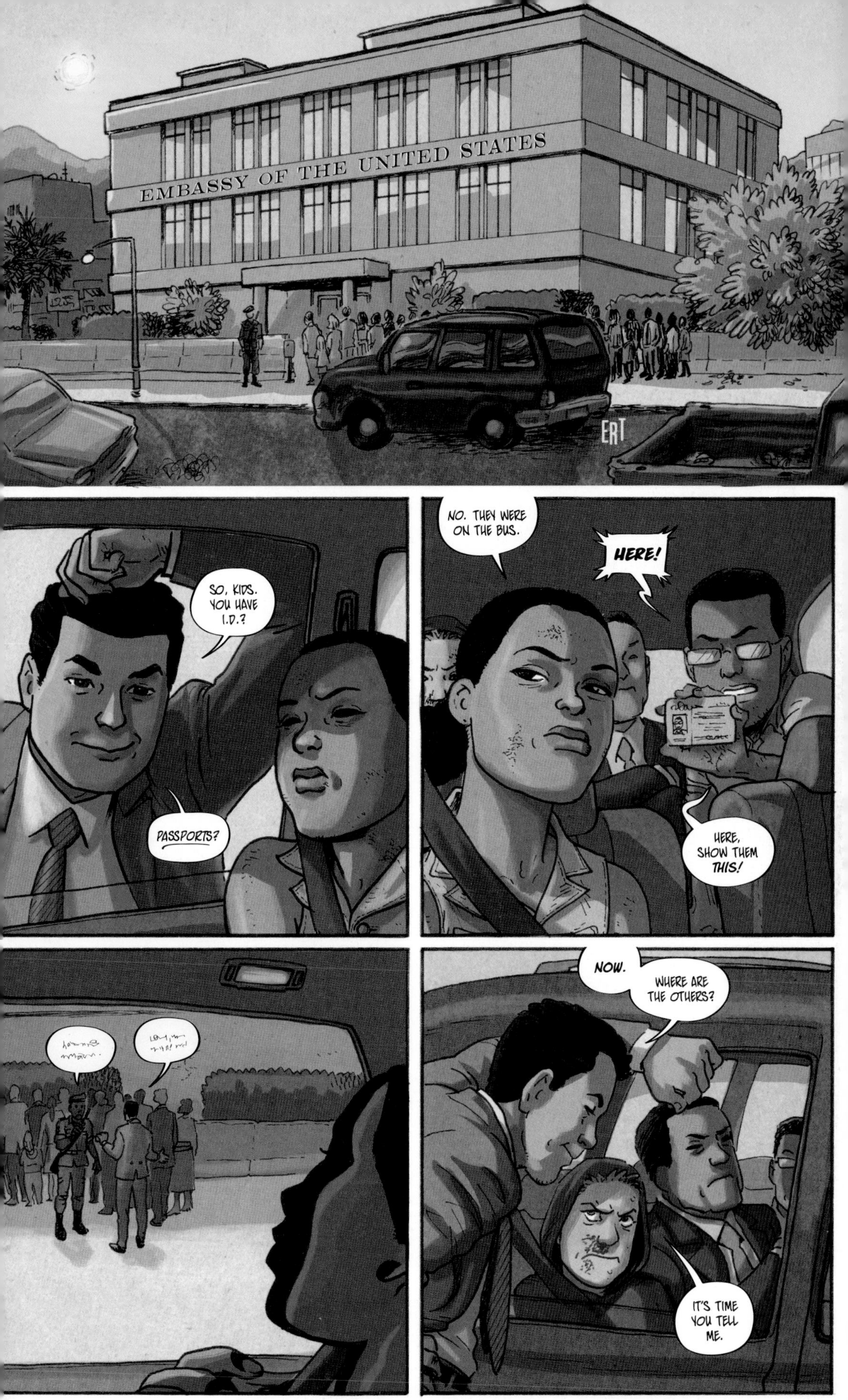
EMBASSY OF THE UNITED STATES
SO, KIDS. YOU HAVE I.D.?
PASSPORTS?
NO. THEY WERE ON THE BUS.
HERE!
HERE, SHOW THEM THIS!
NOW.
WHERE ARE THE OTHERS?
IT'S TIME YOU TELL ME.

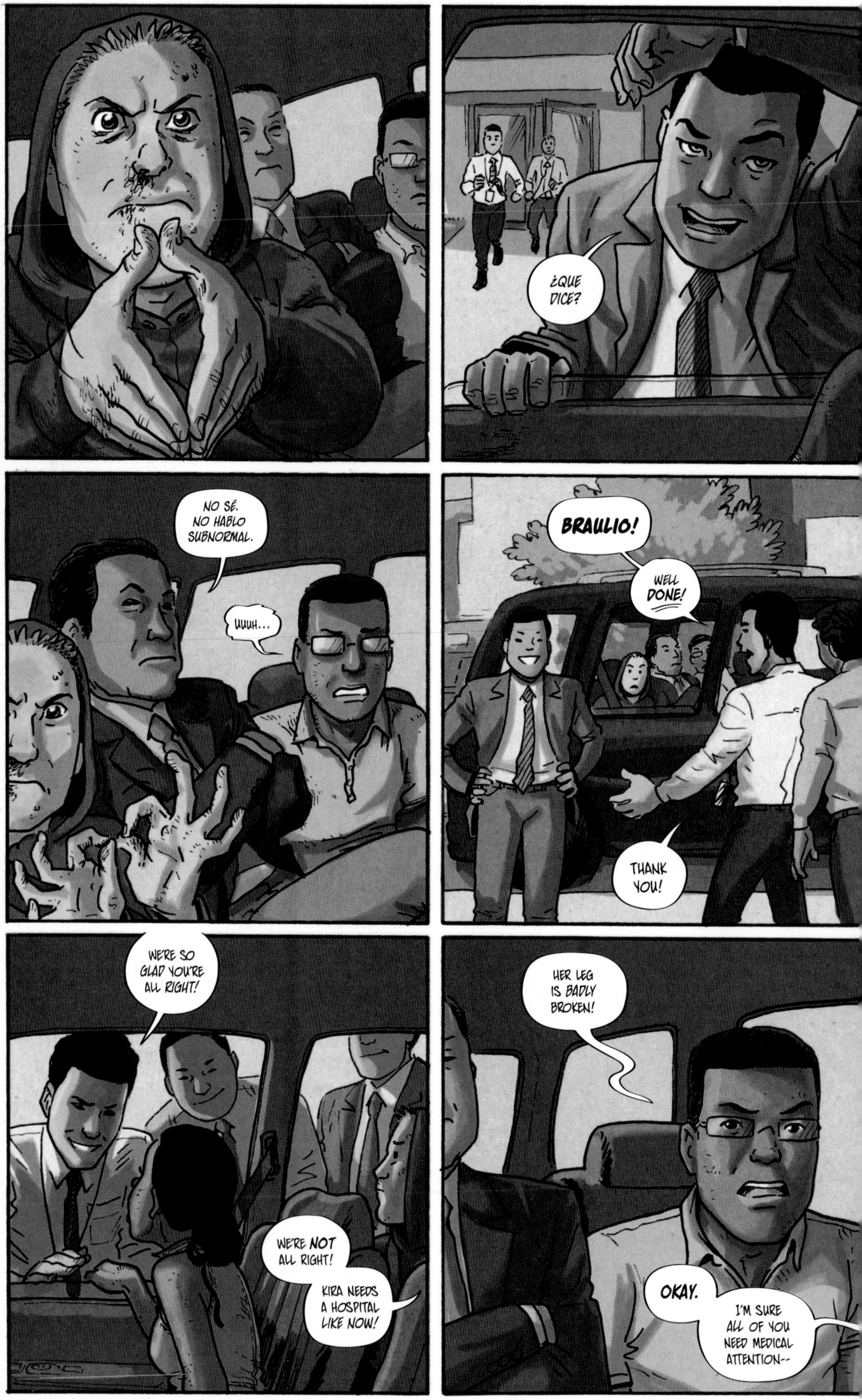
¿QUE DICE?
NO SÉ. NO HABLO SUBNORMAL.
UUUH...
BRAULIO!
WELL DONE!
THANK YOU!
WE'RE SO GLAD YOU'RE ALL RIGHT!
WE'RE NOT ALL RIGHT!
KIRA NEEDS A HOSPITAL LIKE NOW!
HER LEG IS BADLY BROKEN!
OKAY.
I'M SURE ALL OF YOU NEED MEDICAL ATTENTION--

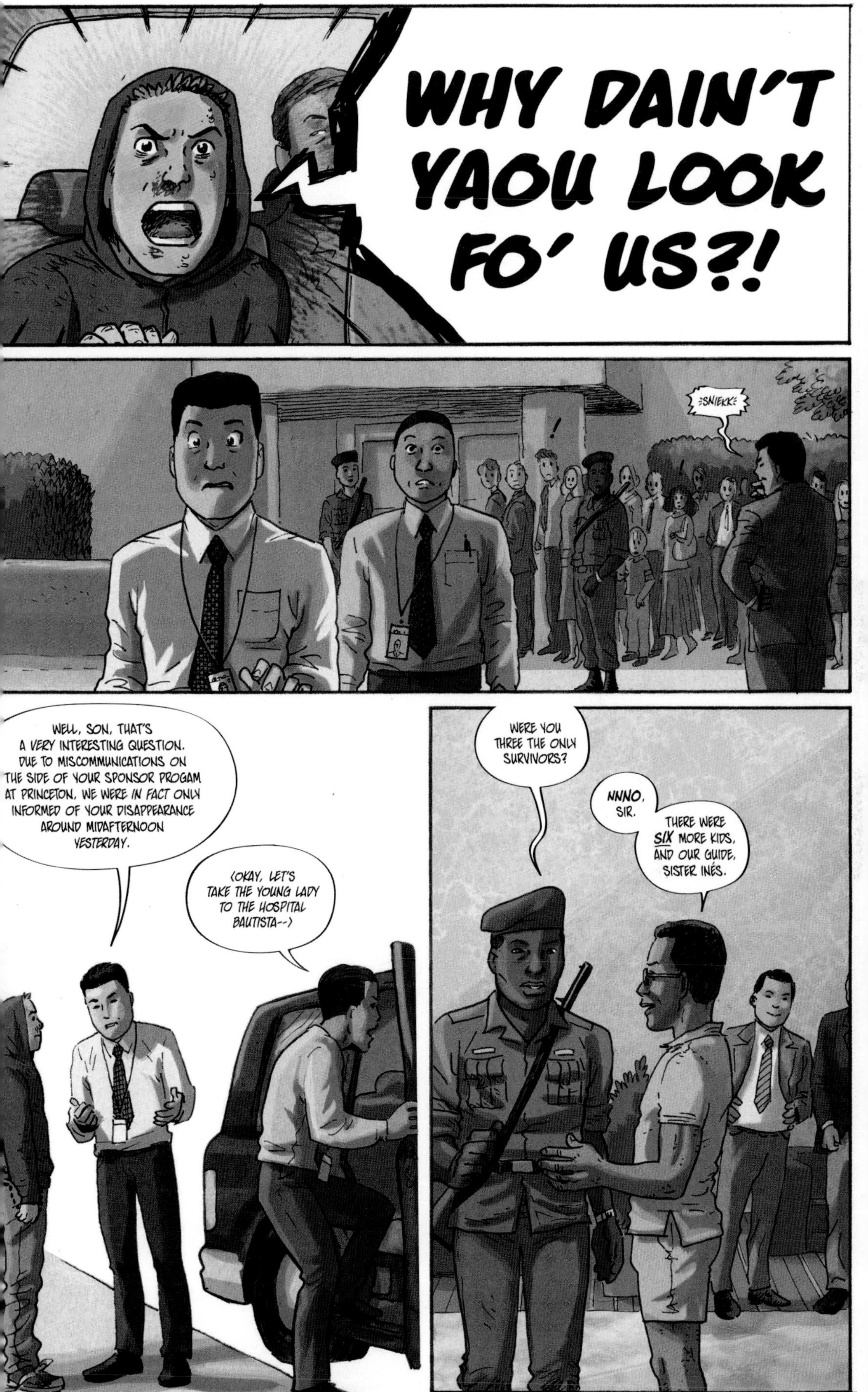
WHY DAIN'T YAOU LOOK FO' US?!
≶SNIEKK≷
WELL, SON, THAT'S A VERY INTERESTING QUESTION. DUE TO MISCOMMUNICATIONS ON THE SIDE OF YOUR SPONSOR PROGAM AT PRINCETON, WE WERE IN FACT ONLY INFORMED OF YOUR DISAPPEARANCE AROUND MIDAFTERNOON YESTERDAY.
‹OKAY, LET'S TAKE THE YOUNG LADY TO THE HOSPITAL BAUTISTA--›
WERE YOU THREE THE ONLY SURVIVORS?
NNNO, SIR.
THERE WERE SIX MORE KIDS, AND OUR GUIDE, SISTER INÉS.

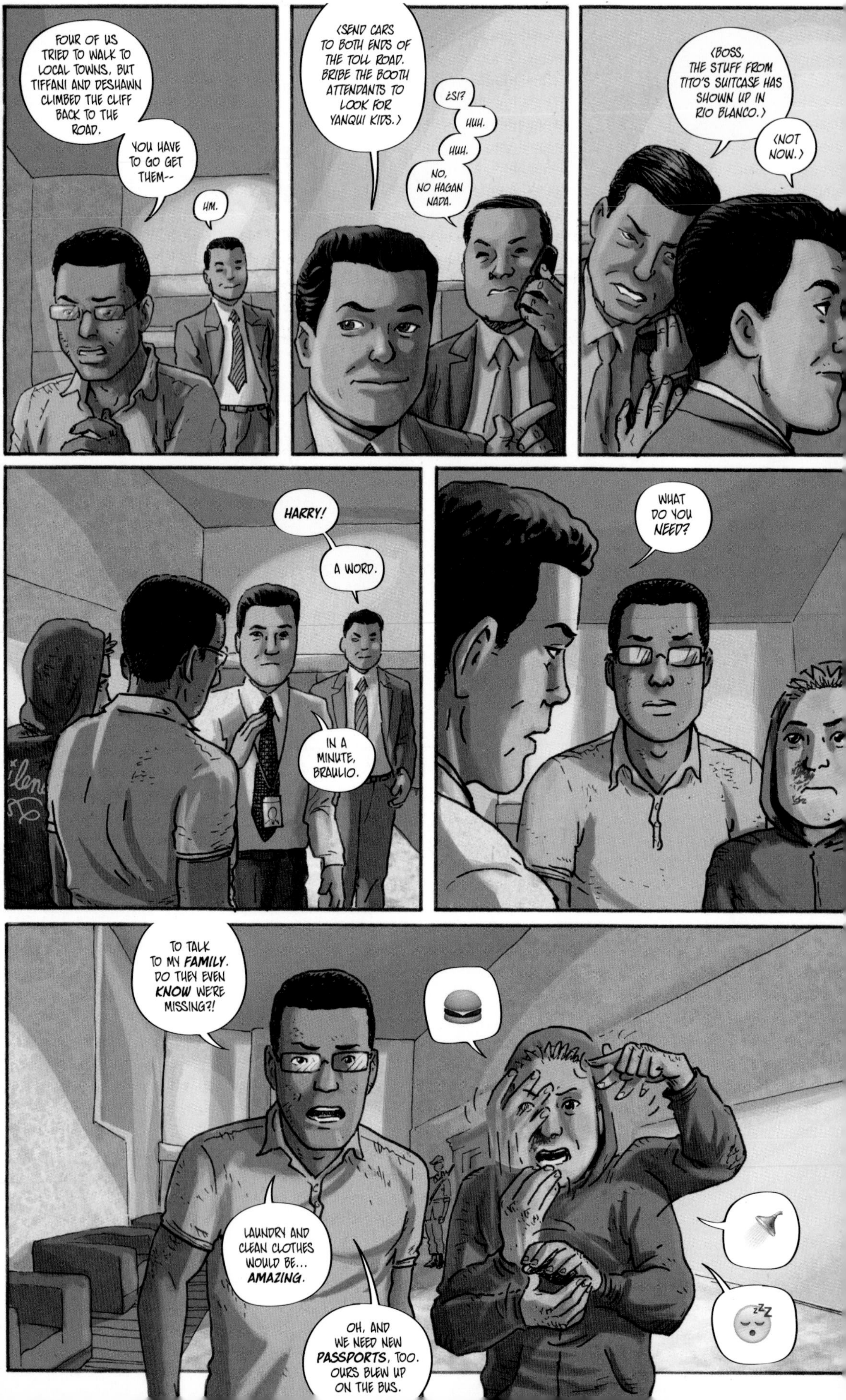
FOUR OF US TRIED TO WALK TO LOCAL TOWNS, BUT TIFFANI AND DESHAWN CLIMBED THE CLIFF BACK TO THE ROAD.
YOU HAVE TO GO GET THEM--
HM.
‹SEND CARS TO BOTH ENDS OF THE TOLL ROAD. BRIBE THE BOOTH ATTENDANTS TO LOOK FOR YANQUI KIDS.›
¿SI?
HUH.
HUH.
NO, NO HAGAN NADA.
‹BOSS, THE STUFF FROM TITO'S SUITCASE HAS SHOWN UP IN RIO BLANCO.›
‹NOT NOW.›
HARRY!
A WORD.
IN A MINUTE, BRAULIO.
WHAT DO YOU NEED?
TO TALK TO MY FAMILY. DO THEY EVEN KNOW WE'RE MISSING?!
LAUNDRY AND CLEAN CLOTHES WOULD BE... AMAZING.
OH, AND WE NEED NEW PASSPORTS, TOO. OURS BLEW UP ON THE BUS.

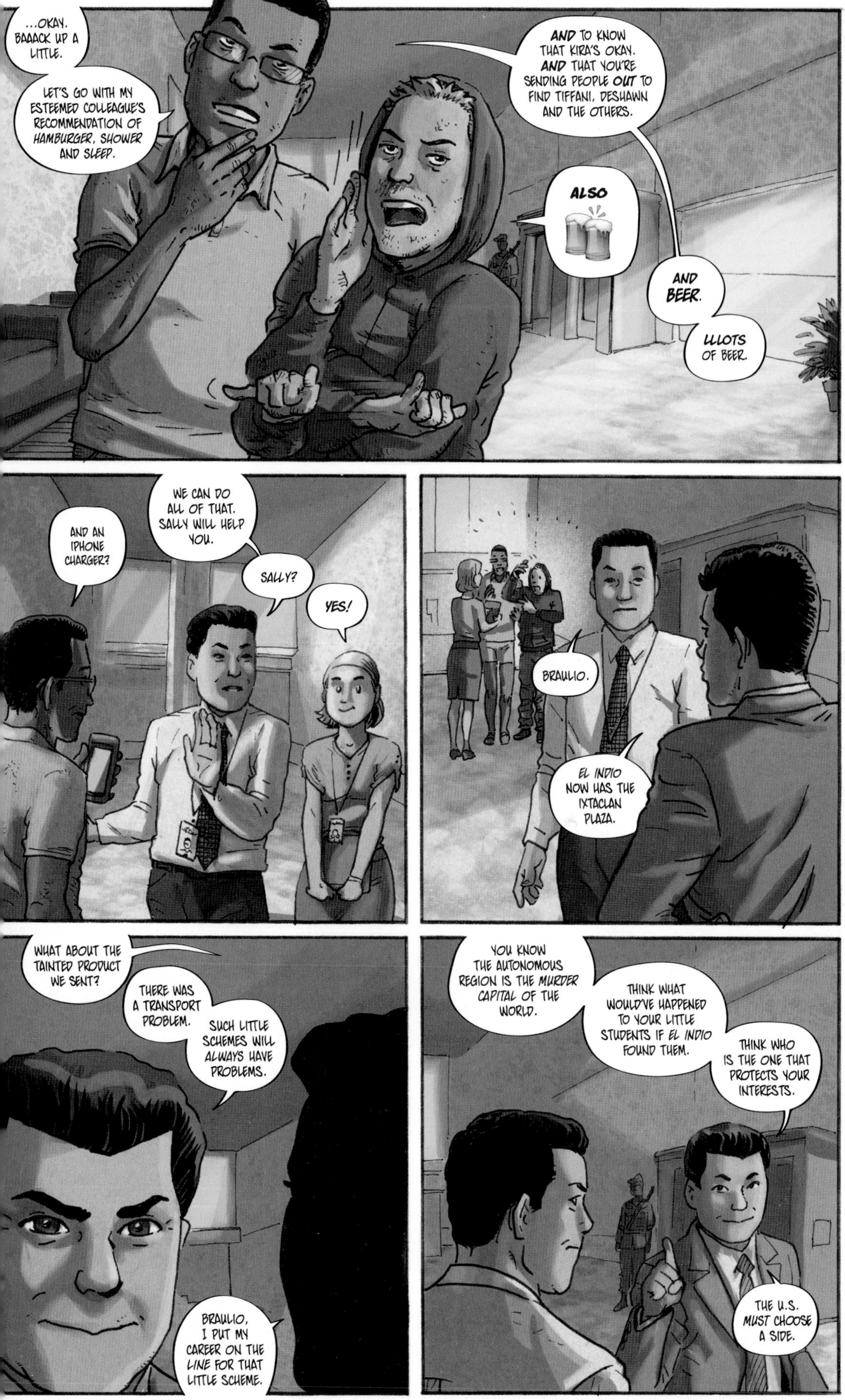
...OKAY. BAAACK UP A LITTLE.
LET'S GO WITH MY ESTEEMED COLLEAGUE'S RECOMMENDATION OF HAMBURGER, SHOWER AND SLEEP.
AND TO KNOW THAT KIRA'S OKAY. AND THAT YOU'RE SENDING PEOPLE OUT TO FIND TIFFANI, DESHAWN AND THE OTHERS.
ALSO
AND BEER.
LLLOTS OF BEER.
AND AN IPHONE CHARGER?
WE CAN DO ALL OF THAT. SALLY WILL HELP YOU.
SALLY?
YES!
BRAULIO.
EL INDIO NOW HAS THE IXTACLAN PLAZA.
WHAT ABOUT THE TAINTED PRODUCT WE SENT?
THERE WAS A TRANSPORT PROBLEM.
SUCH LITTLE SCHEMES WILL ALWAYS HAVE PROBLEMS.
BRAULIO, I PUT MY CAREER ON THE LINE FOR THAT LITTLE SCHEME.
YOU KNOW THE AUTONOMOUS REGION IS THE MURDER CAPITAL OF THE WORLD.
THINK WHAT WOULD'VE HAPPENED TO YOUR LITTLE STUDENTS IF EL INDIO FOUND THEM.
THINK WHO IS THE ONE THAT PROTECTS YOUR INTERESTS.
THE U.S. MUST CHOOSE A SIDE.

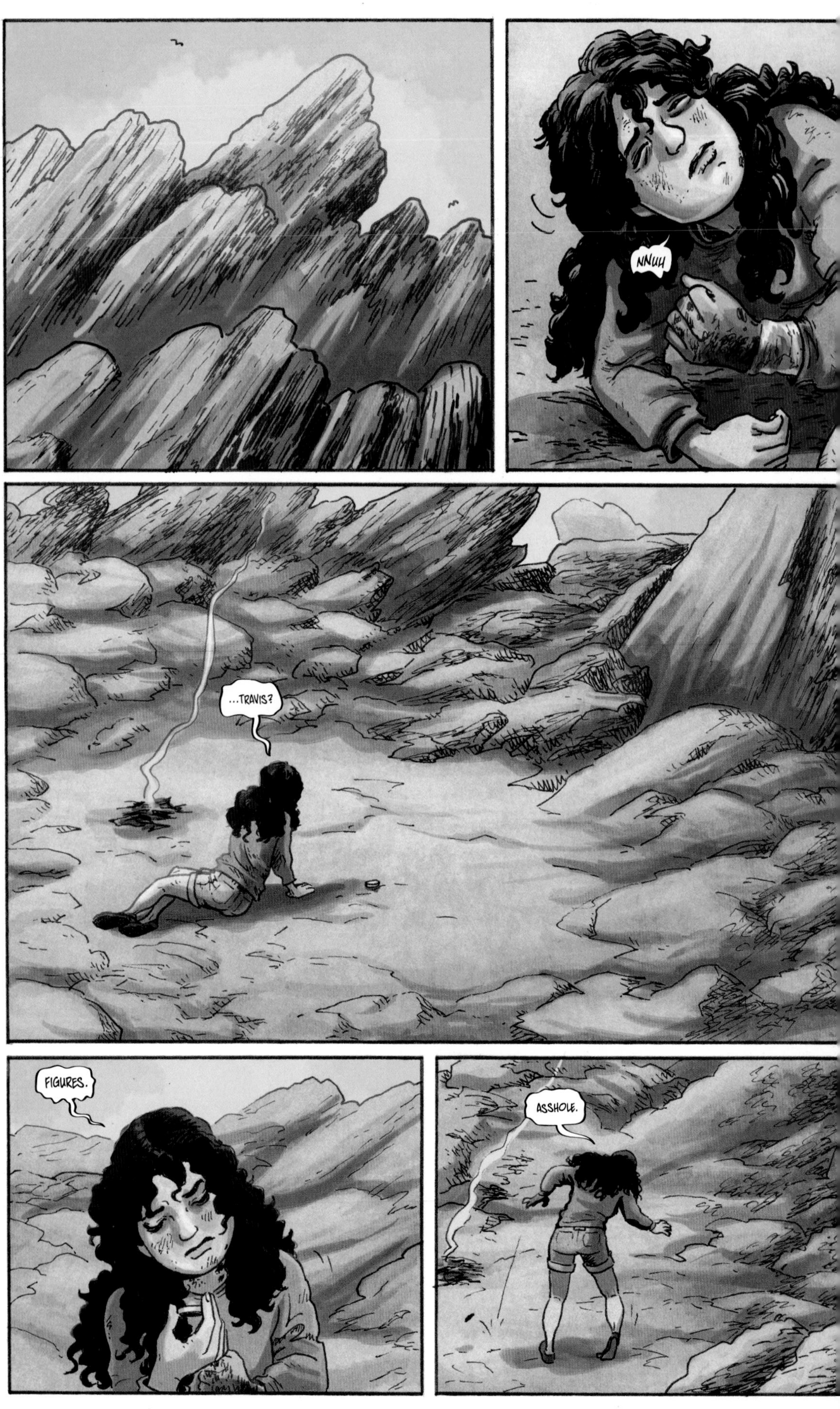
NNUH
...TRAVIS?
FIGURES.
ASSHOLE.

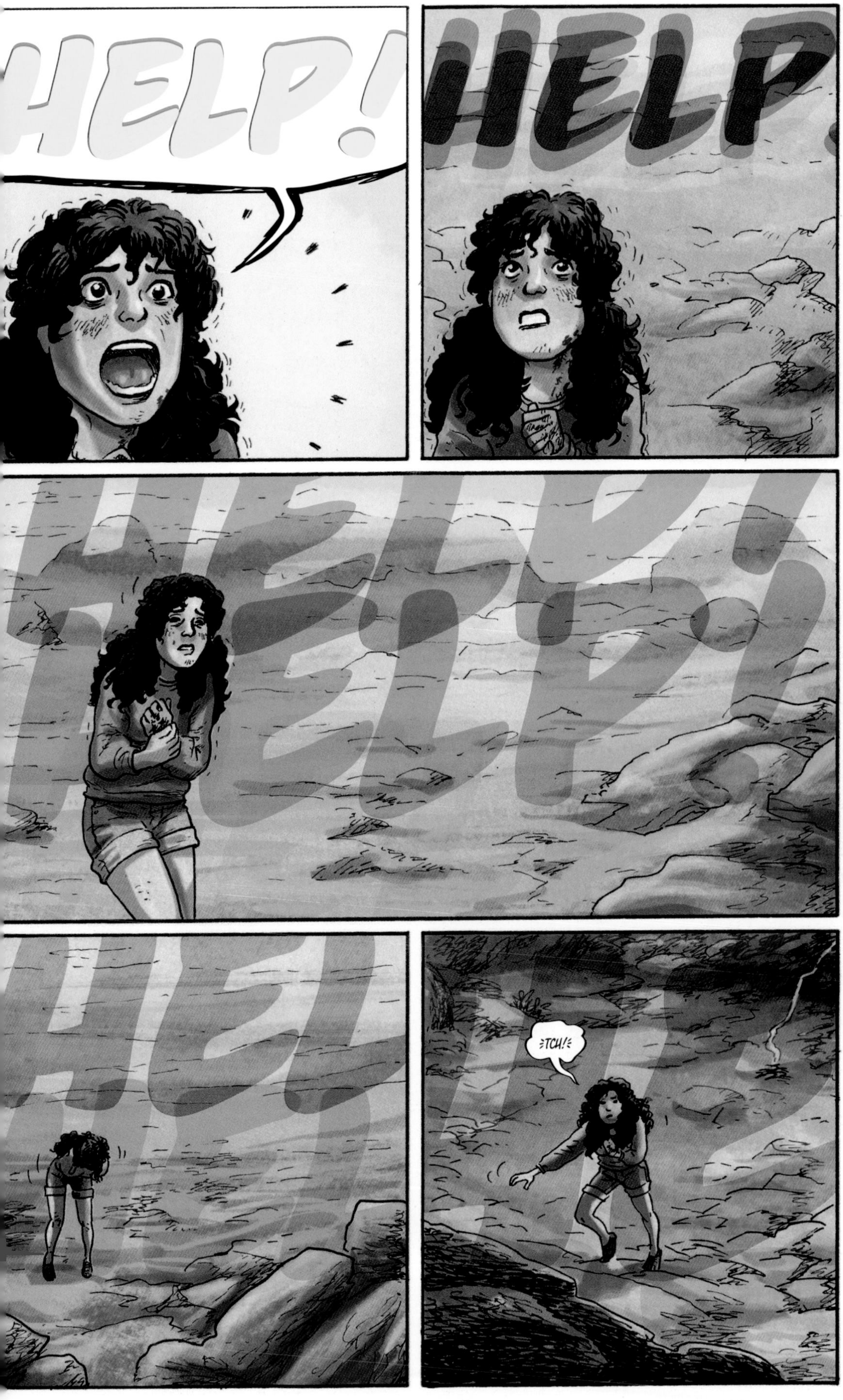
HELP!
HELP!
HELP!
HELP!
HEL
TCH!

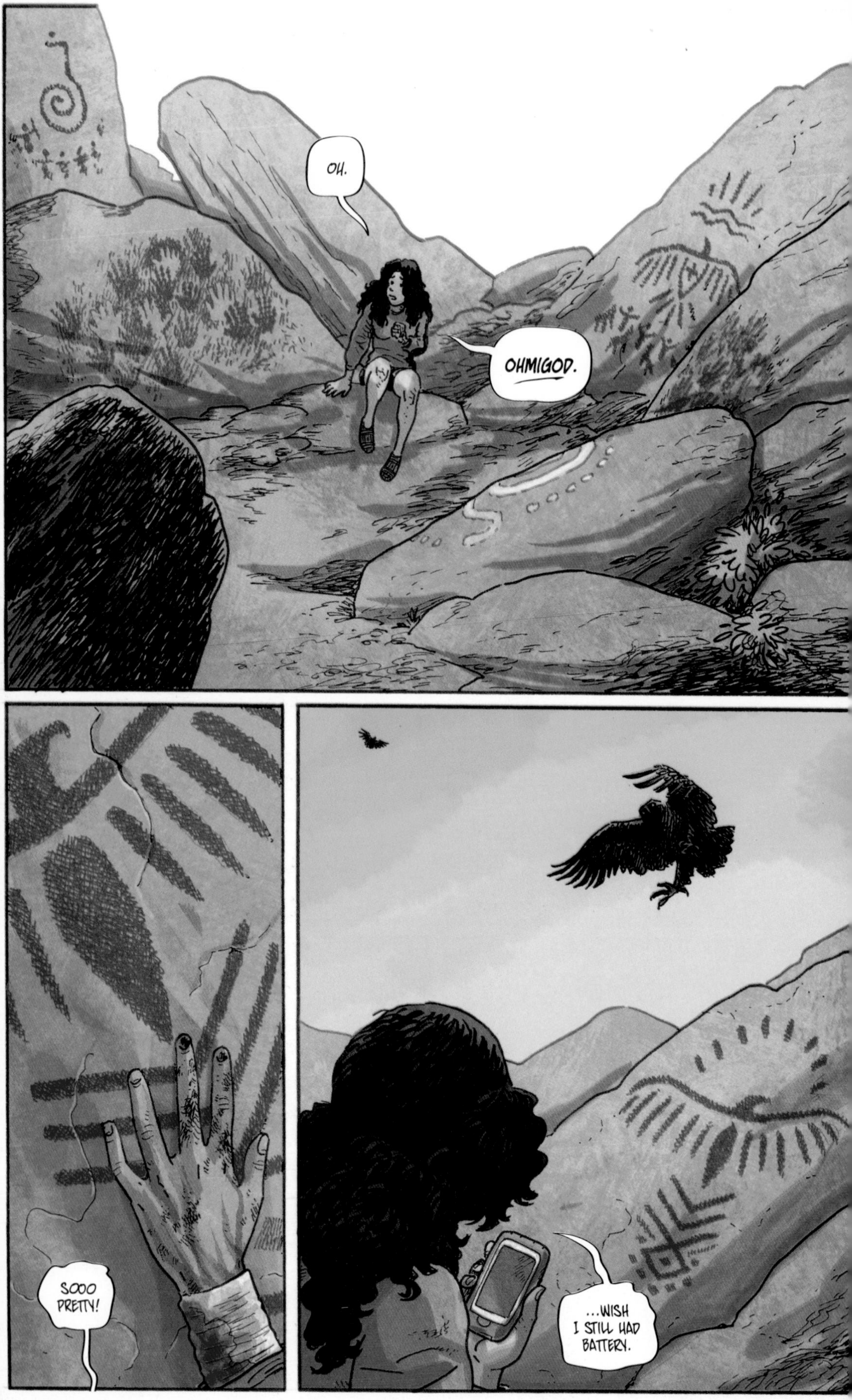
OH.
OHMIGOD.
SOOO PRETTY!
...WISH I STILL HAD BATTERY.

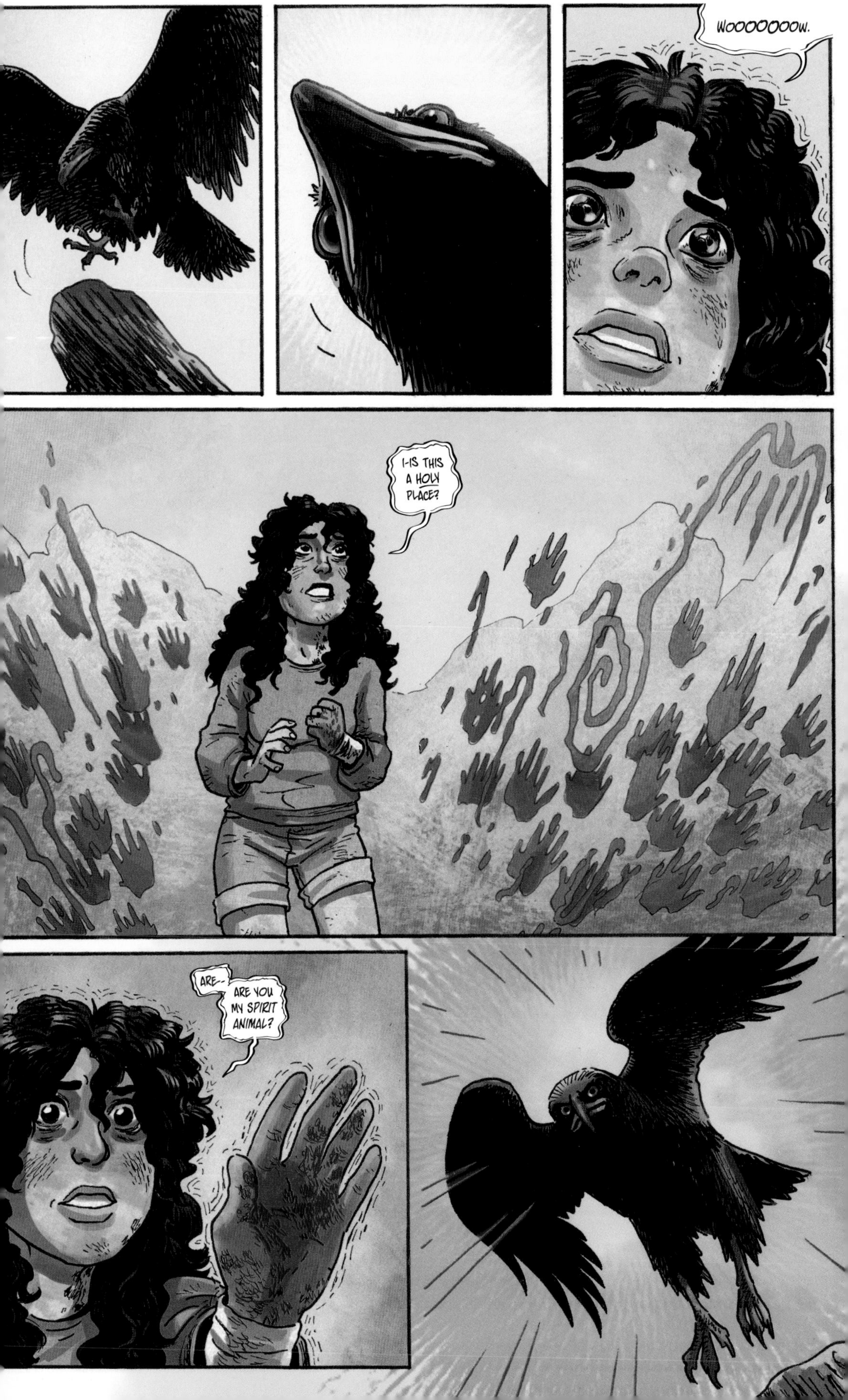
WOOOOOOOW.
I-IS THIS A HOLY PLACE?
ARE--
ARE YOU MY SPIRIT ANIMAL?

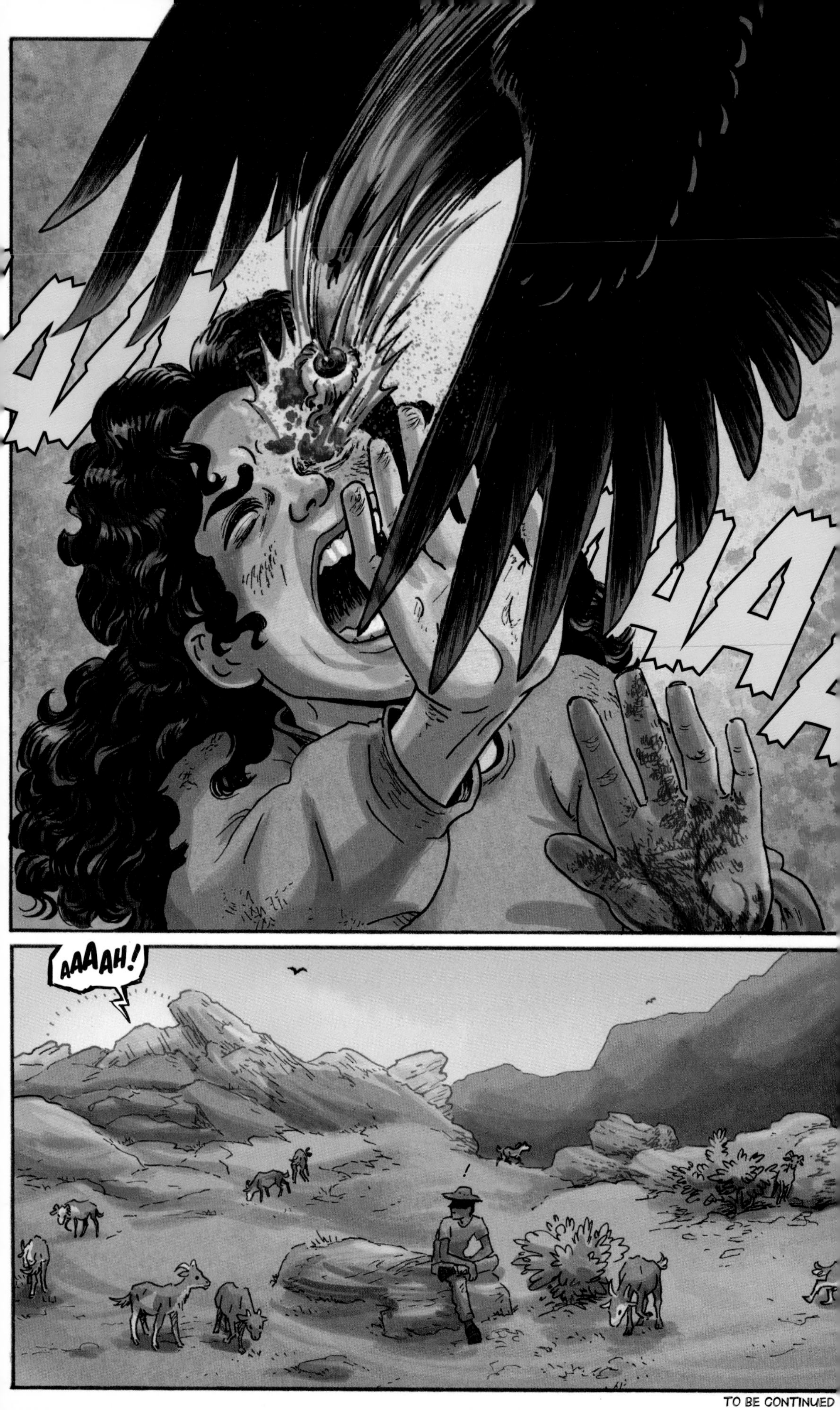
AAAAH!
!

TO BE CONTINUED

MATAGUEY

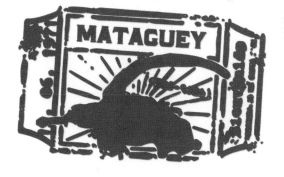

CHILLING TALES OF TEENAGE TERROR!!!

CHAPTER SIX

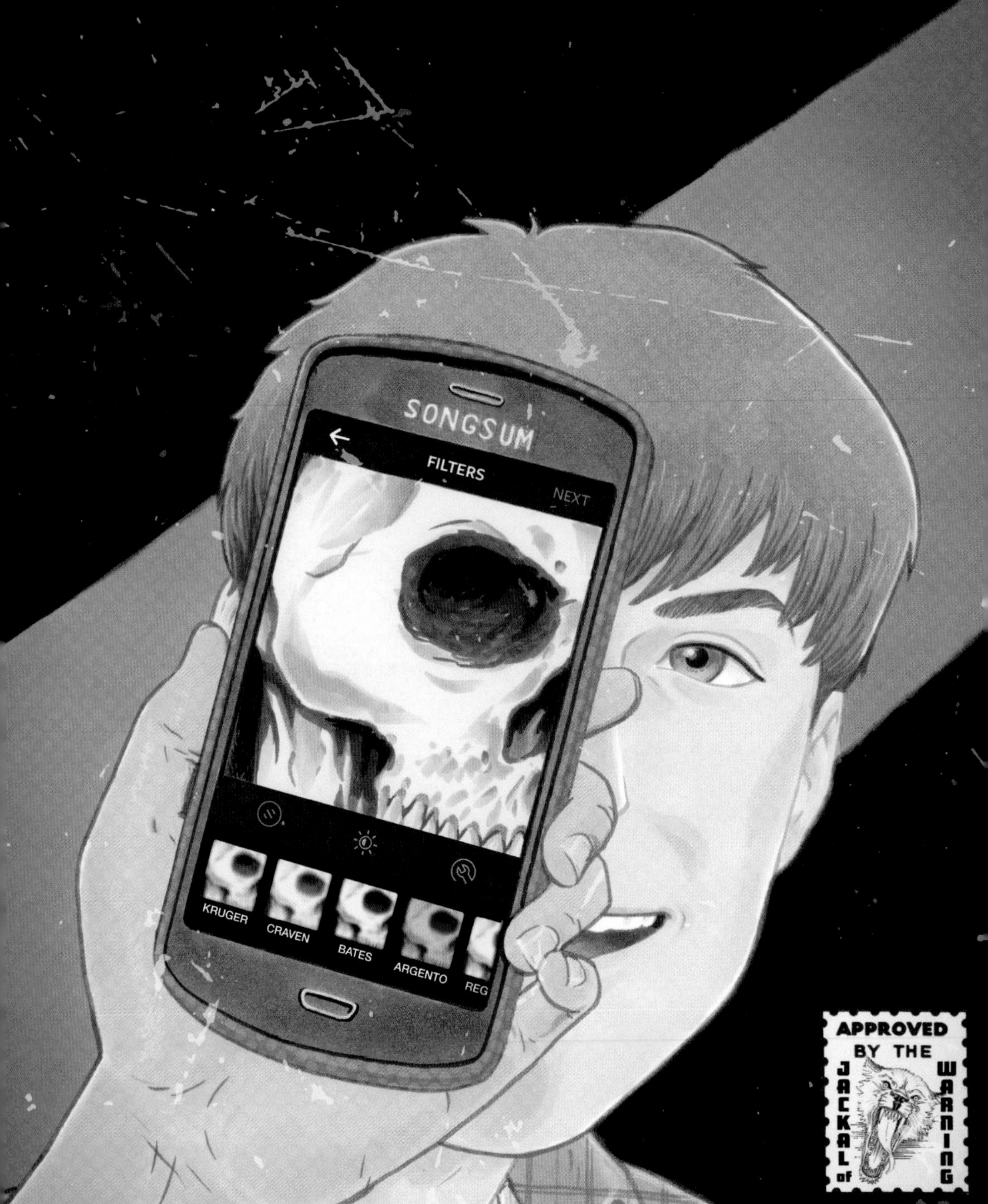
SONGSUM
FILTERS
NEXT
KRUGER
CRAVEN
BATES
ARGENTO
REG
APPROVED BY THE JACKAL of WARNING

WE DARE YOU TO GAZE INTO THE CAMERA... INTO HORROR!

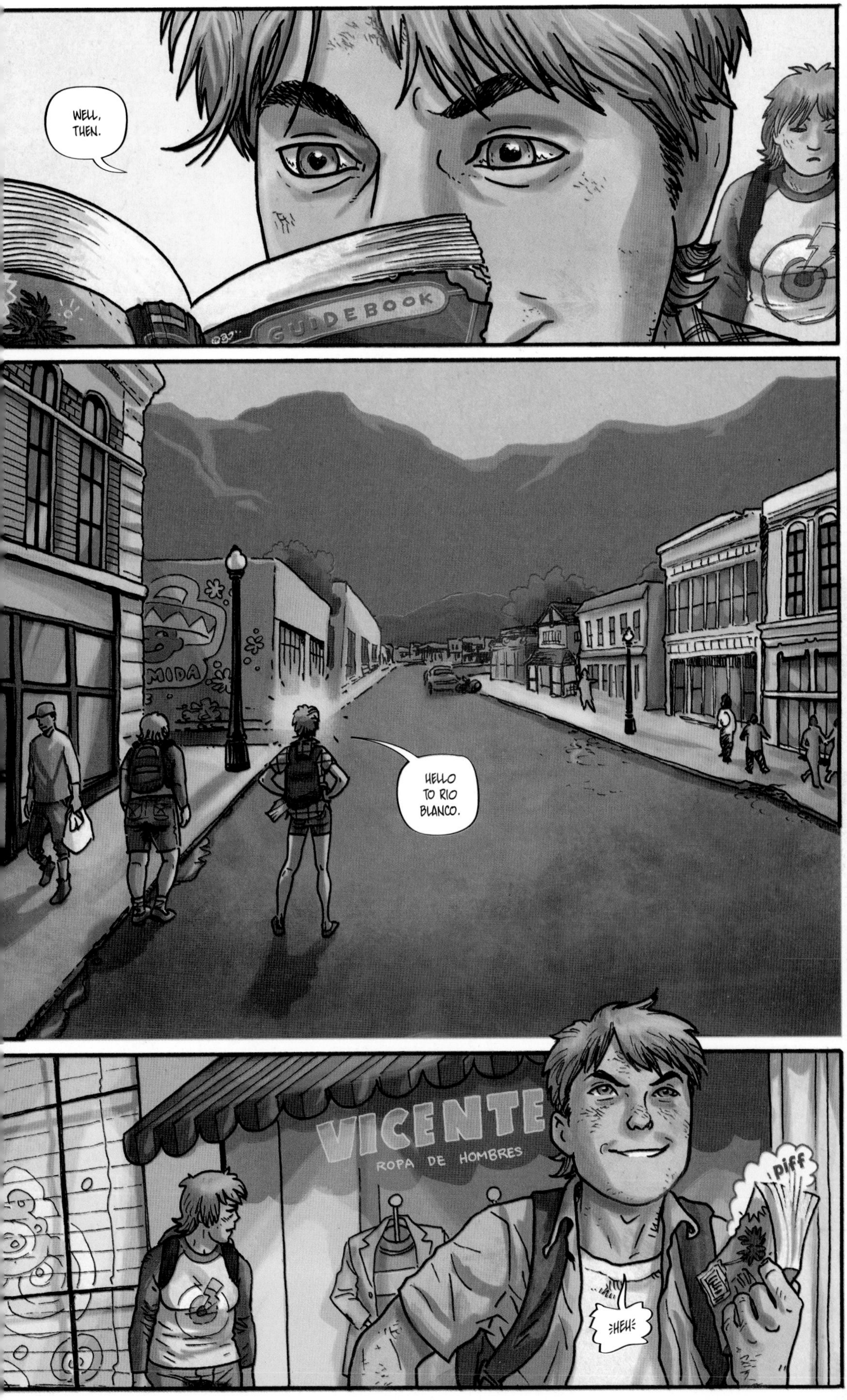
WELL, THEN.
GUIDEBOOK
MIDA
HELLO TO RIO BLANCO.
VICENTE
ROPA DE HOMBRES
piff
HEH

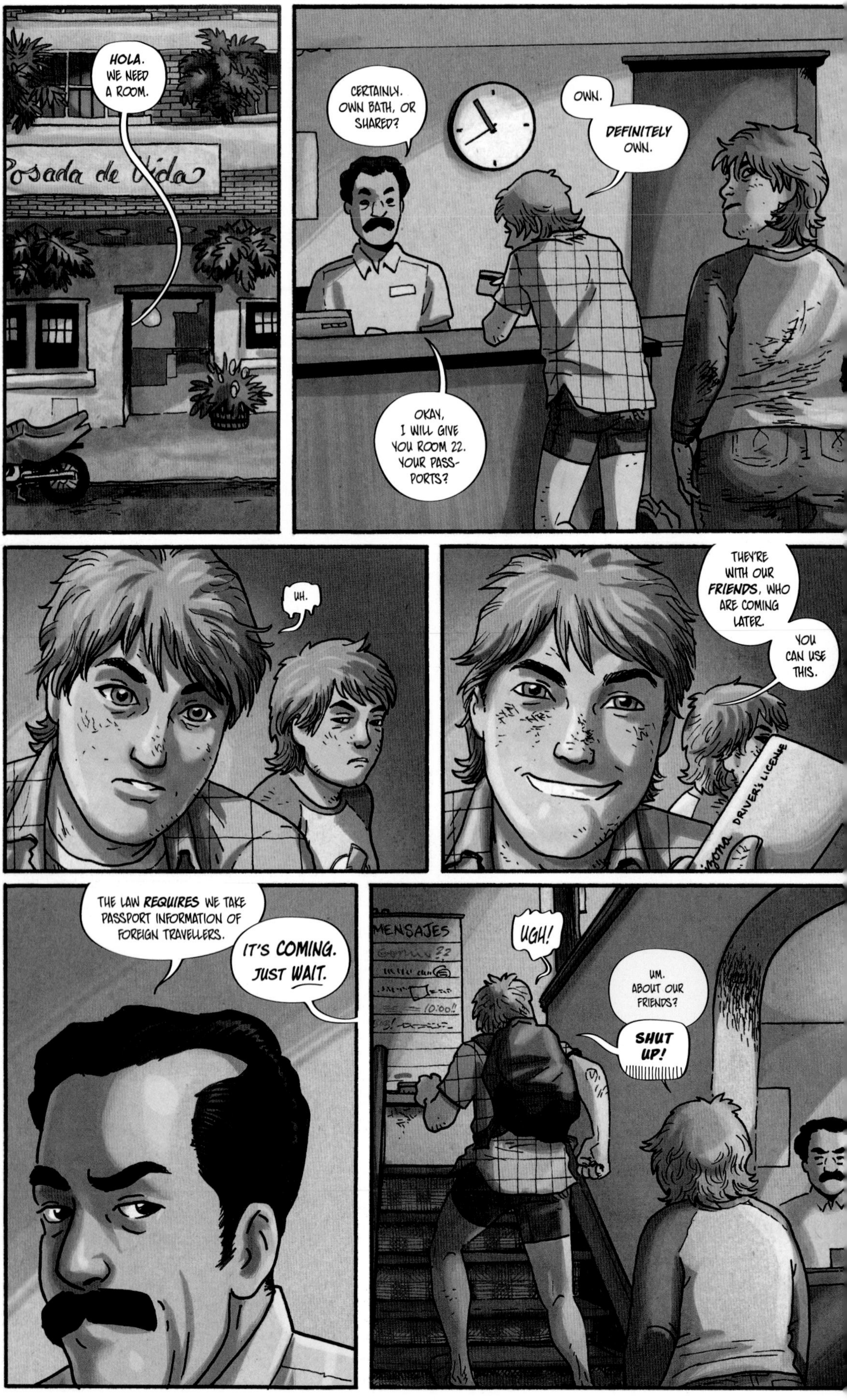
HOLA. WE NEED A ROOM.
Posada de Vida
CERTAINLY. OWN BATH, OR SHARED?
OWN.
DEFINITELY OWN.
OKAY, I WILL GIVE YOU ROOM 22. YOUR PASSPORTS?
UH.
THEY'RE WITH OUR FRIENDS, WHO ARE COMING LATER.
YOU CAN USE THIS.
DRIVER'S LICENSE
THE LAW REQUIRES WE TAKE PASSPORT INFORMATION OF FOREIGN TRAVELLERS.
IT'S COMING. JUST WAIT.
MENSAJES
UGH!
UM. ABOUT OUR FRIENDS?
SHUT UP!

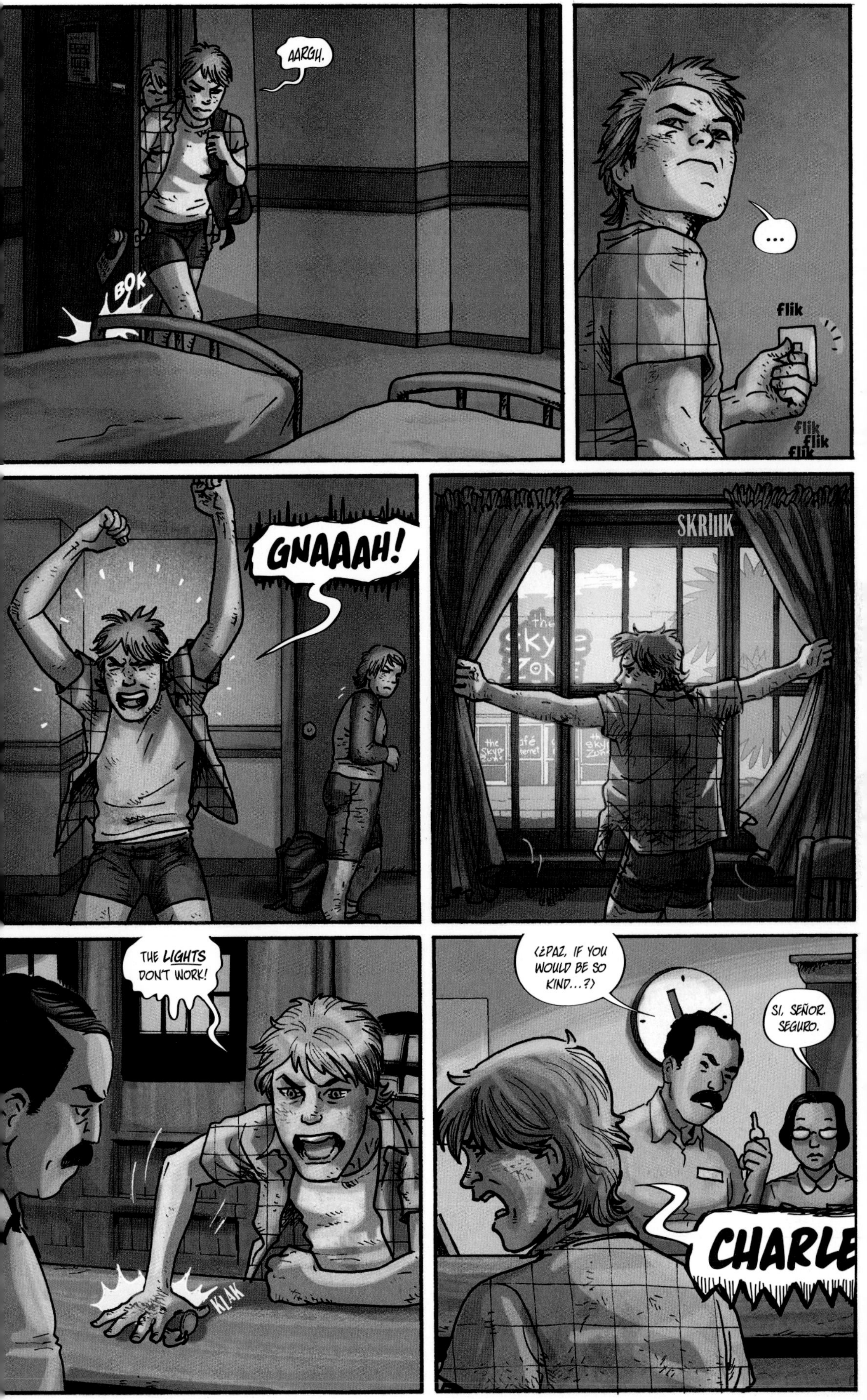
AARGH.
BOK
...
flik
flik
flik
flik
GNAAAH!
SKRIIIK
THE LIGHTS DON'T WORK!
KLAK
‹¿PAZ, IF YOU WOULD BE SO KIND...?›
SI, SEÑOR. SEGURO.
CHARLE

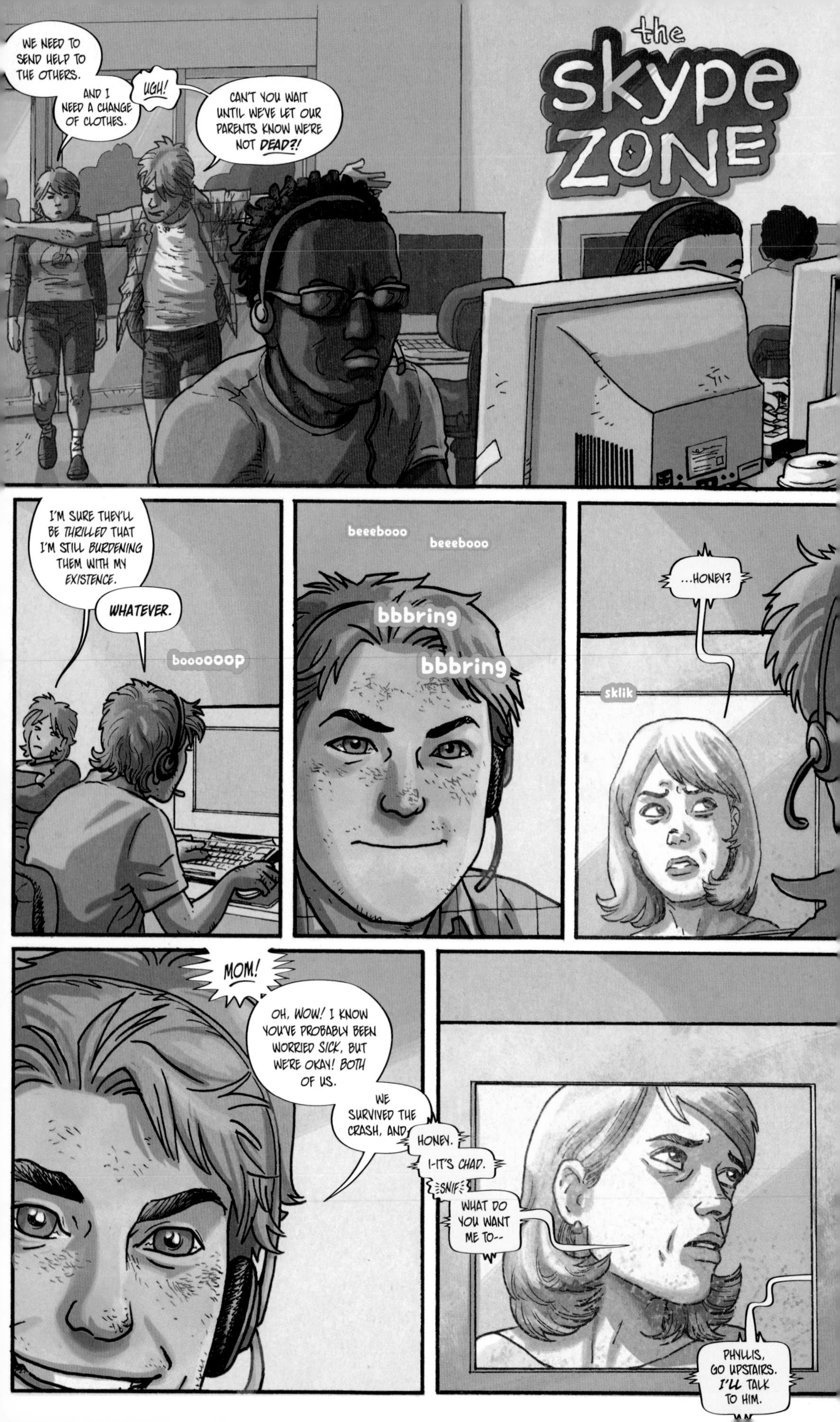
WE NEED TO SEND HELP TO THE OTHERS.
AND I NEED A CHANGE OF CLOTHES.
UGH!
CAN'T YOU WAIT UNTIL WE'VE LET OUR PARENTS KNOW WE'RE NOT DEAD?!
the skype ZONE
I'M SURE THEY'LL BE THRILLED THAT I'M STILL BURDENING THEM WITH MY EXISTENCE.
WHATEVER.
boooooop
beeeboo
beeeboo
bbbring
bbbring
...HONEY?
sklik
MOM!
OH, WOW! I KNOW YOU'VE PROBABLY BEEN WORRIED SICK, BUT WE'RE OKAY! BOTH OF US.
WE SURVIVED THE CRASH, AND
HONEY.
I-IT'S CHAD.
SNIF
WHAT DO YOU WANT ME TO--
PHYLLIS, GO UPSTAIRS. I'LL TALK TO HIM.

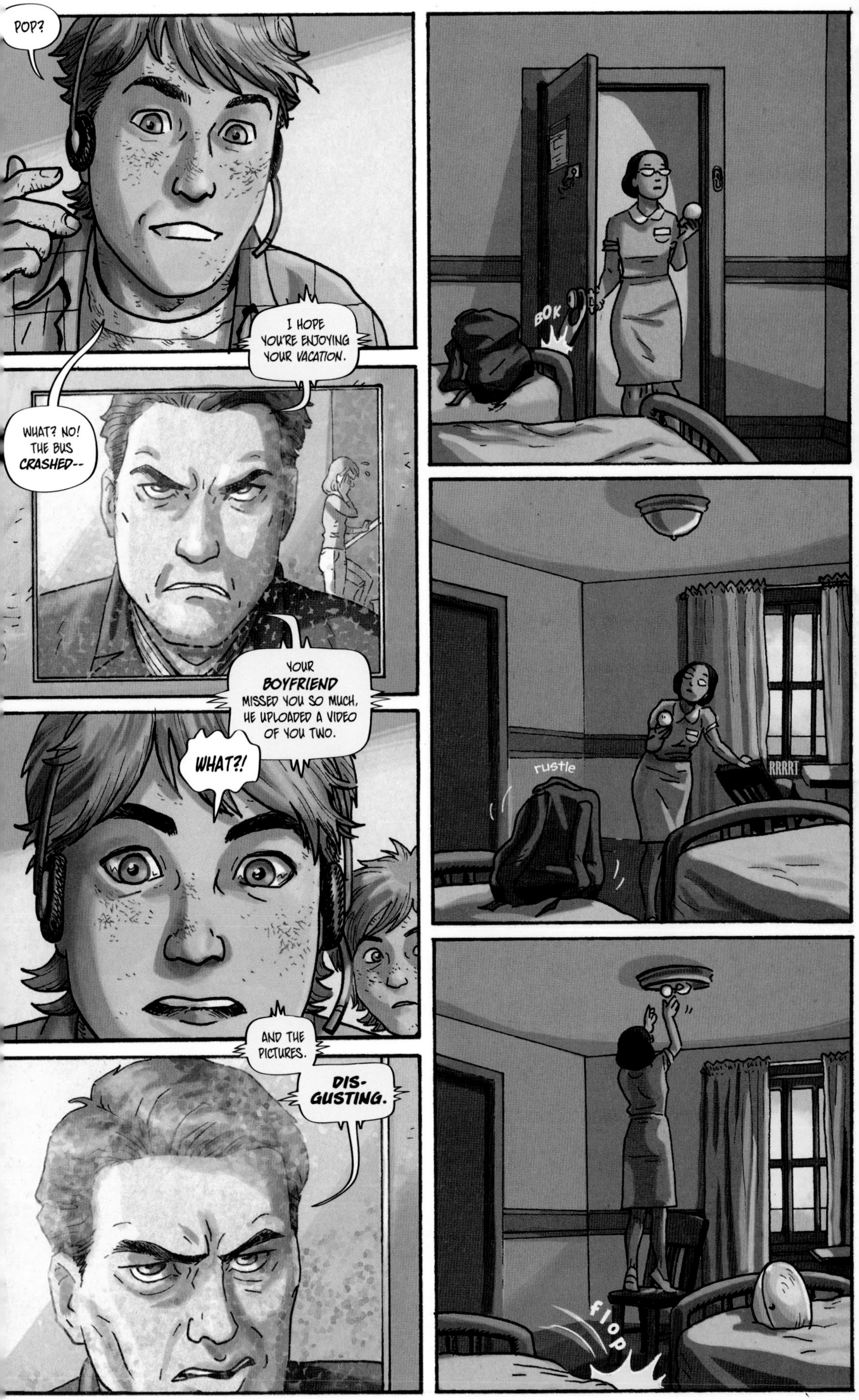
POP?
I HOPE YOU'RE ENJOYING YOUR VACATION.
WHAT? NO! THE BUS CRASHED--
YOUR BOYFRIEND MISSED YOU SO MUCH, HE UPLOADED A VIDEO OF YOU TWO.
WHAT?!
AND THE PICTURES.
DIS-GUSTING.
BOK
rustle
RRRRT
flop

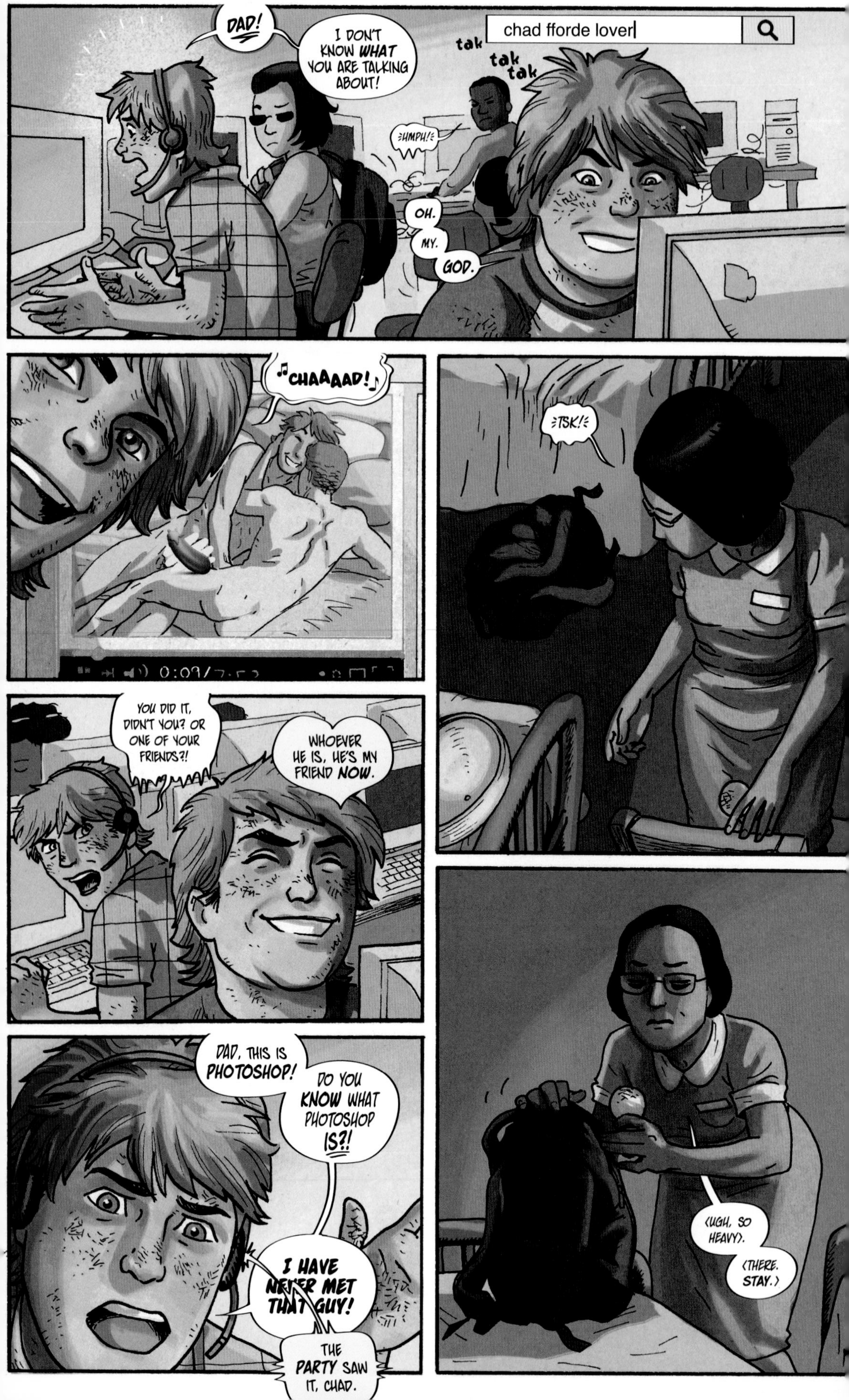
DAD!
I DON'T KNOW WHAT YOU ARE TALKING ABOUT!
chad fforde lover
tak
tak
tak
HMPH!
OH. MY. GOD.
CHAAAAD!
TSK!
YOU DID IT, DIDN'T YOU? OR ONE OF YOUR FRIENDS?!
WHOEVER HE IS, HE'S MY FRIEND NOW.
DAD, THIS IS PHOTOSHOP!
DO YOU KNOW WHAT PHOTOSHOP IS?!
I HAVE NEVER MET THAT GUY!
THE PARTY SAW IT, CHAD.
<UGH, SO HEAVY>.
<THERE. STAY.>

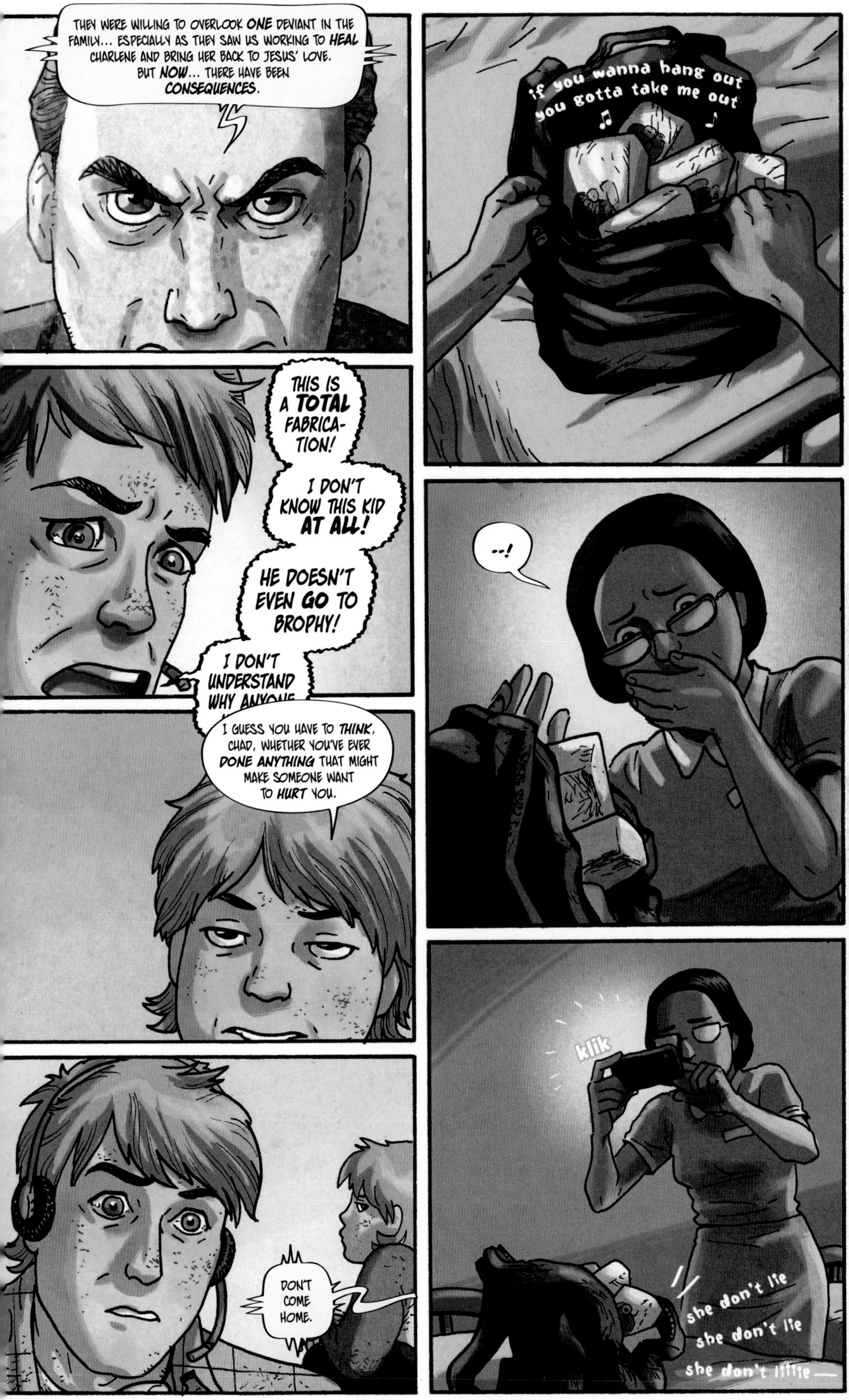
THEY WERE WILLING TO OVERLOOK ONE DEVIANT IN THE FAMILY... ESPECIALLY AS THEY SAW US WORKING TO HEAL CHARLENE AND BRING HER BACK TO JESUS' LOVE. BUT NOW... THERE HAVE BEEN CONSEQUENCES.
THIS IS A TOTAL FABRICATION!
I DON'T KNOW THIS KID AT ALL!
HE DOESN'T EVEN GO TO BROPHY!
I DON'T UNDERSTAND WHY ANYONE
I GUESS YOU HAVE TO THINK, CHAD, WHETHER YOU'VE EVER DONE ANYTHING THAT MIGHT MAKE SOMEONE WANT TO HURT YOU.
DON'T COME HOME.
if you wanna hang out you gotta take me out
--!
klik
she don't lie
she don't lie
she don't liiiie

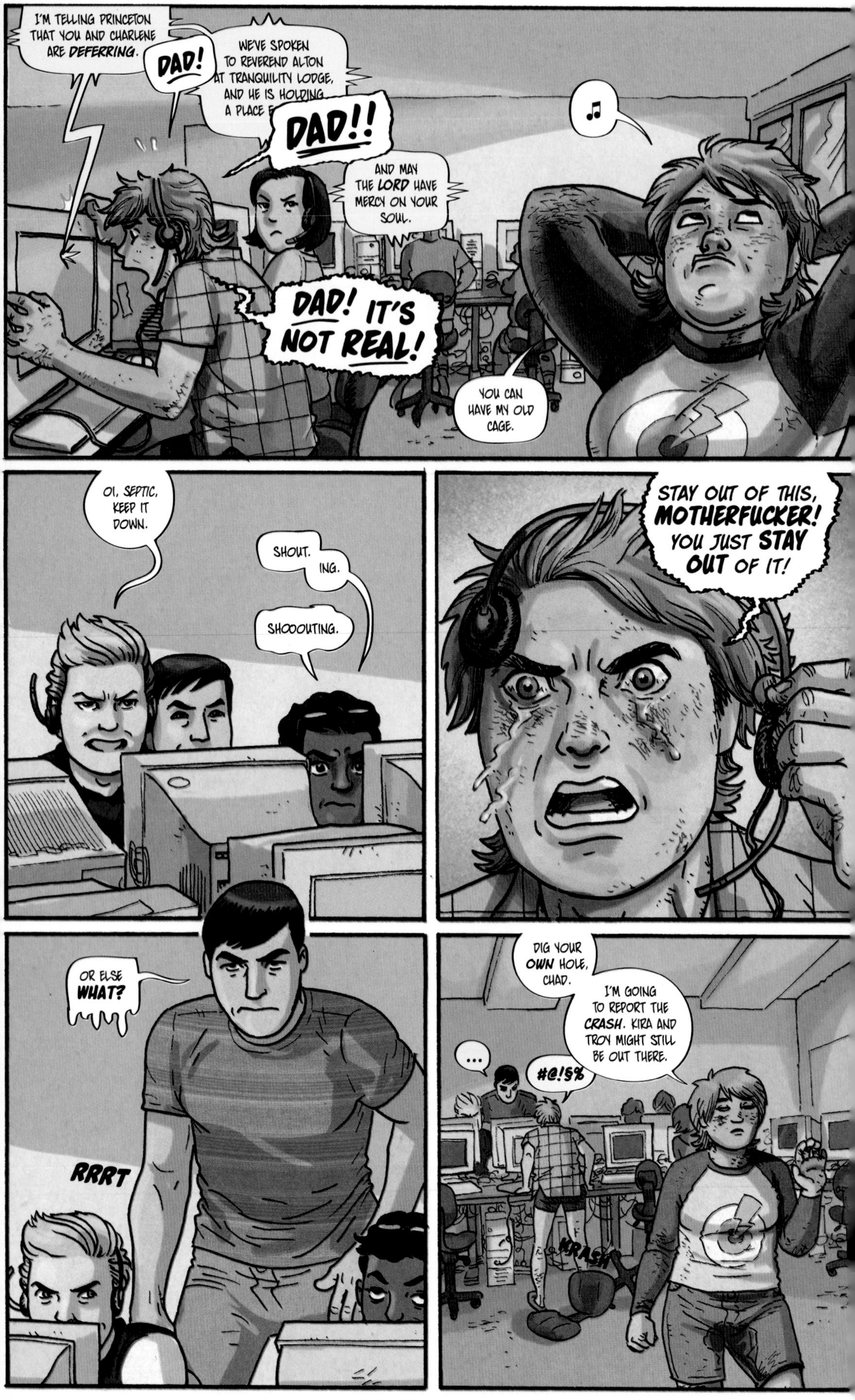
I'M TELLING PRINCETON THAT YOU AND CHARLENE ARE DEFERRING.
DAD!
WE'VE SPOKEN TO REVEREND ALTON AT TRANQUILITY LODGE, AND HE IS HOLDING A PLACE F
DAD!!
AND MAY THE LORD HAVE MERCY ON YOUR SOUL.
DAD! IT'S NOT REAL!
♪
YOU CAN HAVE MY OLD CAGE.
OI, SEPTIC, KEEP IT DOWN.
SHOUT.
ING.
SHOOOUTING.
STAY OUT OF THIS, MOTHERFUCKER! YOU JUST STAY OUT OF IT!
OR ELSE WHAT?
RRRT
DIG YOUR OWN HOLE, CHAD.
I'M GOING TO REPORT THE CRASH. KIRA AND TROY MIGHT STILL BE OUT THERE.
...
#@!§%
KRASH

FUCK FUCK FUCK FUCK FUCK FUCK FUCK FUCK

osada de Viaju

R-ROOM 22.

ONE MOMENT, PLEASE.

UGH, WHAT IS IT WITH *YANKS* AND VOLUME CONTROL?!

I DUNNO, MATE.

BIG COUNTRY? THEY'RE ALL FAR AWAY FROM EACH OTHER?

SO, WE GOING TO LOOK AT ROCK CARVINGS, OR WHAT?

OR CERVEZA!

THE TWO ARE *NOT* MUTUALLY EXCLUSIVE, SIMON.

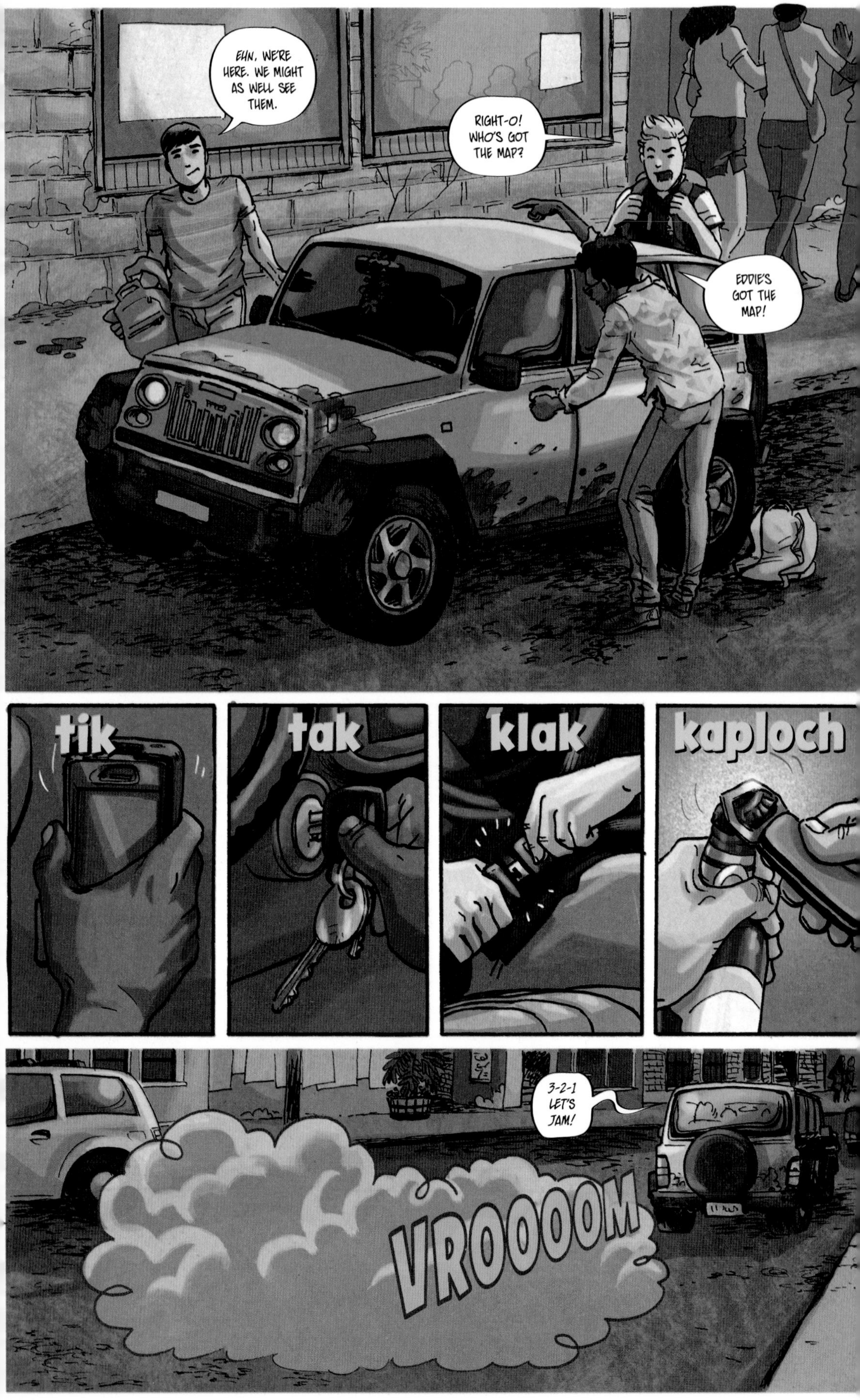
EHN, WE'RE HERE. WE MIGHT AS WELL SEE THEM.
RIGHT-O! WHO'S GOT THE MAP?
EDDIE'S GOT THE MAP!
tik
tak
klak
kaploch
3-2-1 LET'S JAM!
VROOOOM

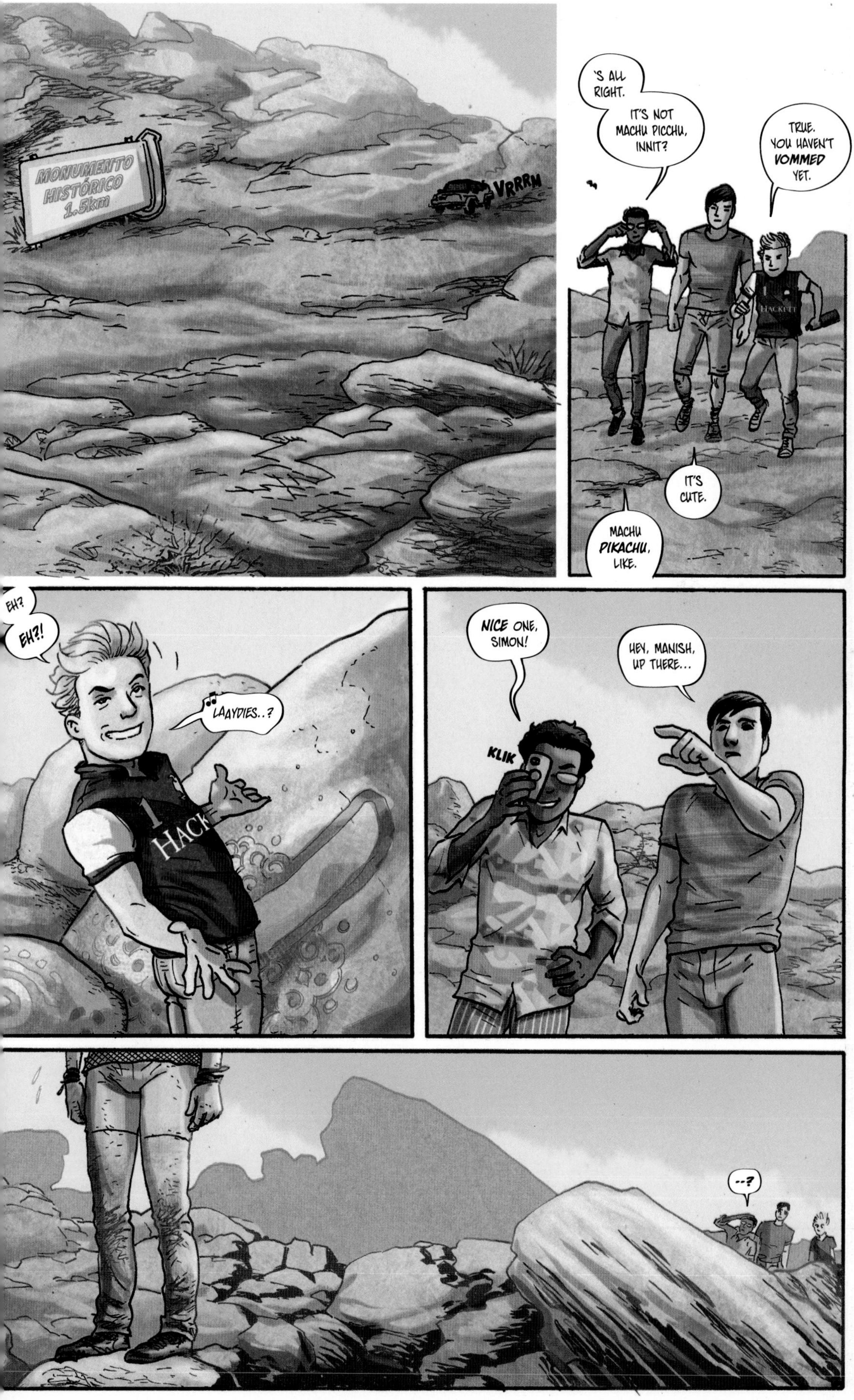
MONUMENTO HISTÓRICO 1.5km
VRRRN
'S ALL RIGHT.
IT'S NOT MACHU PICCHU, INNIT?
TRUE. YOU HAVEN'T VOMMED YET.
HACKETT
IT'S CUTE.
MACHU PIKACHU, LIKE.
EH?
EH?!
LAAYDIES..?
1 HACK
NICE ONE, SIMON!
HEY, MANISH, UP THERE...
KLIK
--?

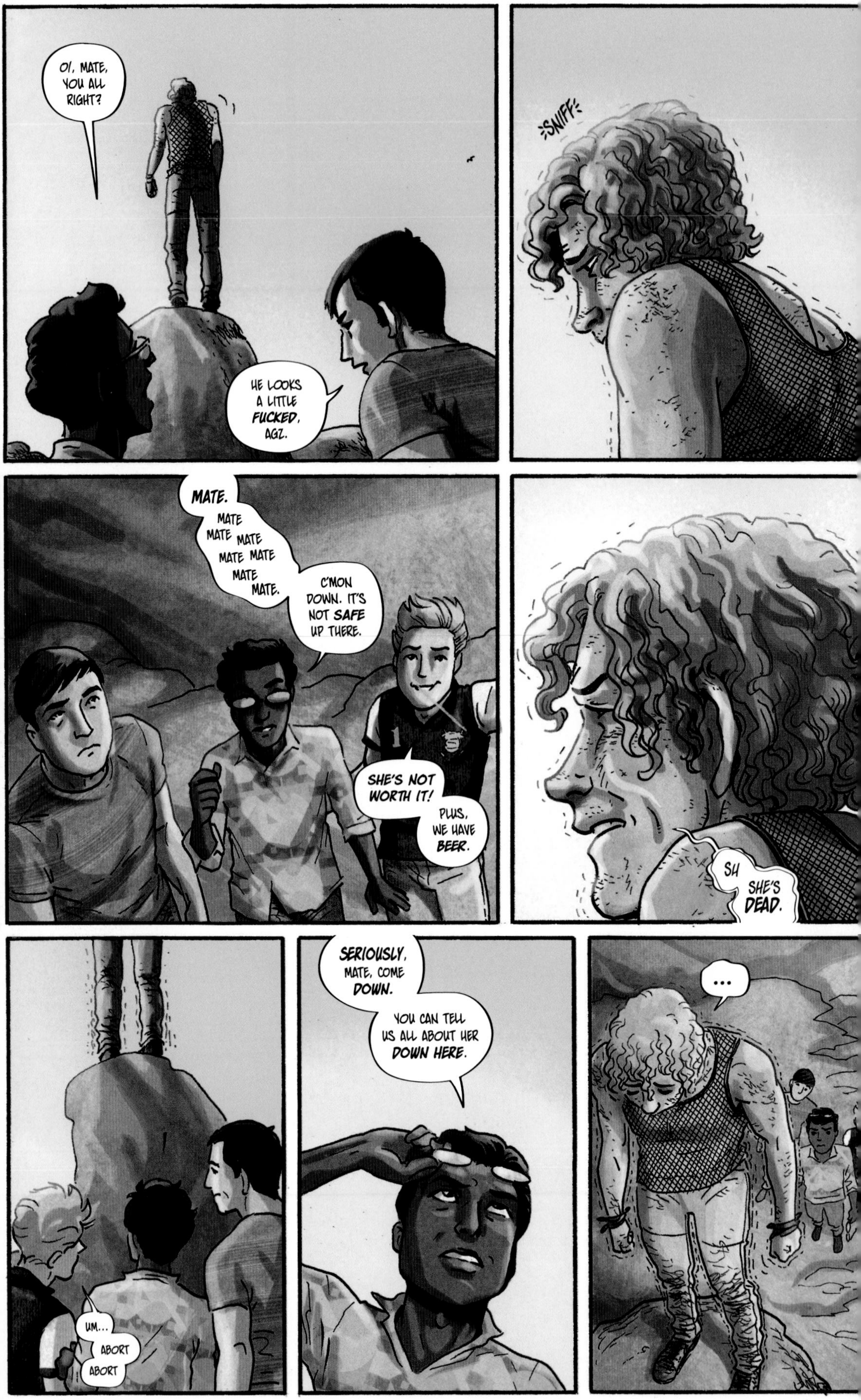
OI, MATE, YOU ALL RIGHT?
HE LOOKS A LITTLE FUCKED, AGZ.
SNIFF
MATE.
MATE MATE MATE MATE MATE MATE MATE.
C'MON DOWN. IT'S NOT SAFE UP THERE.
SHE'S NOT WORTH IT!
PLUS, WE HAVE BEER.
SH SHE'S DEAD.
UM... ABORT ABORT
SERIOUSLY, MATE, COME DOWN.
YOU CAN TELL US ALL ABOUT HER DOWN HERE.
...

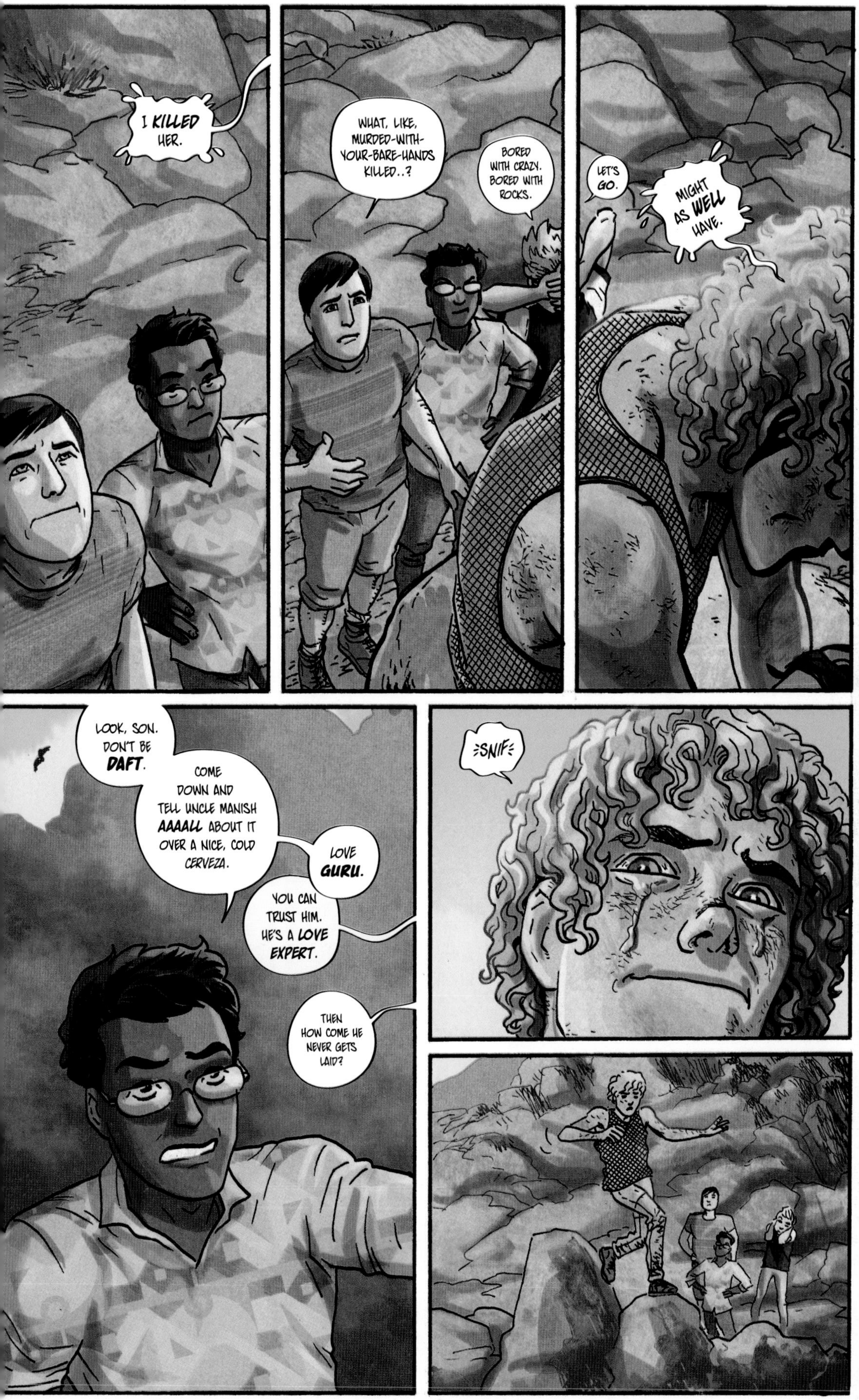

I KILLED HER.
WHAT, LIKE, MURDED-WITH-YOUR-BARE-HANDS KILLED..?
BORED WITH CRAZY. BORED WITH ROCKS.
LET'S GO.
MIGHT AS WELL HAVE.
LOOK, SON. DON'T BE DAFT.
COME DOWN AND TELL UNCLE MANISH AAAALL ABOUT IT OVER A NICE, COLD CERVEZA.
LOVE GURU.
YOU CAN TRUST HIM. HE'S A LOVE EXPERT.
THEN HOW COME HE NEVER GETS LAID?
SNIF

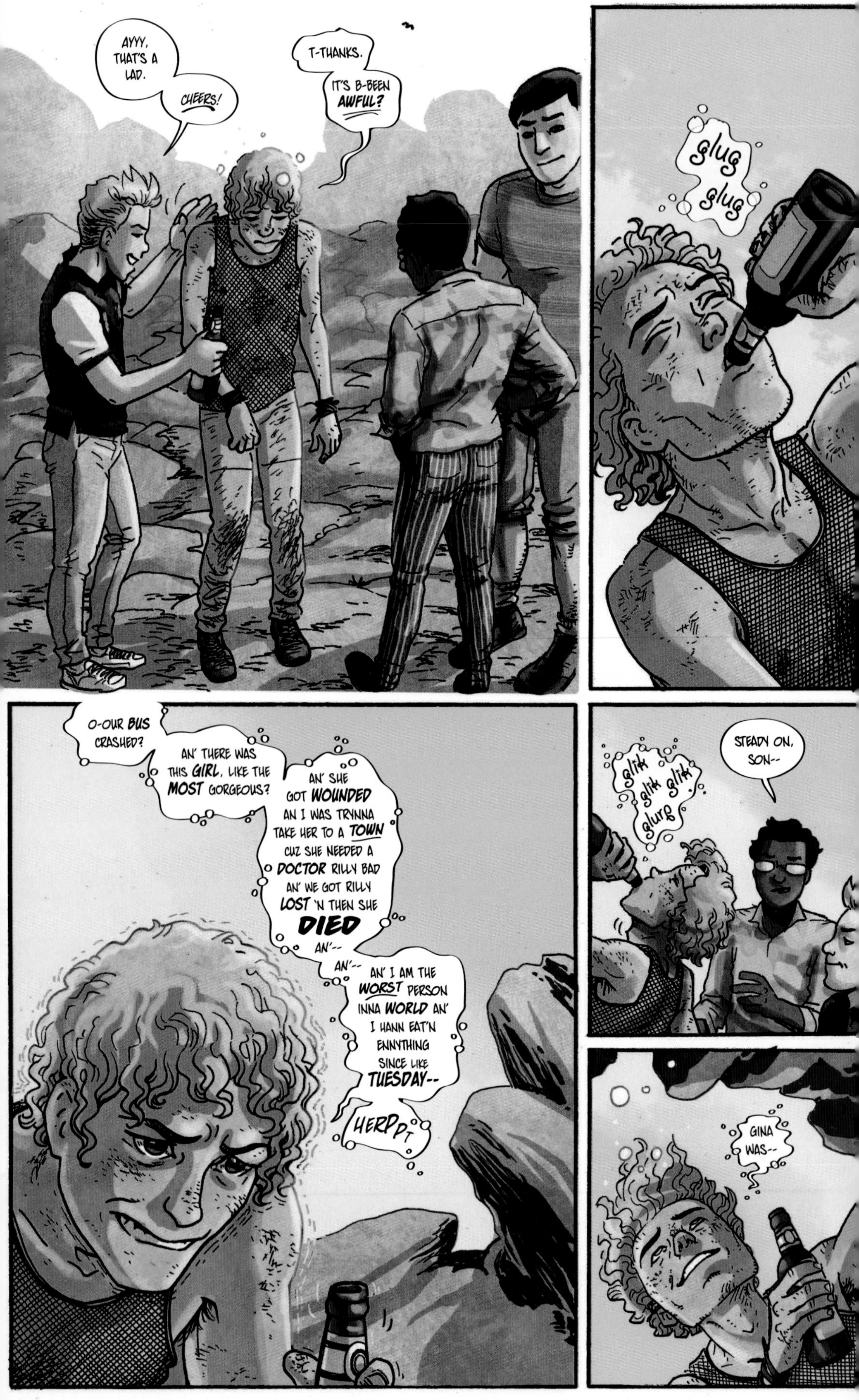
AYYY, THAT'S A LAD.
CHEERS!
T-THANKS.
IT'S B-BEEN AWFUL?
glug glug
O-OUR BUS CRASHED?
AN' THERE WAS THIS GIRL, LIKE THE MOST GORGEOUS?
AN' SHE GOT WOUNDED AN I WAS TRYNNA TAKE HER TO A TOWN CUZ SHE NEEDED A DOCTOR RILLY BAD AN' WE GOT RILLY LOST 'N THEN SHE DIED
AN'--
AN'--
AN' I AM THE WORST PERSON INNA WORLD AN' I HANN EAT'N ENNYTHING SINCE LIKE TUESDAY--
HERPPT
glik glik glik glurg
STEADY ON, SON--
GINA WAS--

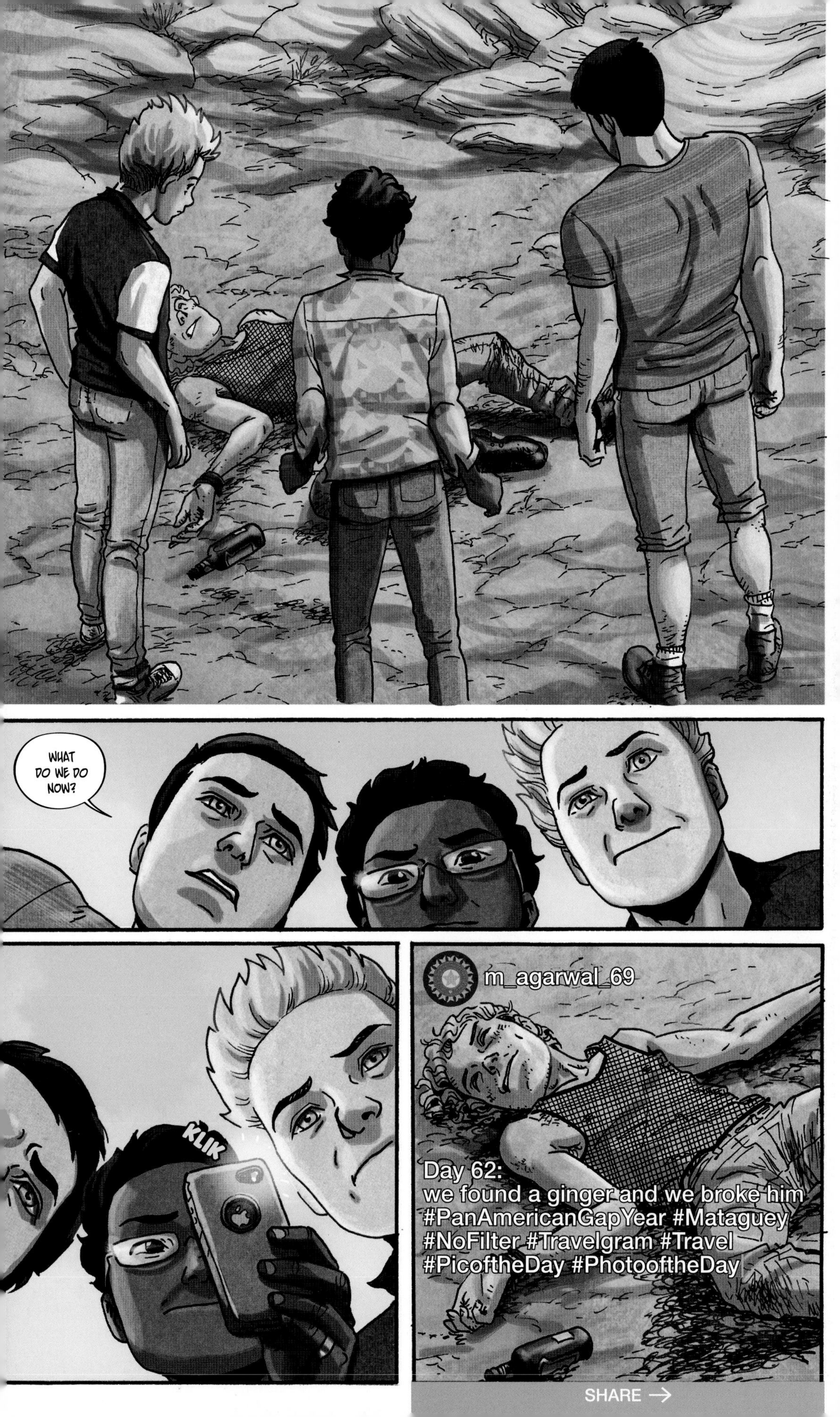
WHAT DO WE DO NOW?
KLIK
m_agarwal_69
Day 62:
we found a ginger and we broke him
#PanAmericanGapYear #Mataguey
#NoFilter #Travelgram #Travel
#PicoftheDay #PhotooftheDay
SHARE →

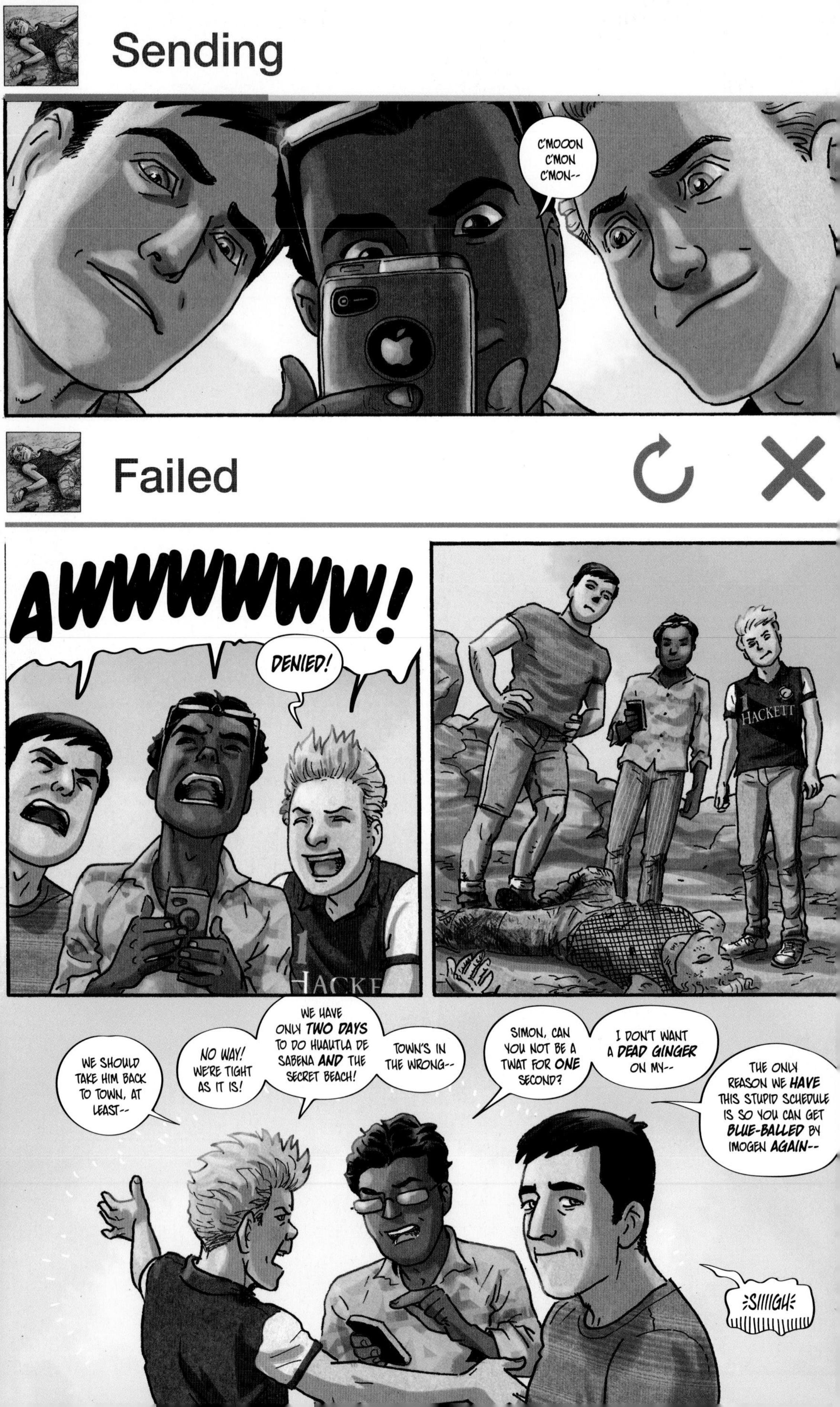
Sending
C'MOOON C'MON C'MON--
Failed
AWWWWWW!
DENIED!
HACKETT
WE SHOULD TAKE HIM BACK TO TOWN, AT LEAST--
NO WAY! WE'RE TIGHT AS IT IS!
WE HAVE ONLY TWO DAYS TO DO HUAUTLA DE SABENA AND THE SECRET BEACH!
TOWN'S IN THE WRONG--
SIMON, CAN YOU NOT BE A TWAT FOR ONE SECOND?
I DON'T WANT A DEAD GINGER ON MY--
THE ONLY REASON WE HAVE THIS STUPID SCHEDULE IS SO YOU CAN GET BLUE-BALLED BY IMOGEN AGAIN--
SIIIIGH

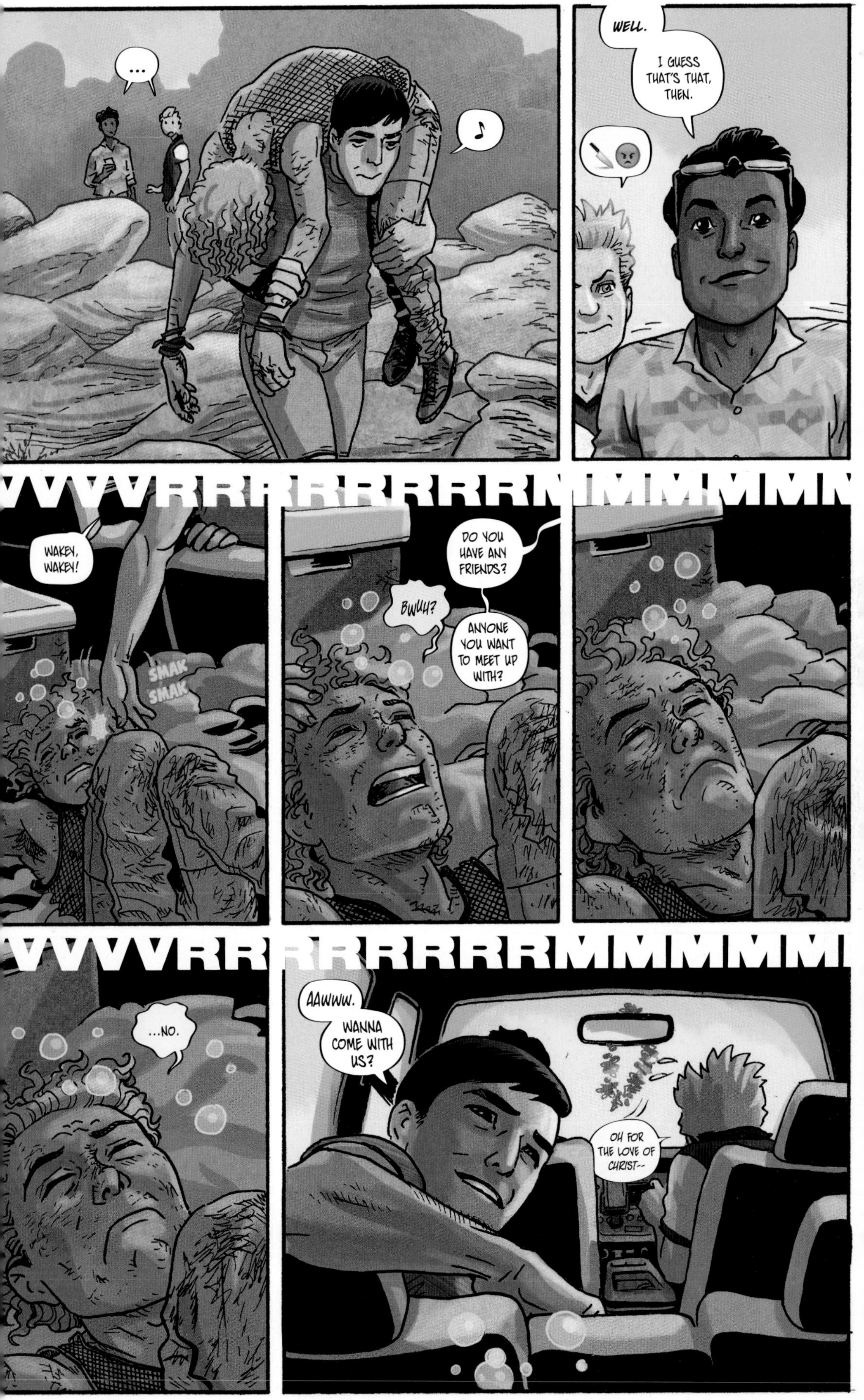
...
♪
WELL.
I GUESS THAT'S THAT, THEN.
VVVVRRRRRRRRMMMMMMM
WAKEY, WAKEY!
SMAK
SMAK
DO YOU HAVE ANY FRIENDS?
BWUH?
ANYONE YOU WANT TO MEET UP WITH?
VVVVRRRRRRRRMMMMMMM
...NO.
AAWWW.
WANNA COME WITH US?
OH FOR THE LOVE OF CHRIST--

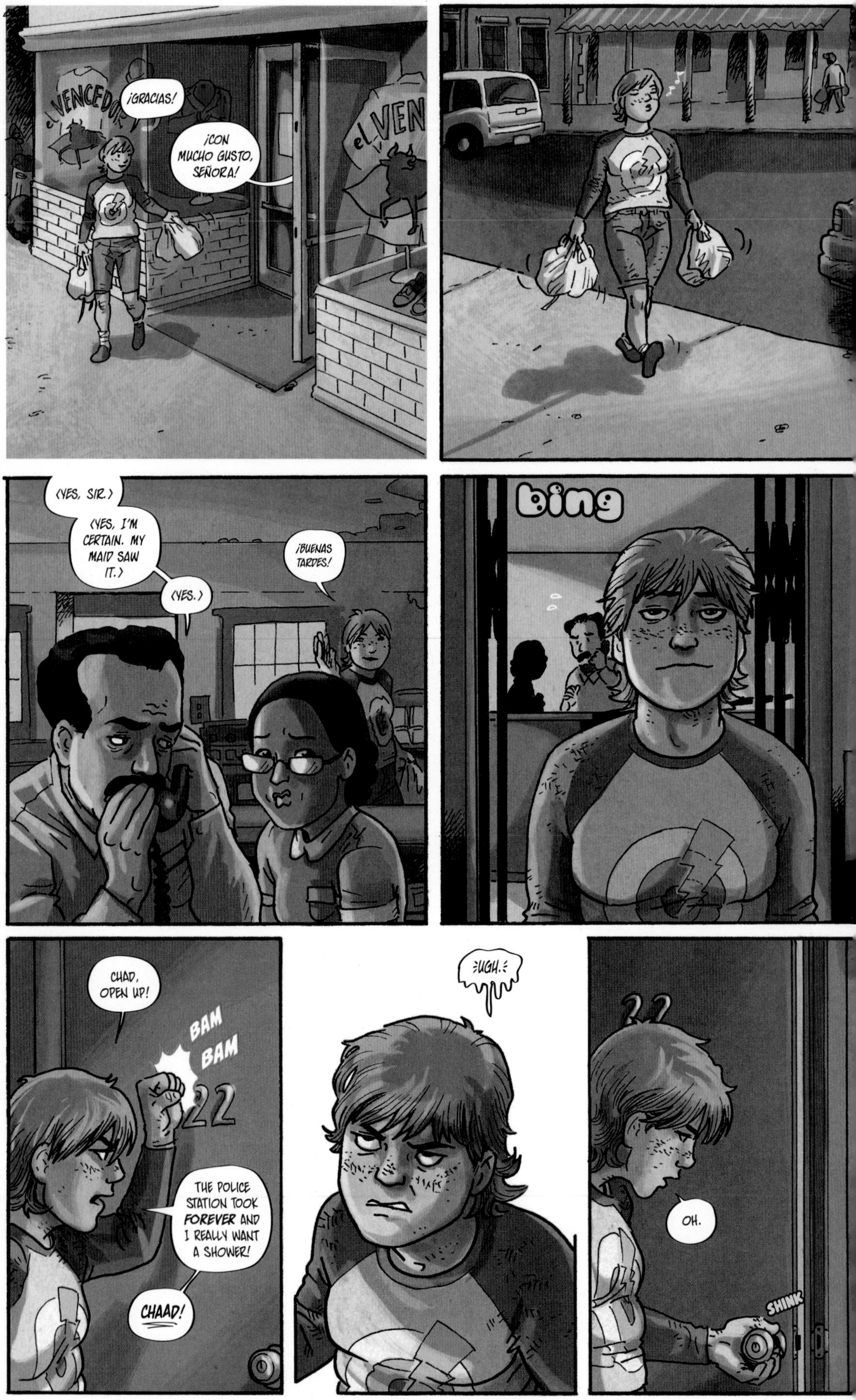
el VENCEDOR
¡GRACIAS!
¡CON MUCHO GUSTO, SEÑORA!
el VEN
‹YES, SIR.›
‹YES, I'M CERTAIN. MY MAID SAW IT.›
‹YES.›
¡BUENAS TARDES!
bing
CHAD, OPEN UP!
BAM BAM
22
THE POLICE STATION TOOK FOREVER AND I REALLY WANT A SHOWER!
CHAAD!
UGH.
OH.
SHINK

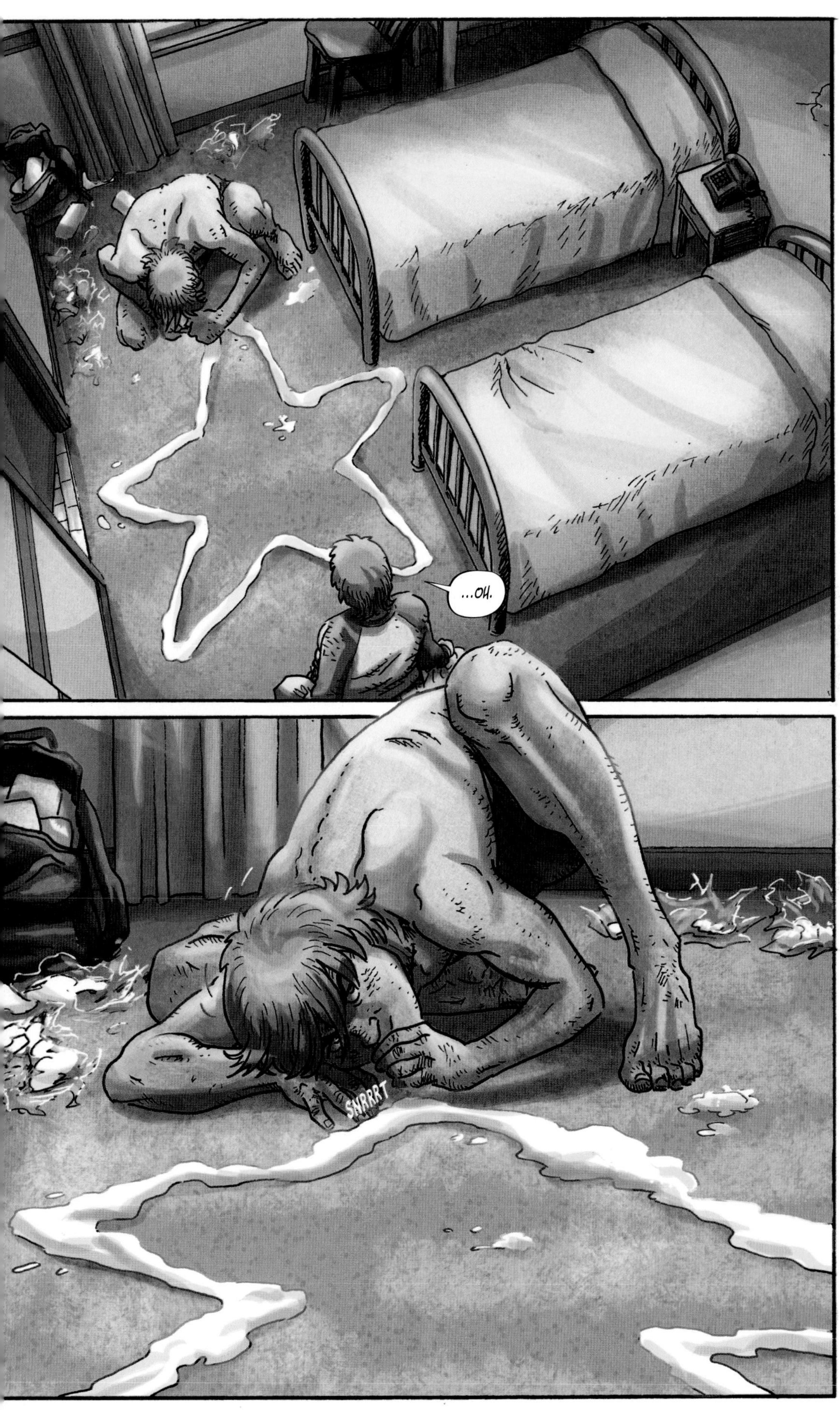
...OH.
SNRRRT

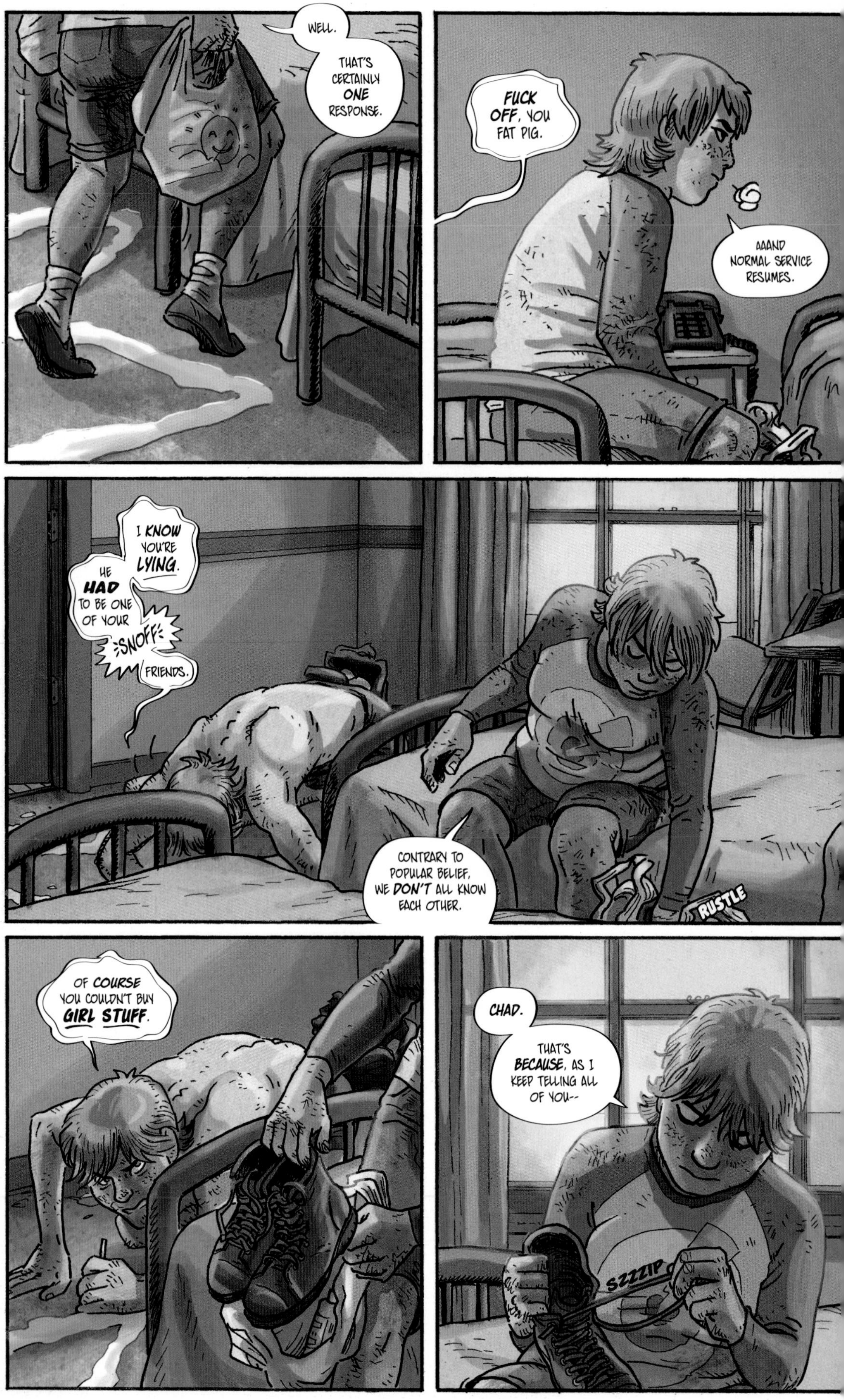
WELL.
THAT'S CERTAINLY ONE RESPONSE.
FUCK OFF, YOU FAT PIG.
AAAND NORMAL SERVICE RESUMES.
I KNOW YOU'RE LYING.
HE HAD TO BE ONE OF YOUR
SNOFF
FRIENDS.
CONTRARY TO POPULAR BELIEF, WE DON'T ALL KNOW EACH OTHER.
RUSTLE
OF COURSE YOU COULDN'T BUY GIRL STUFF.
CHAD.
THAT'S BECAUSE, AS I KEEP TELLING ALL OF YOU--
SZZZIP

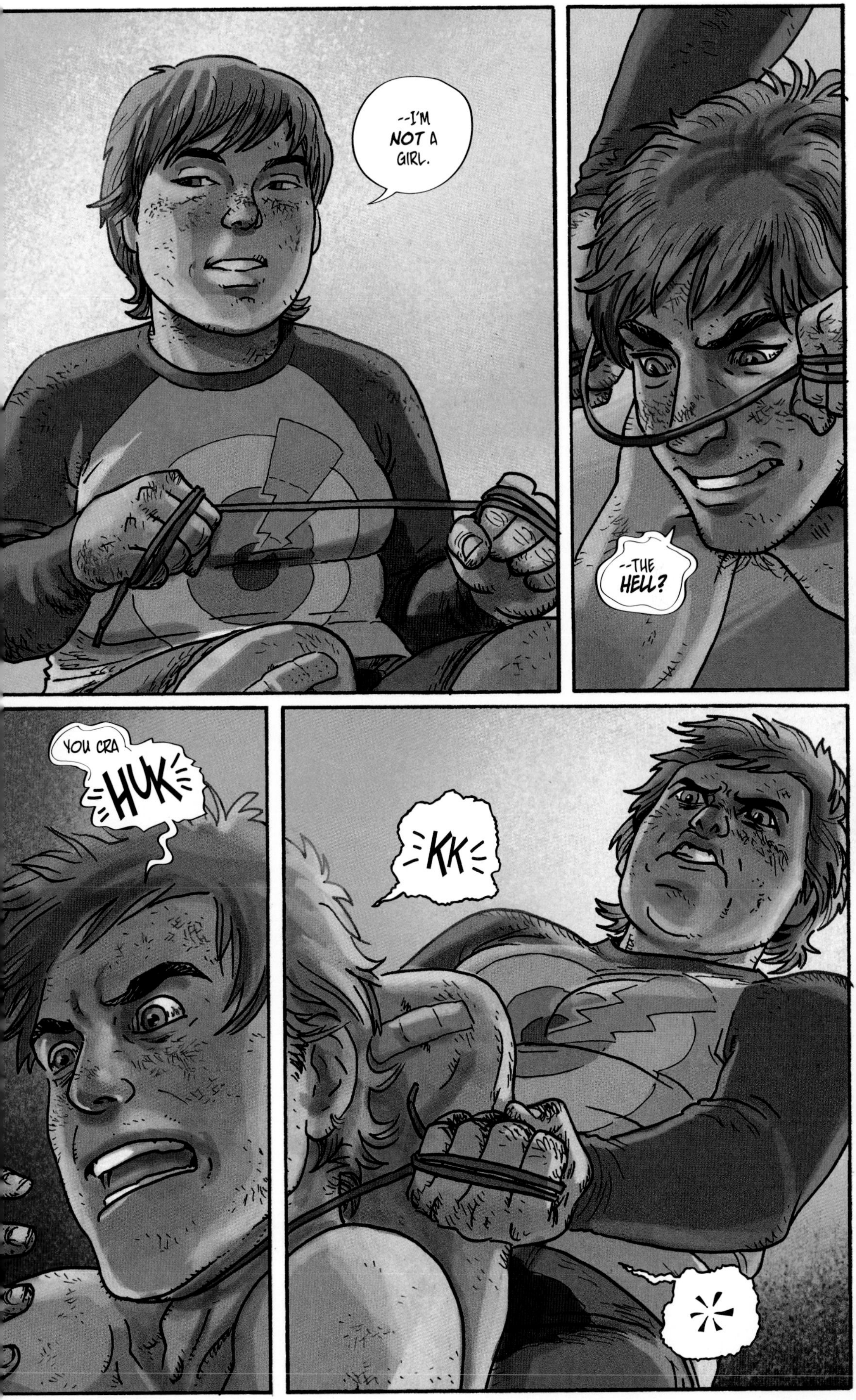
--I'M NOT A GIRL.
--THE HELL?
YOU CRA
HUK
KK
*!

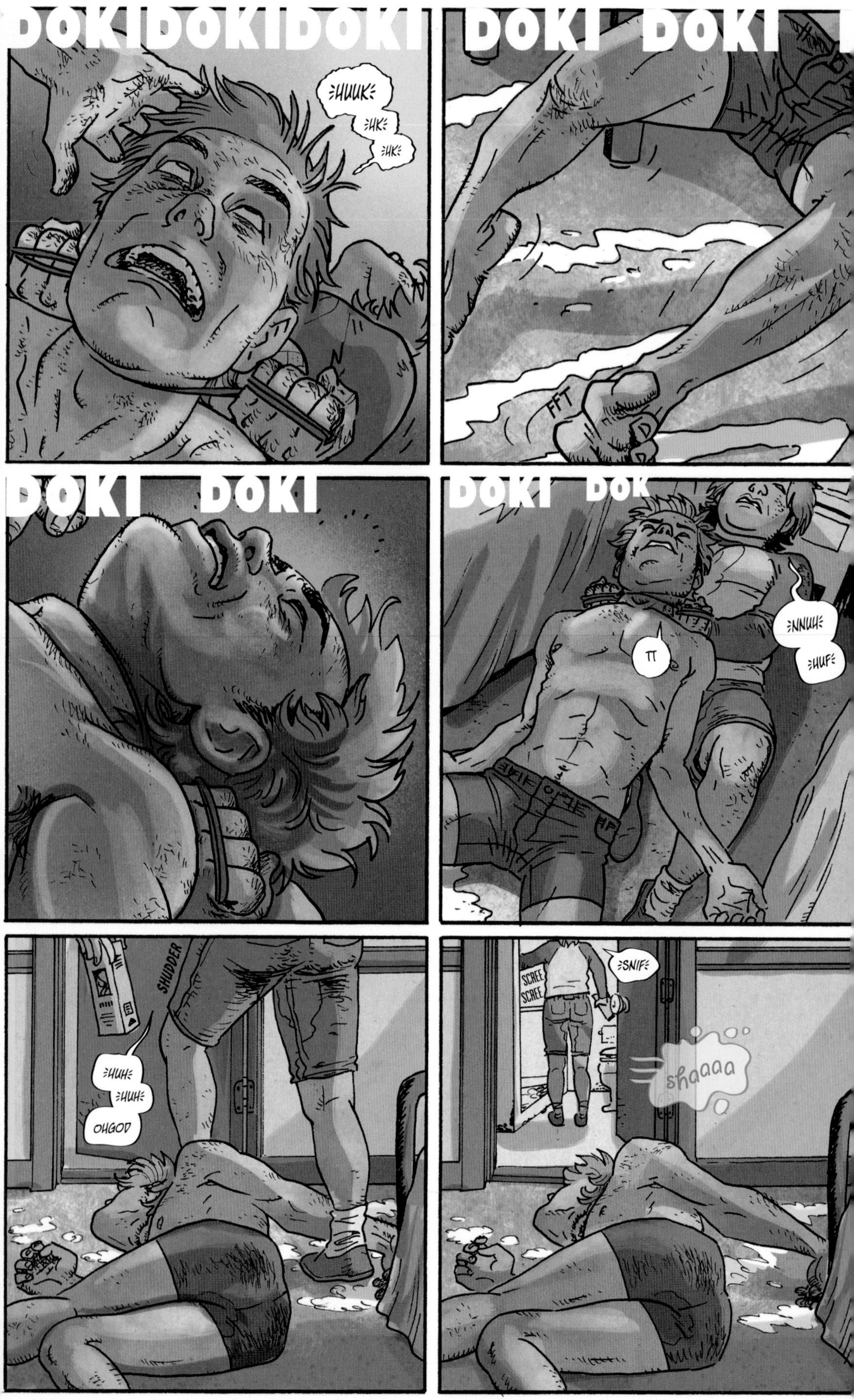
DOKIDOKIDOKI
HUUK
HK
HK
DOKI DOKI
FFT
DOKI DOKI
DOKI DOK
TT
NNUH
HUF
SHUDDER
HUH
HUH
OHGOD
SCREE
SCREE
SNIF
shaaaa

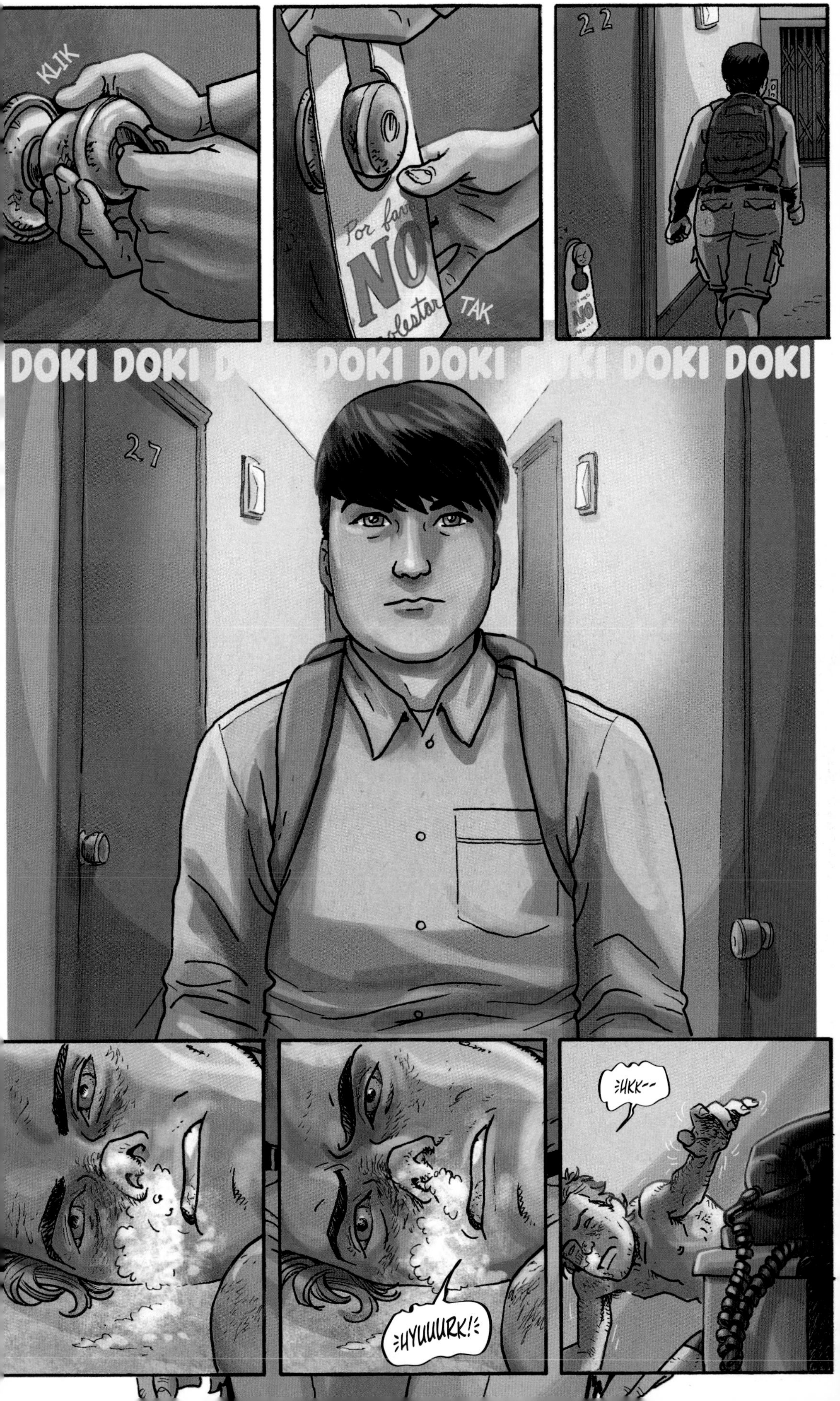
KLIK
Por favor NO molestar
TAK
22
NO
DOKI DOKI DOKI DOKI DOKI DOKI DOKI DOKI
27
HYUUURK!
HKK--

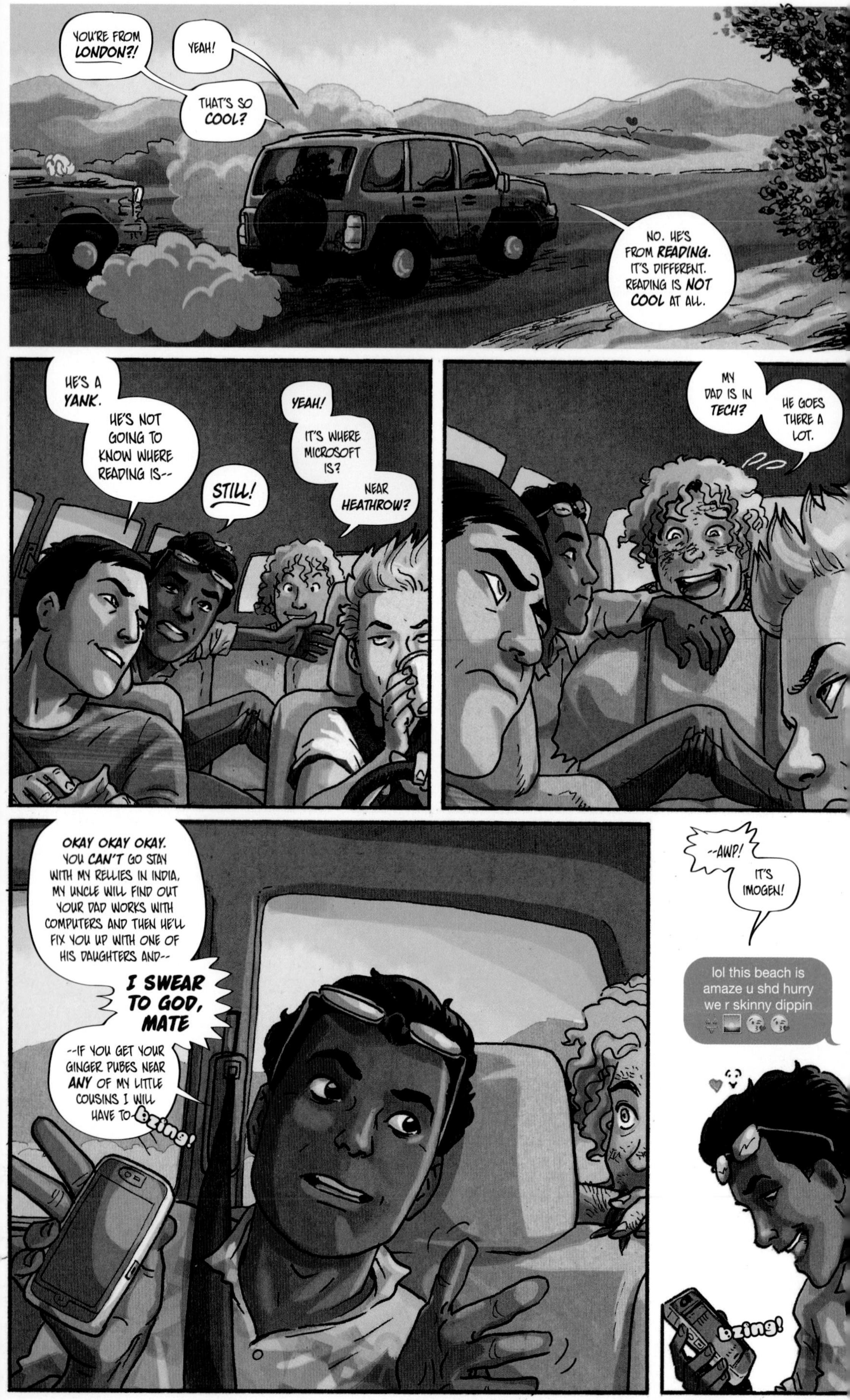
YOU'RE FROM LONDON?!
YEAH!
THAT'S SO COOL?
NO. HE'S FROM READING. IT'S DIFFERENT. READING IS NOT COOL AT ALL.
HE'S A YANK.
HE'S NOT GOING TO KNOW WHERE READING IS--
STILL!
YEAH!
IT'S WHERE MICROSOFT IS?
NEAR HEATHROW?
MY DAD IS IN TECH?
HE GOES THERE A LOT.
OKAY OKAY OKAY. YOU CAN'T GO STAY WITH MY RELLIES IN INDIA. MY UNCLE WILL FIND OUT YOUR DAD WORKS WITH COMPUTERS AND THEN HE'LL FIX YOU UP WITH ONE OF HIS DAUGHTERS AND--
I SWEAR TO GOD, MATE
--IF YOU GET YOUR GINGER PUBES NEAR ANY OF MY LITTLE COUSINS I WILL HAVE TO--
bzing!
--AWP!
IT'S IMOGEN!
lol this beach is amaze u shd hurry we r skinny dippin
bzing!

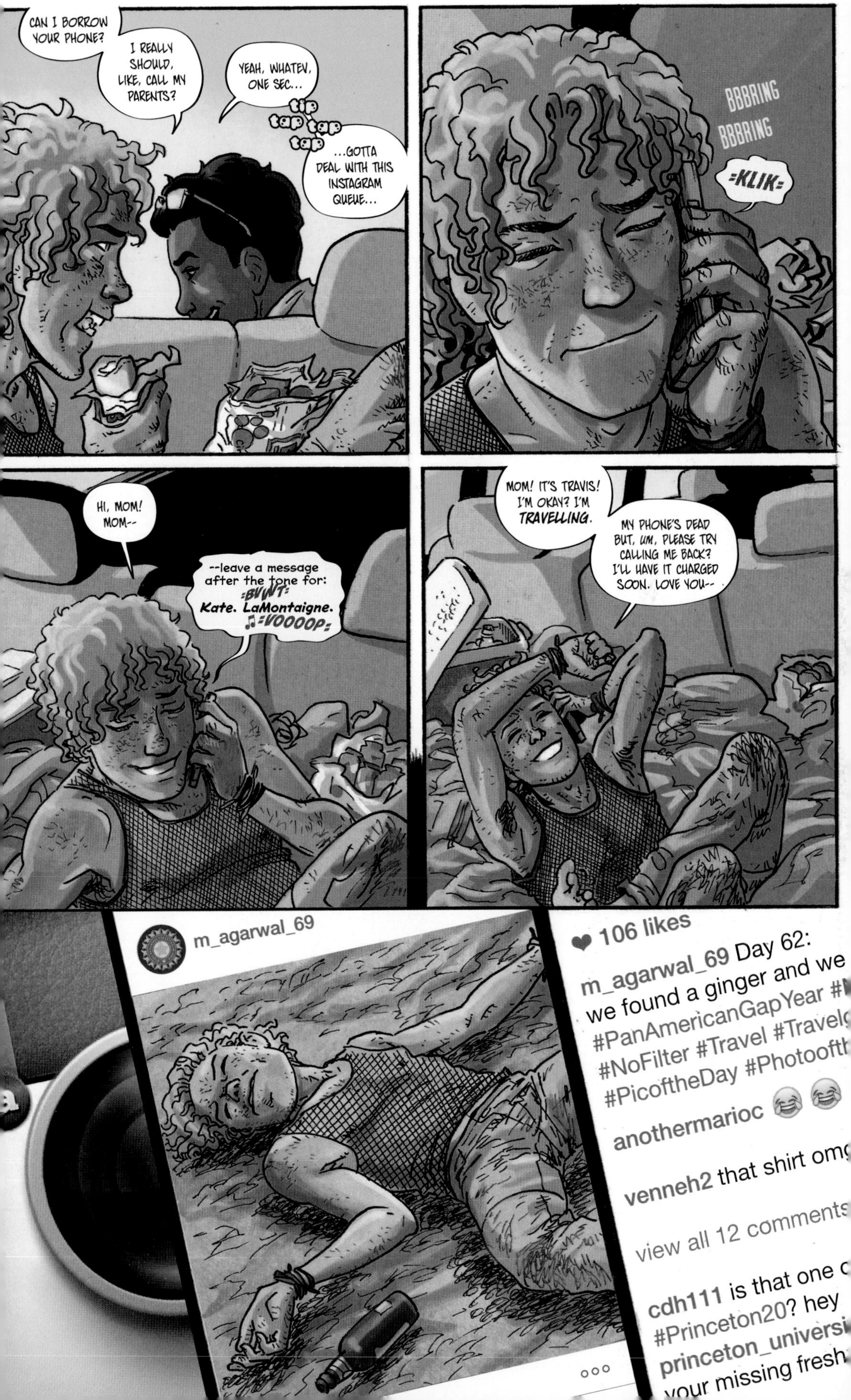

CAN I BORROW YOUR PHONE?
I REALLY SHOULD, LIKE, CALL MY PARENTS?
YEAH, WHATEV, ONE SEC...
tip tap tap tap
...GOTTA DEAL WITH THIS INSTAGRAM QUEUE...
BBBRING
BBBRING
=KLIK=
HI, MOM! MOM--
--leave a message after the tone for: =BVVVT= Kate. LaMontaigne. =VOOOOP=
MOM! IT'S TRAVIS! I'M OKAY? I'M TRAVELLING.
MY PHONE'S DEAD BUT, UM, PLEASE TRY CALLING ME BACK? I'LL HAVE IT CHARGED SOON. LOVE YOU--
m_agarwal_69
106 likes
m_agarwal_69 Day 62: we found a ginger and we
#PanAmericanGapYear
#NoFilter #Travel
#PicoftheDay
anothermarioc
venneh2 that shirt
view all 12 comments
cdh111 is that one
#Princeton20? hey
princeton_
your missing

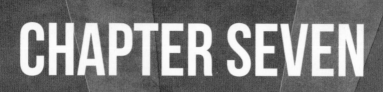

CHAPTER SEVEN

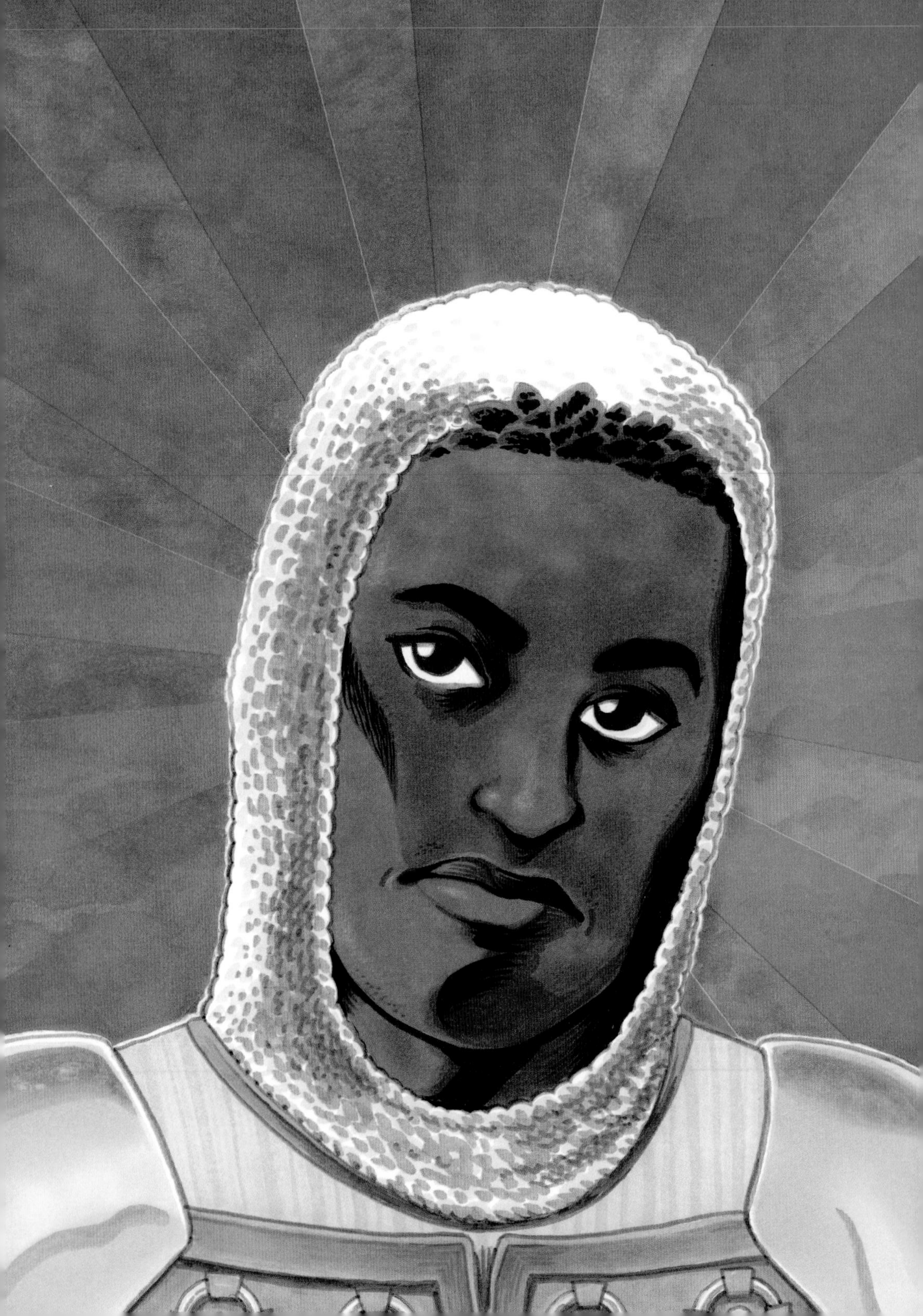

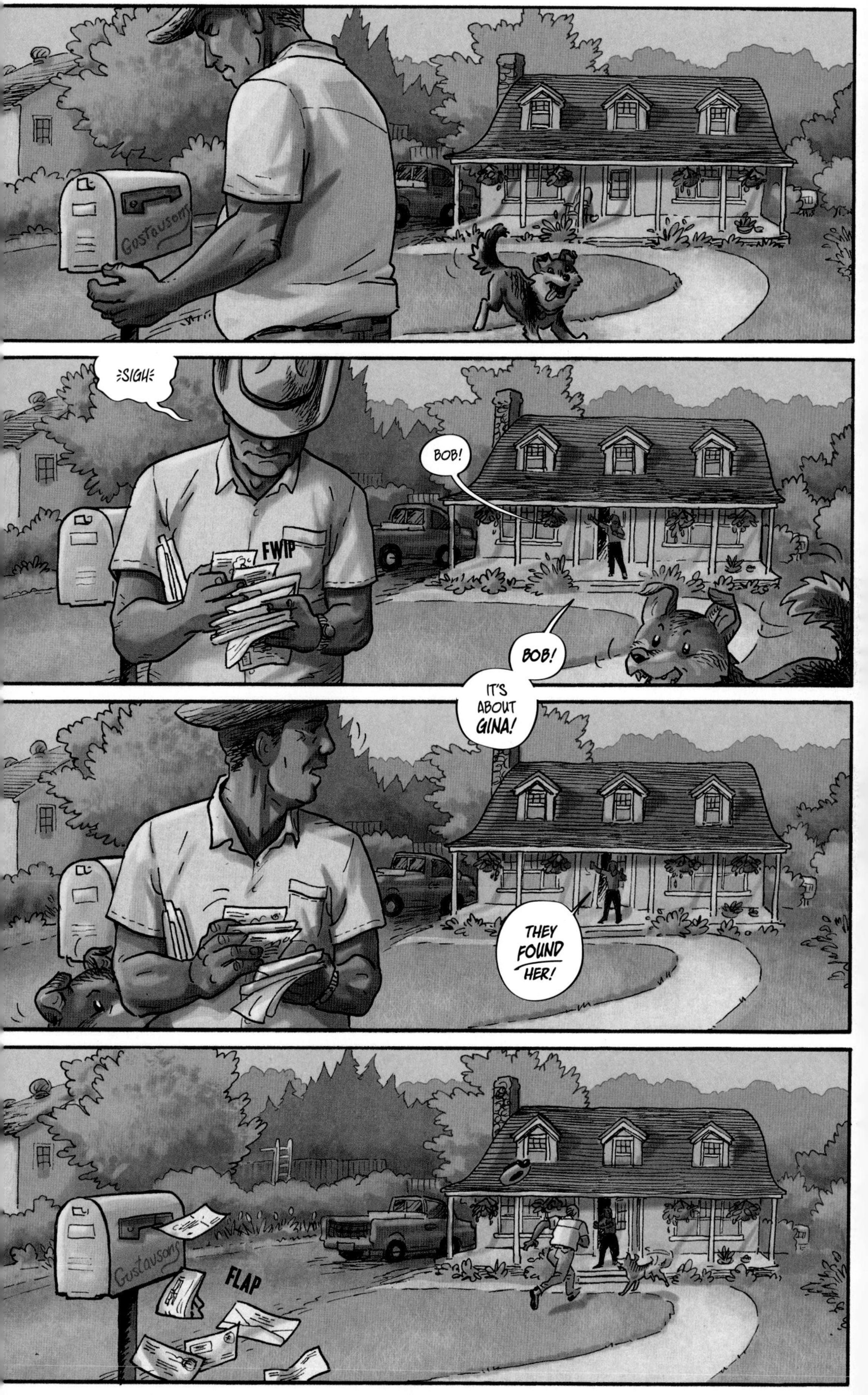

Gustausons
SIGH
FWIP
BOB!
BOB!
IT'S ABOUT GINA!
THEY FOUND HER!
Gustausons
FLAP

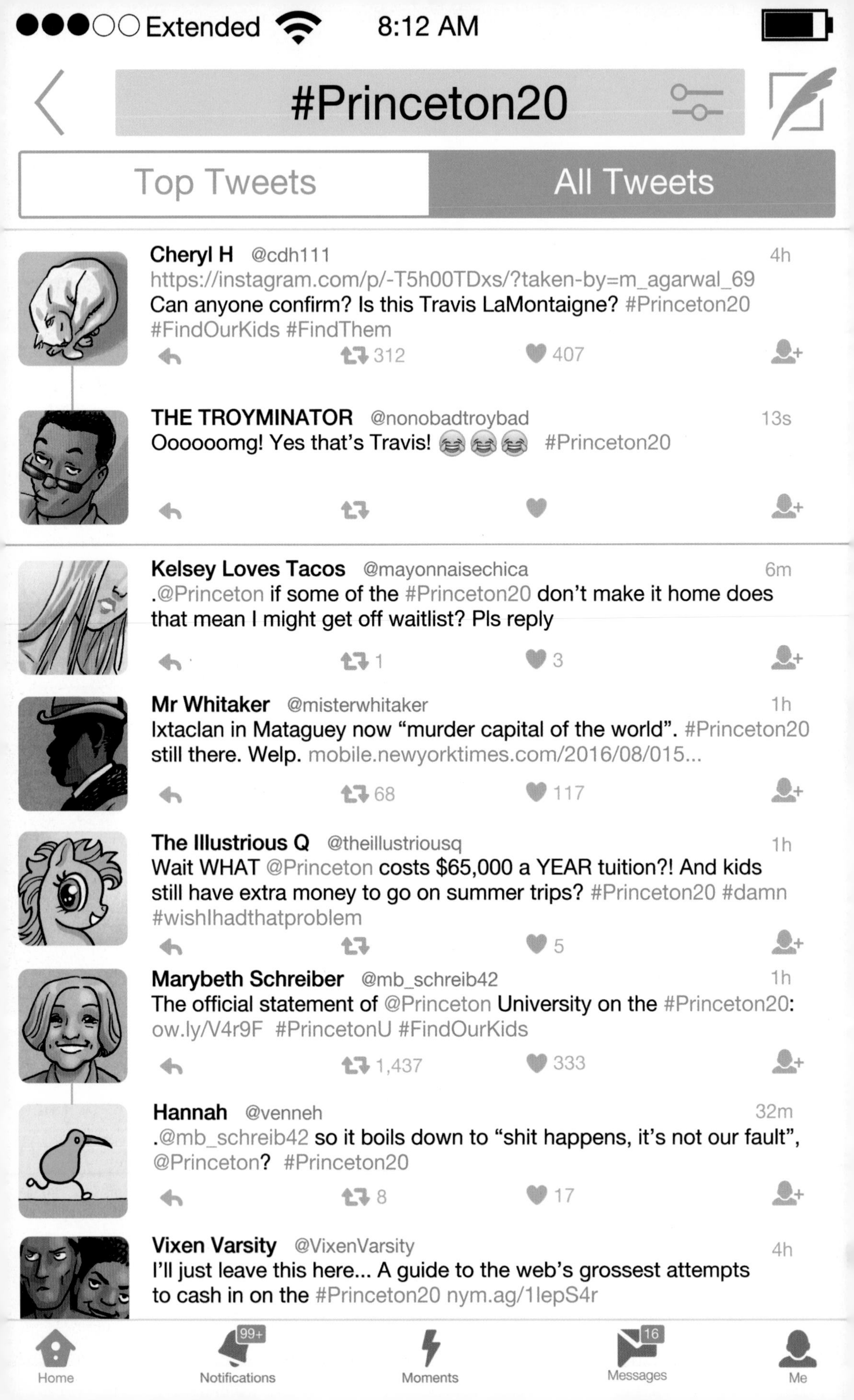

Extended
8:12 AM
#Princeton20
Top Tweets
All Tweets
Cheryl H @cdh111 4h
https://instagram.com/p/-T5h00TDxs/?taken-by=m_agarwal_69
Can anyone confirm? Is this Travis LaMontaigne? #Princeton20 #FindOurKids #FindThem
312
407
THE TROYMINATOR @nonobadtroybad 13s
Ooooooomg! Yes that's Travis! 😂😂😂 #Princeton20
Kelsey Loves Tacos @mayonnaisechica 6m
.@Princeton if some of the #Princeton20 don't make it home does that mean I might get off waitlist? Pls reply
1
3
Mr Whitaker @misterwhitaker 1h
Ixtaclan in Mataguey now "murder capital of the world". #Princeton20 still there. Welp. mobile.newyorktimes.com/2016/08/015...
68
117
The Illustrious Q @theillustriousq 1h
Wait WHAT @Princeton costs $65,000 a YEAR tuition?! And kids still have extra money to go on summer trips? #Princeton20 #damn #wishIhadthatproblem
5
Marybeth Schreiber @mb_schreib42 1h
The official statement of @Princeton University on the #Princeton20: ow.ly/V4r9F #PrincetonU #FindOurKids
1,437
333
Hannah @venneh 32m
.@mb_schreib42 so it boils down to "shit happens, it's not our fault", @Princeton? #Princeton20
8
17
Vixen Varsity @VixenVarsity 4h
I'll just leave this here... A guide to the web's grossest attempts to cash in on the #Princeton20 nym.ag/1lepS4r
Home
99+
Notifications
Moments
16
Messages
Me

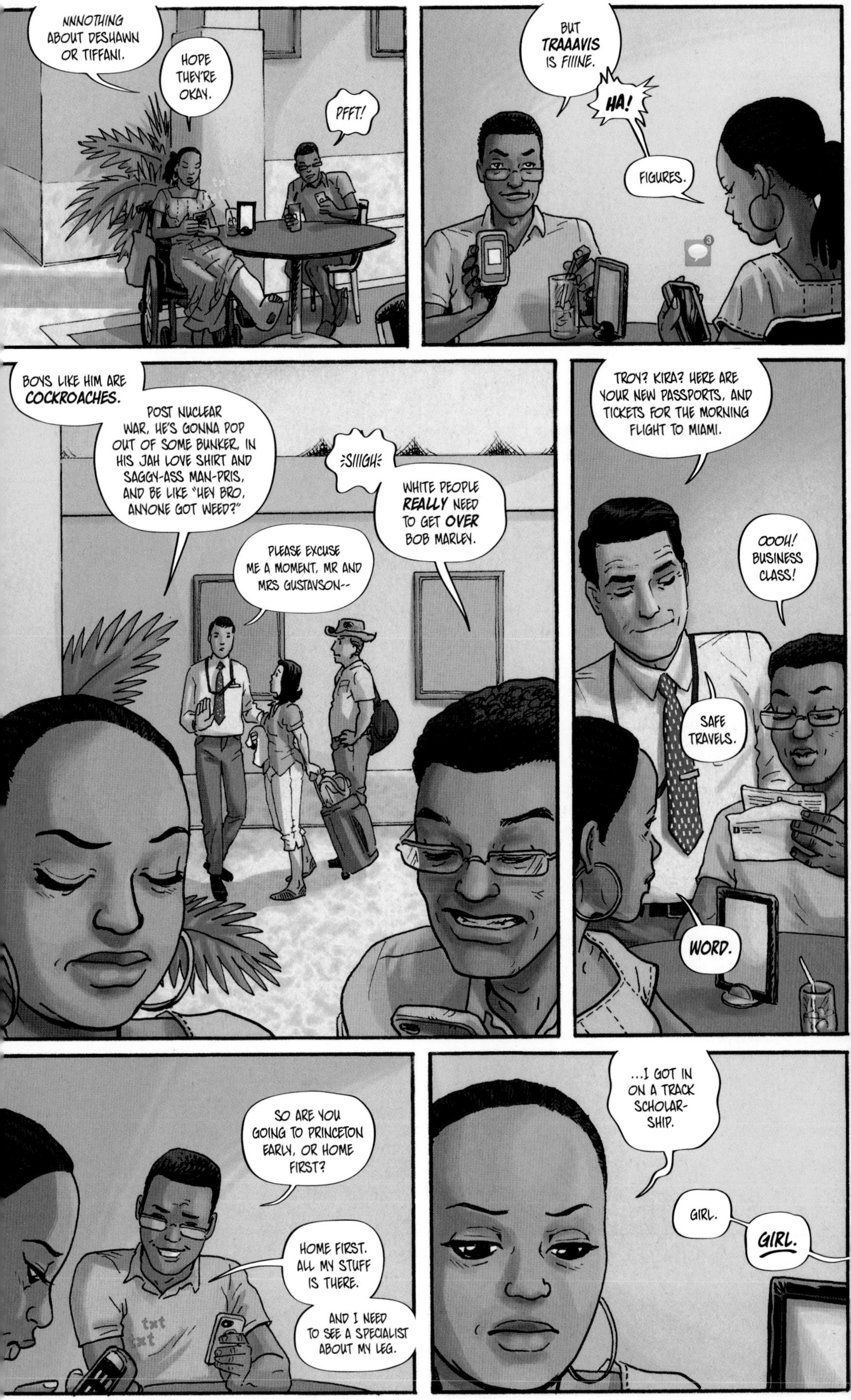

NNNOTHING ABOUT DESHAWN OR TIFFANI.
HOPE THEY'RE OKAY.
PFFT!
txt txt
BUT TRAAAVIS IS FIIINE.
HA!
FIGURES.
3
BOYS LIKE HIM ARE COCKROACHES.
POST NUCLEAR WAR, HE'S GONNA POP OUT OF SOME BUNKER, IN HIS JAH LOVE SHIRT AND SAGGY-ASS MAN-PRIS, AND BE LIKE "HEY BRO, ANYONE GOT WEED?"
SIIIGH
WHITE PEOPLE REALLY NEED TO GET OVER BOB MARLEY.
PLEASE EXCUSE ME A MOMENT, MR AND MRS GUSTAVSON--
TROY? KIRA? HERE ARE YOUR NEW PASSPORTS, AND TICKETS FOR THE MORNING FLIGHT TO MIAMI.
OOOH! BUSINESS CLASS!
SAFE TRAVELS.
WORD.
SO ARE YOU GOING TO PRINCETON EARLY, OR HOME FIRST?
HOME FIRST. ALL MY STUFF IS THERE.
AND I NEED TO SEE A SPECIALIST ABOUT MY LEG.
txt txt
...I GOT IN ON A TRACK SCHOLAR-SHIP.
GIRL.
GIRL.

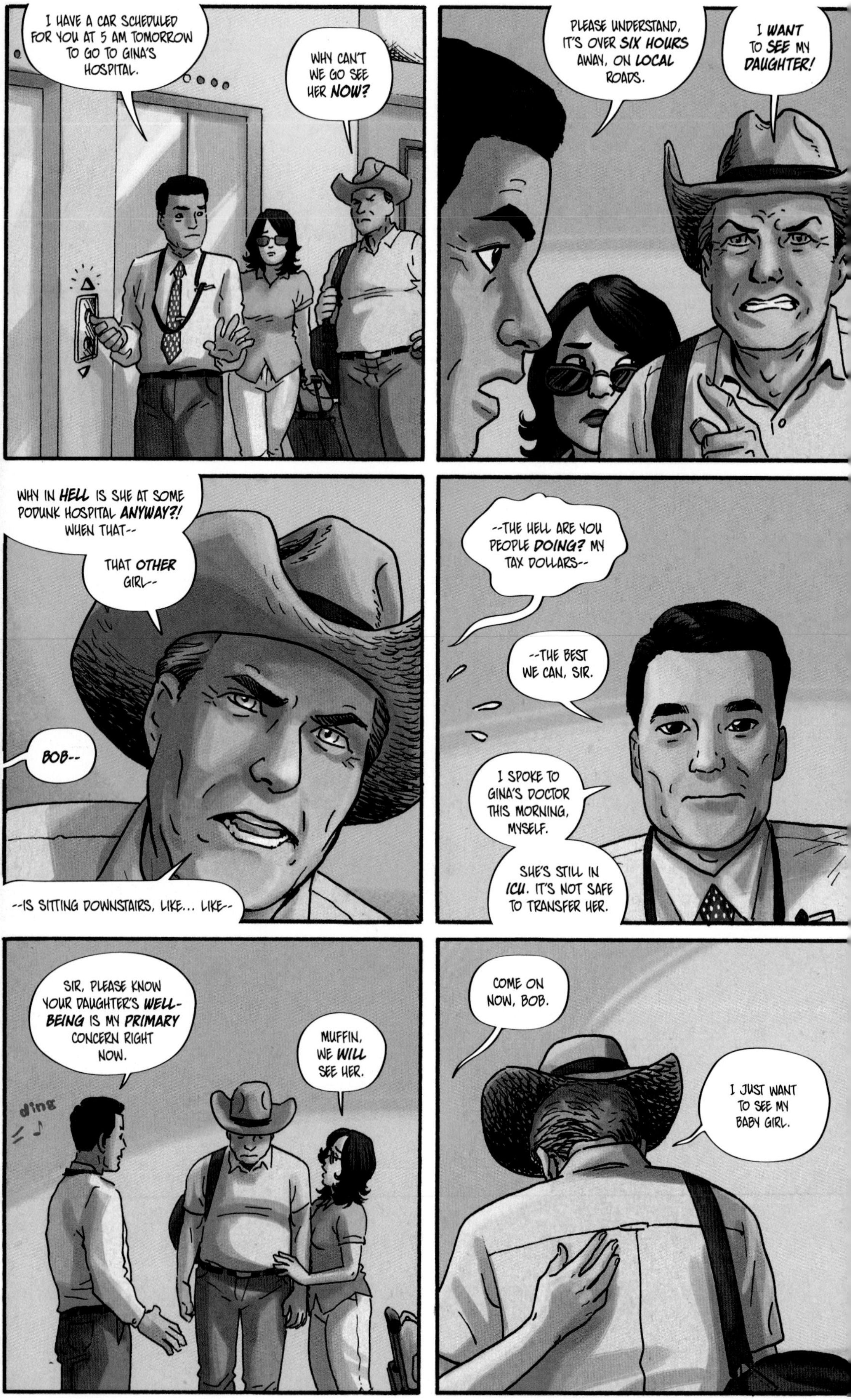
I HAVE A CAR SCHEDULED FOR YOU AT 5 AM TOMORROW TO GO TO GINA'S HOSPITAL.
WHY CAN'T WE GO SEE HER **NOW?**
PLEASE UNDERSTAND, IT'S OVER **SIX HOURS** AWAY, ON **LOCAL** ROADS.
I **WANT** TO **SEE** MY **DAUGHTER!**
WHY IN **HELL** IS SHE AT SOME PODUNK HOSPITAL **ANYWAY?!** WHEN THAT--
THAT **OTHER** GIRL--
BOB--
--IS SITTING DOWNSTAIRS, LIKE... LIKE--
--THE HELL ARE YOU PEOPLE **DOING?** MY TAX DOLLARS--
--THE BEST WE CAN, SIR.
I SPOKE TO GINA'S DOCTOR THIS MORNING, MYSELF.
SHE'S STILL IN **ICU**. IT'S NOT SAFE TO TRANSFER HER.
SIR, PLEASE KNOW YOUR DAUGHTER'S **WELL-BEING** IS MY **PRIMARY** CONCERN RIGHT NOW.
ding
MUFFIN, WE **WILL** SEE HER.
COME ON NOW, BOB.
I JUST WANT TO SEE MY BABY GIRL.

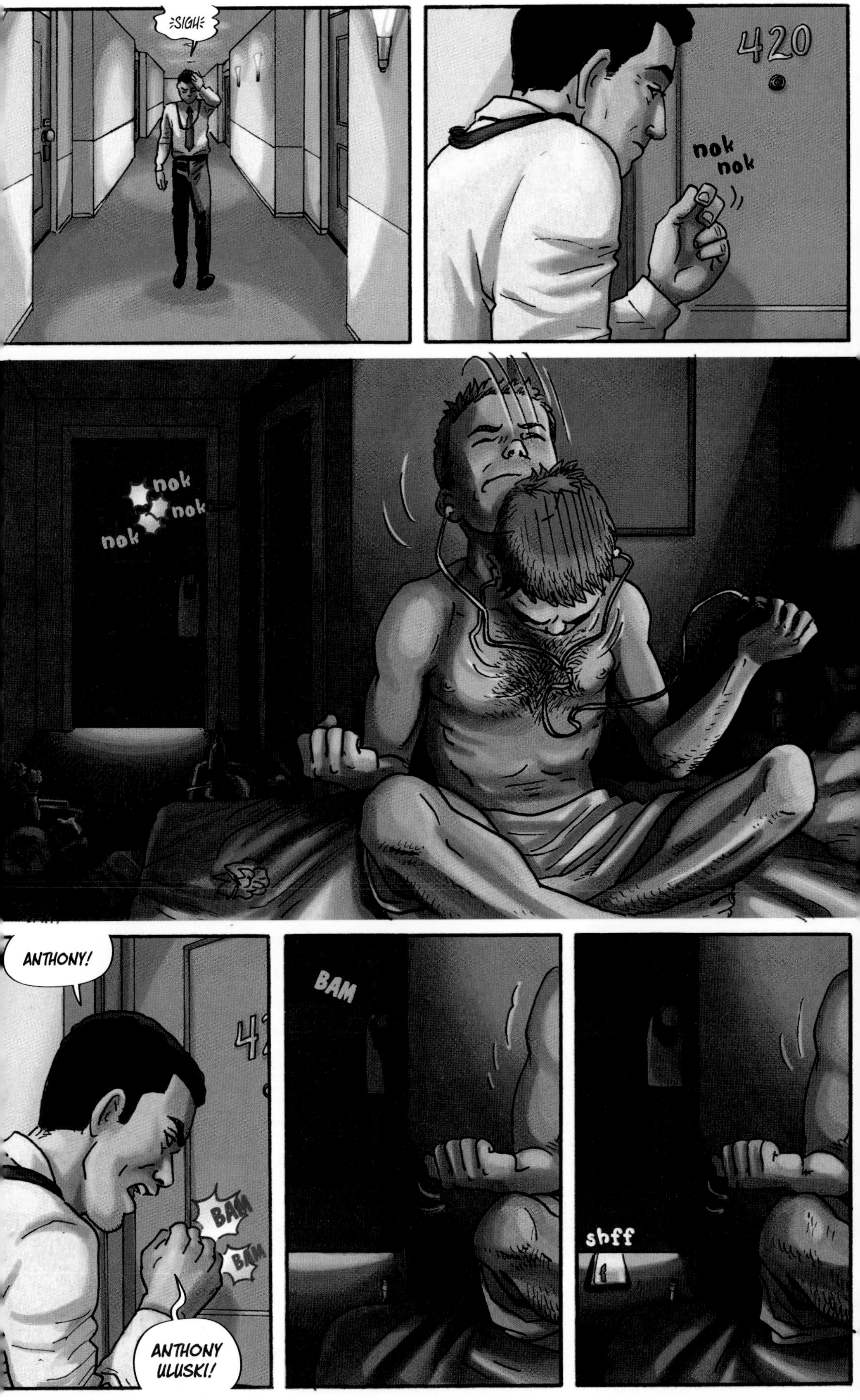

SIGH
420
nok
nok
nok
nok
nok
ANTHONY!
BAM
BAM
ANTHONY ULUSKI!
BAM
shff

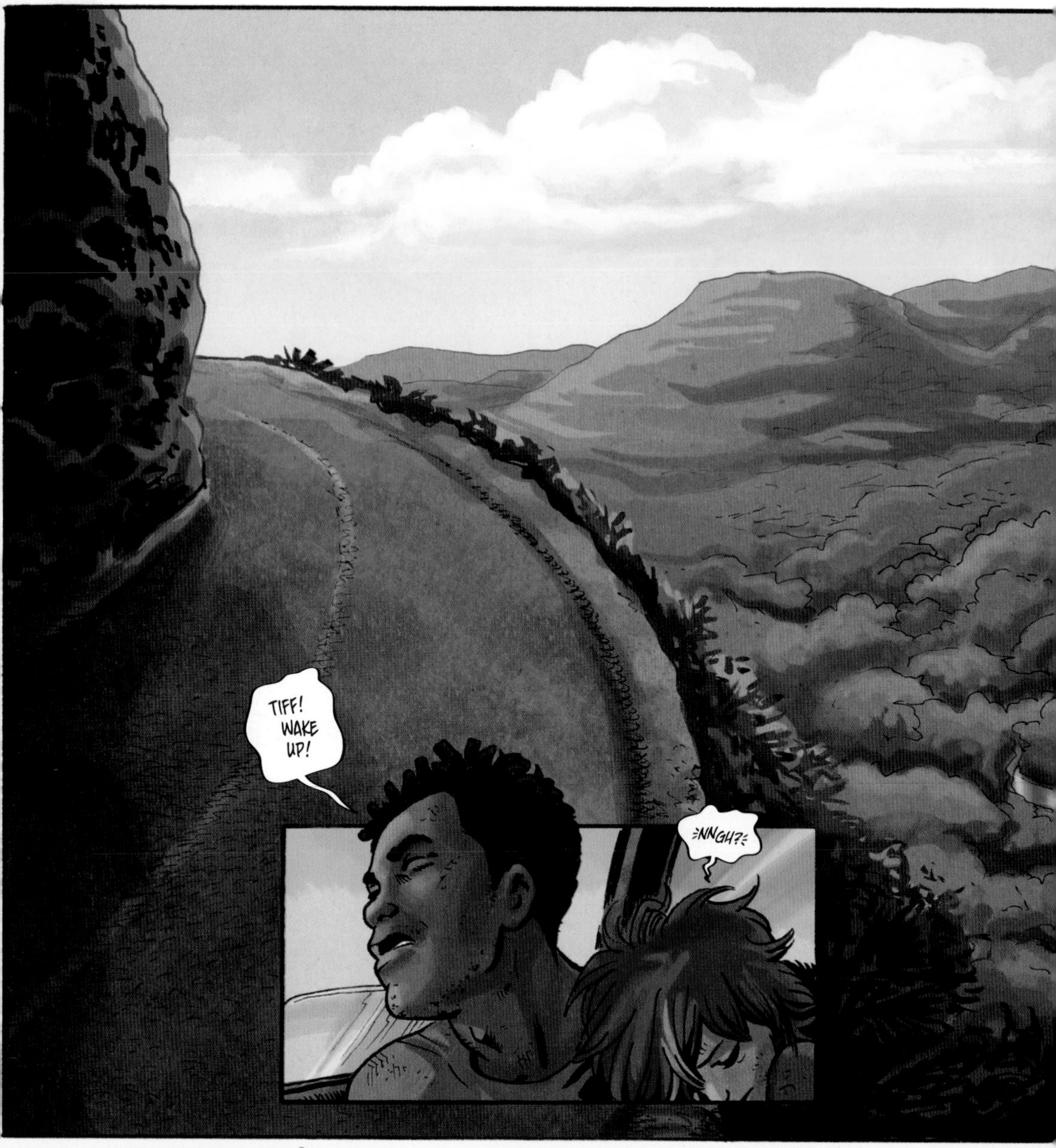
TIFF! WAKE UP!
NNGH?
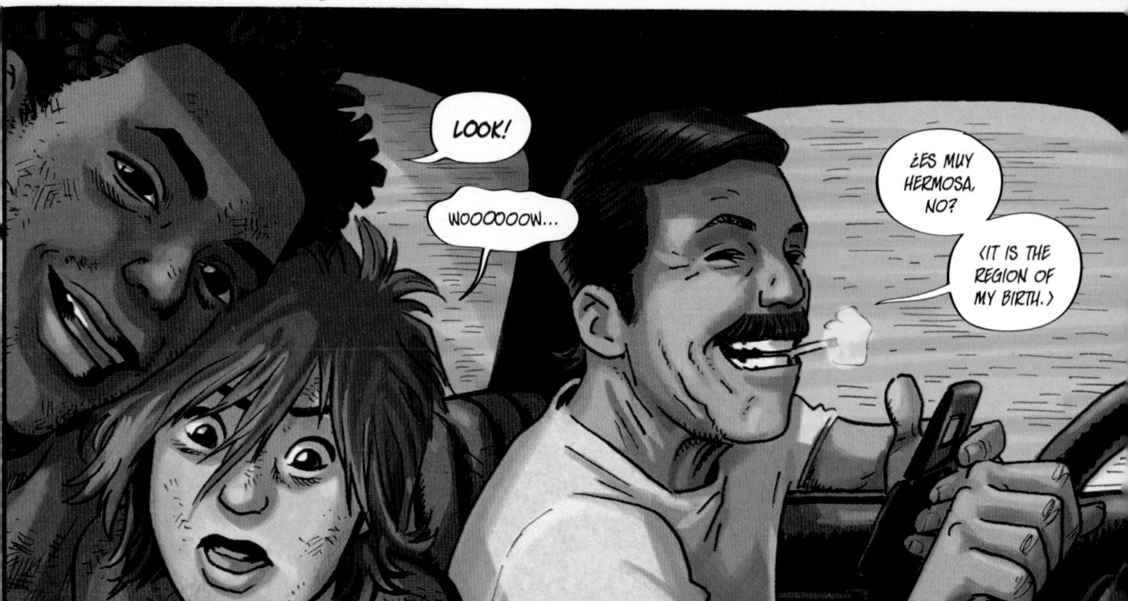
LOOK!
WOOOOOOW...
¿ES MUY HERMOSA, NO?
‹IT IS THE REGION OF MY BIRTH.›

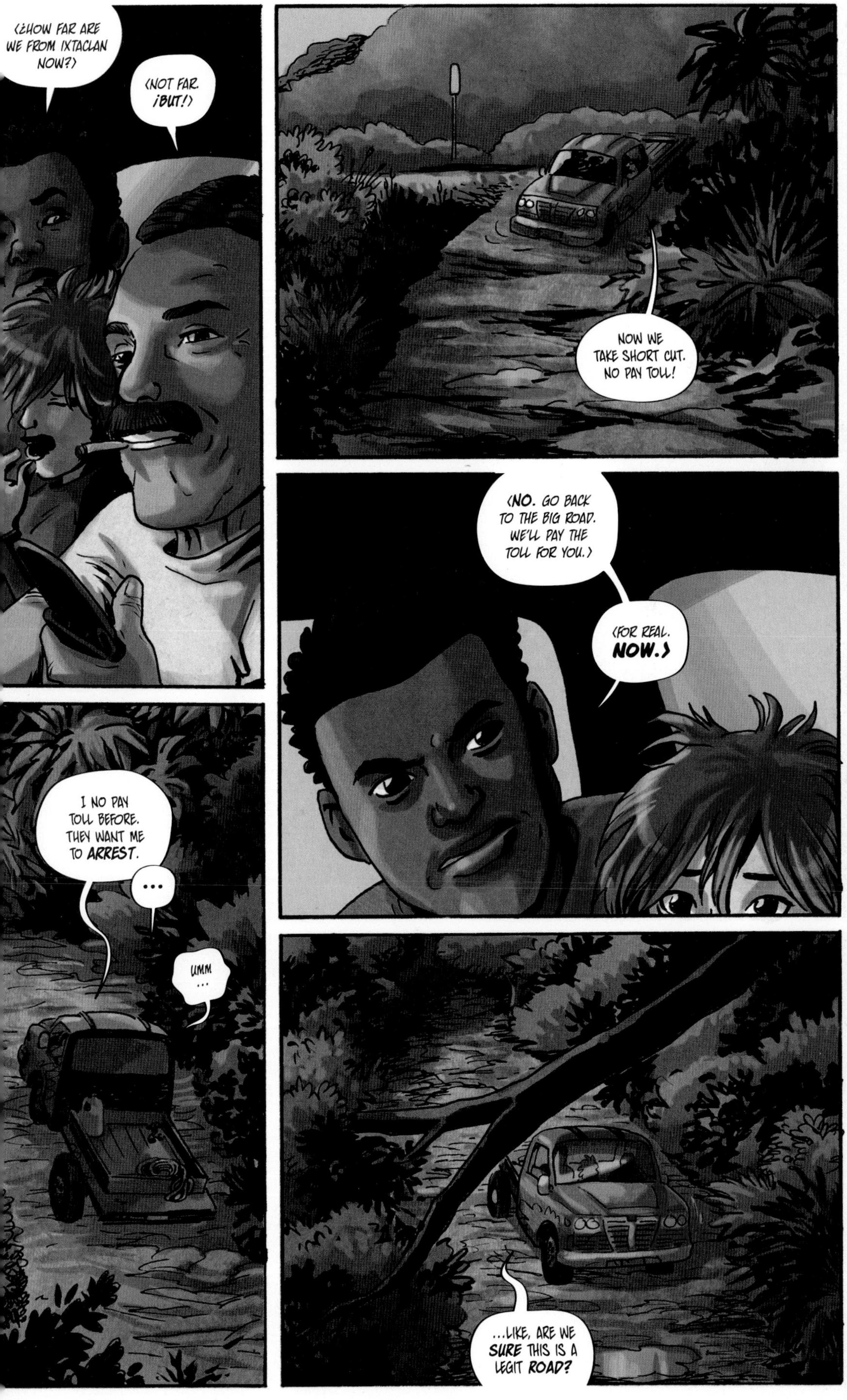
‹¿HOW FAR ARE WE FROM IXTACLAN NOW?›
‹NOT FAR. ¡BUT!›
NOW WE TAKE SHORT CUT. NO PAY TOLL!
I NO PAY TOLL BEFORE. THEY WANT ME TO ARREST.
...
UMM ...
‹NO. GO BACK TO THE BIG ROAD. WE'LL PAY THE TOLL FOR YOU.›
‹FOR REAL. NOW.›
...LIKE, ARE WE SURE THIS IS A LEGIT ROAD?

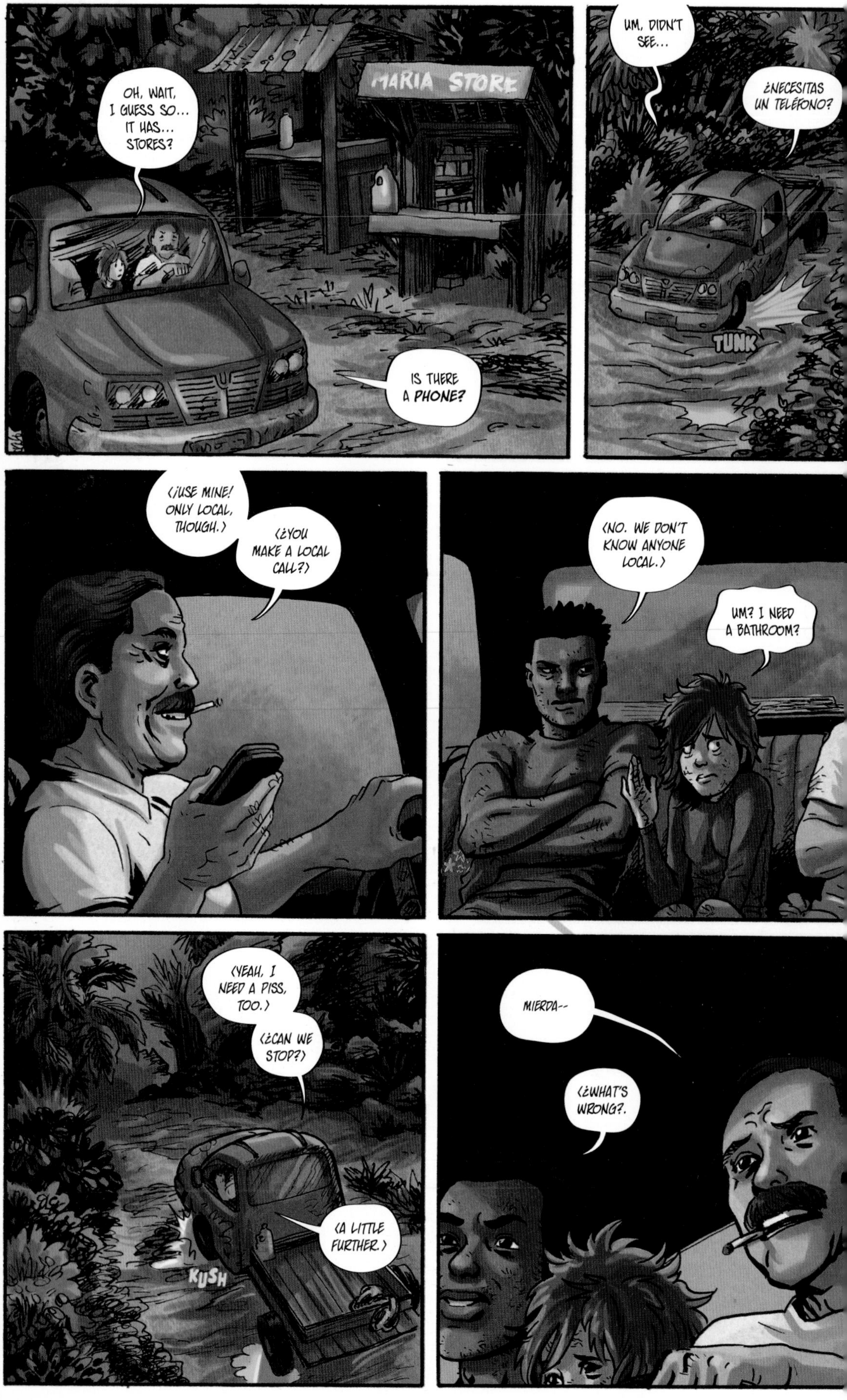
MARIA STORE
OH, WAIT, I GUESS SO... IT HAS... STORES?
IS THERE A PHONE?
UM, DIDN'T SEE...
¿NECESITAS UN TELÉFONO?
TUNK
⟨¡USE MINE! ONLY LOCAL, THOUGH.⟩
⟨¿YOU MAKE A LOCAL CALL?⟩
⟨NO. WE DON'T KNOW ANYONE LOCAL.⟩
UM? I NEED A BATHROOM?
⟨YEAH, I NEED A PISS, TOO.⟩
⟨¿CAN WE STOP?⟩
⟨A LITTLE FURTHER.⟩
KUSH
MIERDA--
⟨¿WHAT'S WRONG?.

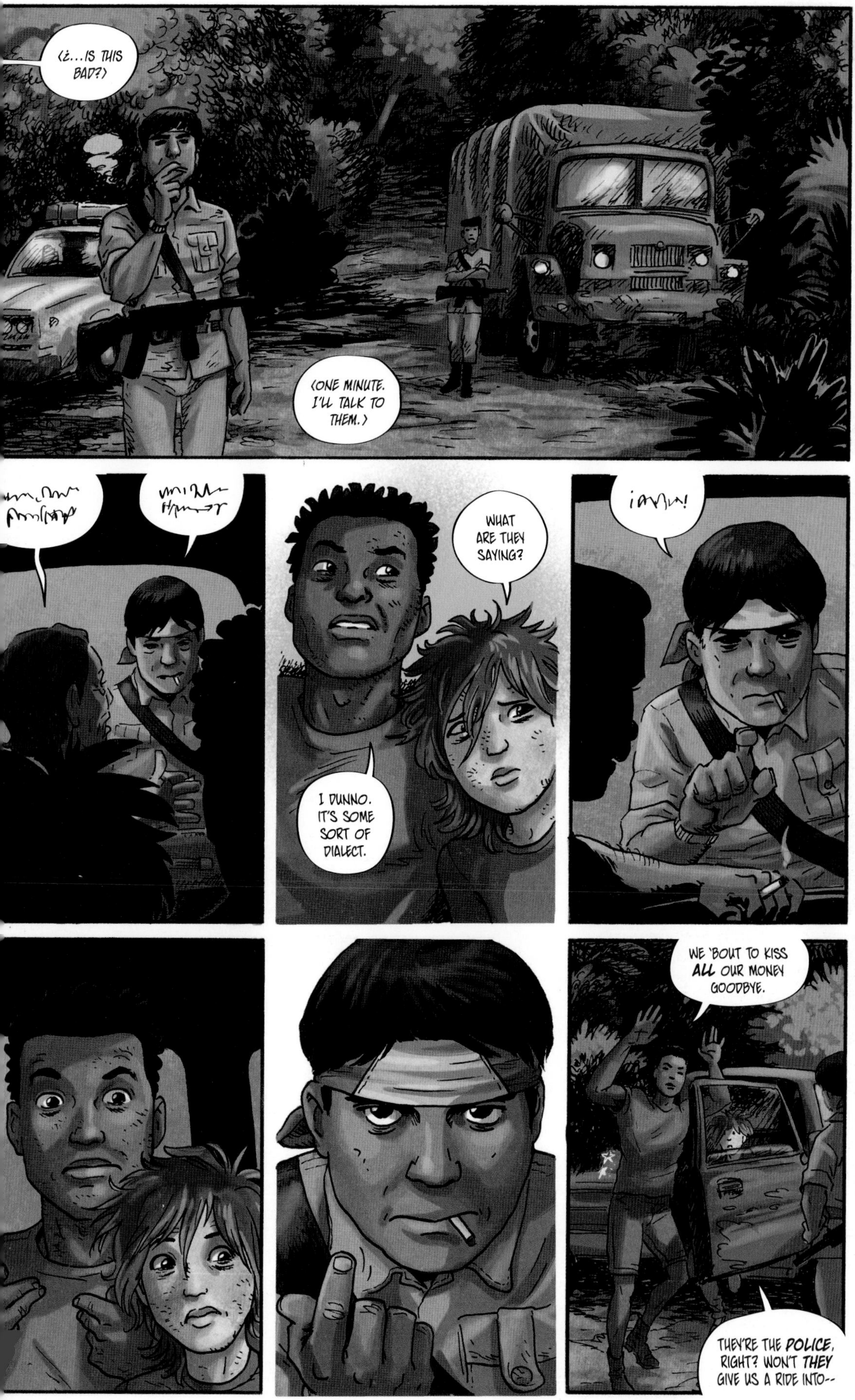
‹¿...IS THIS BAD?›
‹ONE MINUTE. I'LL TALK TO THEM.›
WHAT ARE THEY SAYING?
I DUNNO. IT'S SOME SORT OF DIALECT.
WE 'BOUT TO KISS **ALL** OUR MONEY GOODBYE.
THEY'RE THE ***POLICE***, RIGHT? WON'T ***THEY*** GIVE US A RIDE INTO--

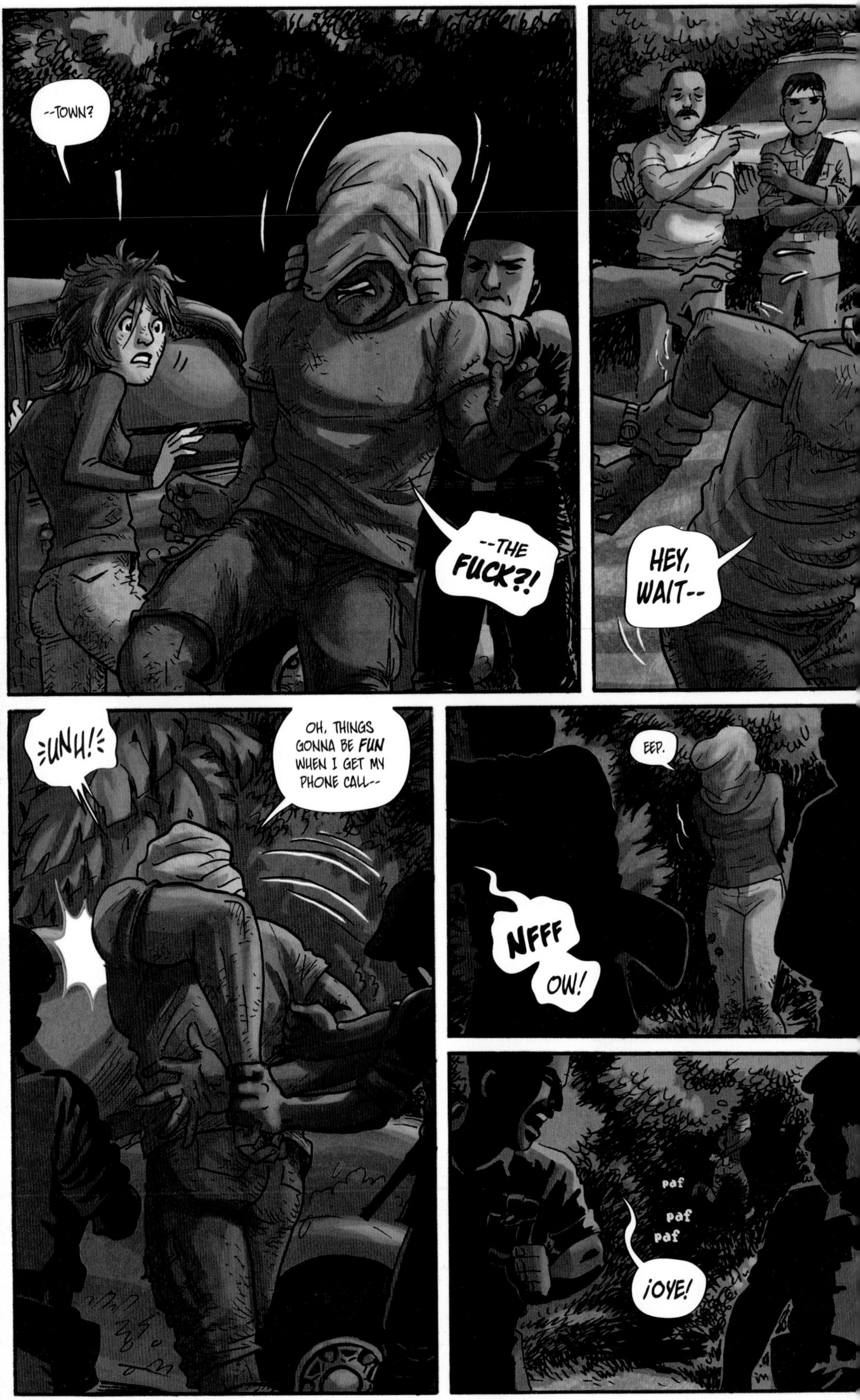
--TOWN?
--THE FUCK?!
HEY, WAIT--
UNH!
OH, THINGS GONNA BE FUN WHEN I GET MY PHONE CALL--
EEP.
NFFF
OW!
paf
paf
paf
¡OYE!

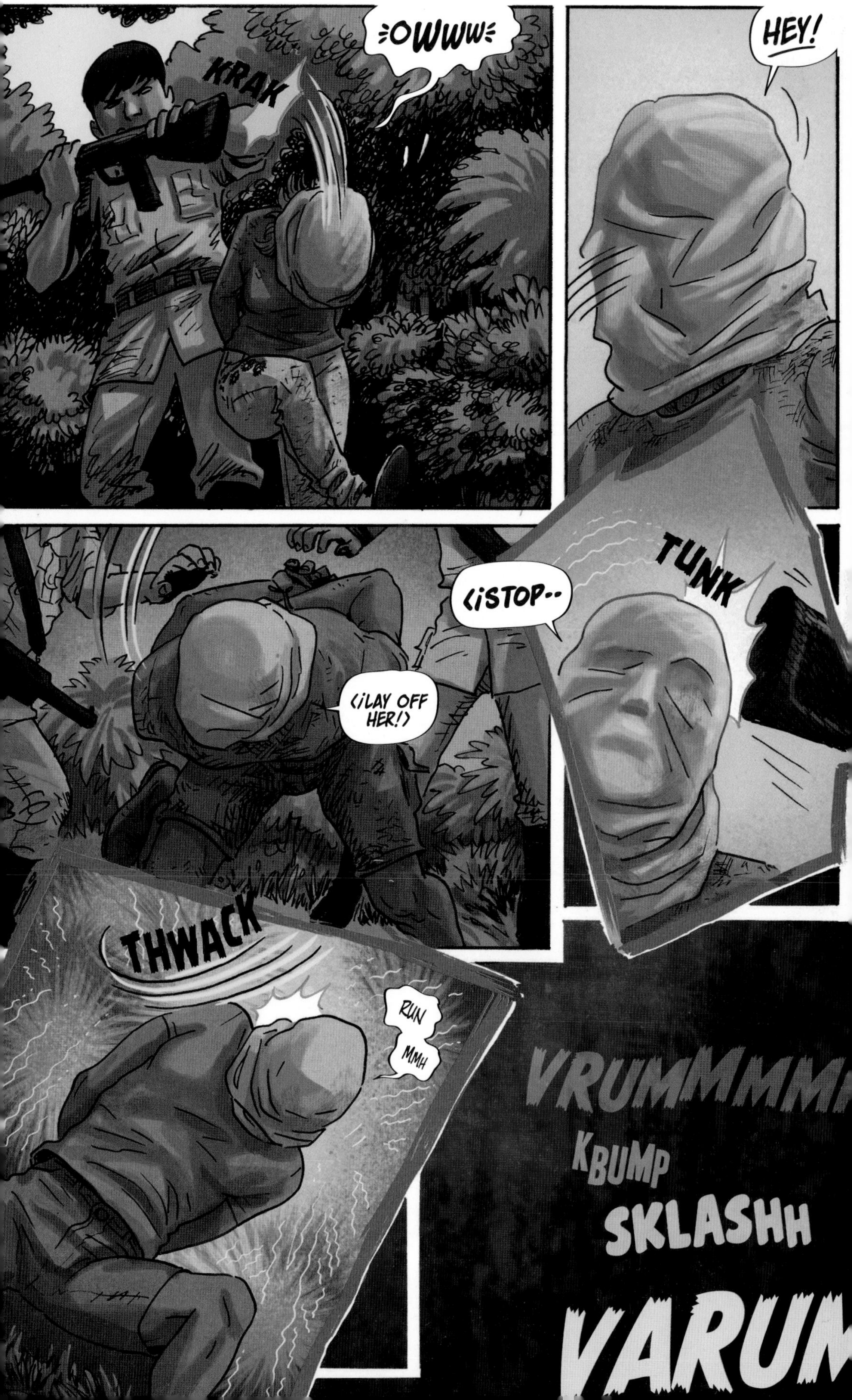
KRAK
OWWW
HEY!
TUNK
<¡STOP..
<¡LAY OFF HER!>
THWACK
RUN
MMH
VRUMMMMM
KBUMP
SKLASHH
VARUM

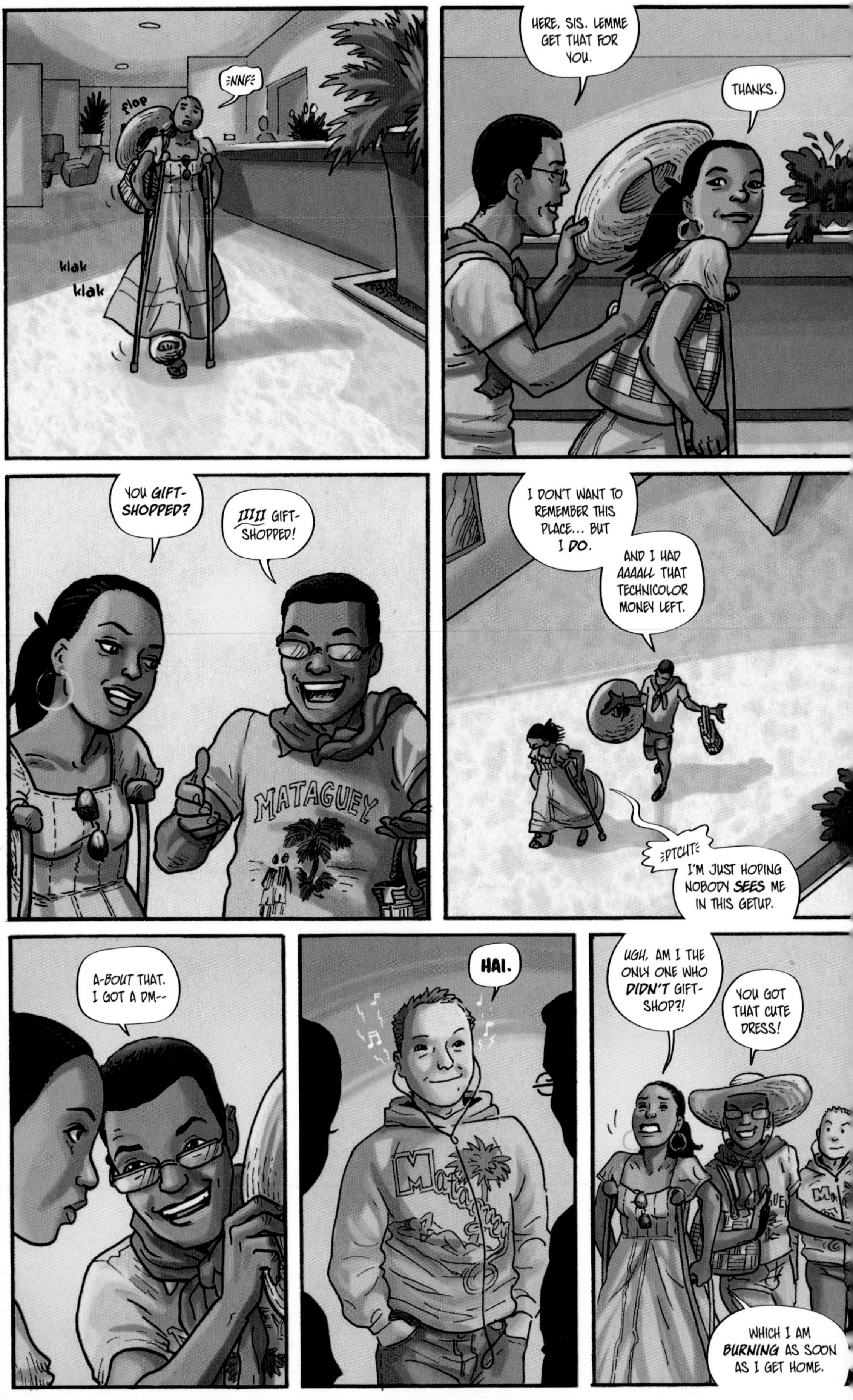
flop
NNF
klak
klak
HERE, SIS. LEMME GET THAT FOR YOU.
THANKS.
YOU GIFT-SHOPPED?
IIIII GIFT-SHOPPED!
I DON'T WANT TO REMEMBER THIS PLACE... BUT I DO.
AND I HAD AAAALL THAT TECHNICOLOR MONEY LEFT.
PTCHT
I'M JUST HOPING NOBODY SEES ME IN THIS GETUP.
A-BOUT THAT. I GOT A DM--
HAI.
UGH, AM I THE ONLY ONE WHO DIDN'T GIFT-SHOP?!
YOU GOT THAT CUTE DRESS!
WHICH I AM BURNING AS SOON AS I GET HOME.

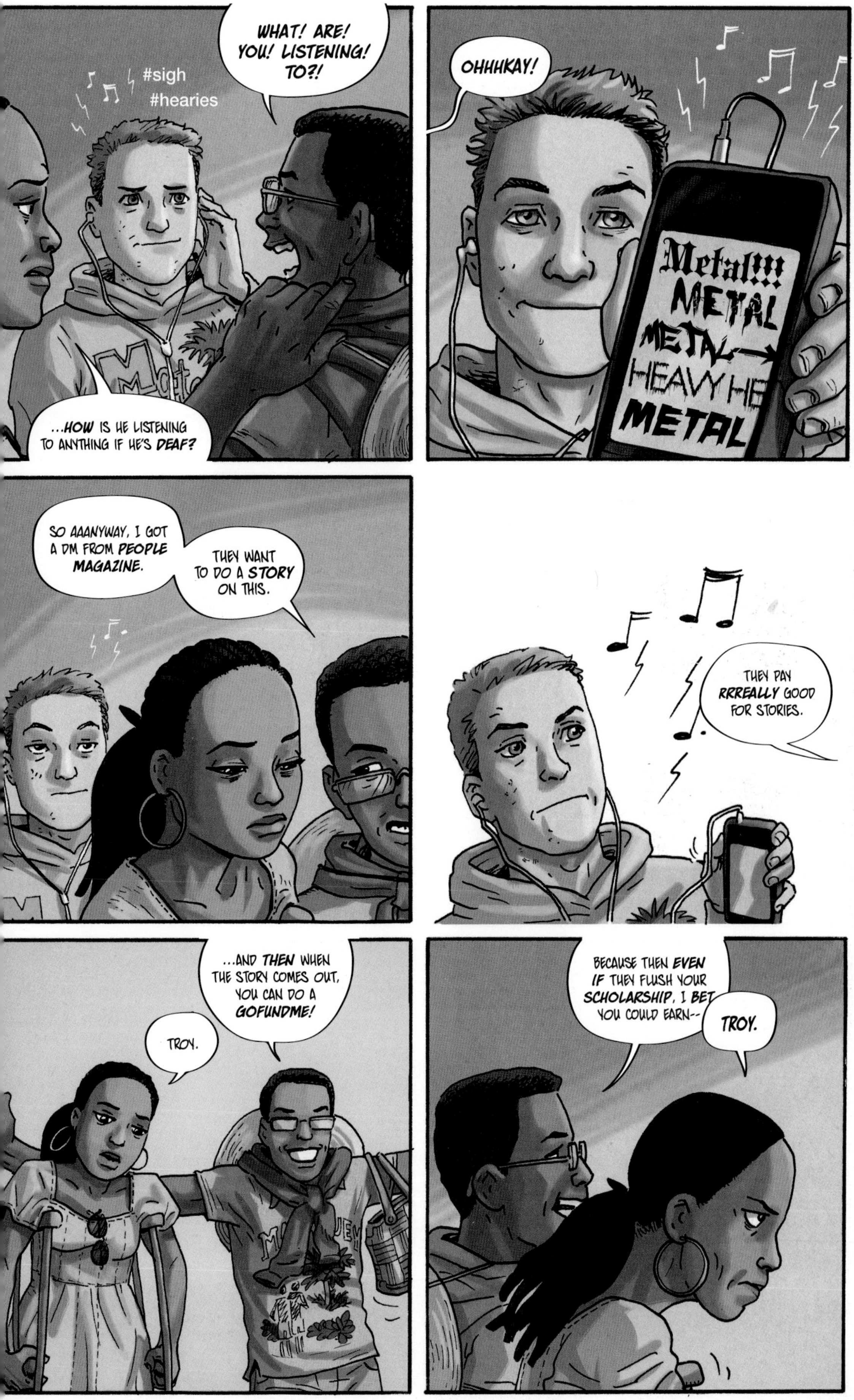

#sigh
#hearies
WHAT! ARE! YOU! LISTENING! TO?!
...HOW IS HE LISTENING TO ANYTHING IF HE'S DEAF?
OHHHKAY!
Metal!!! METAL METAL HEAVY HE METAL
SO AAANYWAY, I GOT A DM FROM PEOPLE MAGAZINE.
THEY WANT TO DO A STORY ON THIS.
THEY PAY RRREALLY GOOD FOR STORIES.
...AND THEN WHEN THE STORY COMES OUT, YOU CAN DO A GOFUNDME!
TROY.
BECAUSE THEN EVEN IF THEY FLUSH YOUR SCHOLARSHIP, I BET YOU COULD EARN--
TROY.

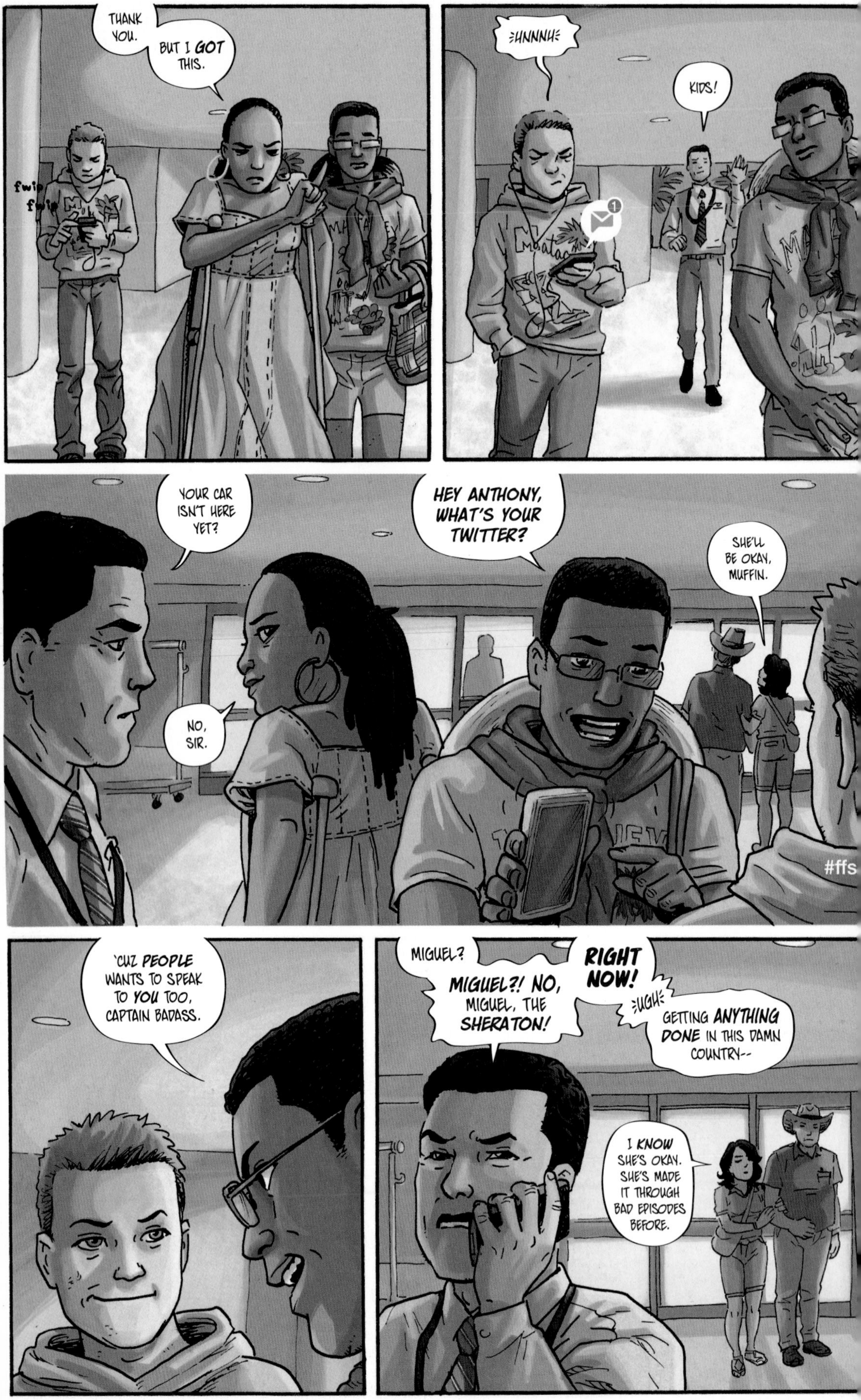
THANK YOU.
BUT I GOT THIS.
fwip fwip
≡HNNNH≡
KIDS!
YOUR CAR ISN'T HERE YET?
HEY ANTHONY, WHAT'S YOUR TWITTER?
NO, SIR.
SHE'LL BE OKAY, MUFFIN.
#ffs
'CUZ PEOPLE WANTS TO SPEAK TO YOU TOO, CAPTAIN BADASS.
MIGUEL?
MIGUEL?! NO, MIGUEL, THE SHERATON!
RIGHT NOW!
≡UGH≡
GETTING ANYTHING DONE IN THIS DAMN COUNTRY--
I KNOW SHE'S OKAY. SHE'S MADE IT THROUGH BAD EPISODES BEFORE.

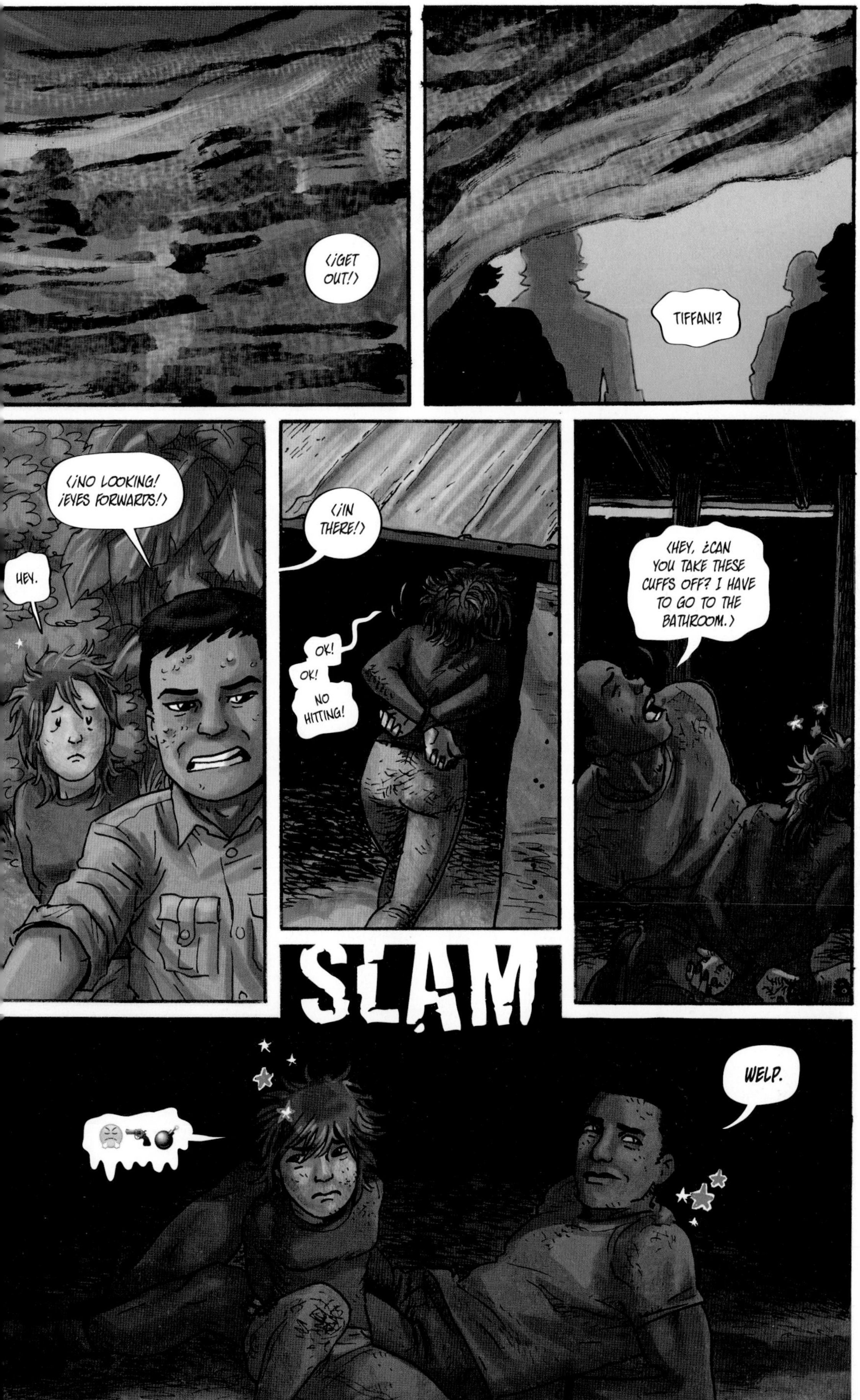
‹¡GET OUT!›
TIFFANI?
‹¡NO LOOKING! ¡EYES FORWARDS!›
HEY.
‹¡IN THERE!›
OK!
OK!
NO HITTING!
‹HEY, ¿CAN YOU TAKE THESE CUFFS OFF? I HAVE TO GO TO THE BATHROOM.›
SLAM
WELP.

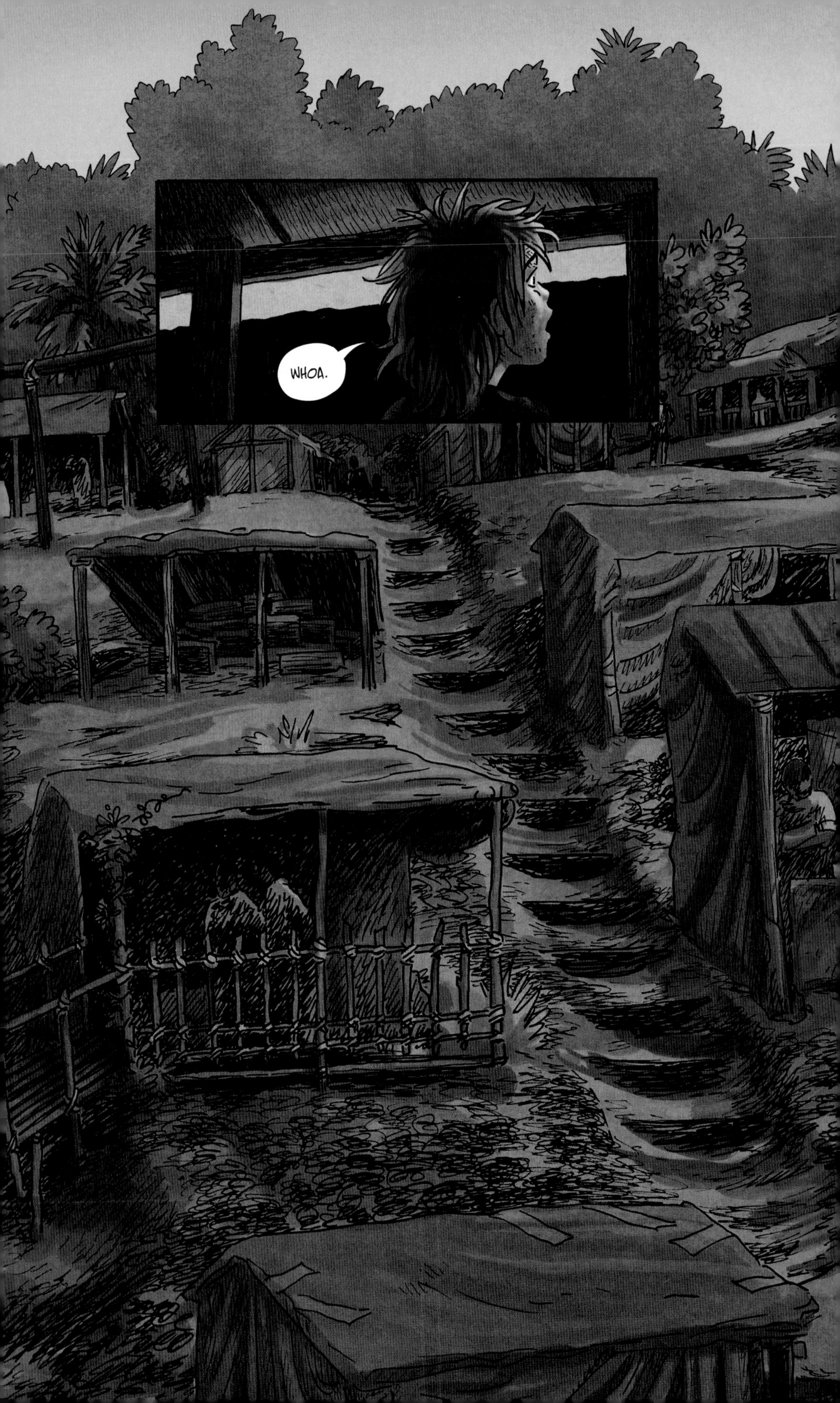
WHOA.

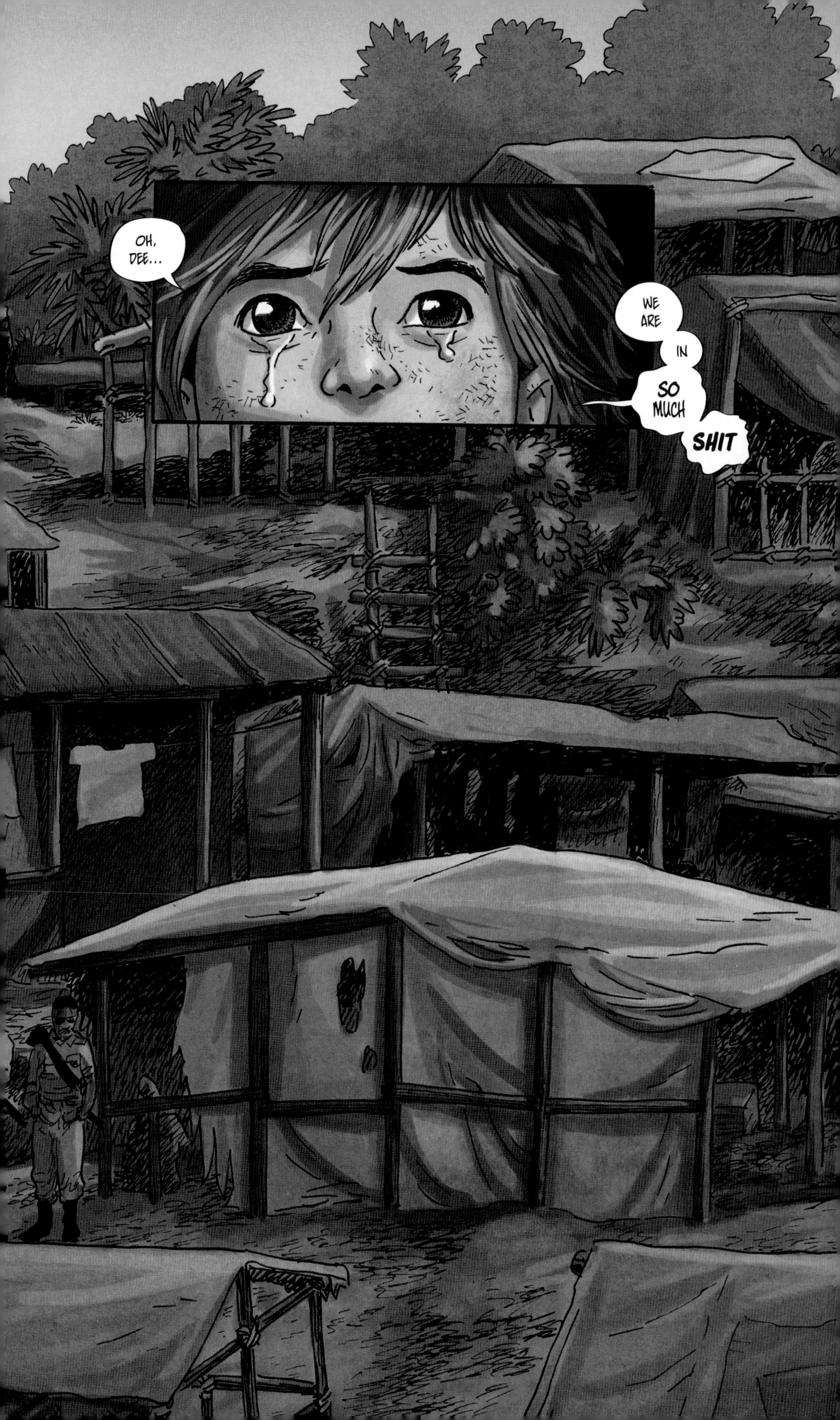
OH, DEE...
WE ARE IN SO MUCH SHIT

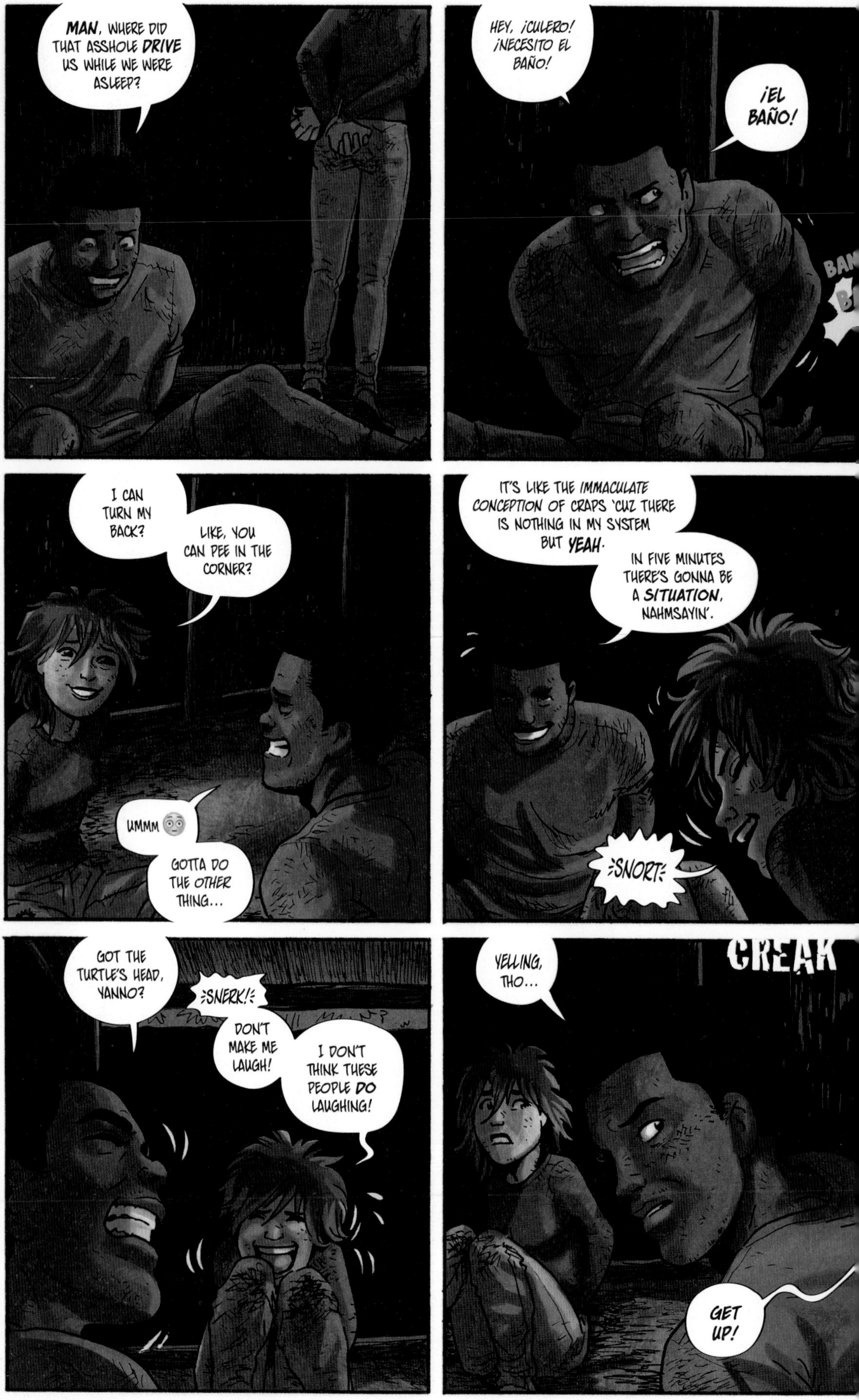
MAN, WHERE DID THAT ASSHOLE DRIVE US WHILE WE WERE ASLEEP?
HEY, ¡CULERO! ¡NECESITO EL BAÑO!
¡EL BAÑO!
I CAN TURN MY BACK?
LIKE, YOU CAN PEE IN THE CORNER?
UMMM
GOTTA DO THE OTHER THING...
IT'S LIKE THE IMMACULATE CONCEPTION OF CRAPS 'CUZ THERE IS NOTHING IN MY SYSTEM BUT YEAH.
IN FIVE MINUTES THERE'S GONNA BE A SITUATION, NAHMSAYIN'.
SNORT
GOT THE TURTLE'S HEAD, YANNO?
SNERK!
DON'T MAKE ME LAUGH!
I DON'T THINK THESE PEOPLE DO LAUGHING!
YELLING, THO...
CREAK
GET UP!

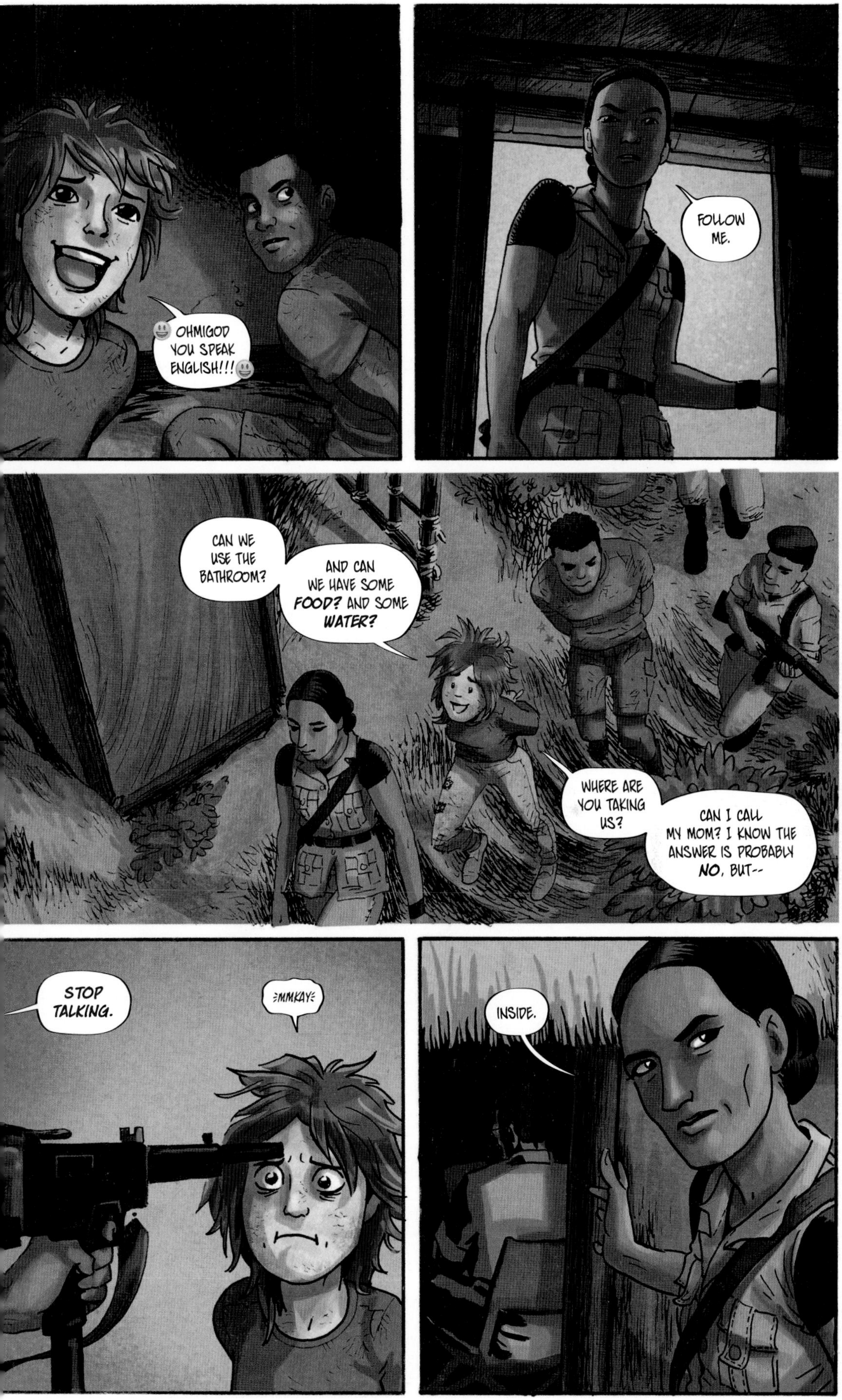
OHMIGOD YOU SPEAK ENGLISH!!!
FOLLOW ME.
CAN WE USE THE BATHROOM?
AND CAN WE HAVE SOME FOOD? AND SOME WATER?
WHERE ARE YOU TAKING US?
CAN I CALL MY MOM? I KNOW THE ANSWER IS PROBABLY NO, BUT--
STOP TALKING.
MMKAY
INSIDE.

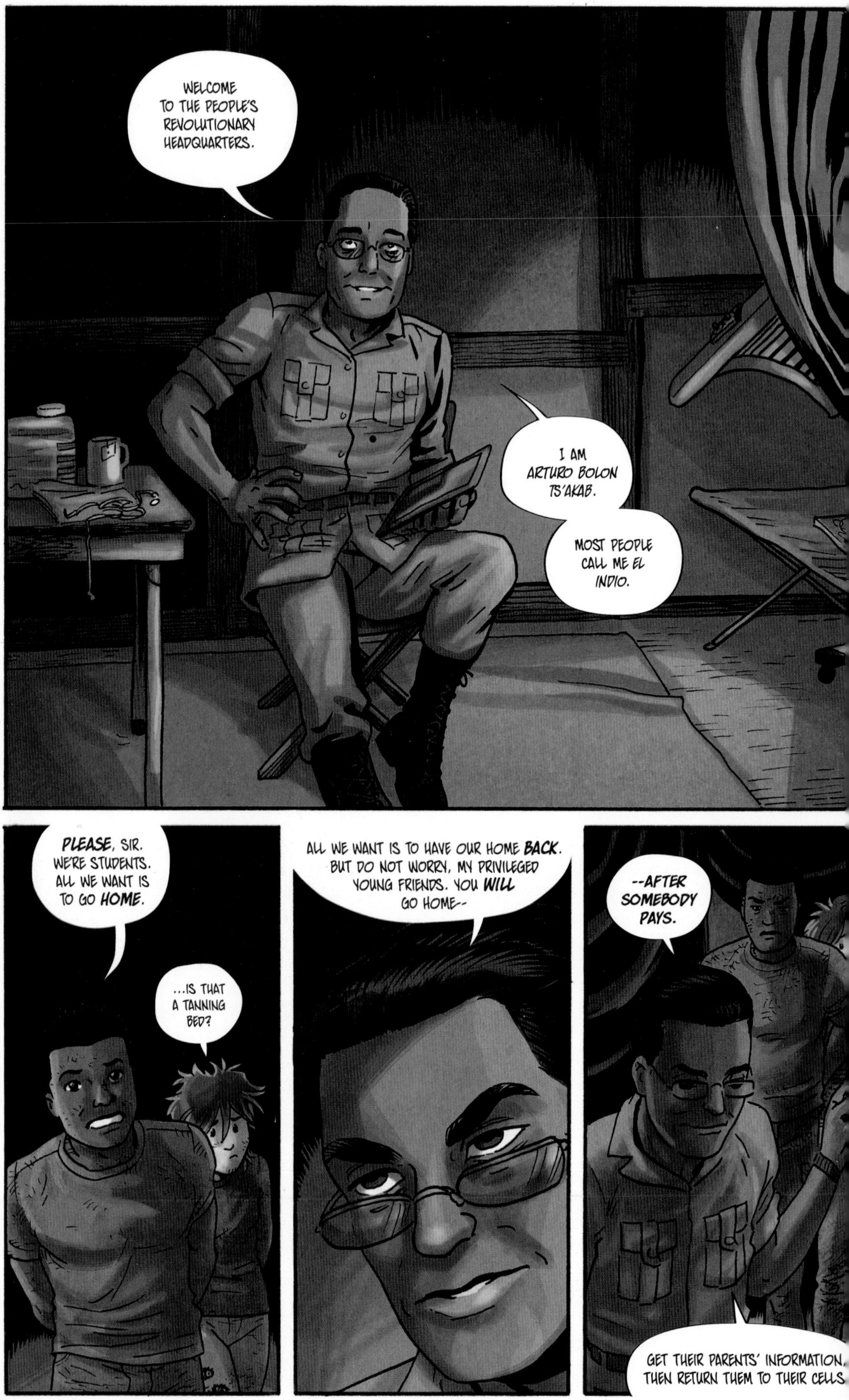
WELCOME TO THE PEOPLE'S REVOLUTIONARY HEADQUARTERS.
I AM ARTURO BOLON TS'AKAB.
MOST PEOPLE CALL ME EL INDIO.
PLEASE, SIR. WE'RE STUDENTS. ALL WE WANT IS TO GO **HOME**.
...IS THAT A TANNING BED?
ALL WE WANT IS TO HAVE OUR HOME **BACK**. BUT DO NOT WORRY, MY PRIVILEGED YOUNG FRIENDS. YOU **WILL** GO HOME--
--AFTER SOMEBODY PAYS.
GET THEIR PARENTS' INFORMATION, THEN RETURN THEM TO THEIR CELLS.

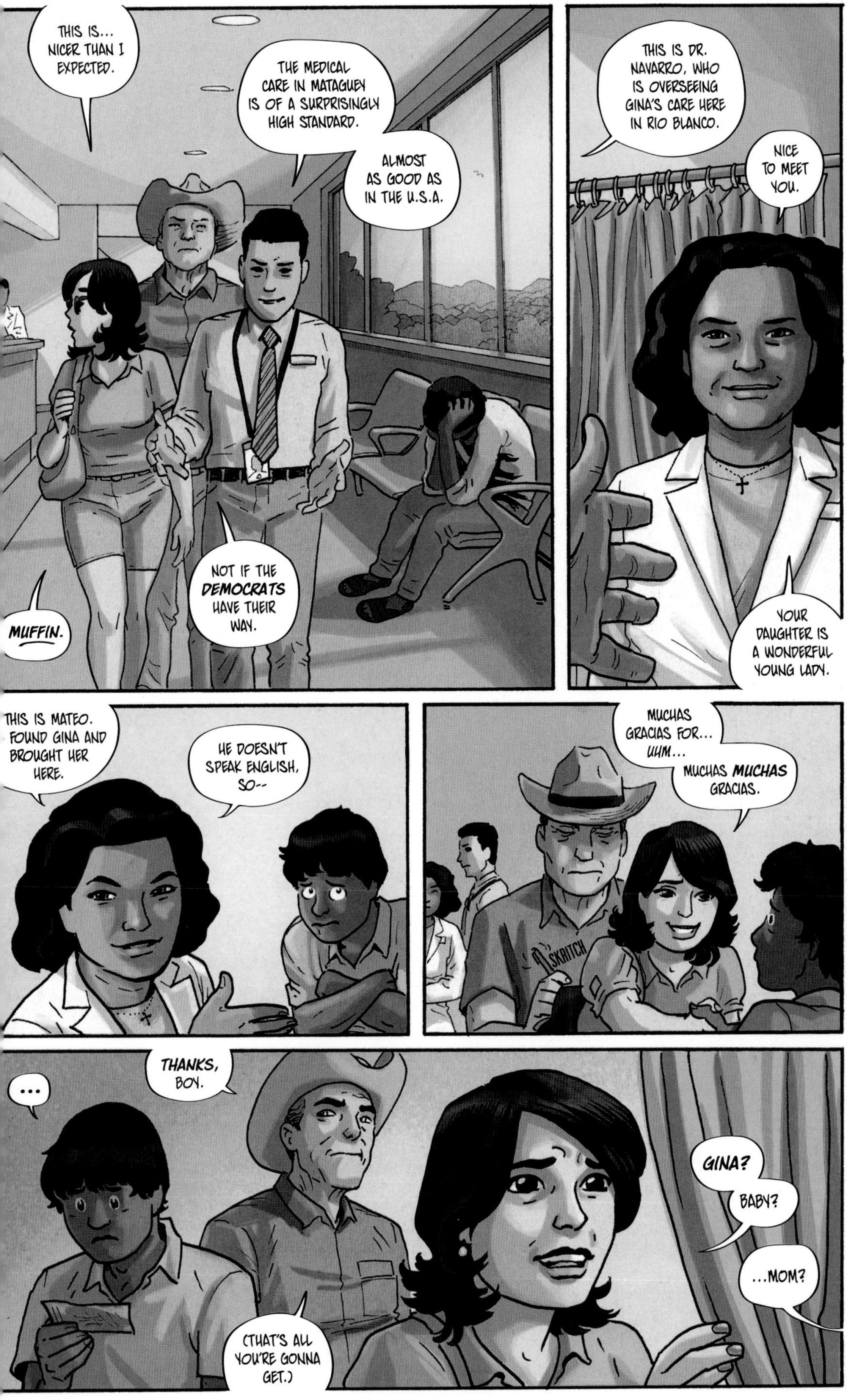

THIS IS... NICER THAN I EXPECTED.
THE MEDICAL CARE IN MATAGUEY IS OF A SURPRISINGLY HIGH STANDARD.
ALMOST AS GOOD AS IN THE U.S.A.
NOT IF THE DEMOCRATS HAVE THEIR WAY.
MUFFIN.
THIS IS DR. NAVARRO, WHO IS OVERSEEING GINA'S CARE HERE IN RIO BLANCO.
NICE TO MEET YOU.
YOUR DAUGHTER IS A WONDERFUL YOUNG LADY.
THIS IS MATEO. FOUND GINA AND BROUGHT HER HERE.
HE DOESN'T SPEAK ENGLISH, SO--
MUCHAS GRACIAS FOR... UHM...
MUCHAS MUCHAS GRACIAS.
SKRITCH
...
THANKS, BOY.
(THAT'S ALL YOU'RE GONNA GET.)
GINA?
BABY?
...MOM?

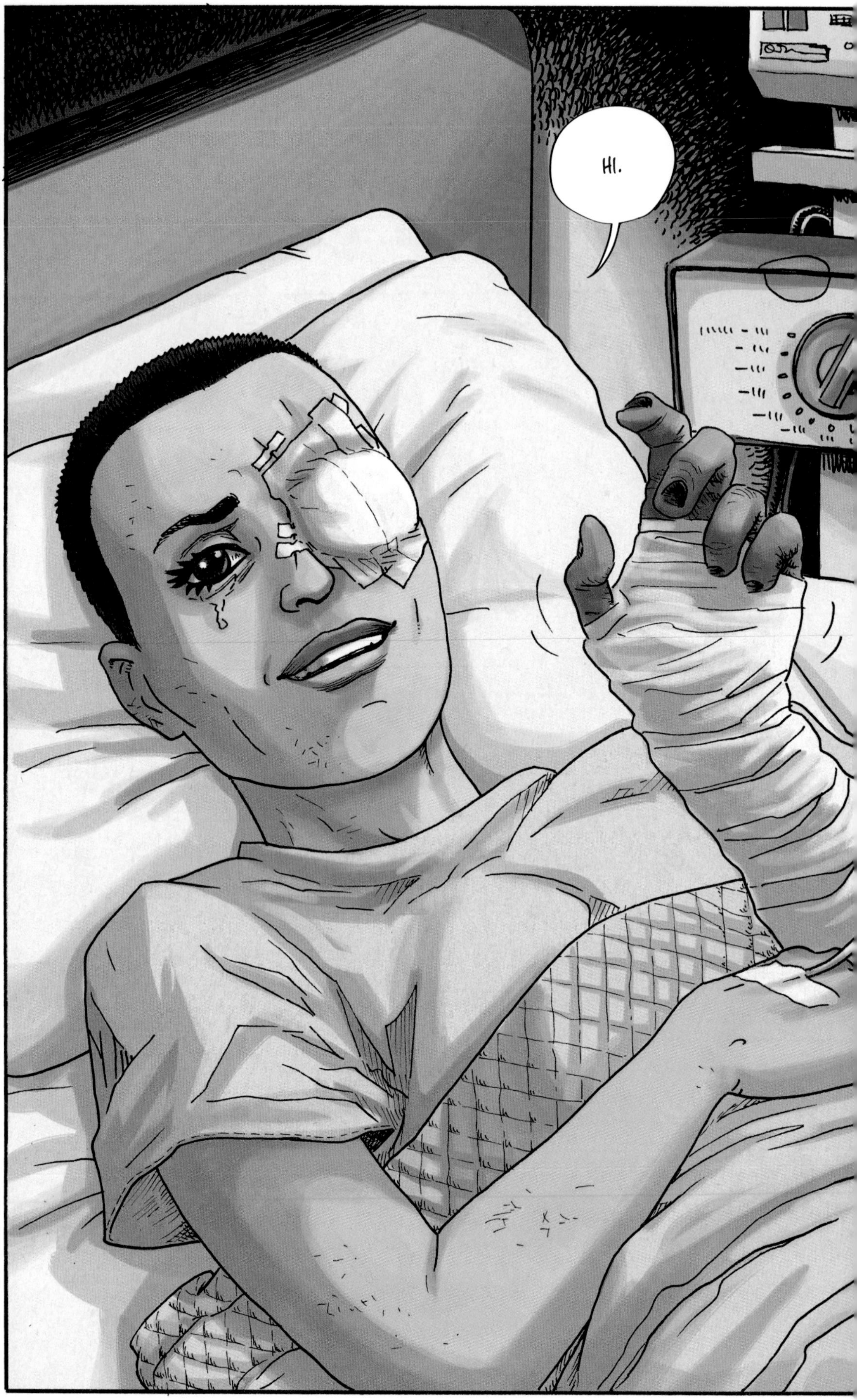
HI.

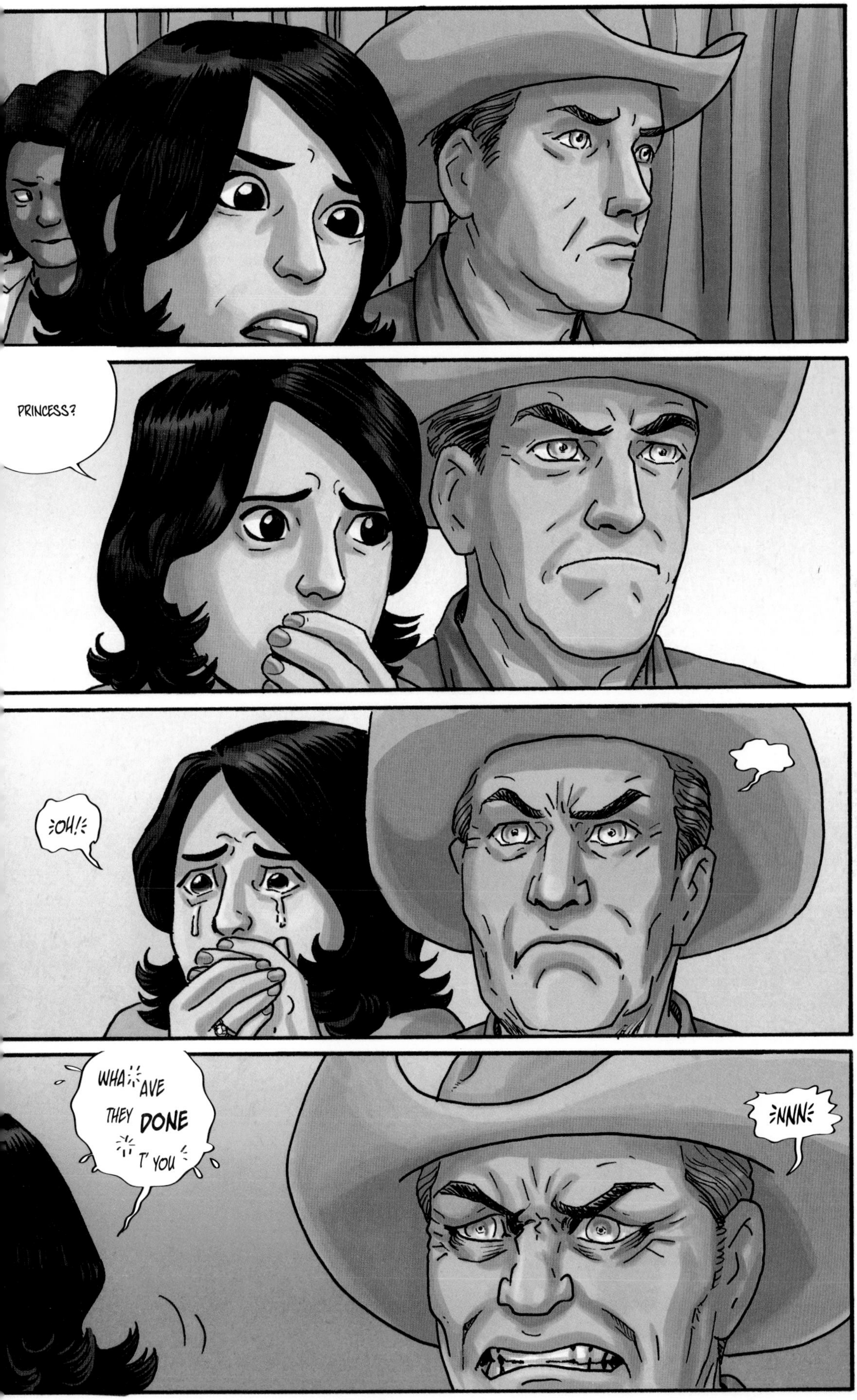
PRINCESS?
OH!
WHA' 'AVE THEY DONE T' YOU
NNN

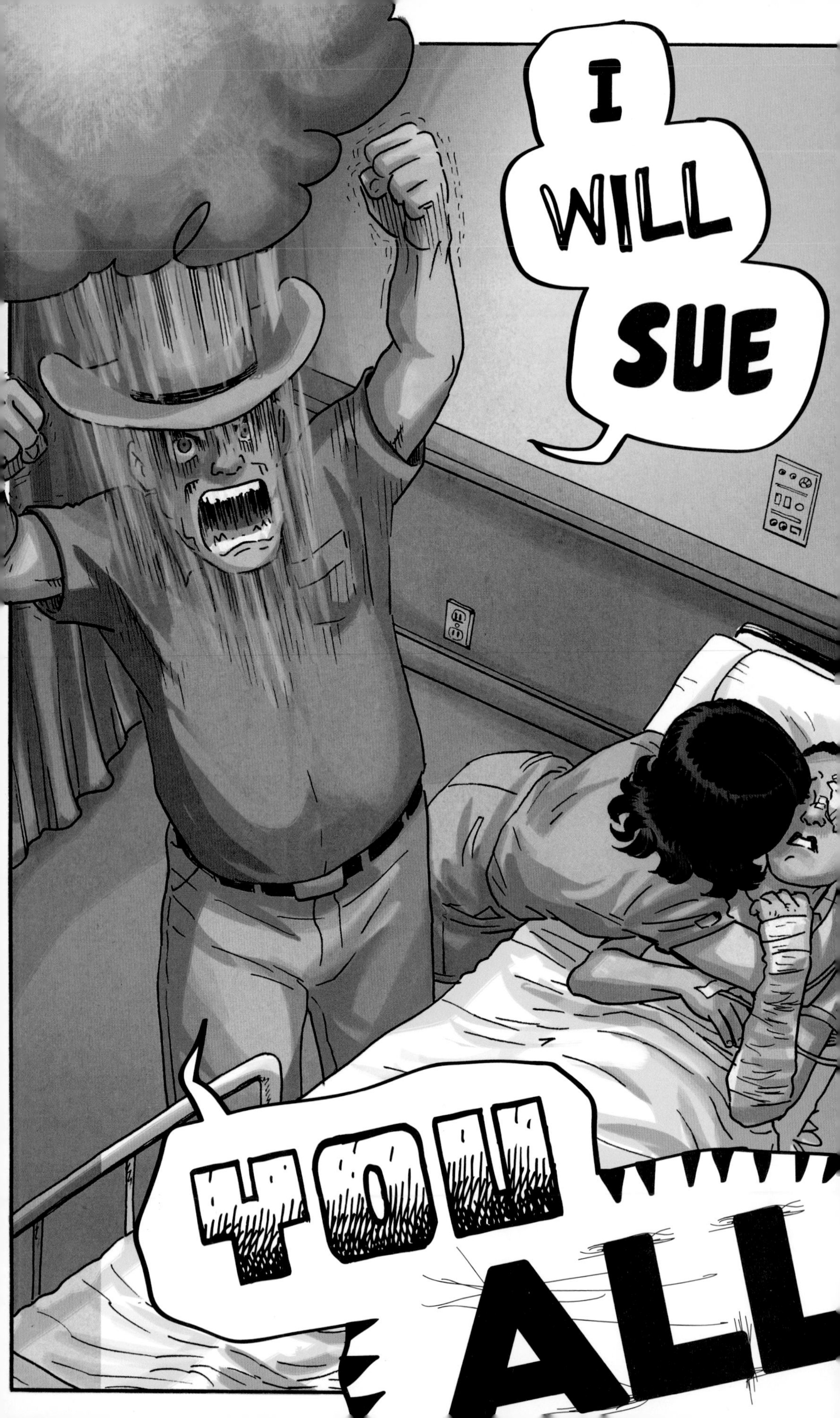
I WILL SUE
YOU ALL

CHAPTER EIGHT

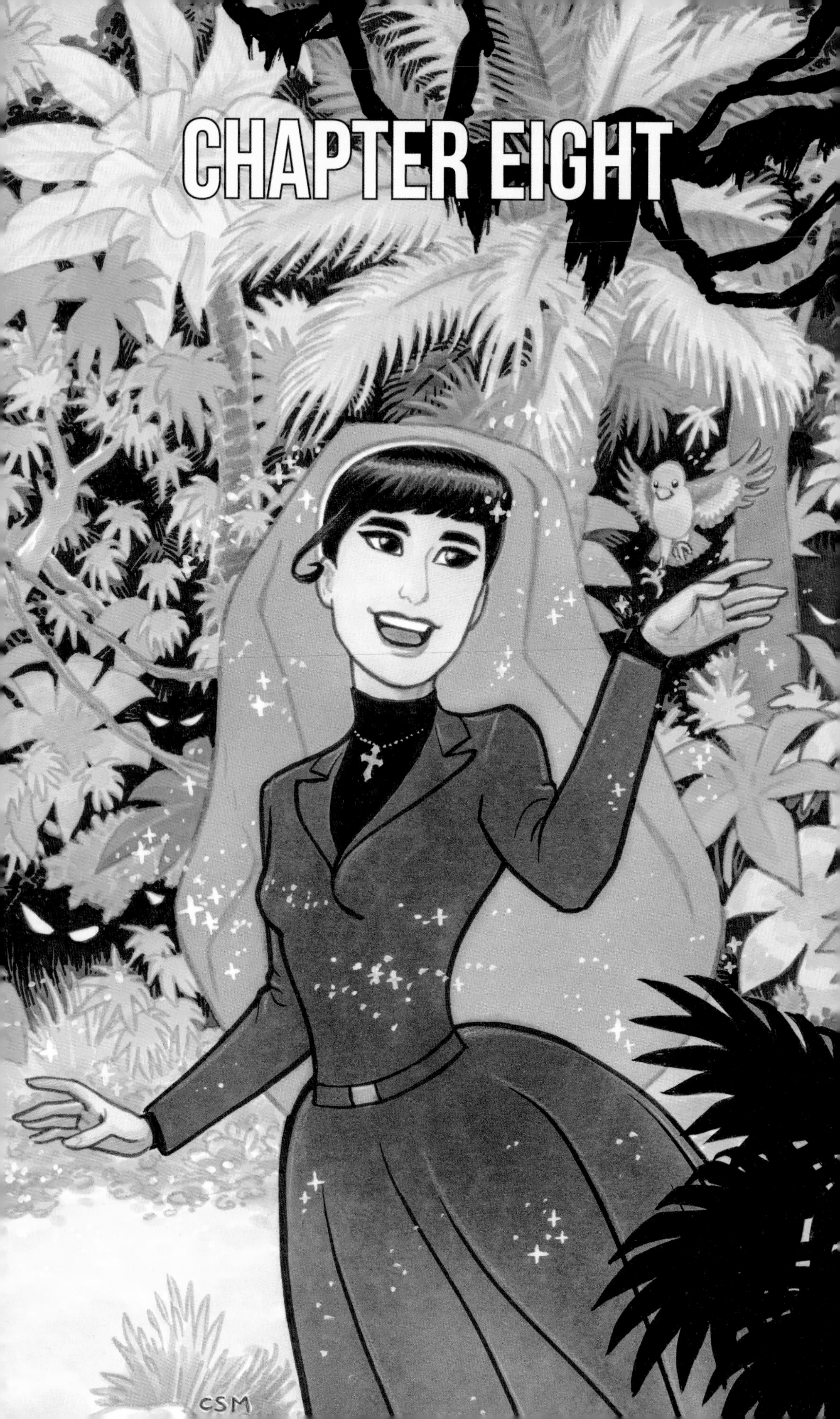
CSM

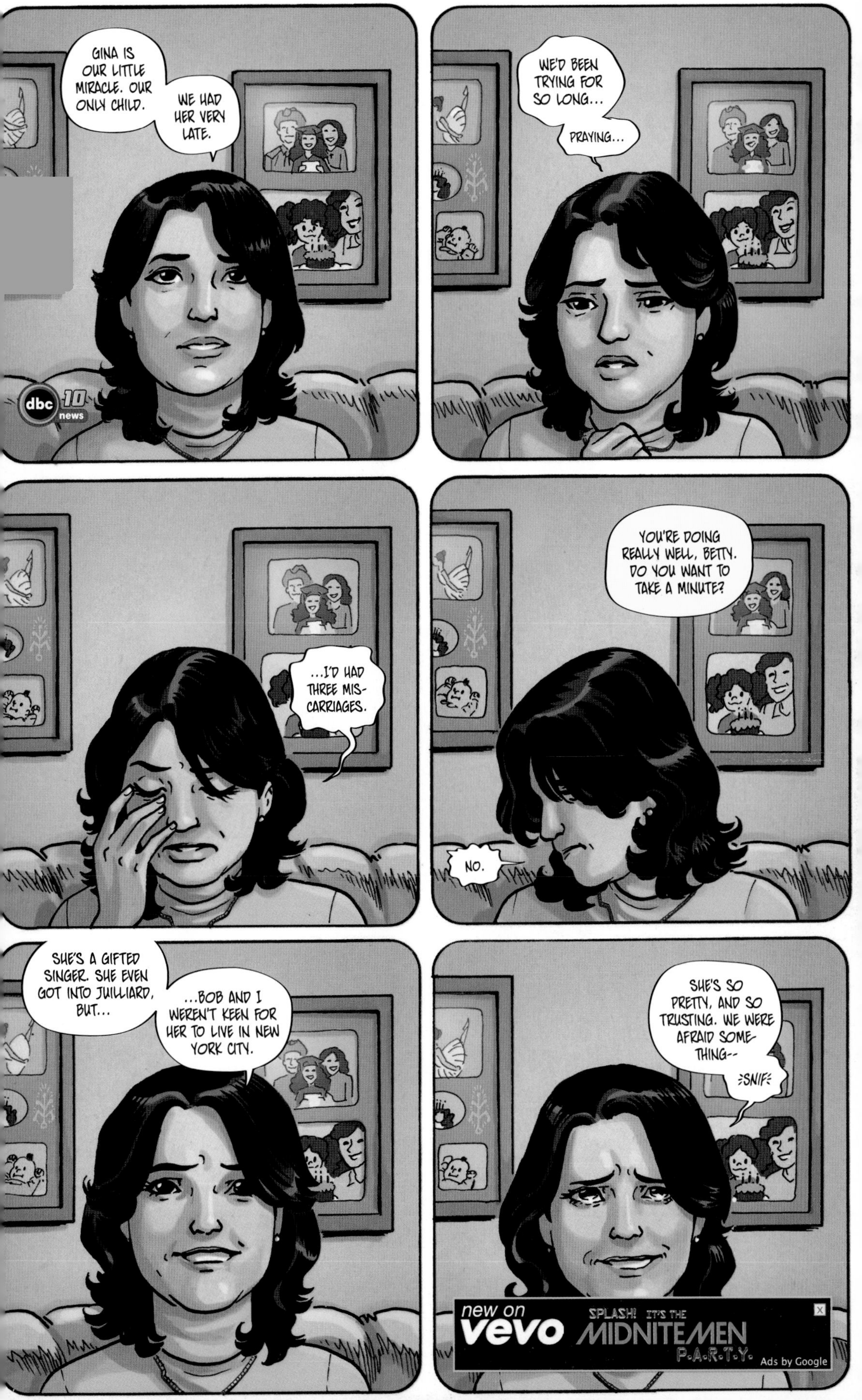
GINA IS OUR LITTLE MIRACLE. OUR ONLY CHILD.
WE HAD HER VERY LATE.
dbc 10 news
WE'D BEEN TRYING FOR SO LONG...
PRAYING...
...I'D HAD THREE MIS-CARRIAGES.
YOU'RE DOING REALLY WELL, BETTY. DO YOU WANT TO TAKE A MINUTE?
NO.
SHE'S A GIFTED SINGER. SHE EVEN GOT INTO JUILLIARD, BUT...
...BOB AND I WEREN'T KEEN FOR HER TO LIVE IN NEW YORK CITY.
SHE'S SO PRETTY, AND SO TRUSTING. WE WERE AFRAID SOME-THING--
SNIF
new on vevo
SPLASH! IT'S THE MIDNITEMEN P.A.R.T.Y.
Ads by Google

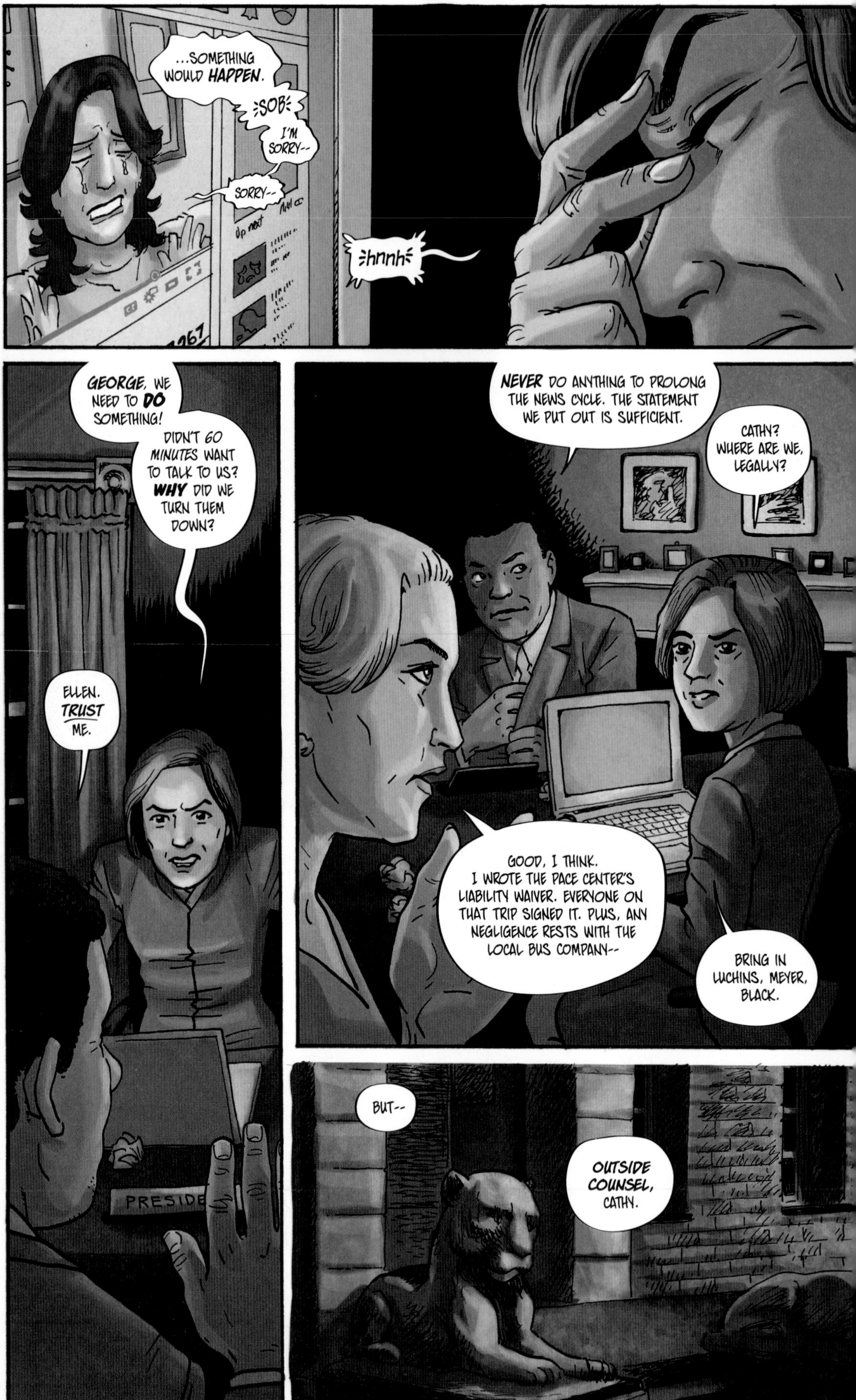
...SOMETHING WOULD **HAPPEN**.
SOB
I'M SORRY--
SORRY--
Up next
hnnh
GEORGE, WE NEED TO **DO** SOMETHING!
DIDN'T 60 MINUTES WANT TO TALK TO US? **WHY** DID WE TURN THEM DOWN?
NEVER DO ANYTHING TO PROLONG THE NEWS CYCLE. THE STATEMENT WE PUT OUT IS SUFFICIENT.
CATHY? WHERE ARE WE, LEGALLY?
ELLEN. **TRUST** ME.
GOOD, I THINK. I WROTE THE PACE CENTER'S LIABILITY WAIVER. EVERYONE ON THAT TRIP SIGNED IT. PLUS, ANY NEGLIGENCE RESTS WITH THE LOCAL BUS COMPANY--
BRING IN LUCHINS, MEYER, BLACK.
PRESIDE
BUT--
OUTSIDE COUNSEL, CATHY.

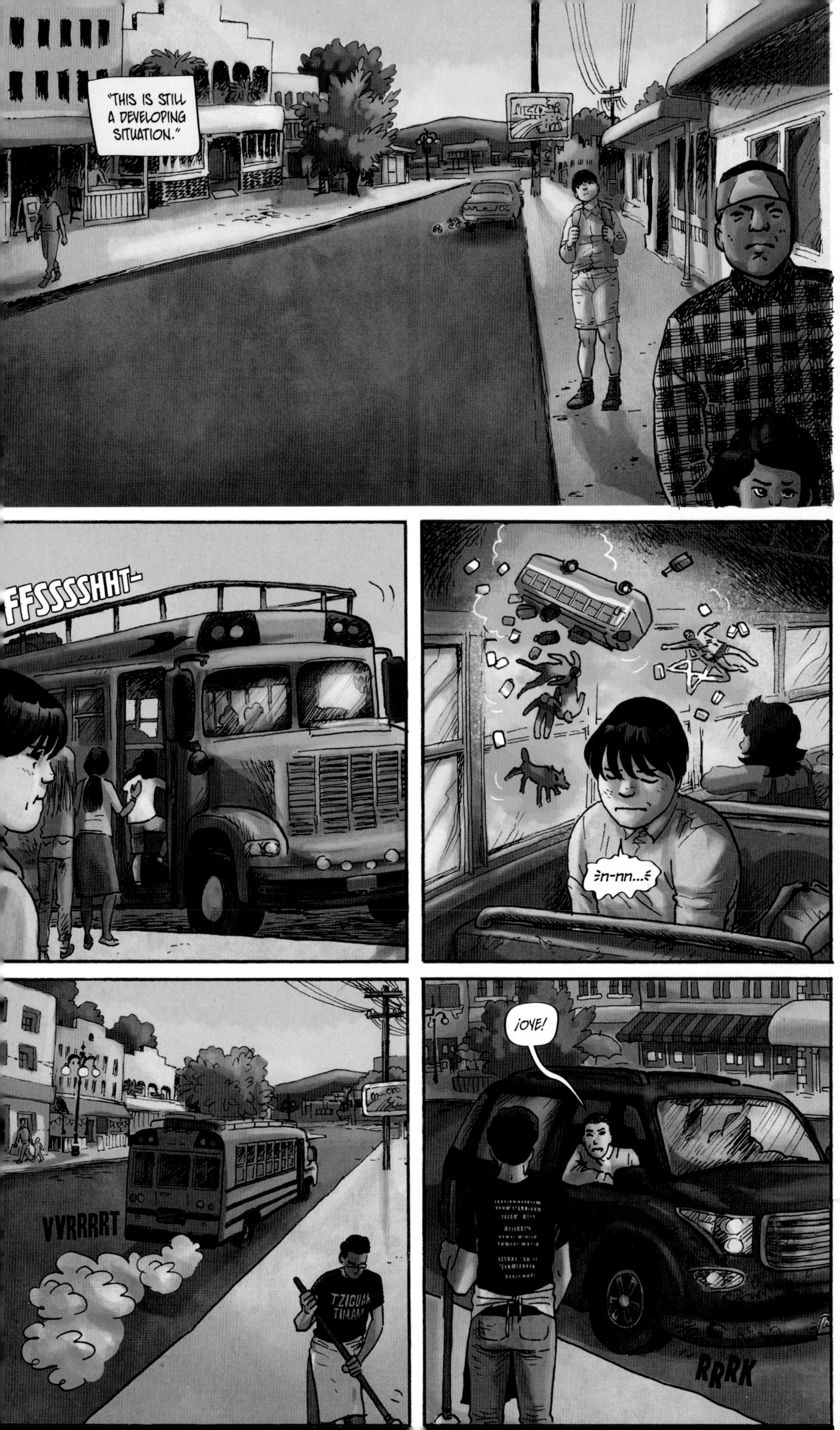
"THIS IS STILL A DEVELOPING SITUATION."
FFSSSSHHT-
n-nn...
VVRRRRT
TZIGUAN TIJIAM
¡OYE!
RRRK

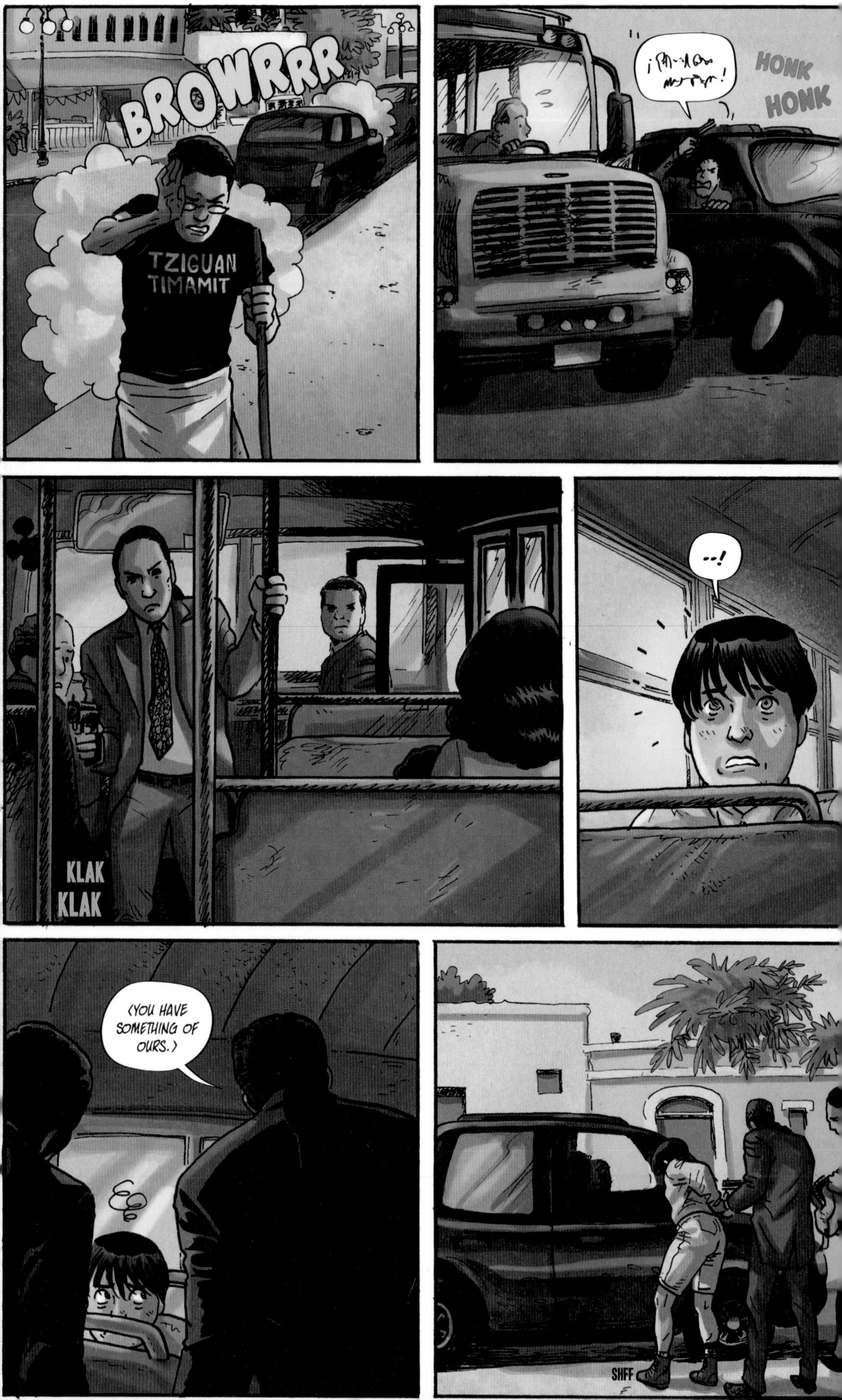
BROWRRR
TZIGUAN TIMAMIT
HONK
HONK
KLAK
KLAK
--!
<YOU HAVE SOMETHING OF OURS.>
SHFF

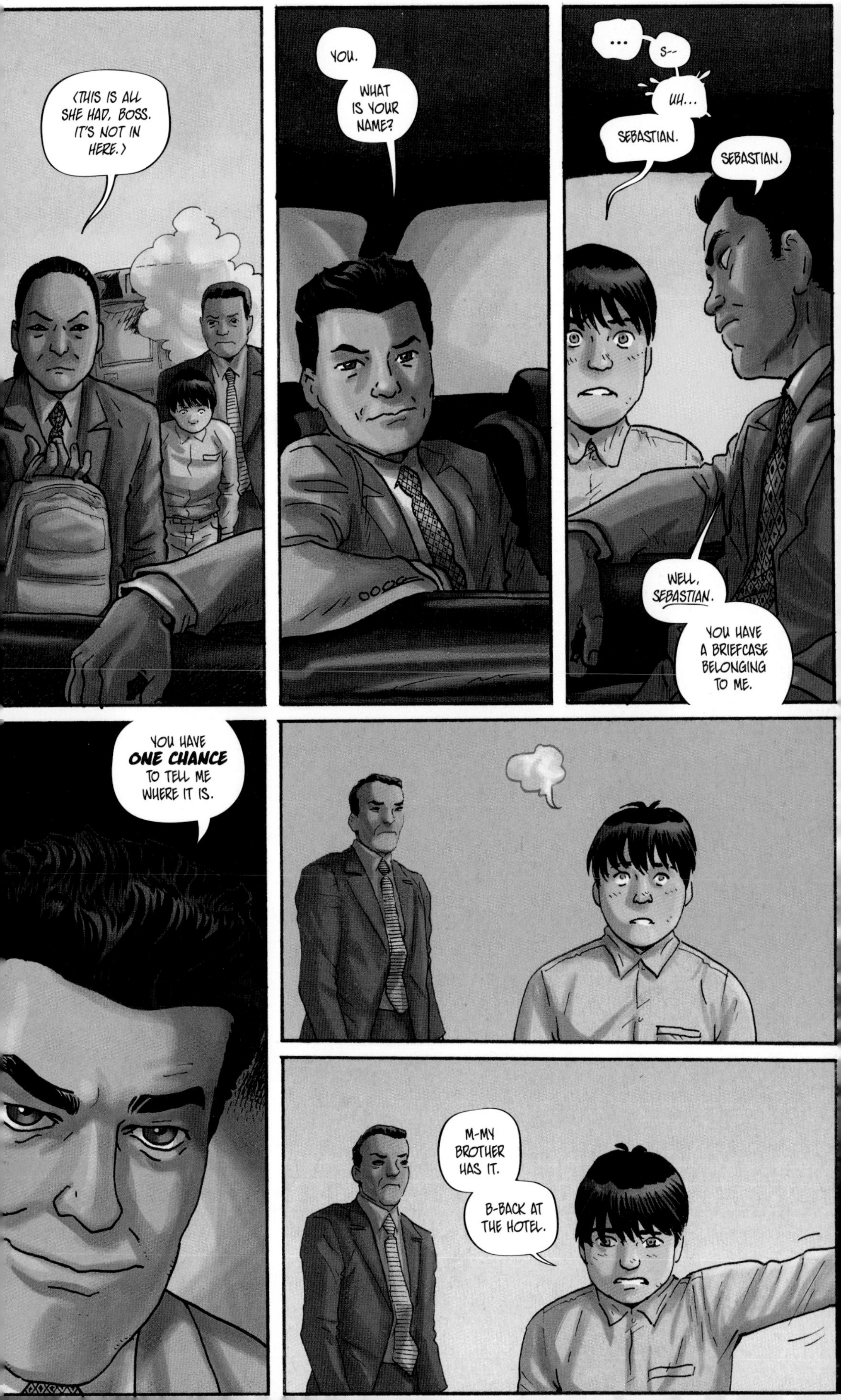

‹THIS IS ALL SHE HAD, BOSS. IT'S NOT IN HERE.›
YOU.
WHAT IS YOUR NAME?
...
S--
UH...
SEBASTIAN.
SEBASTIAN.
WELL, SEBASTIAN.
YOU HAVE A BRIEFCASE BELONGING TO ME.
YOU HAVE ONE CHANCE TO TELL ME WHERE IT IS.
M-MY BROTHER HAS IT.
B-BACK AT THE HOTEL.

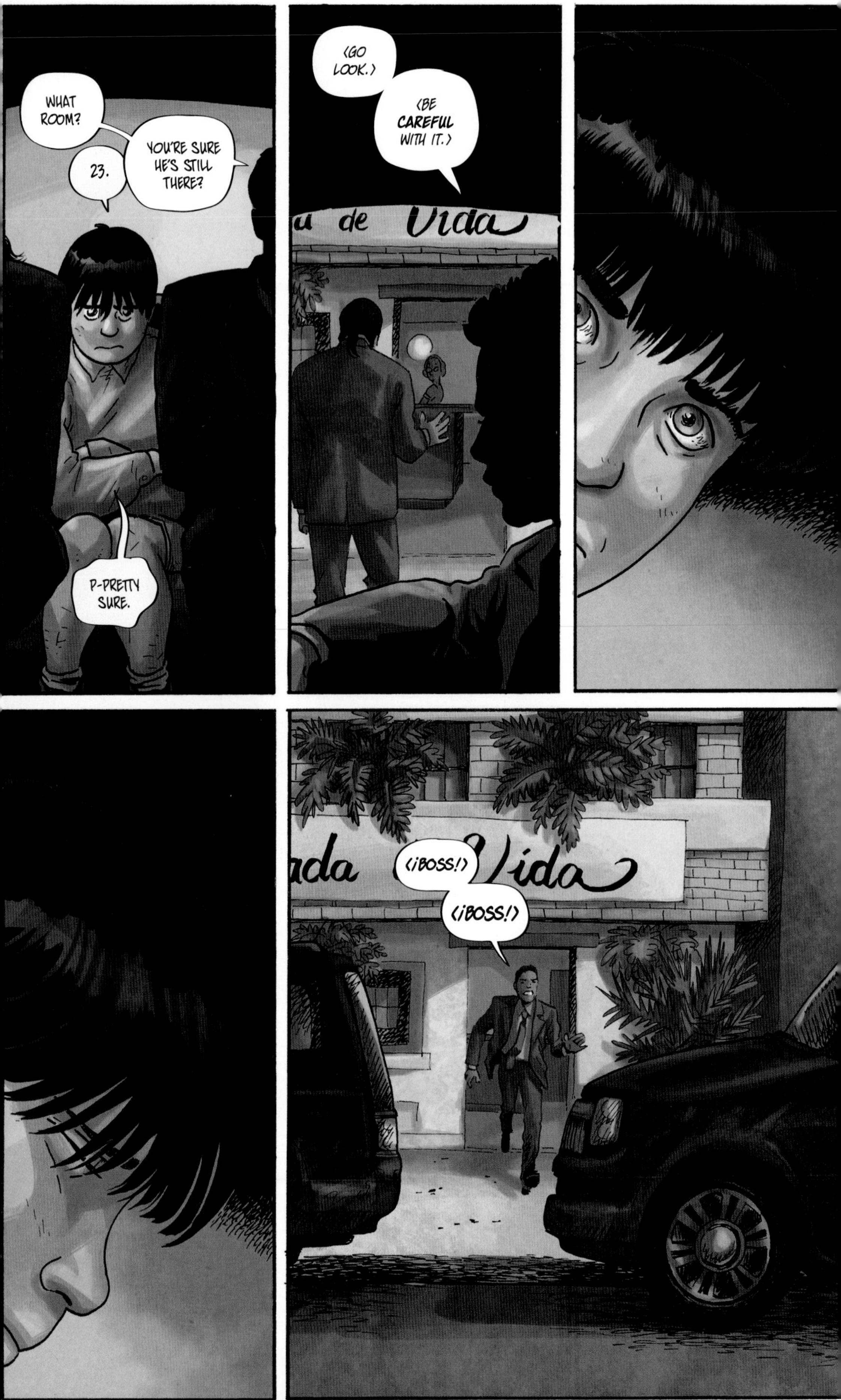
WHAT ROOM?
23.
YOU'RE SURE HE'S STILL THERE?
P-PRETTY SURE.
‹GO LOOK.›
‹BE CAREFUL WITH IT.›
u de Vida
ada Vida
‹¡BOSS!›
‹¡BOSS!›

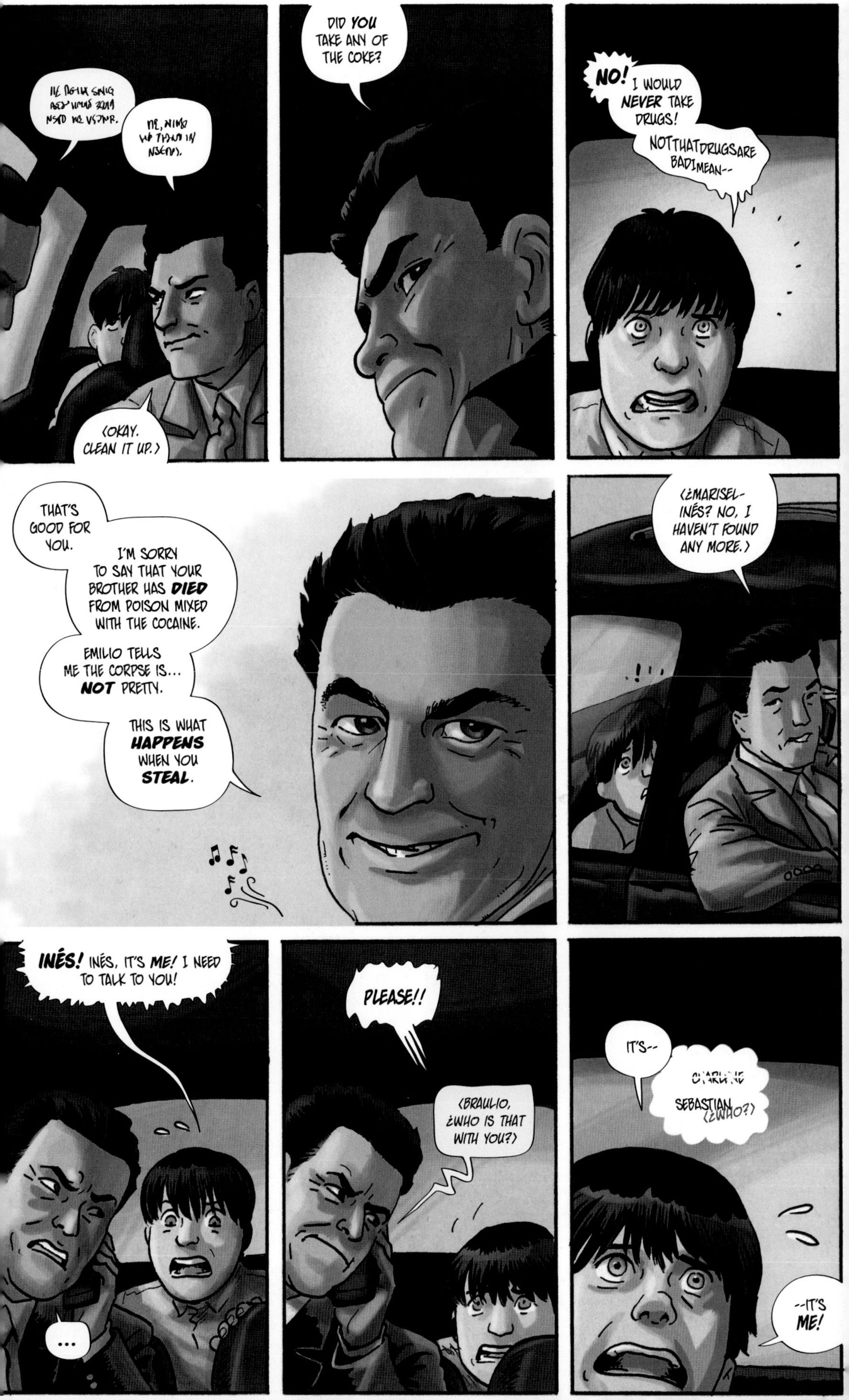

<OKAY. CLEAN IT UP.>
DID YOU TAKE ANY OF THE COKE?
NO! I WOULD NEVER TAKE DRUGS!
NOTTHATDRUGSARE BADIMEAN--
THAT'S GOOD FOR YOU.
I'M SORRY TO SAY THAT YOUR BROTHER HAS DIED FROM POISON MIXED WITH THE COCAINE.
EMILIO TELLS ME THE CORPSE IS... NOT PRETTY.
THIS IS WHAT HAPPENS WHEN YOU STEAL.
<¿MARISEL-INÉS? NO, I HAVEN'T FOUND ANY MORE.>
!!
INÉS! INÉS, IT'S ME! I NEED TO TALK TO YOU!
...
PLEASE!!
<BRAULIO, ¿WHO IS THAT WITH YOU?>
IT'S--
SEBASTIAN
<¿WHO?>
--IT'S ME!

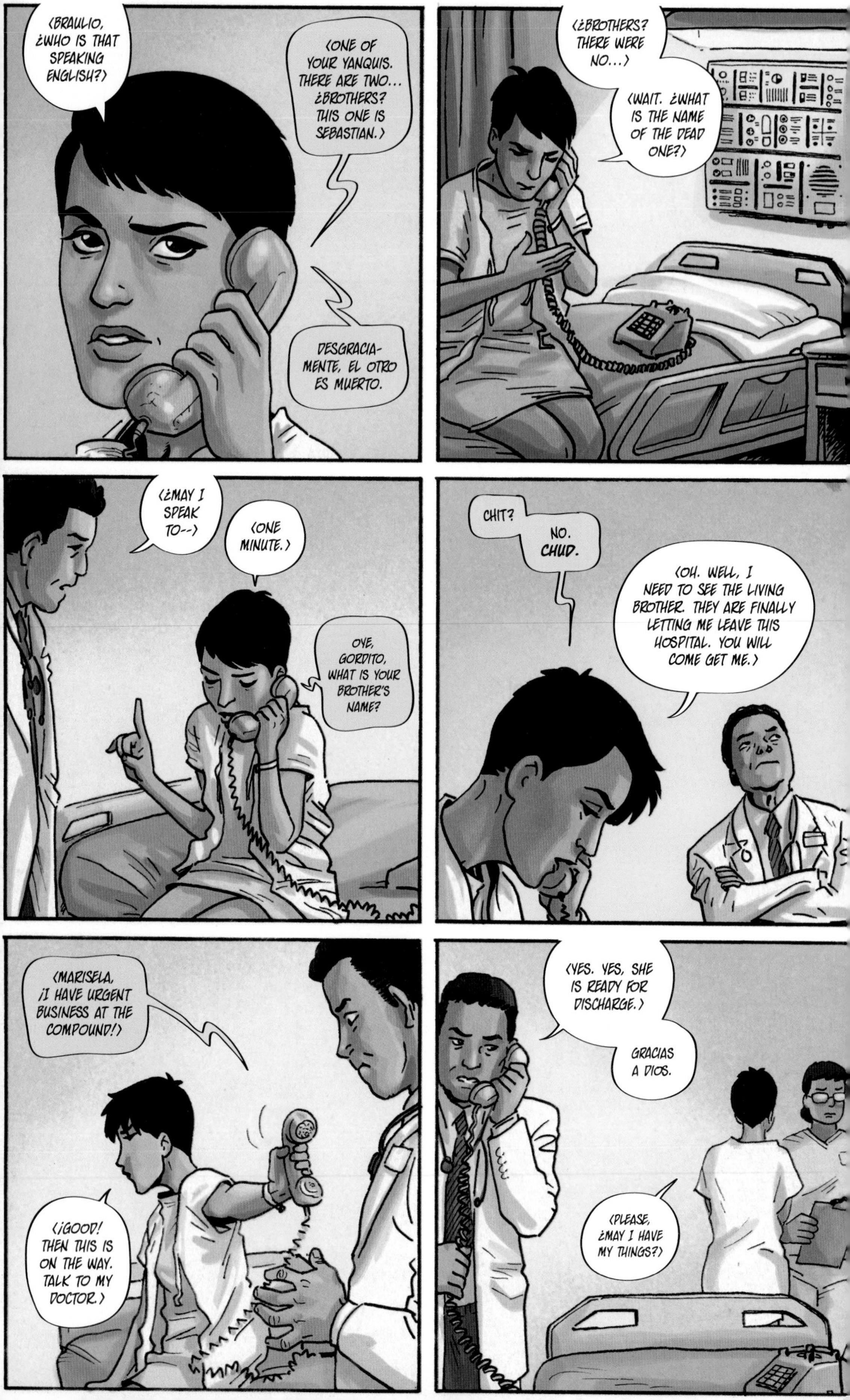
⟨BRAULIO, ¿WHO IS THAT SPEAKING ENGLISH?⟩
⟨ONE OF YOUR YANQUIS. THERE ARE TWO... ¿BROTHERS? THIS ONE IS SEBASTIAN.⟩
DESGRACIAMENTE, EL OTRO ES MUERTO.
⟨¿BROTHERS? THERE WERE NO...⟩
⟨WAIT. ¿WHAT IS THE NAME OF THE DEAD ONE?⟩
⟨¿MAY I SPEAK TO--⟩
⟨ONE MINUTE.⟩
OYE, GORDITO, WHAT IS YOUR BROTHER'S NAME?
CHIT?
NO. CHUD.
⟨OH. WELL, I NEED TO SEE THE LIVING BROTHER. THEY ARE FINALLY LETTING ME LEAVE THIS HOSPITAL. YOU WILL COME GET ME.⟩
⟨MARISELA, ¡I HAVE URGENT BUSINESS AT THE COMPOUND!⟩
⟨¡GOOD! THEN THIS IS ON THE WAY. TALK TO MY DOCTOR.⟩
⟨YES. YES, SHE IS READY FOR DISCHARGE.⟩
GRACIAS A DIOS.
⟨PLEASE, ¿MAY I HAVE MY THINGS?⟩

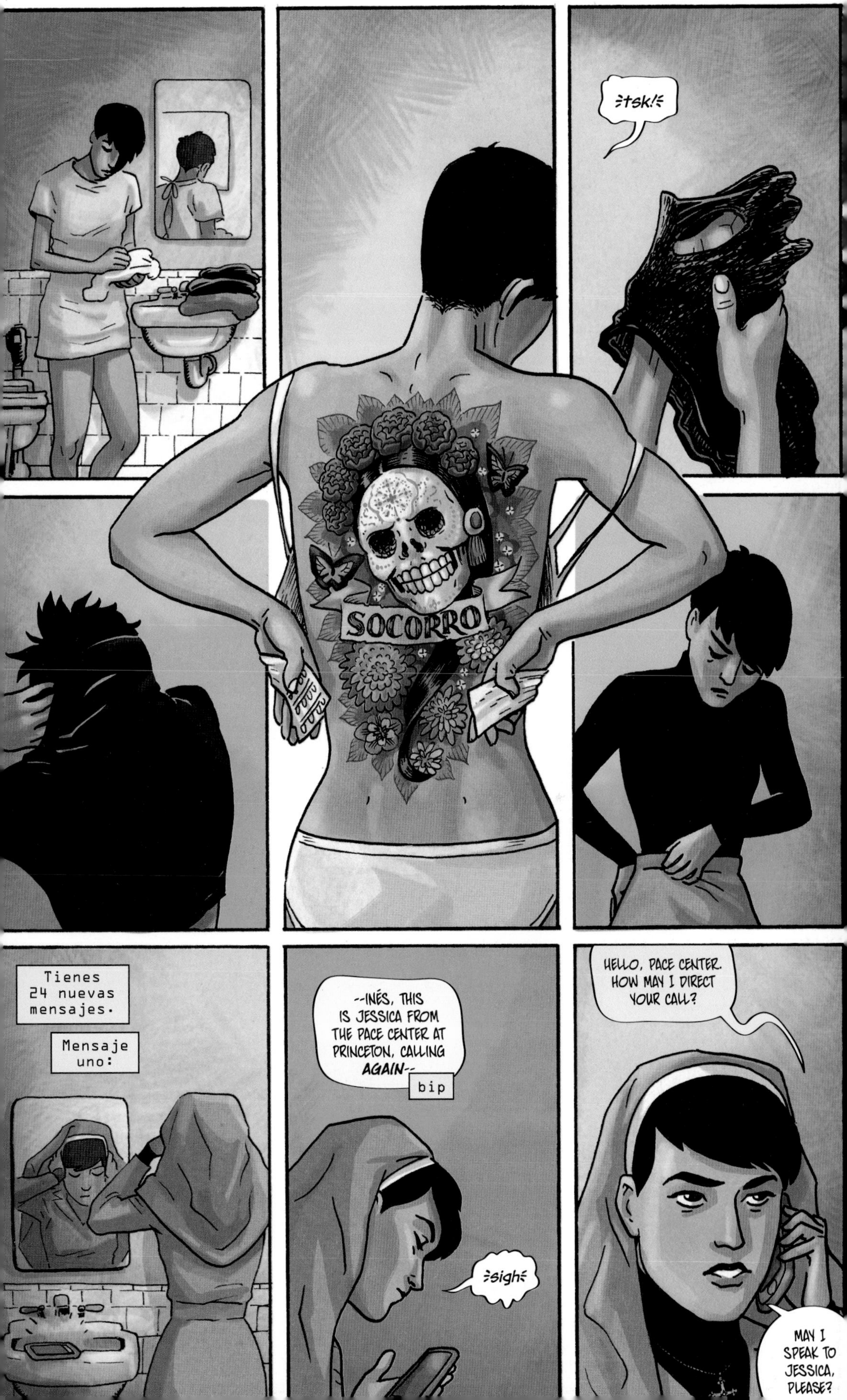

=tsk!=
Tienes 24 nuevas mensajes.
Mensaje uno:
--INÉS, THIS IS JESSICA FROM THE PACE CENTER AT PRINCETON, CALLING **AGAIN**--
bip
=sigh=
HELLO, PACE CENTER. HOW MAY I DIRECT YOUR CALL?
MAY I SPEAK TO JESSICA, PLEASE?

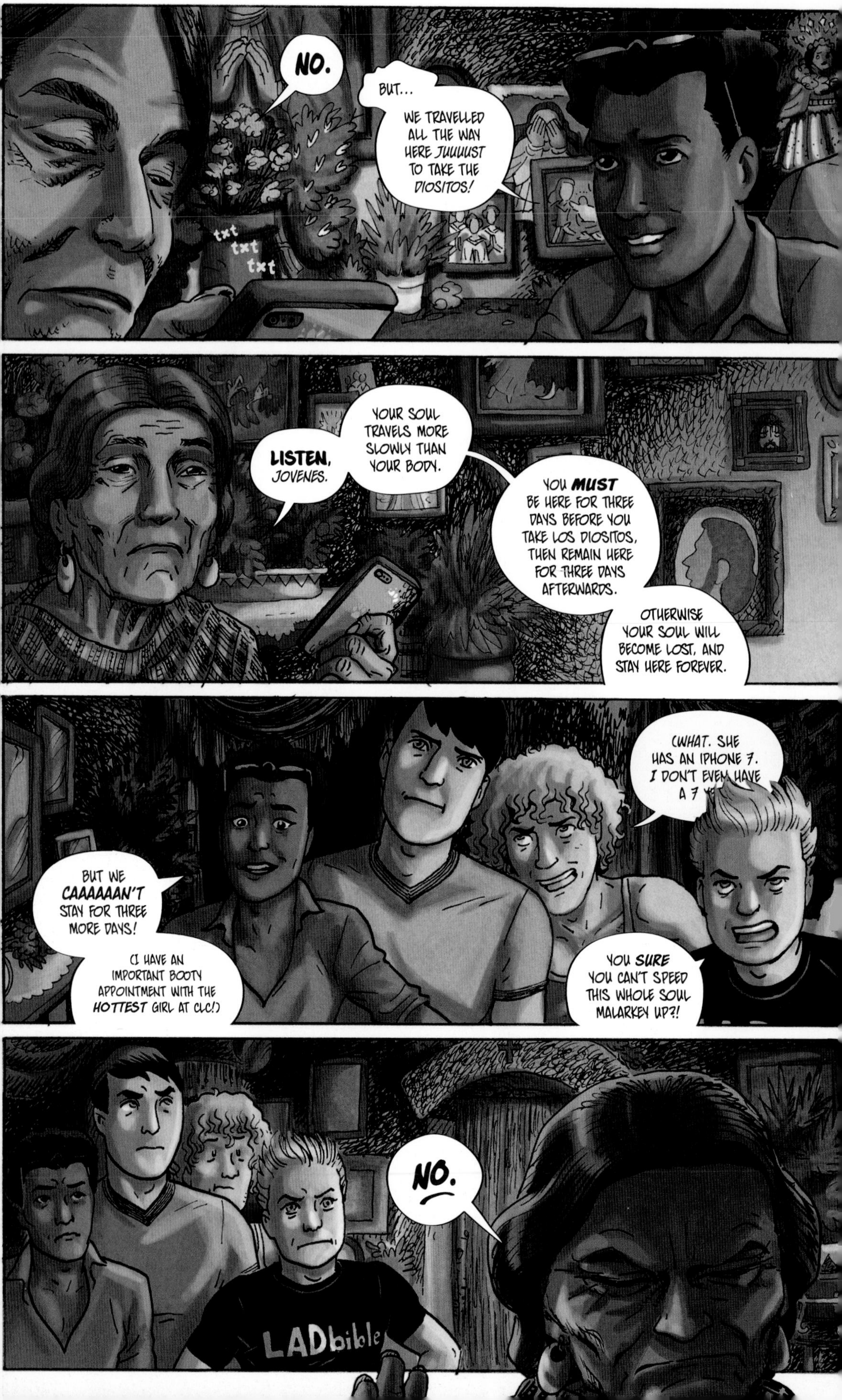
NO.
BUT...
WE TRAVELLED ALL THE WAY HERE JUUUUST TO TAKE THE DIOSITOS!
txt txt txt
LISTEN, JOVENES.
YOUR SOUL TRAVELS MORE SLOWLY THAN YOUR BODY.
YOU MUST BE HERE FOR THREE DAYS BEFORE YOU TAKE LOS DIOSITOS, THEN REMAIN HERE FOR THREE DAYS AFTERWARDS.
OTHERWISE YOUR SOUL WILL BECOME LOST, AND STAY HERE FOREVER.
BUT WE CAAAAAAN'T STAY FOR THREE MORE DAYS!
(I HAVE AN IMPORTANT BOOTY APPOINTMENT WITH THE HOTTEST GIRL AT CLC!)
(WHAT. SHE HAS AN IPHONE 7. I DON'T EVEN HAVE A 7
YOU SURE YOU CAN'T SPEED THIS WHOLE SOUL MALARKEY UP?!
NO.
LADbible

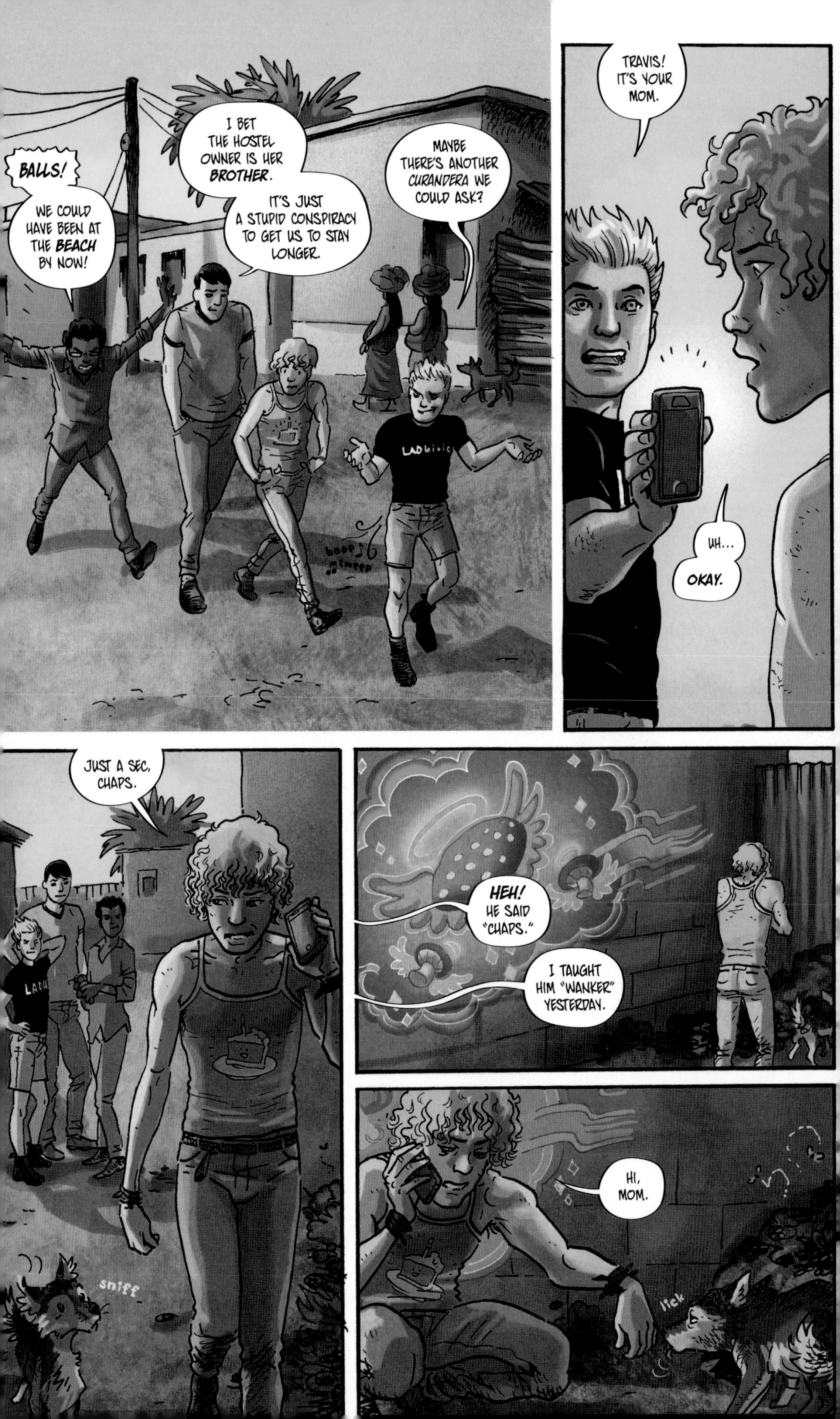
BALLS!
WE COULD HAVE BEEN AT THE BEACH BY NOW!
I BET THE HOSTEL OWNER IS HER BROTHER.
IT'S JUST A STUPID CONSPIRACY TO GET US TO STAY LONGER.
MAYBE THERE'S ANOTHER CURANDERA WE COULD ASK?
LAD
boop tweep
TRAVIS! IT'S YOUR MOM.
UH...
OKAY.
JUST A SEC, CHAPS.
sniff
HEH! HE SAID "CHAPS."
I TAUGHT HIM "WANKER" YESTERDAY.
HI, MOM.
lick

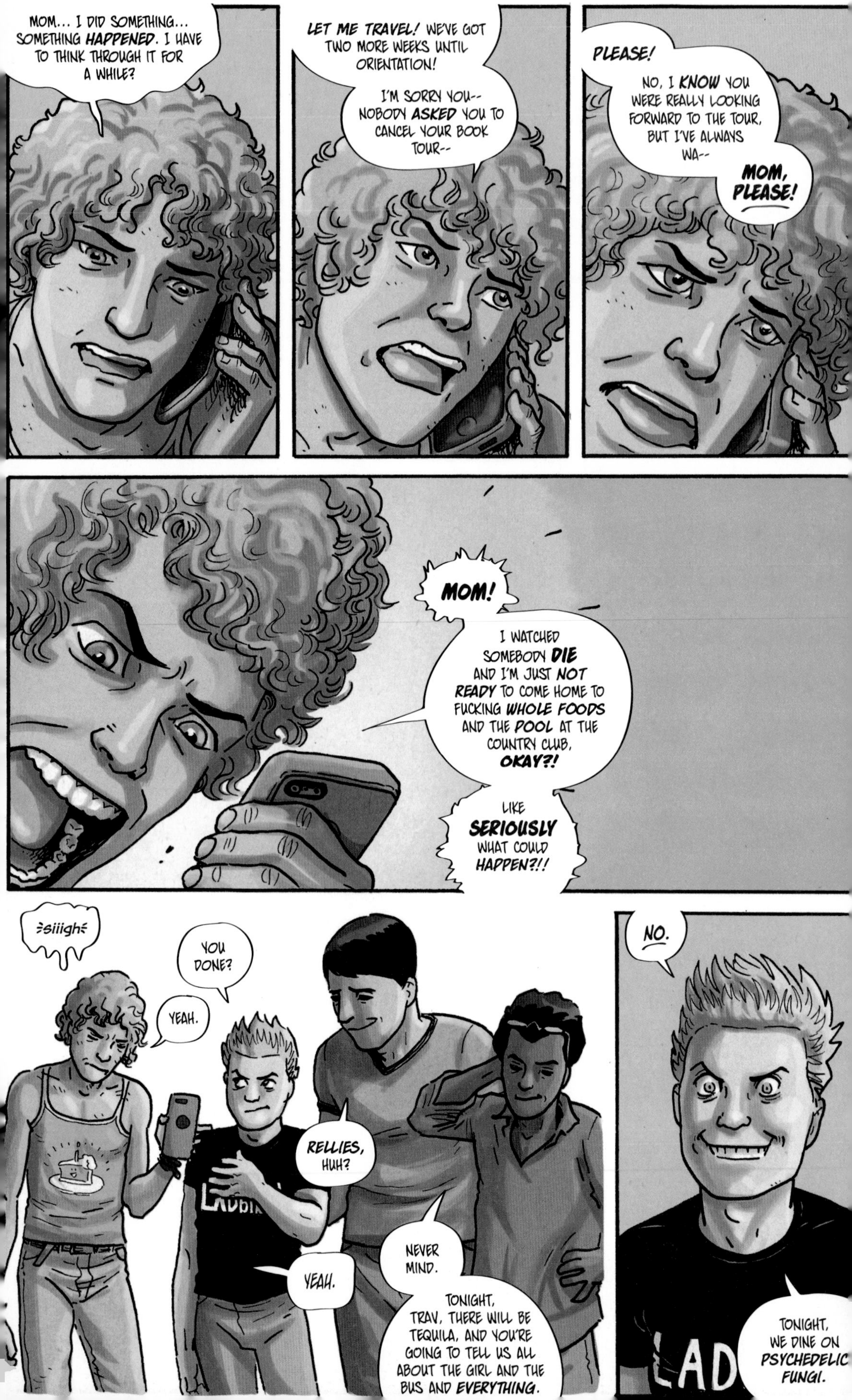
MOM... I DID SOMETHING... SOMETHING HAPPENED. I HAVE TO THINK THROUGH IT FOR A WHILE?
LET ME TRAVEL! WE'VE GOT TWO MORE WEEKS UNTIL ORIENTATION!
I'M SORRY YOU-- NOBODY ASKED YOU TO CANCEL YOUR BOOK TOUR--
PLEASE!
NO, I KNOW YOU WERE REALLY LOOKING FORWARD TO THE TOUR, BUT I'VE ALWAYS WA--
MOM, PLEASE!
MOM!
I WATCHED SOMEBODY DIE AND I'M JUST NOT READY TO COME HOME TO FUCKING WHOLE FOODS AND THE POOL AT THE COUNTRY CLUB, OKAY?!
LIKE SERIOUSLY WHAT COULD HAPPEN?!!
siiigh
YOU DONE?
YEAH.
RELLIES, HUH?
YEAH.
NEVER MIND.
TONIGHT, TRAV, THERE WILL BE TEQUILA, AND YOU'RE GOING TO TELL US ALL ABOUT THE GIRL AND THE BUS AND EVERYTHING.
NO.
TONIGHT, WE DINE ON PSYCHEDELIC FUNGI.

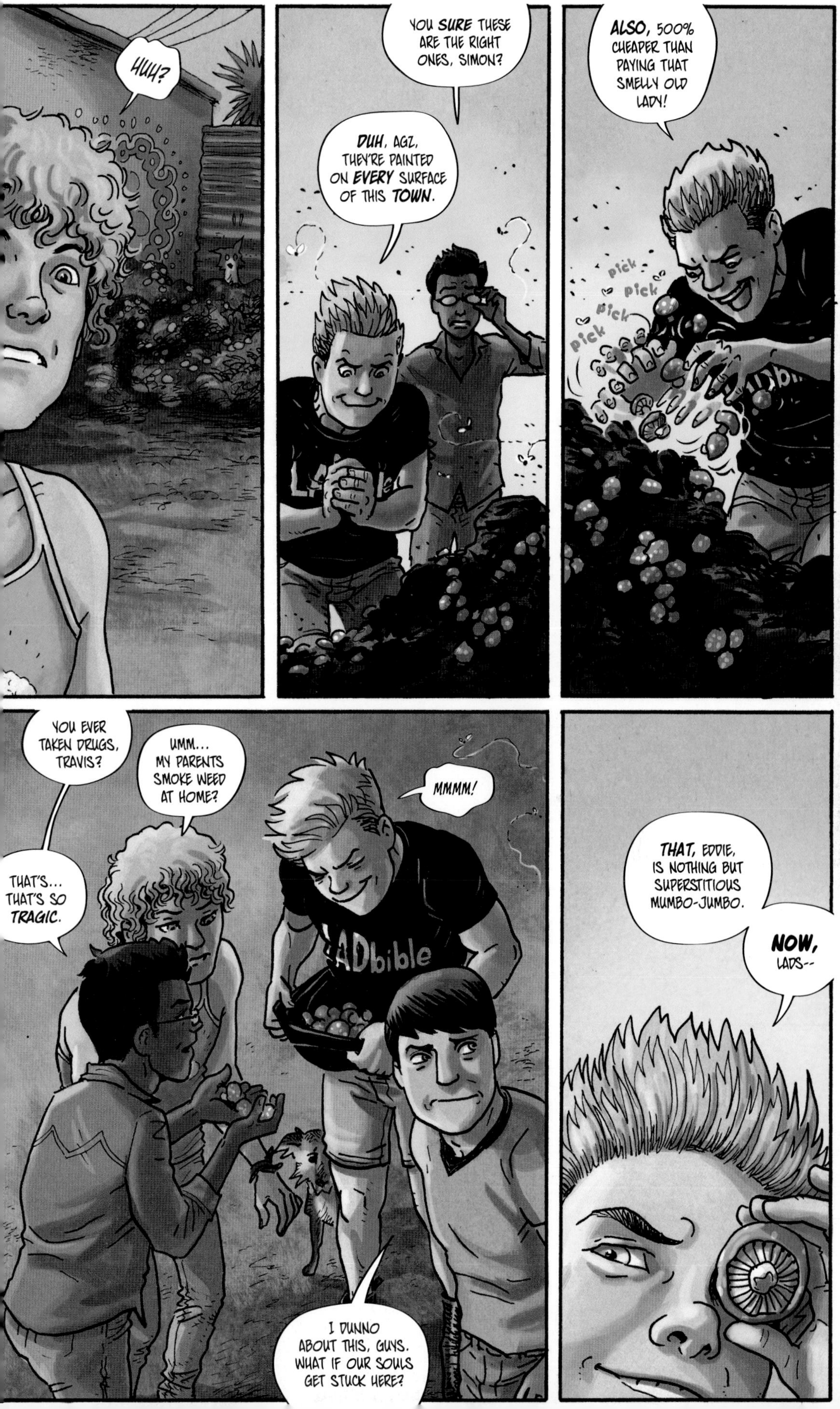
HUH?
YOU SURE THESE ARE THE RIGHT ONES, SIMON?
DUH, AGZ, THEY'RE PAINTED ON EVERY SURFACE OF THIS TOWN.
ALSO, 500% CHEAPER THAN PAYING THAT SMELLY OLD LADY!
pick
pick
pick
pick
YOU EVER TAKEN DRUGS, TRAVIS?
UMM... MY PARENTS SMOKE WEED AT HOME?
THAT'S... THAT'S SO TRAGIC.
MMMM!
LADbible
I DUNNO ABOUT THIS, GUYS. WHAT IF OUR SOULS GET STUCK HERE?
THAT, EDDIE, IS NOTHING BUT SUPERSTITIOUS MUMBO-JUMBO.
NOW, LADS--

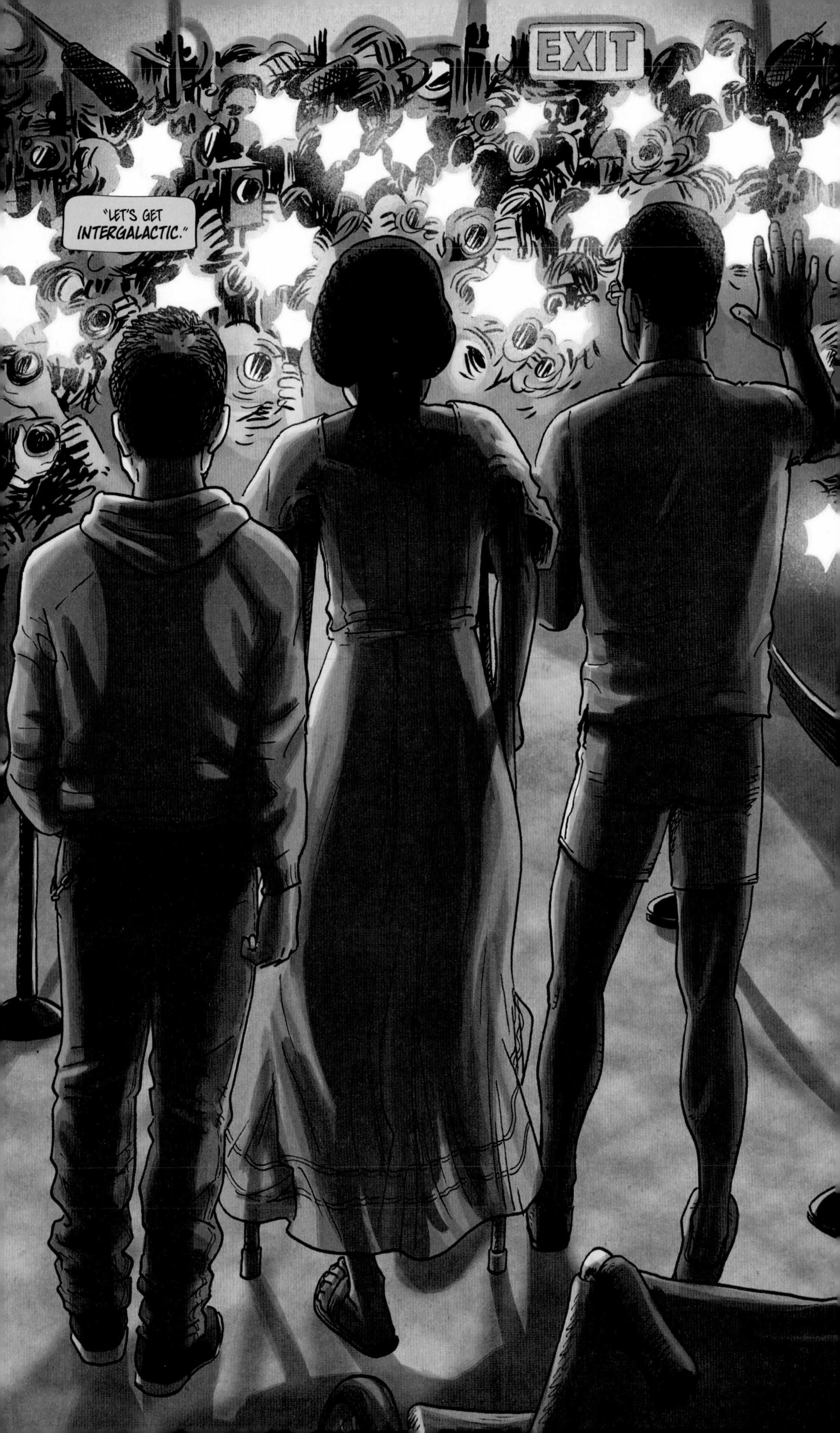
EXIT
"LET'S GET INTERGALACTIC."

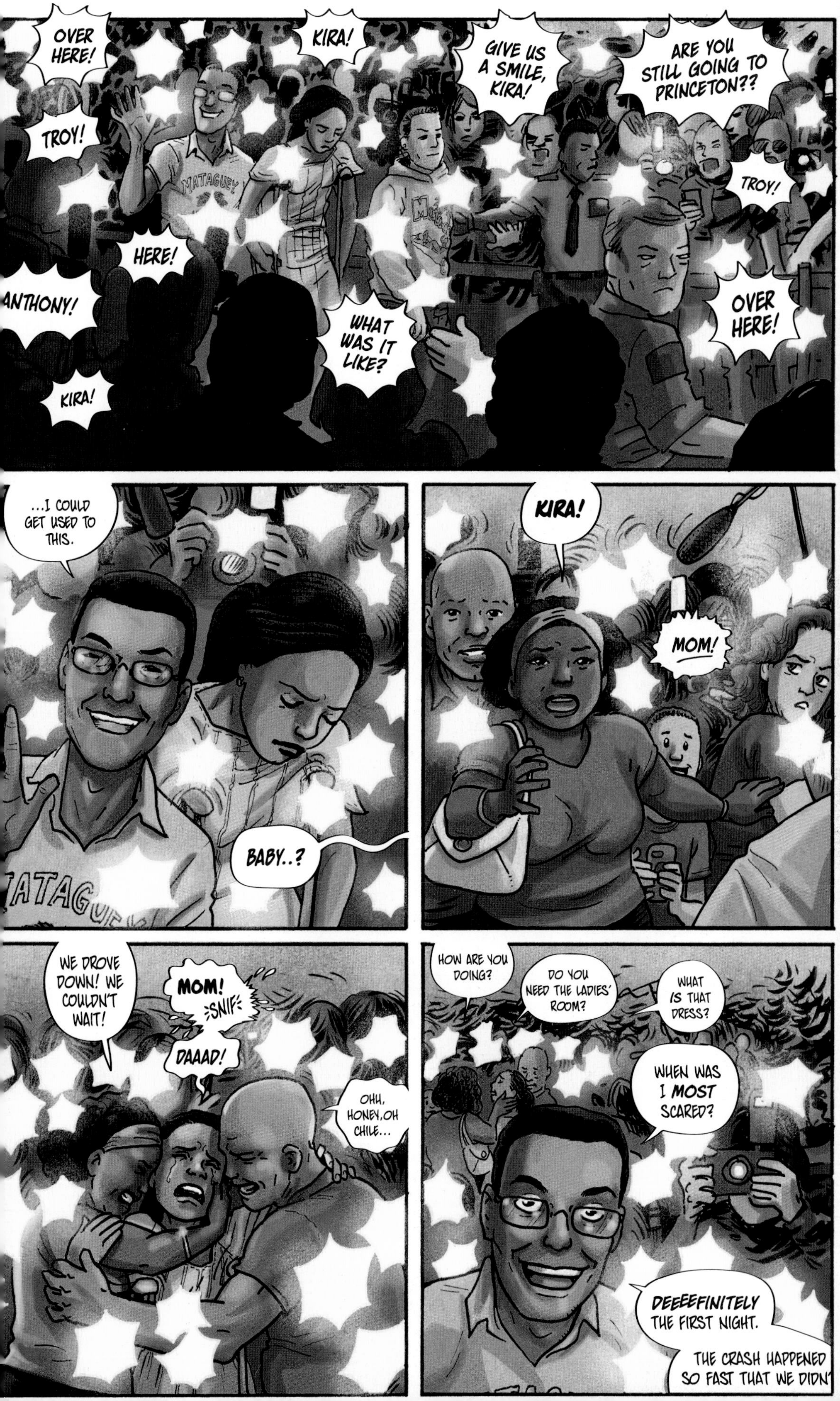

OVER HERE!
KIRA!
GIVE US A SMILE, KIRA!
ARE YOU STILL GOING TO PRINCETON??
TROY!
TROY!
HERE!
ANTHONY!
WHAT WAS IT LIKE?
OVER HERE!
KIRA!
...I COULD GET USED TO THIS.
BABY..?
KIRA!
MOM!
WE DROVE DOWN! WE COULDN'T WAIT!
MOM!
SNIF
DAAAD!
OHH, HONEY, OH CHILE...
HOW ARE YOU DOING?
DO YOU NEED THE LADIES' ROOM?
WHAT IS THAT DRESS?
WHEN WAS I MOST SCARED?
DEEEEFINITELY THE FIRST NIGHT.
THE CRASH HAPPENED SO FAST THAT WE DIDN'

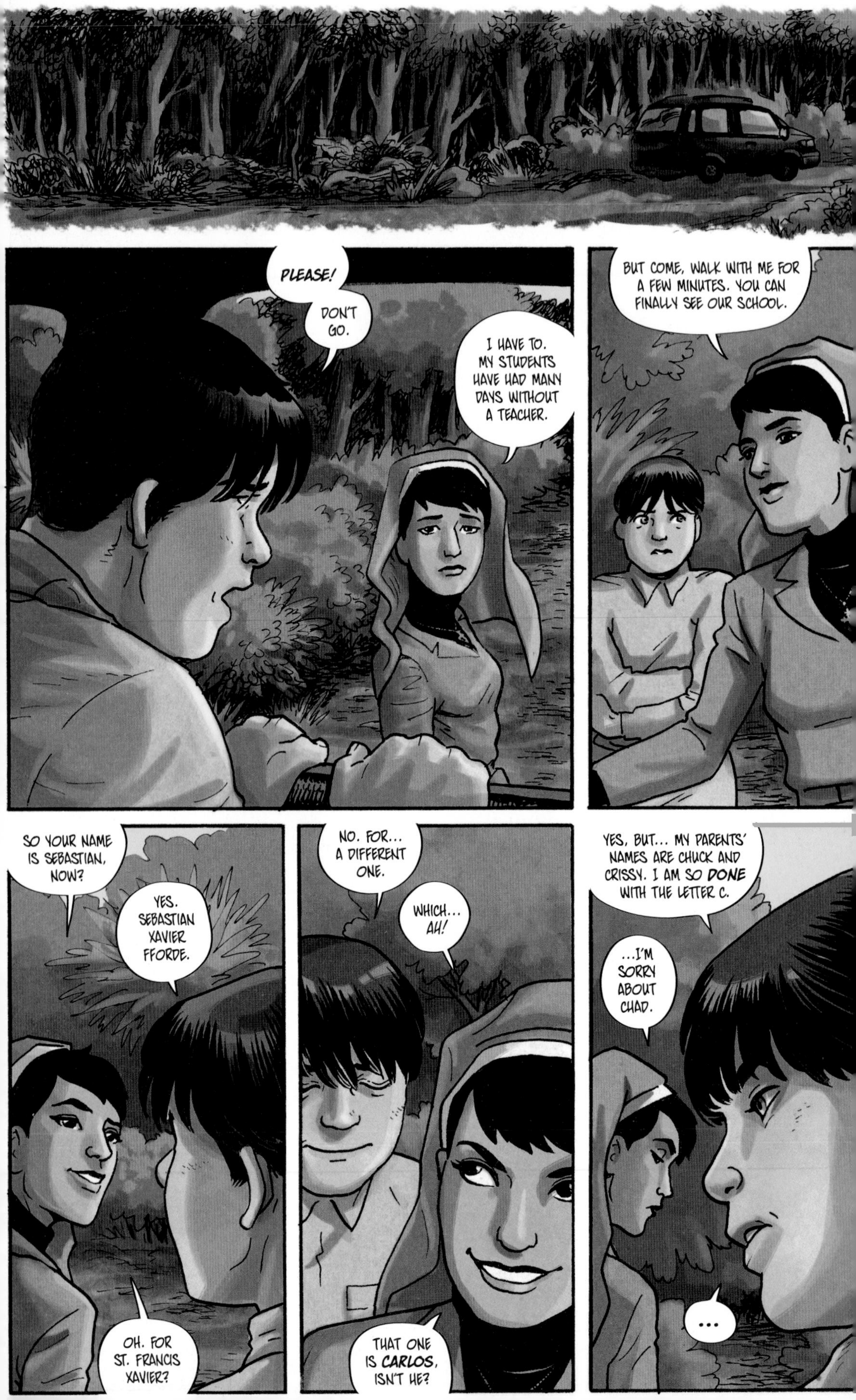

PLEASE!
DON'T GO.
I HAVE TO. MY STUDENTS HAVE HAD MANY DAYS WITHOUT A TEACHER.
BUT COME, WALK WITH ME FOR A FEW MINUTES. YOU CAN FINALLY SEE OUR SCHOOL.
SO YOUR NAME IS SEBASTIAN, NOW?
YES. SEBASTIAN XAVIER FFORDE.
OH. FOR ST. FRANCIS XAVIER?
NO. FOR... A DIFFERENT ONE.
WHICH... AH!
THAT ONE IS CARLOS, ISN'T HE?
YES, BUT... MY PARENTS' NAMES ARE CHUCK AND CRISSY. I AM SO DONE WITH THE LETTER C.
...I'M SORRY ABOUT CHAD.
...

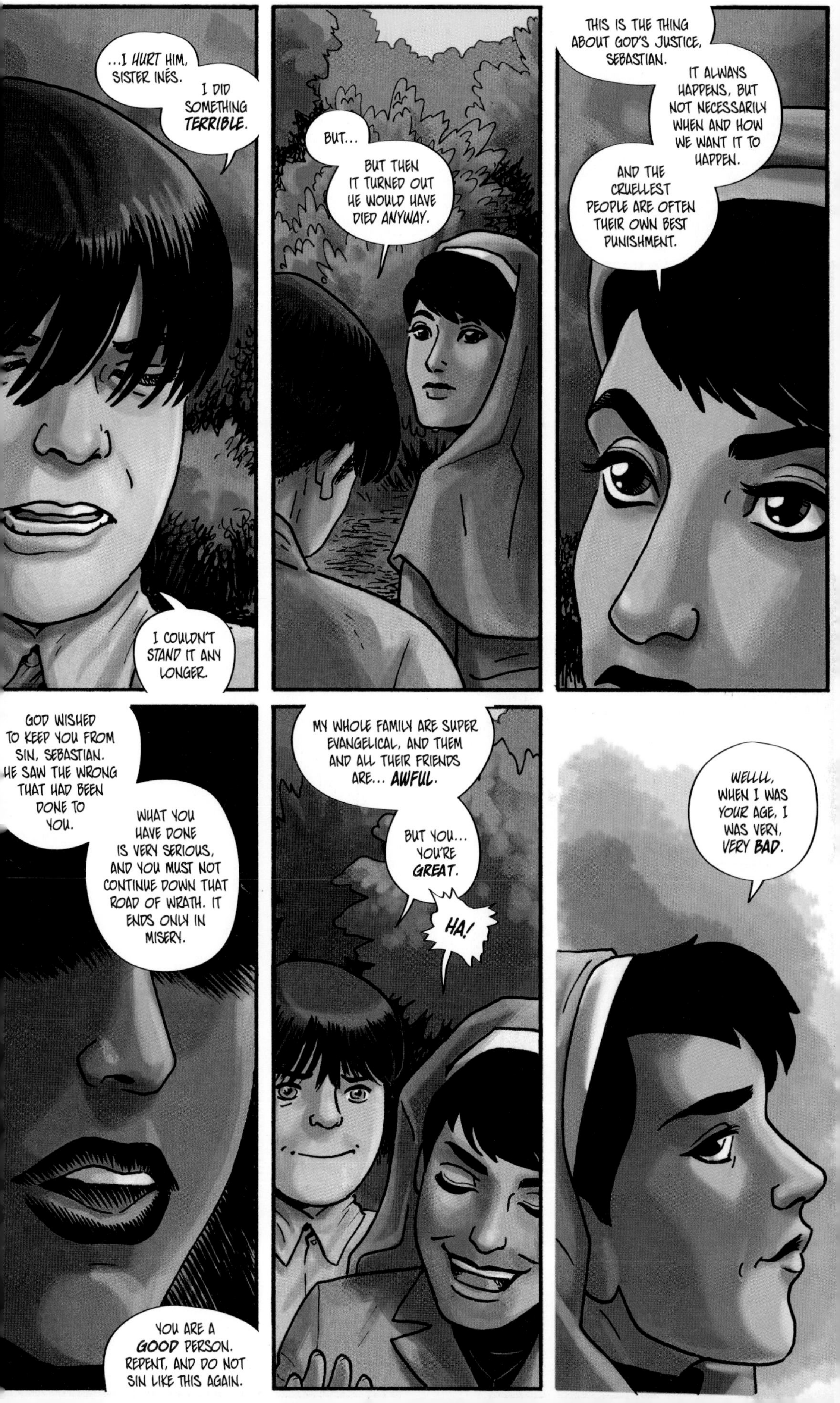
...I HURT HIM, SISTER INÉS.
I DID SOMETHING TERRIBLE.
I COULDN'T STAND IT ANY LONGER.
BUT...
BUT THEN IT TURNED OUT HE WOULD HAVE DIED ANYWAY.
THIS IS THE THING ABOUT GOD'S JUSTICE, SEBASTIAN.
IT ALWAYS HAPPENS, BUT NOT NECESSARILY WHEN AND HOW WE WANT IT TO HAPPEN.
AND THE CRUELLEST PEOPLE ARE OFTEN THEIR OWN BEST PUNISHMENT.
GOD WISHED TO KEEP YOU FROM SIN, SEBASTIAN. HE SAW THE WRONG THAT HAD BEEN DONE TO YOU.
WHAT YOU HAVE DONE IS VERY SERIOUS, AND YOU MUST NOT CONTINUE DOWN THAT ROAD OF WRATH. IT ENDS ONLY IN MISERY.
YOU ARE A GOOD PERSON. REPENT, AND DO NOT SIN LIKE THIS AGAIN.
MY WHOLE FAMILY ARE SUPER EVANGELICAL, AND THEM AND ALL THEIR FRIENDS ARE... AWFUL.
BUT YOU... YOU'RE GREAT.
HA!
WELLLL, WHEN I WAS YOUR AGE, I WAS VERY, VERY BAD.

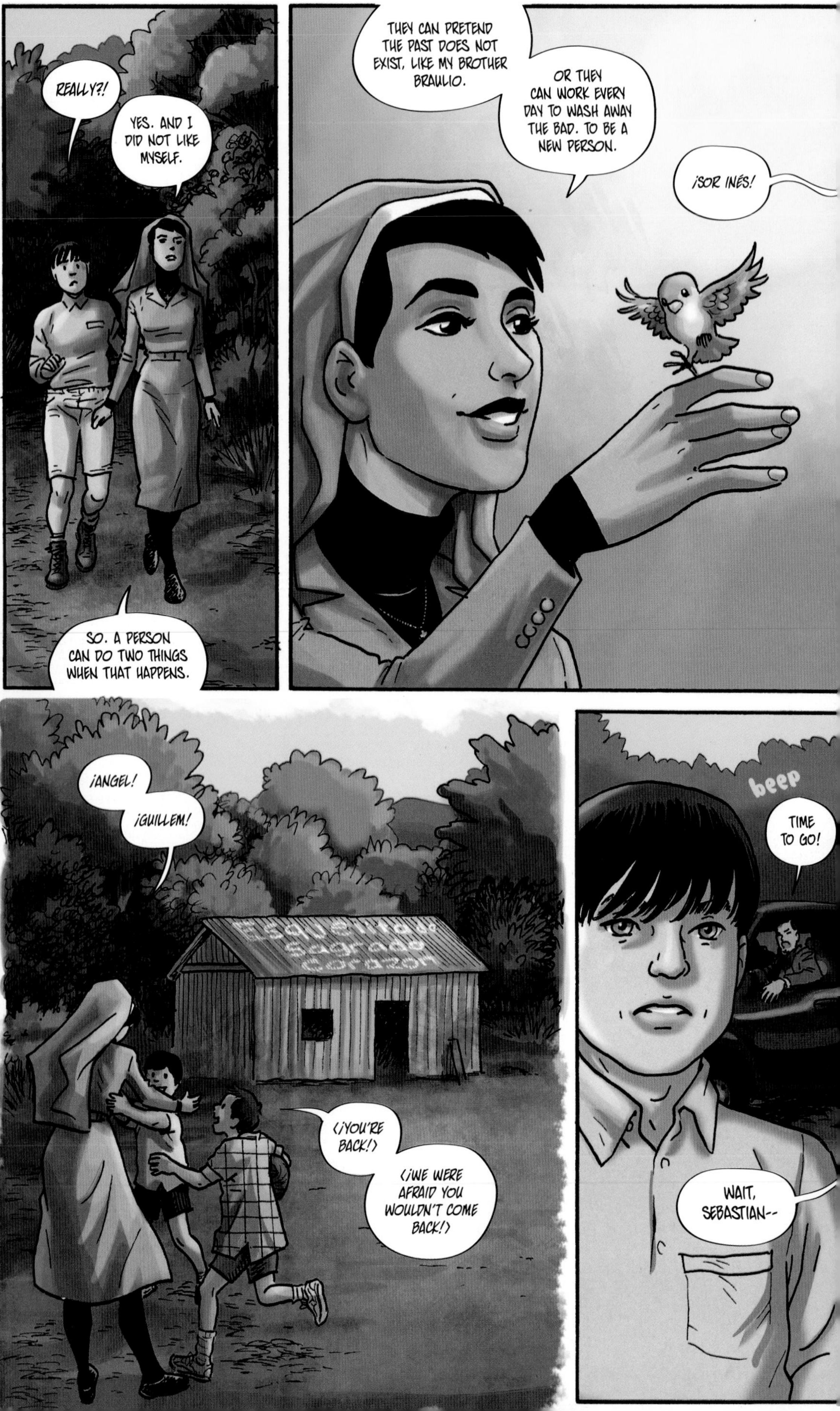
REALLY?!
YES. AND I DID NOT LIKE MYSELF.
SO. A PERSON CAN DO TWO THINGS WHEN THAT HAPPENS.
THEY CAN PRETEND THE PAST DOES NOT EXIST, LIKE MY BROTHER BRAULIO.
OR THEY CAN WORK EVERY DAY TO WASH AWAY THE BAD. TO BE A NEW PERSON.
¡SOR INÉS!
¡ANGEL!
¡GUILLEM!
‹¡YOU'RE BACK!›
‹¡WE WERE AFRAID YOU WOULDN'T COME BACK!›
beep
TIME TO GO!
WAIT, SEBASTIAN--

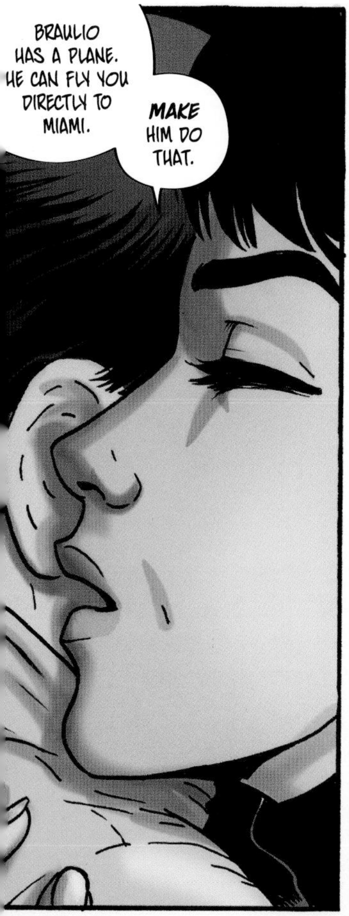
BRAULIO HAS A PLANE. HE CAN FLY YOU DIRECTLY TO MIAMI.
MAKE HIM DO THAT.

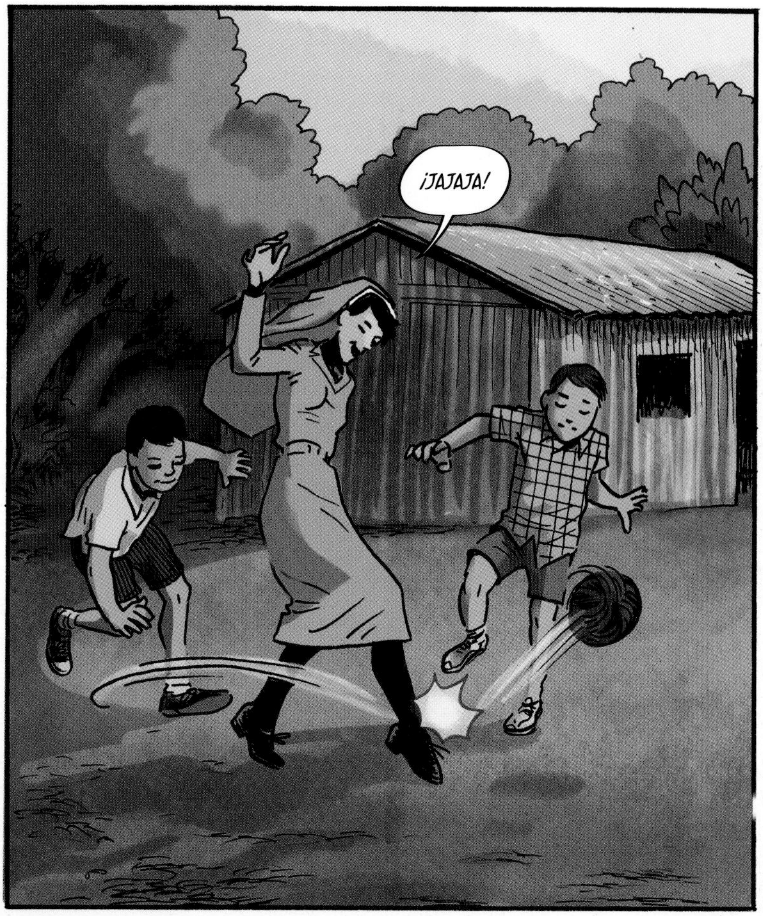
¡JAJAJA!

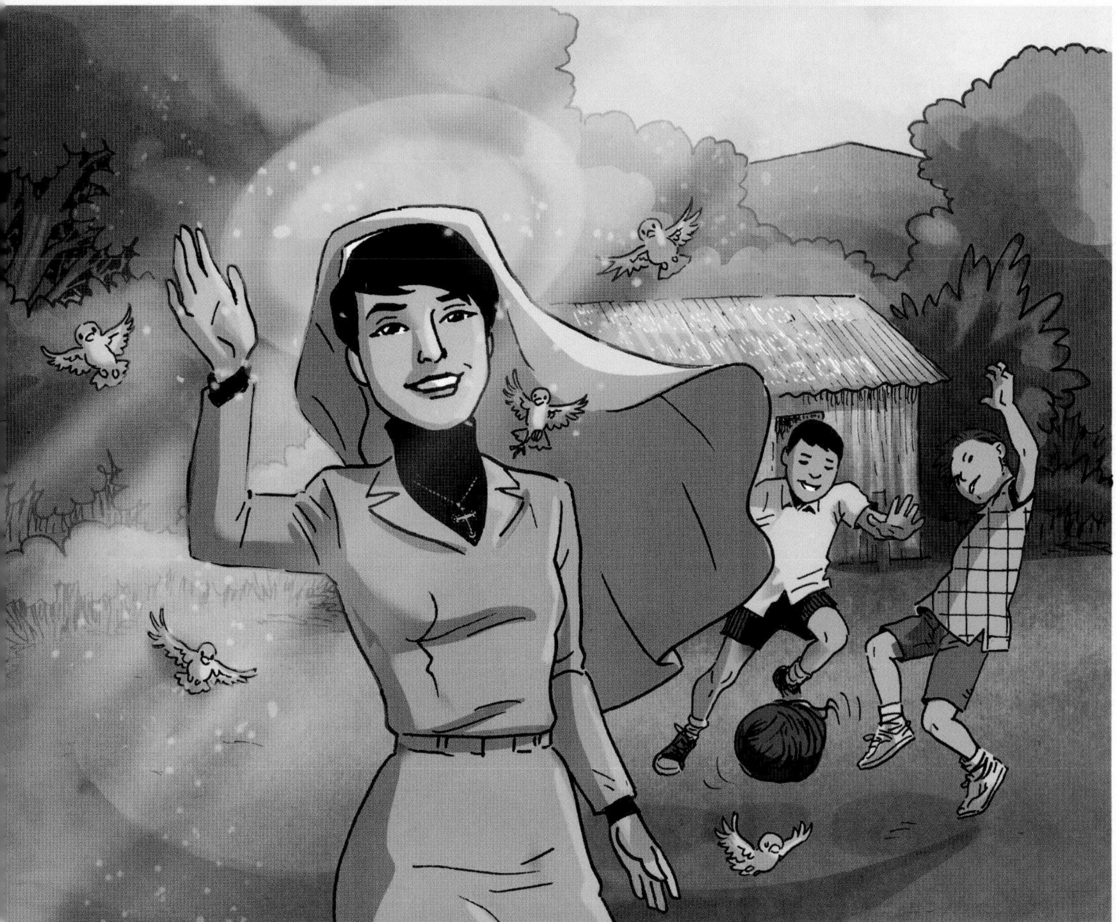

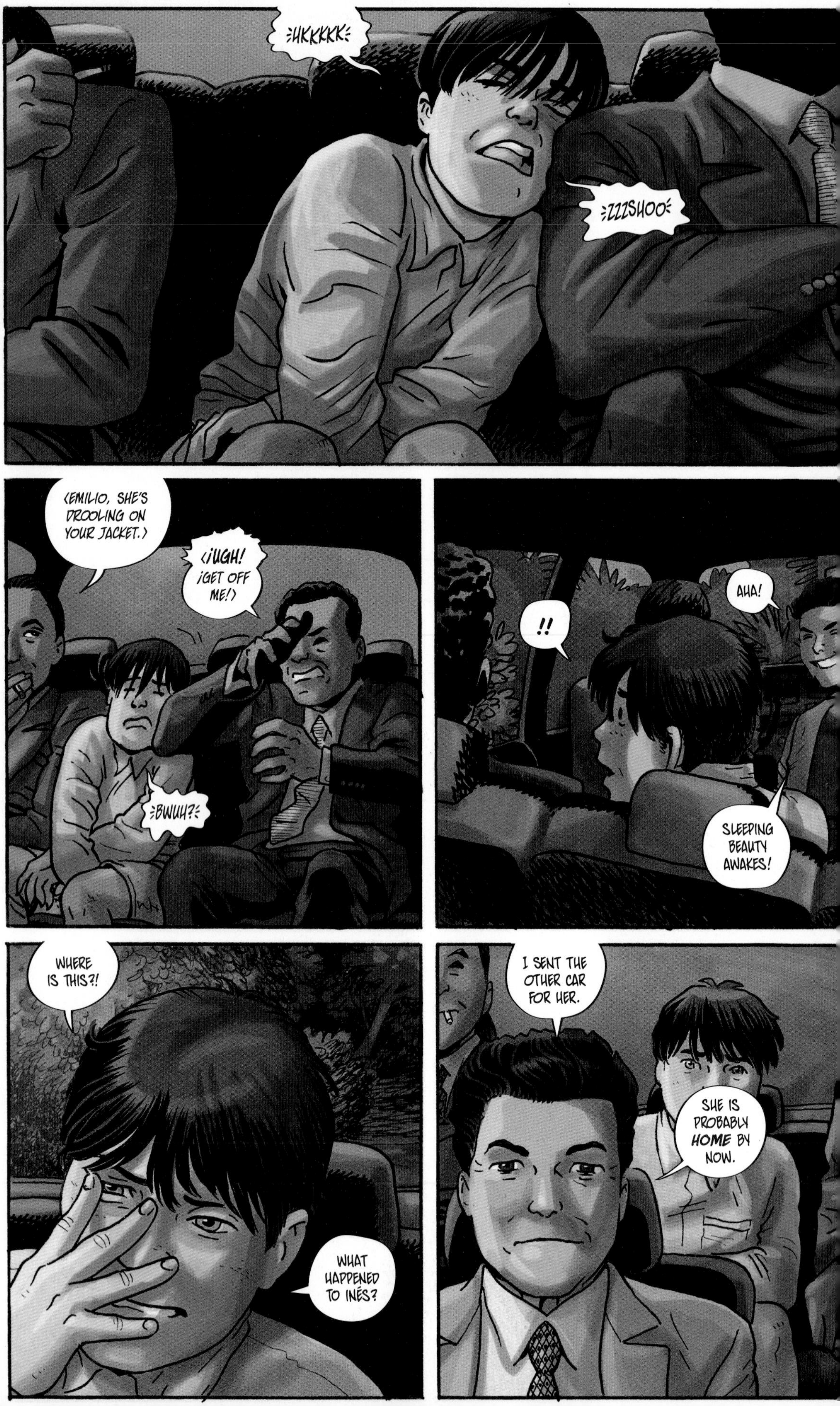
HKKKKK
ZZZSHOO
‹EMILIO, SHE'S DROOLING ON YOUR JACKET.›
‹¡UGH! ¡GET OFF ME!›
BWUH?
!!
AHA!
SLEEPING BEAUTY AWAKES!
WHERE IS THIS?!
WHAT HAPPENED TO INÉS?
I SENT THE OTHER CAR FOR HER.
SHE IS PROBABLY **HOME** BY NOW.

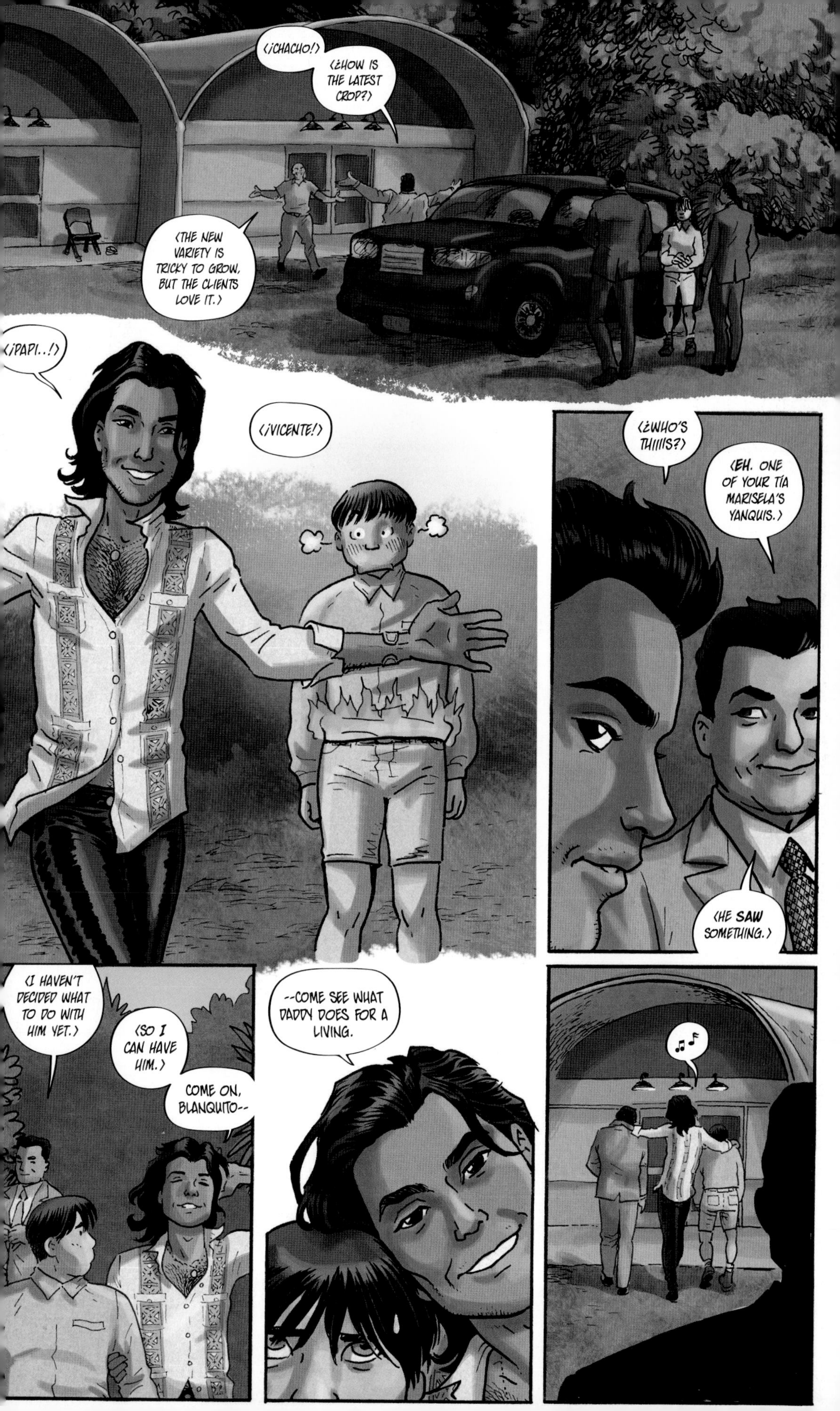

⟨¡CHACHO!⟩
⟨¿HOW IS THE LATEST CROP?⟩
⟨THE NEW VARIETY IS TRICKY TO GROW, BUT THE CLIENTS LOVE IT.⟩
⟨¡PAPI..!⟩
⟨¡VICENTE!⟩
⟨¿WHO'S THIIIIS?⟩
⟨EH. ONE OF YOUR TÍA MARISELA'S YANQUIS.⟩
⟨HE SAW SOMETHING.⟩
⟨I HAVEN'T DECIDED WHAT TO DO WITH HIM YET.⟩
⟨SO I CAN HAVE HIM.⟩
COME ON, BLANQUITO--
--COME SEE WHAT DADDY DOES FOR A LIVING.

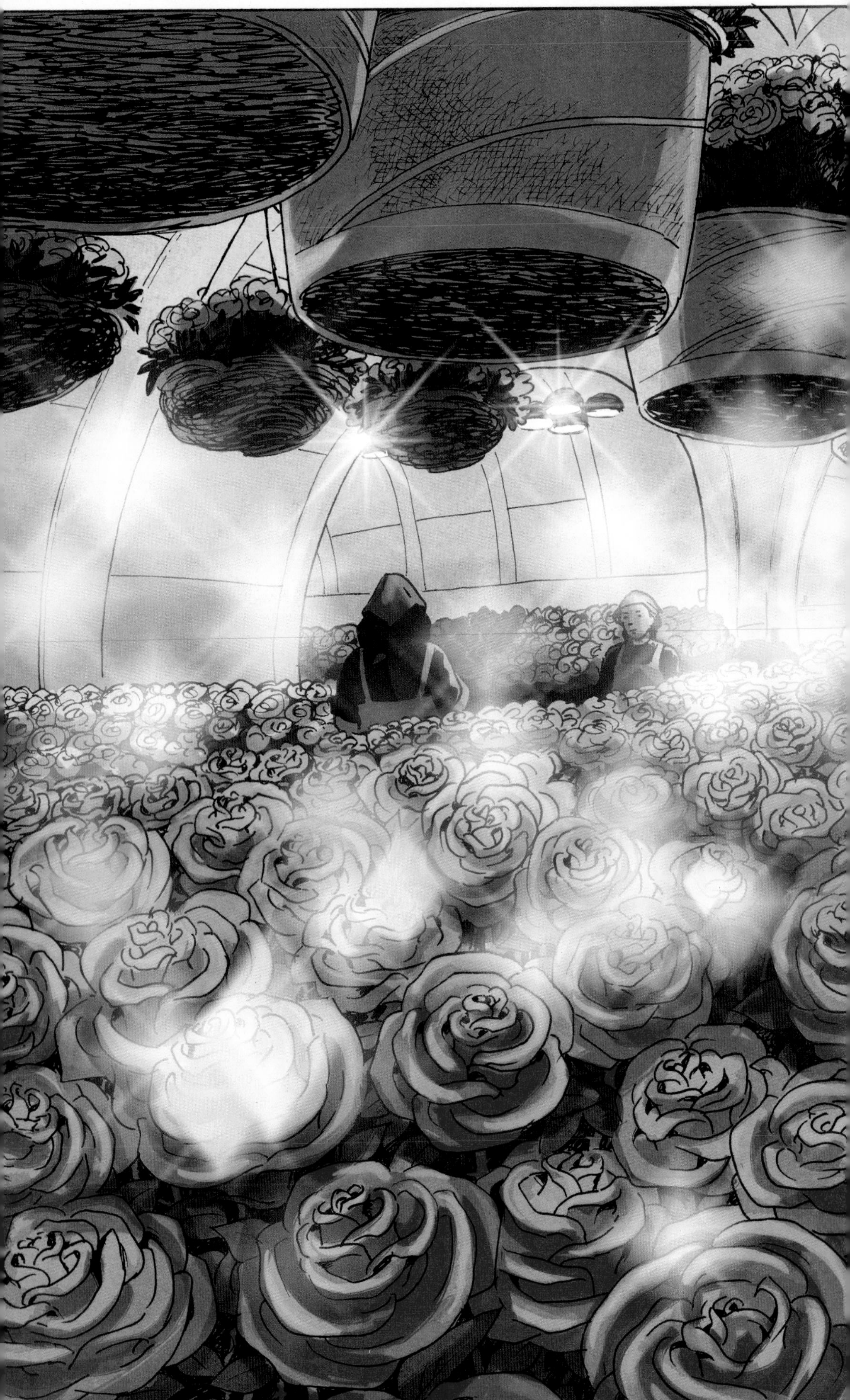

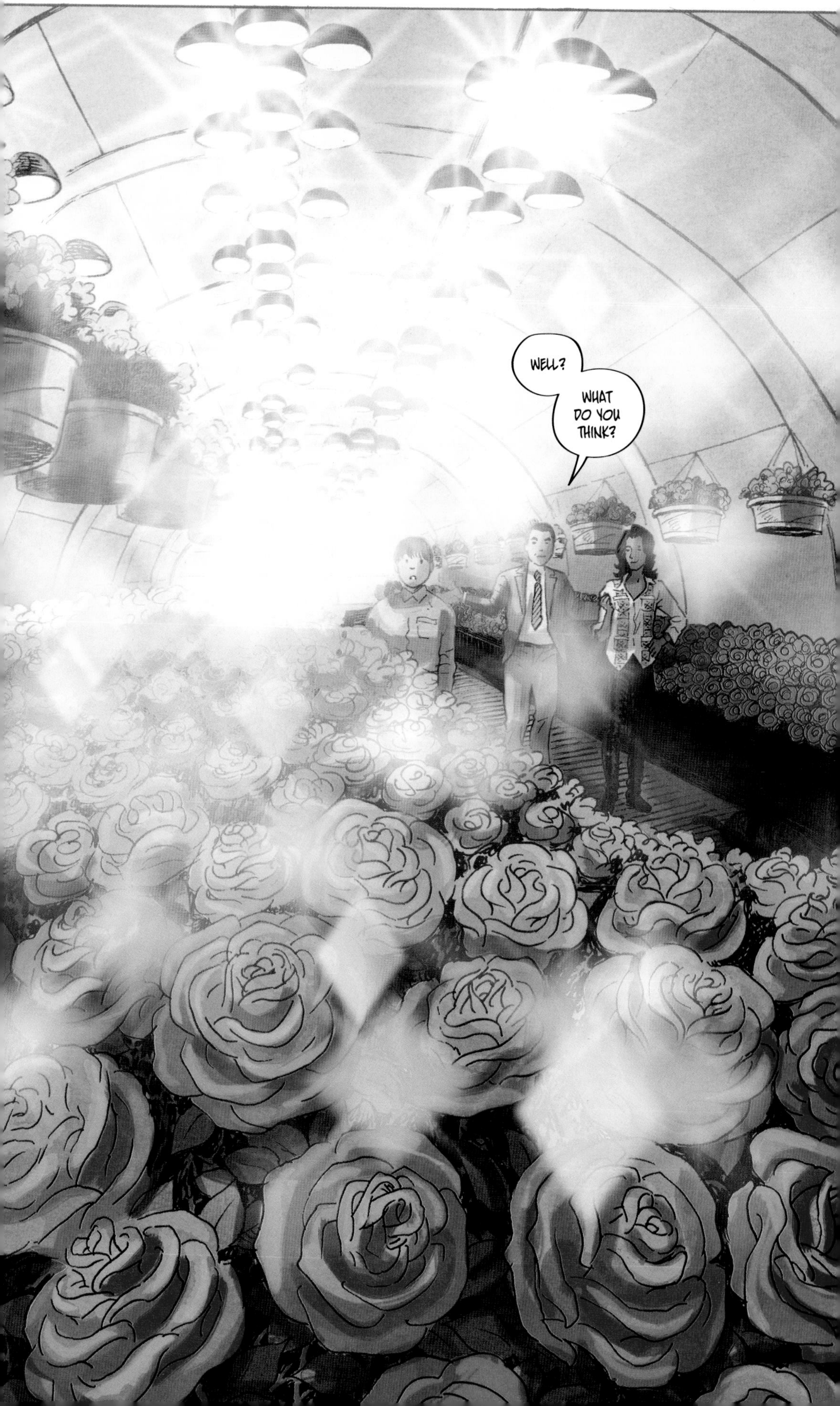
WELL?
WHAT DO YOU THINK?

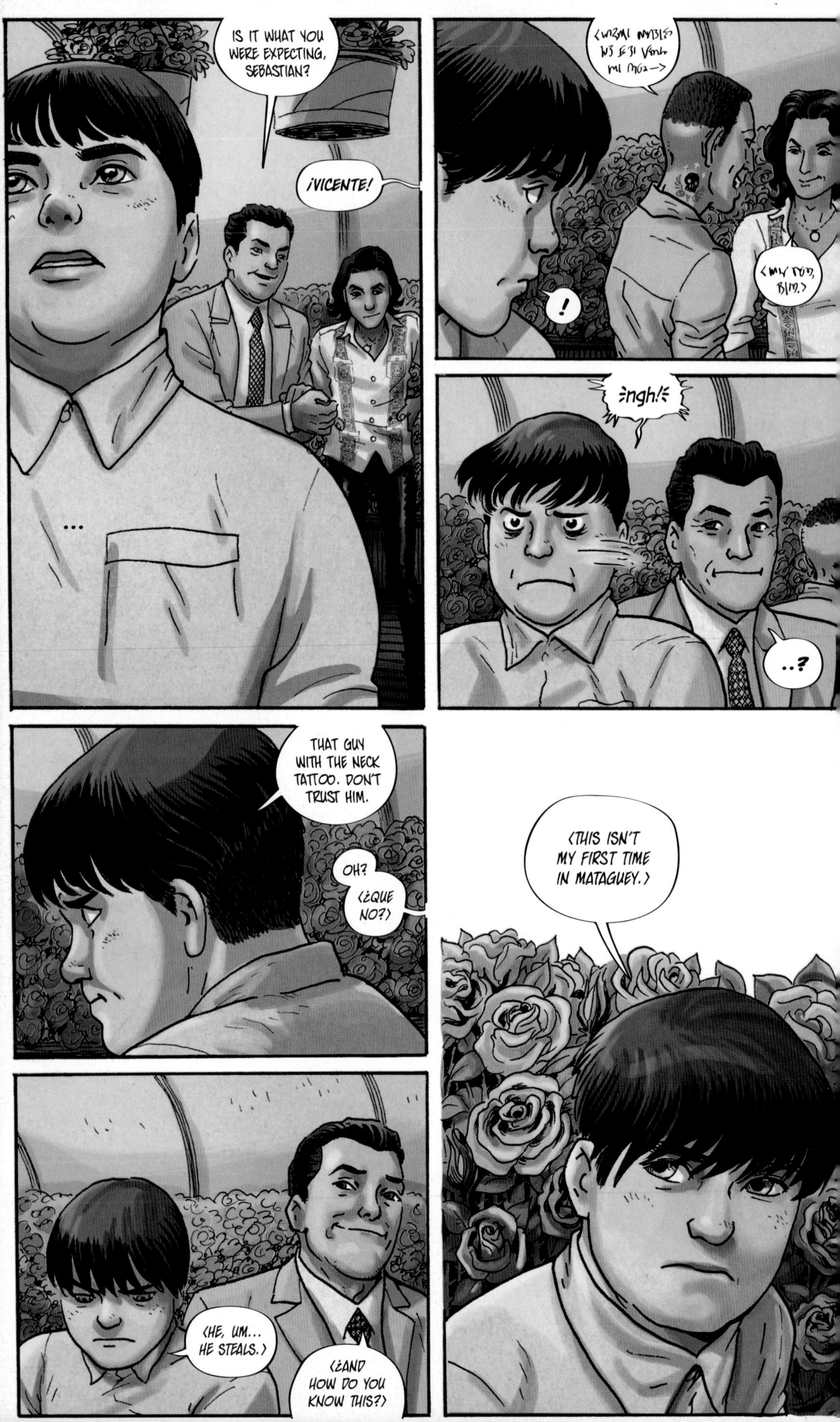
IS IT WHAT YOU WERE EXPECTING, SEBASTIAN?
¡VICENTE!
...
!
ngh!
..?
THAT GUY WITH THE NECK TATTOO. DON'T TRUST HIM.
OH?
⟨¿QUE NO?⟩
⟨HE, UM... HE STEALS.⟩
⟨¿AND HOW DO YOU KNOW THIS?⟩
⟨THIS ISN'T MY FIRST TIME IN MATAGUEY.⟩

bingely ♪
bing--

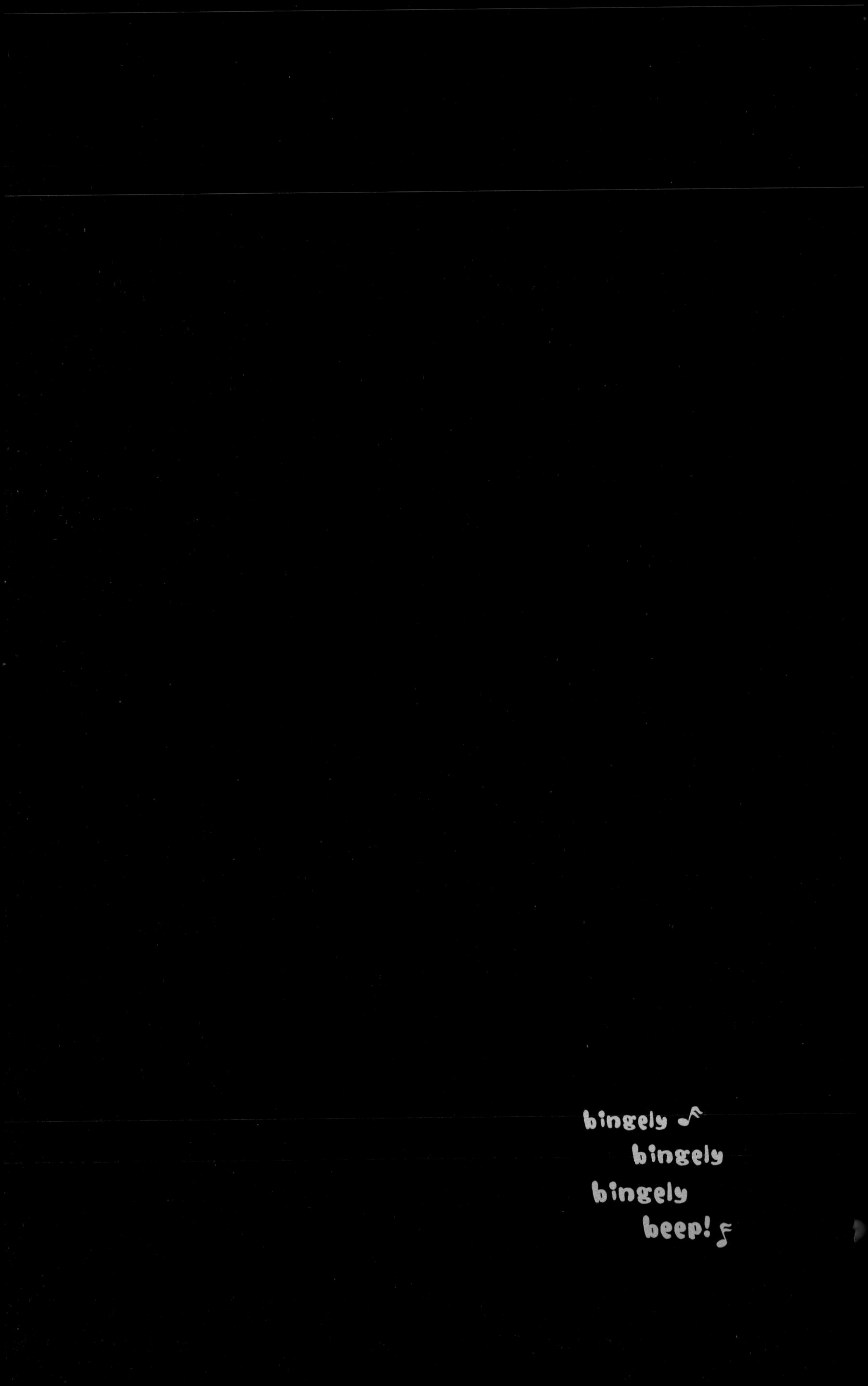
bingely
bingely
bingely
beep!

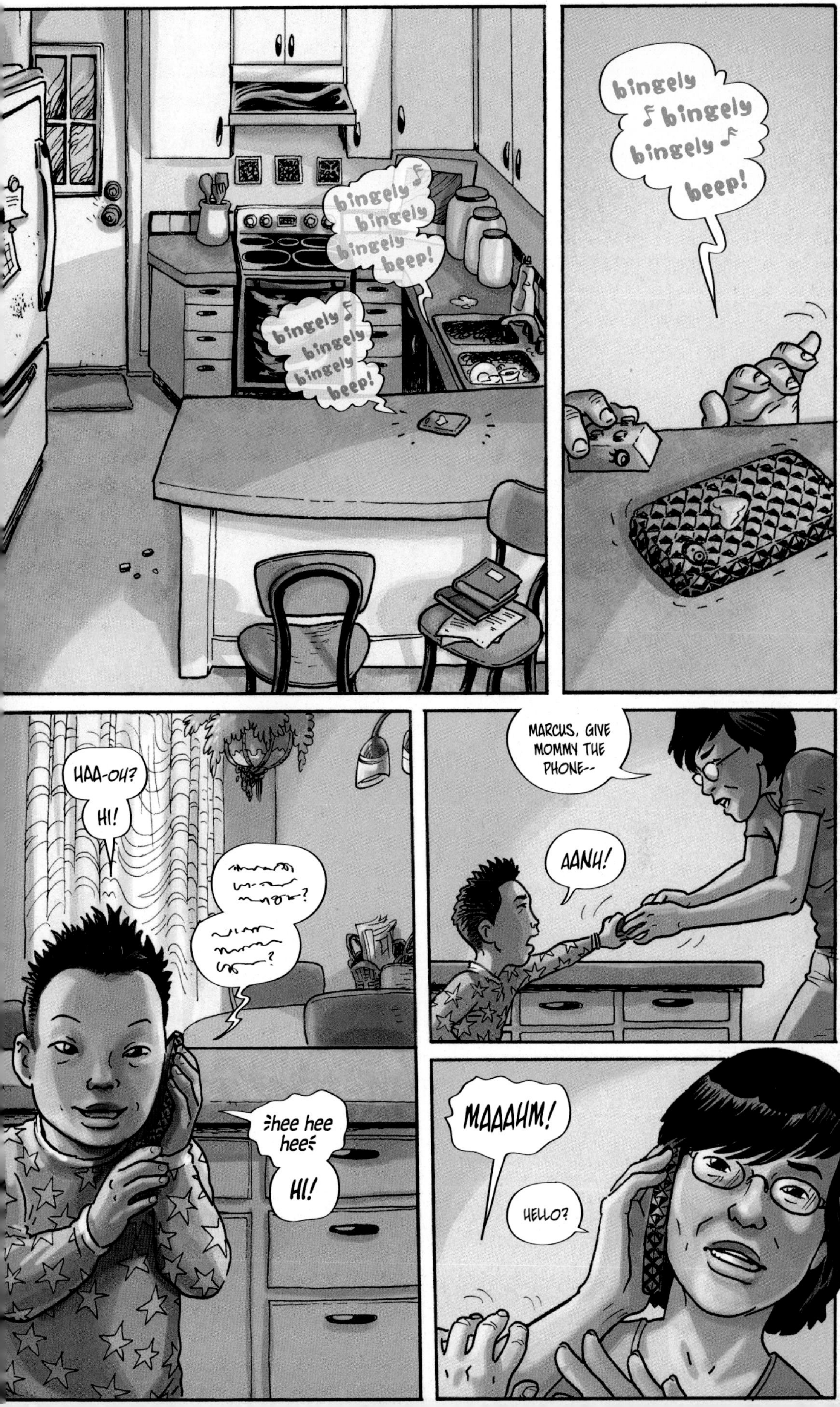
bingely bingely bingely beep!
bingely bingely bingely beep!
bingely bingely bingely beep!
HAA-OH?
HI!
hee hee hee
HI!
MARCUS, GIVE MOMMY THE PHONE--
AANH!
MAAAHM!
HELLO?

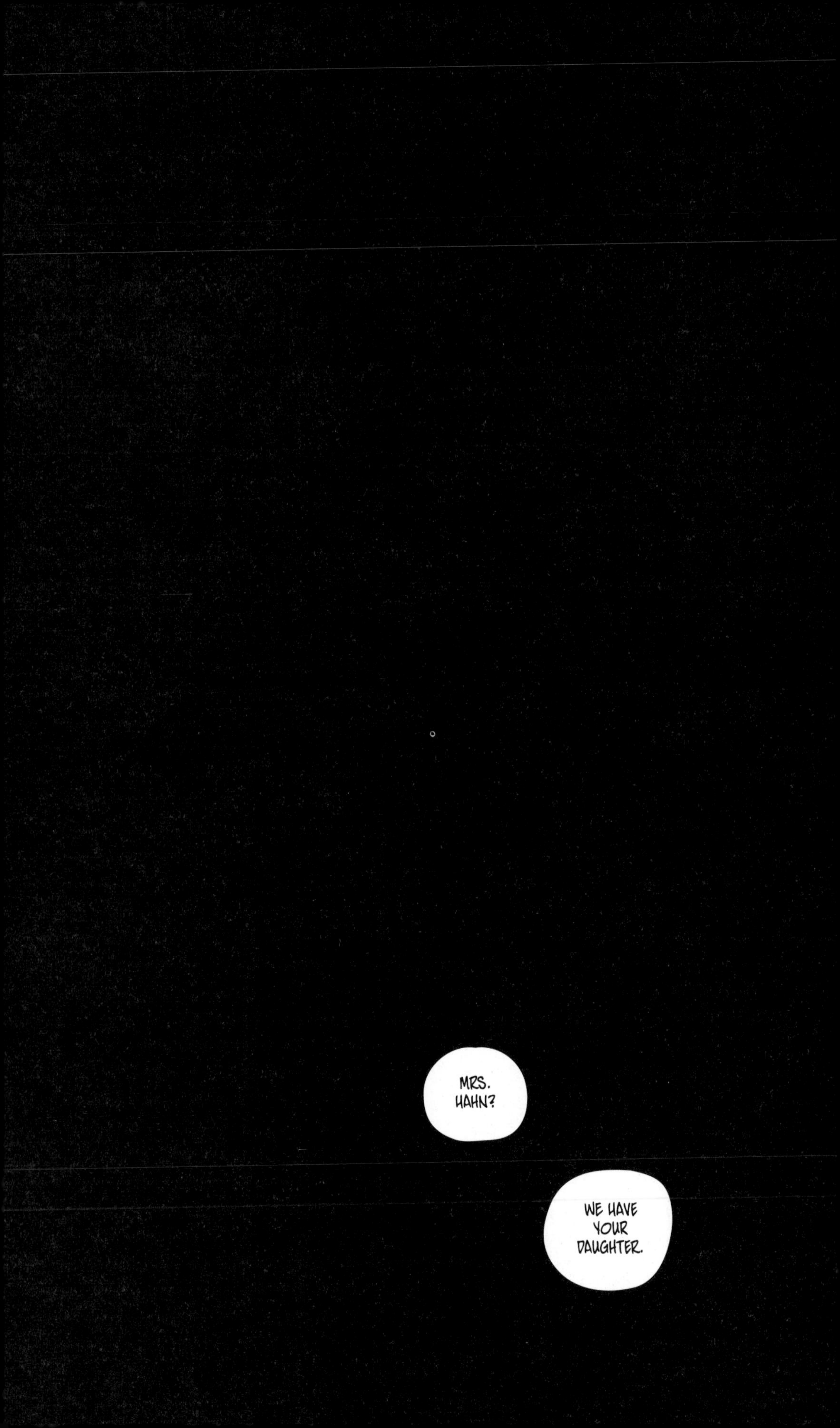
MRS. HAHN?
WE HAVE YOUR DAUGHTER.

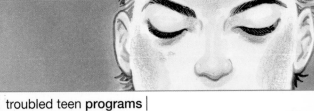

troubled teen programs

Google Search   I'm Feeling Lucky

I AM A GIRL

CHAPTER

NINE

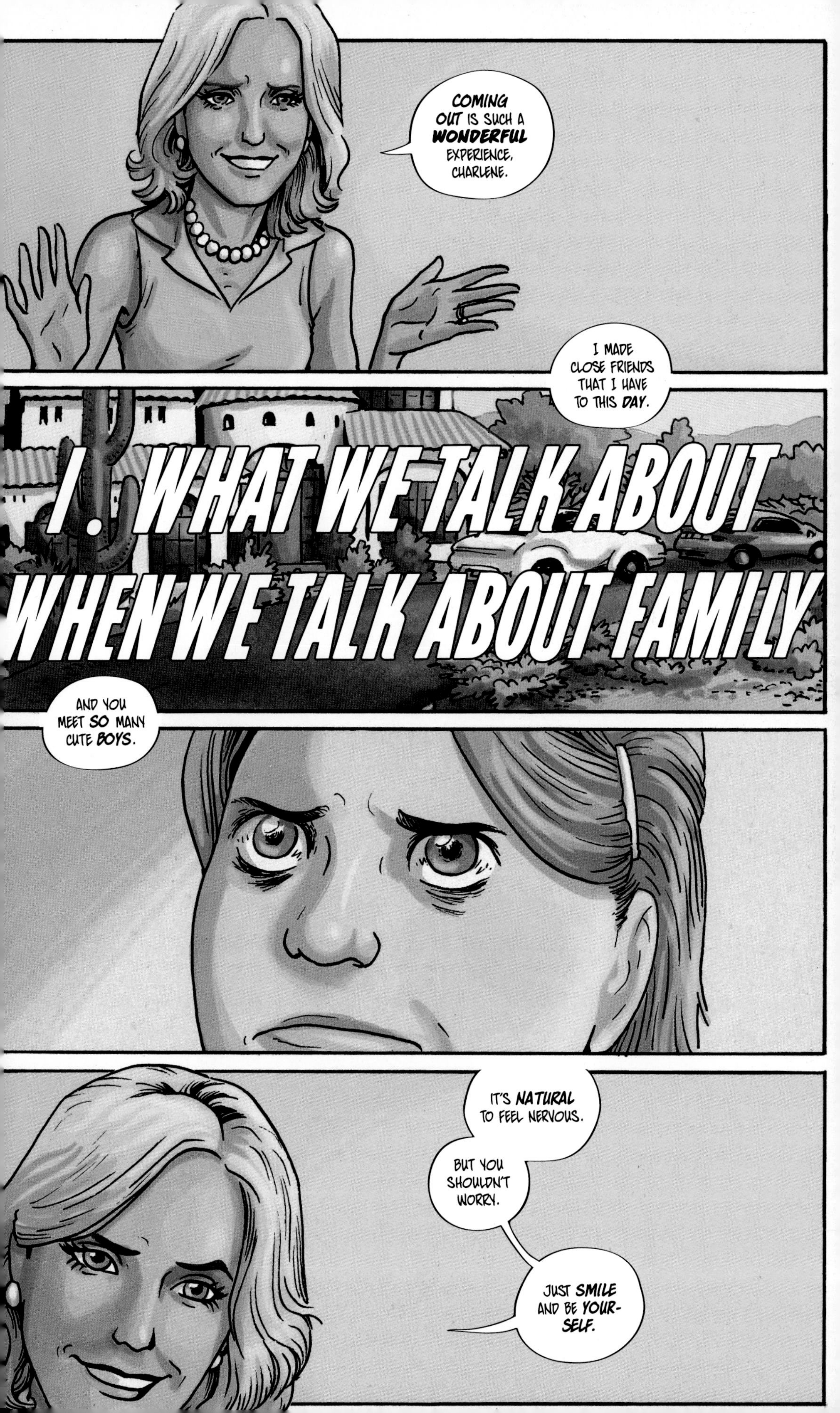
COMING OUT IS SUCH A WONDERFUL EXPERIENCE, CHARLENE.
I MADE CLOSE FRIENDS THAT I HAVE TO THIS DAY.
I. WHAT WE TALK ABOUT WHEN WE TALK ABOUT FAMILY
AND YOU MEET SO MANY CUTE BOYS.
IT'S NATURAL TO FEEL NERVOUS.
BUT YOU SHOULDN'T WORRY.
JUST SMILE AND BE YOURSELF.

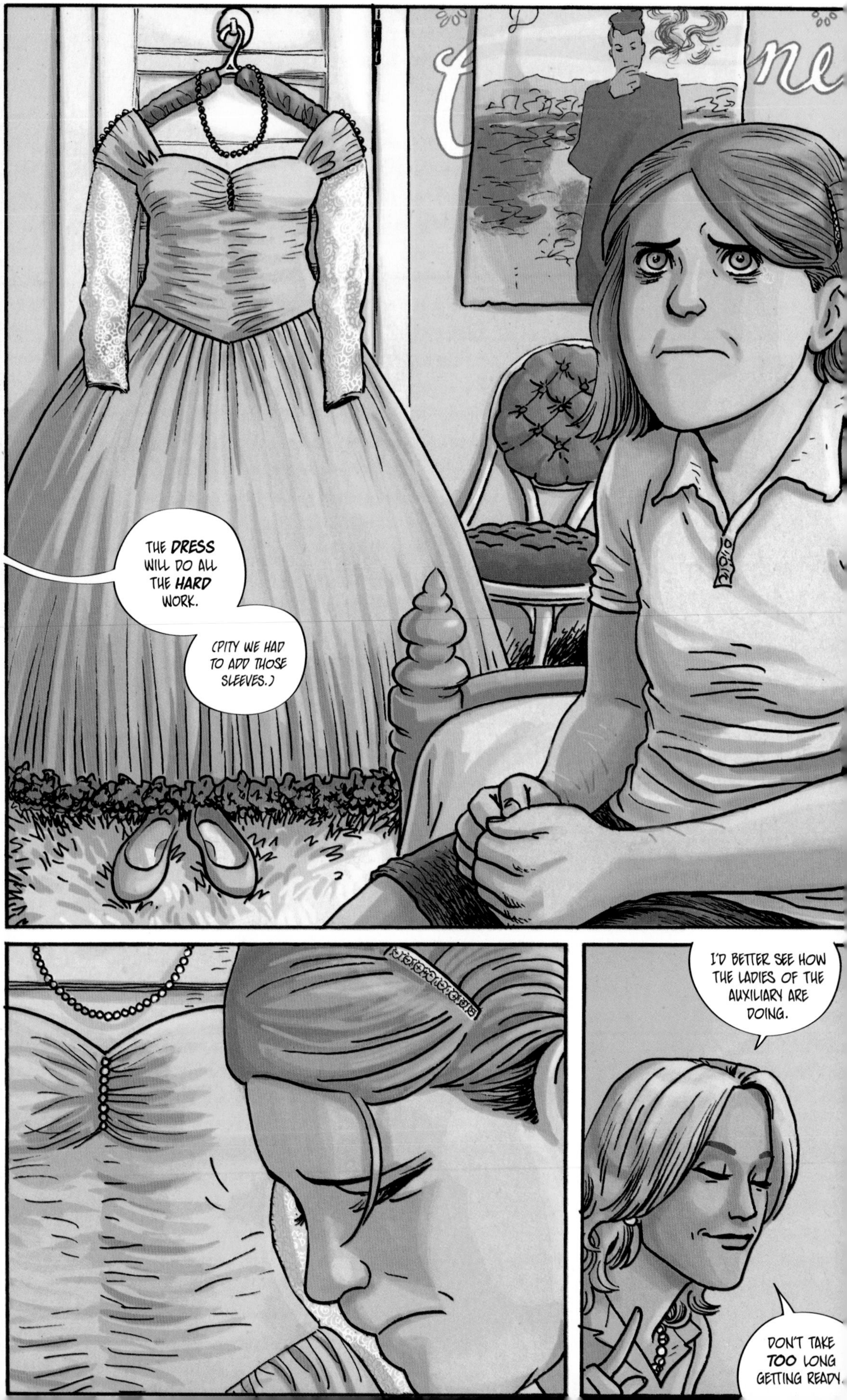
THE **DRESS** WILL DO ALL THE **HARD** WORK.
(PITY WE HAD TO ADD THOSE SLEEVES.)
I'D BETTER SEE HOW THE LADIES OF THE AUXILIARY ARE DOING.
DON'T TAKE **TOO** LONG GETTING READY.

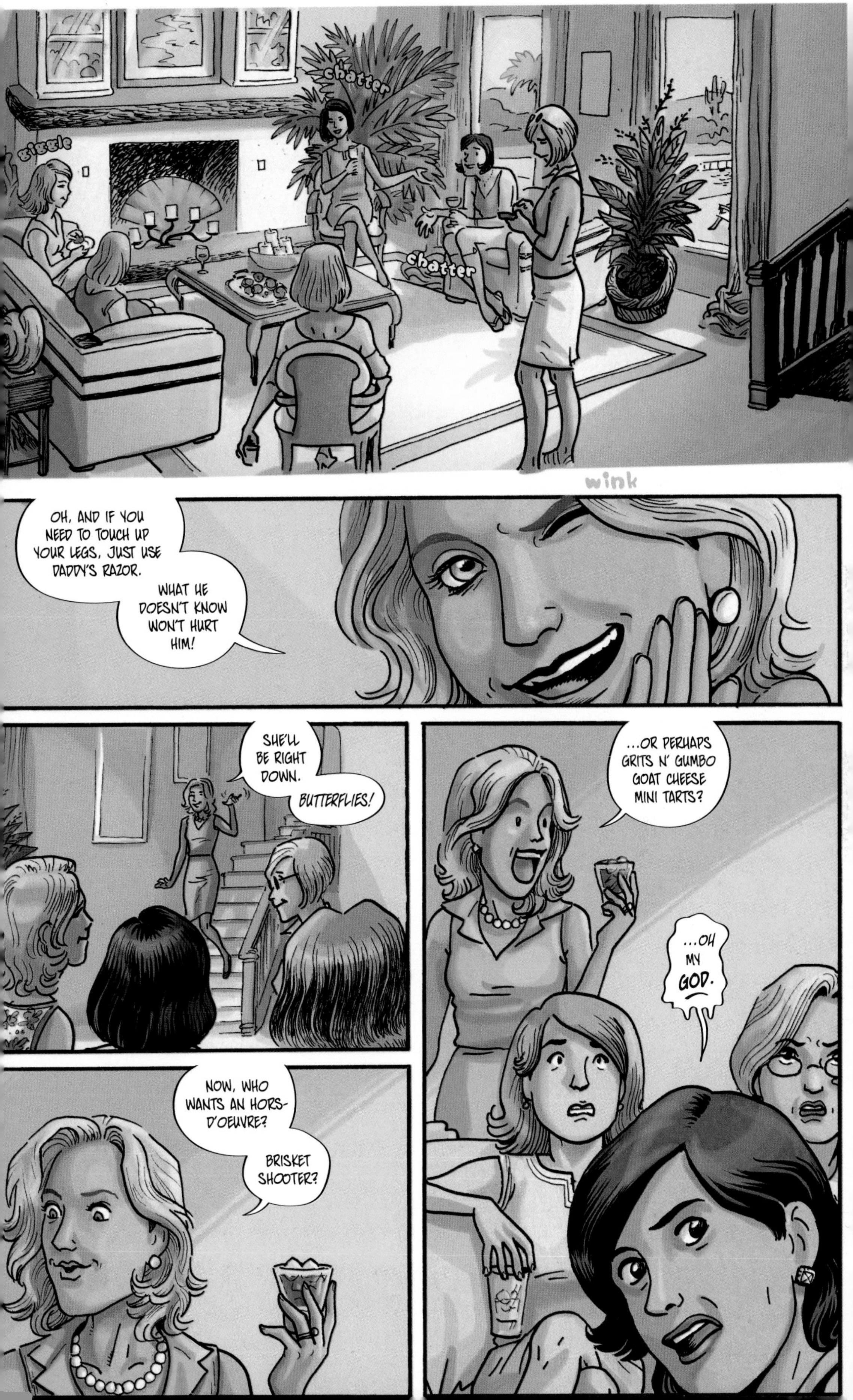
chatter
giggle
chatter
wink
OH, AND IF YOU NEED TO TOUCH UP YOUR LEGS, JUST USE DADDY'S RAZOR.
WHAT HE DOESN'T KNOW WON'T HURT HIM!
SHE'LL BE RIGHT DOWN.
BUTTERFLIES!
NOW, WHO WANTS AN HORS-D'OEUVRE?
BRISKET SHOOTER?
...OR PERHAPS GRITS N' GUMBO GOAT CHEESE MINI TARTS?
...OH MY GOD.

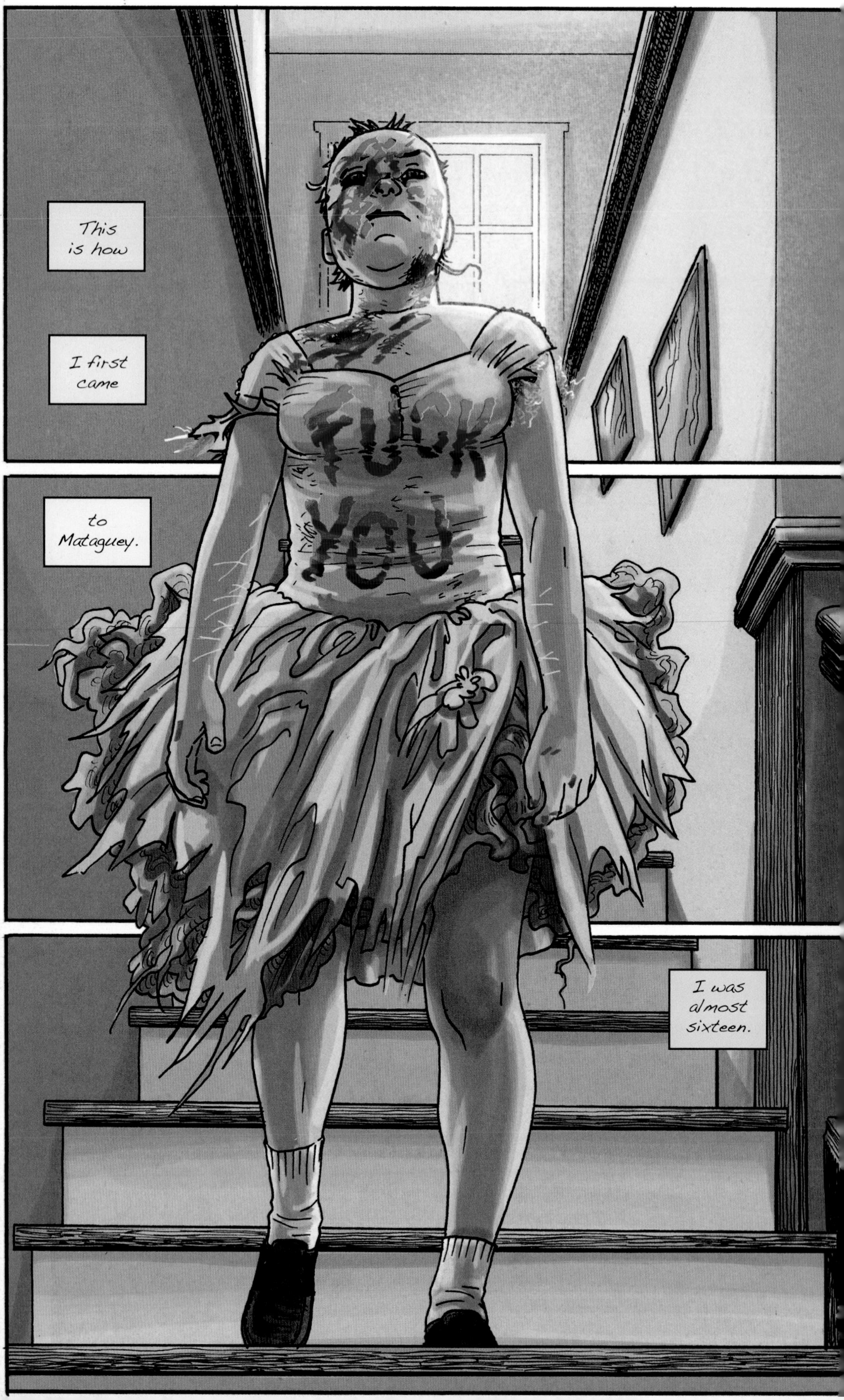
This is how
I first came
to Mataguey.
I was almost sixteen.
FUCK YOU

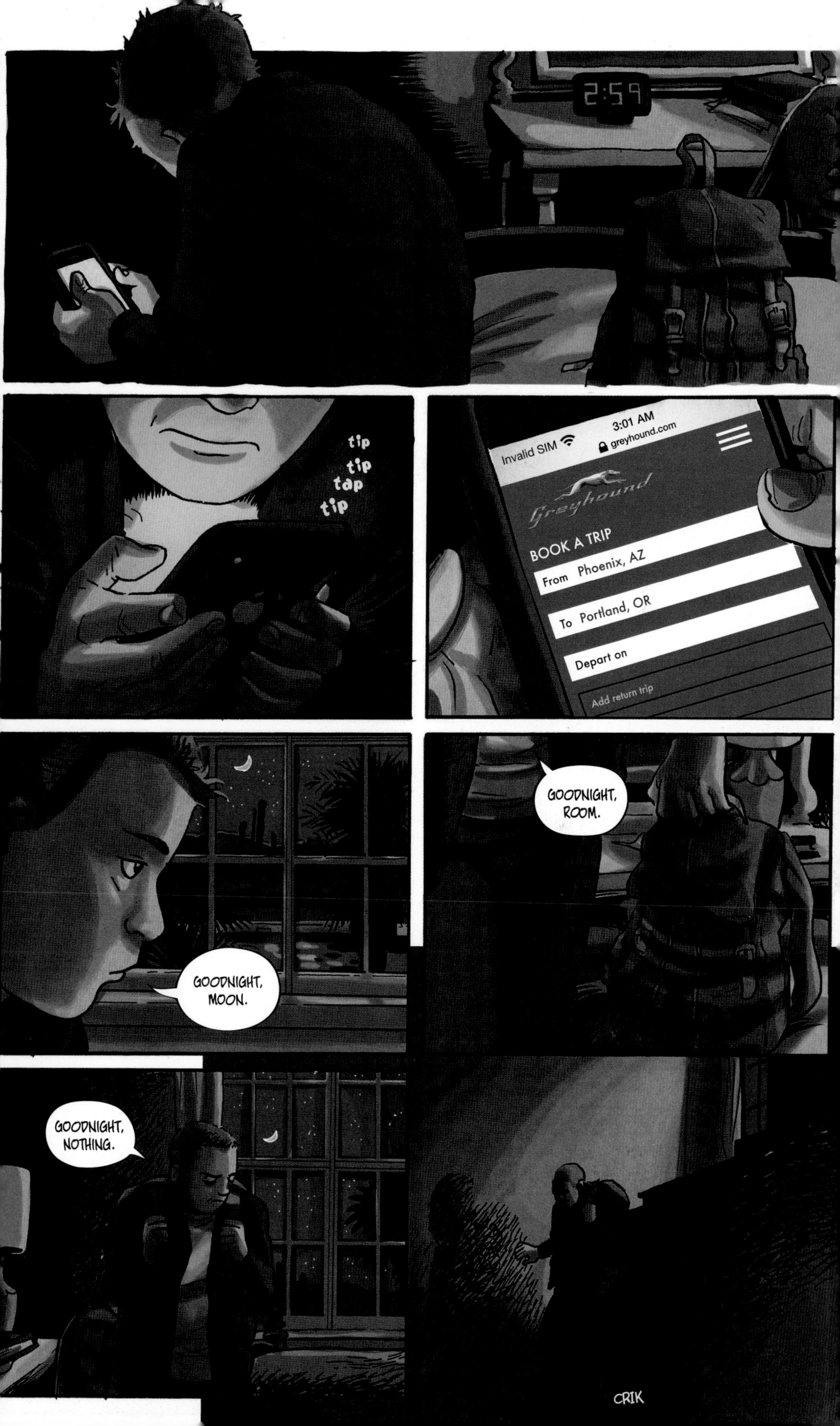
2:59
tip
tip
tap
tip
3:01 AM
Invalid SIM
greyhound.com
Greyhound
BOOK A TRIP
From Phoenix, AZ
To Portland, OR
Depart on
Add return trip
GOODNIGHT, MOON.
GOODNIGHT, ROOM.
GOODNIGHT, NOTHING.
CRIK

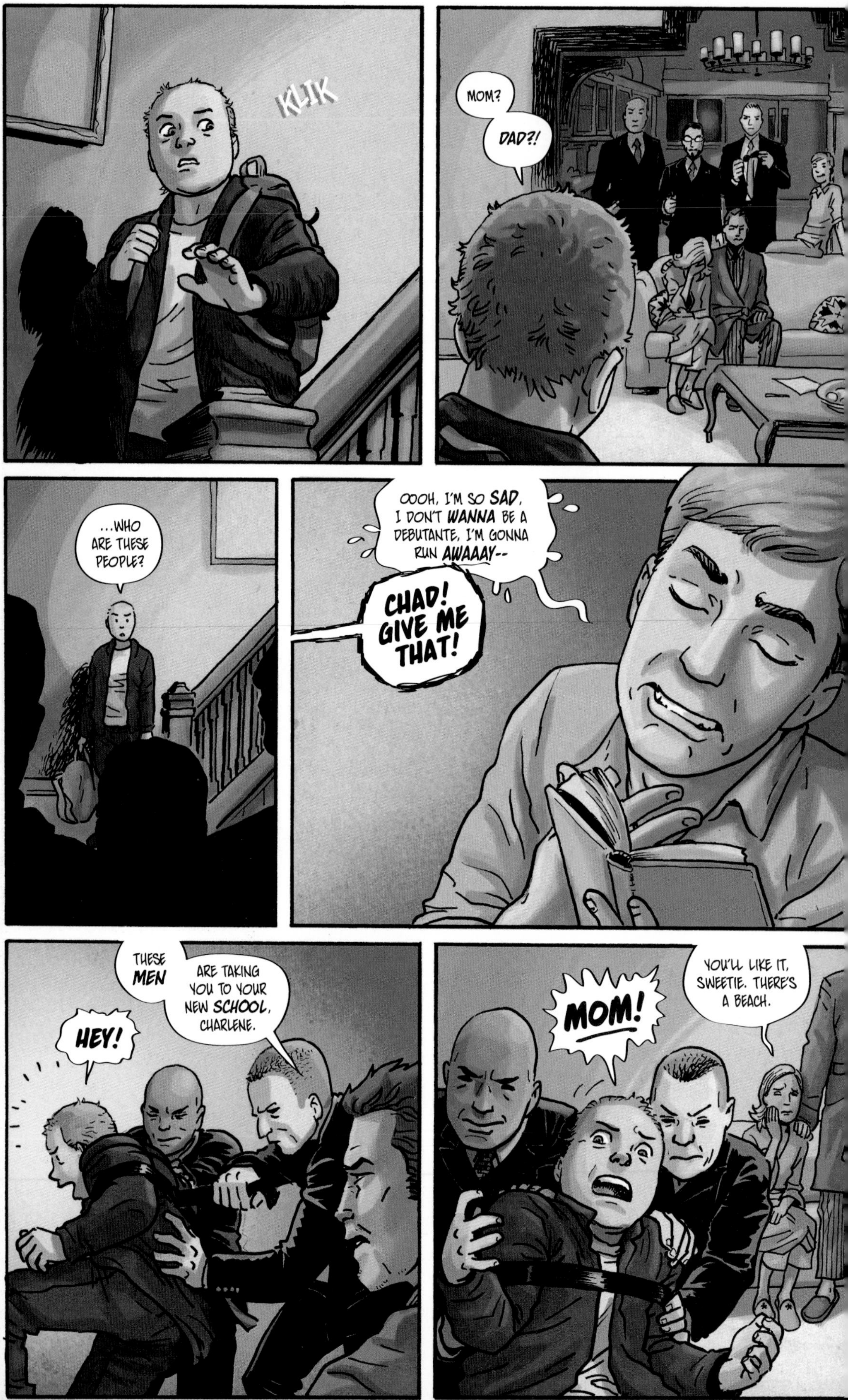
KLIK
MOM?
DAD?!
...WHO ARE THESE PEOPLE?
OOOH, I'M SO SAD, I DON'T WANNA BE A DEBUTANTE, I'M GONNA RUN AWAAAY--
CHAD! GIVE ME THAT!
THESE MEN
ARE TAKING YOU TO YOUR NEW SCHOOL, CHARLENE.
HEY!
MOM!
YOU'LL LIKE IT, SWEETIE. THERE'S A BEACH.

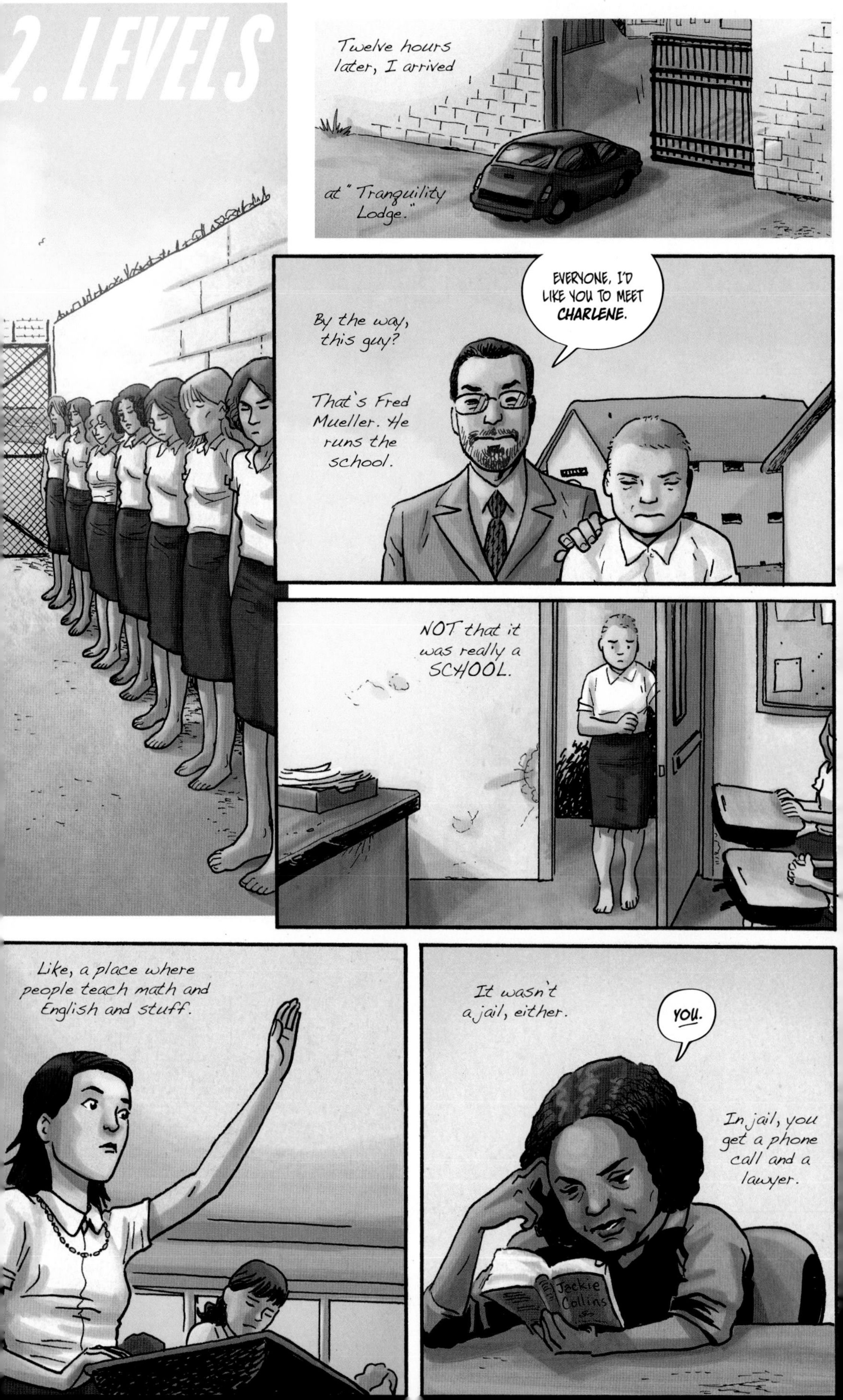
2. LEVELS
Twelve hours later, I arrived
at "Tranquility Lodge."
By the way, this guy?
EVERYONE, I'D LIKE YOU TO MEET CHARLENE.
That's Fred Mueller. He runs the school.
NOT that it was really a SCHOOL.
Like, a place where people teach math and English and stuff.
It wasn't a jail, either.
YOU.
In jail, you get a phone call and a lawyer.
Jackie Collins

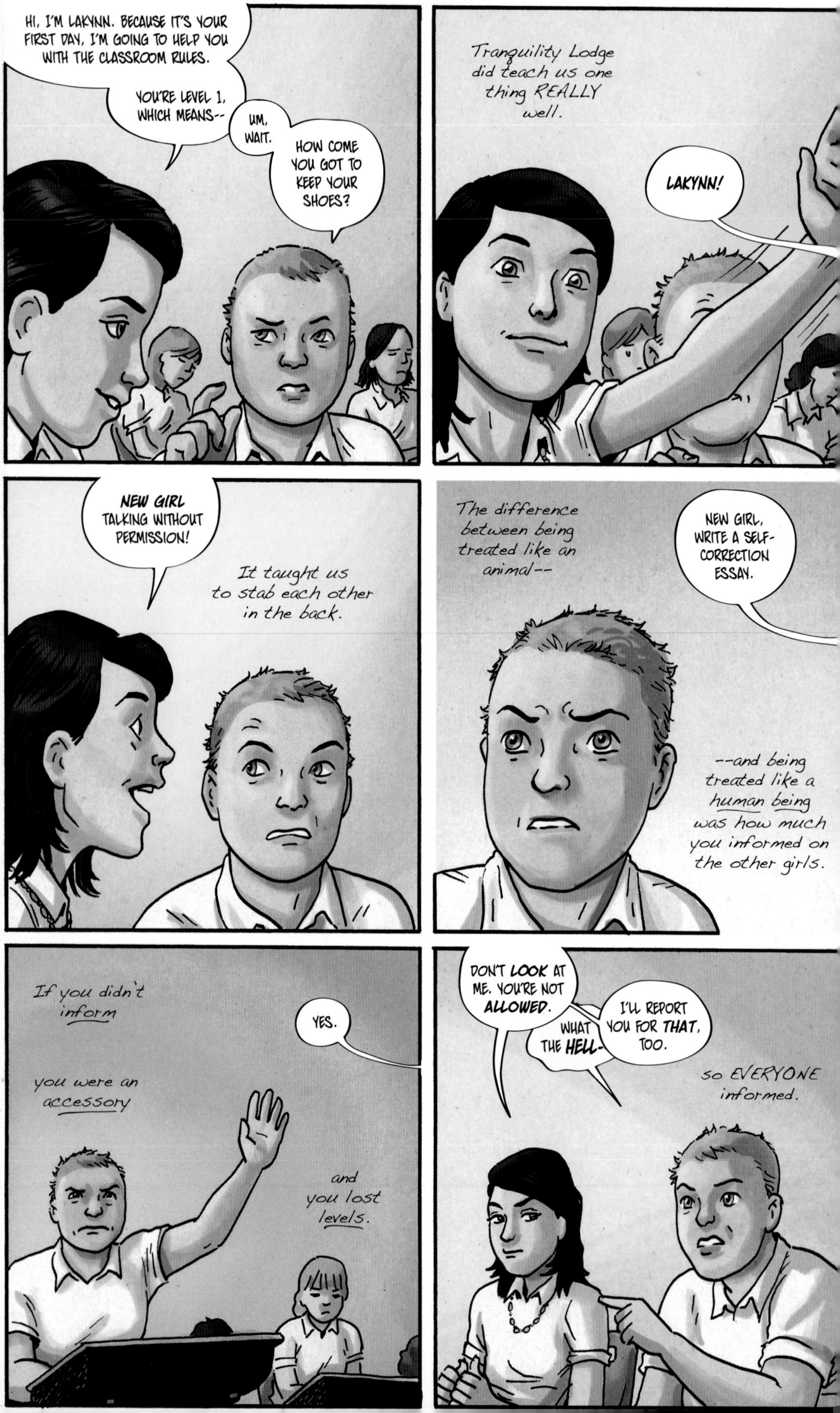
HI, I'M LAKYNN. BECAUSE IT'S YOUR FIRST DAY, I'M GOING TO HELP YOU WITH THE CLASSROOM RULES.
YOU'RE LEVEL 1, WHICH MEANS--
UM, WAIT.
HOW COME YOU GOT TO KEEP YOUR SHOES?
Tranquility Lodge did teach us one thing REALLY well.
LAKYNN!
NEW GIRL TALKING WITHOUT PERMISSION!
It taught us to stab each other in the back.
The difference between being treated like an animal--
NEW GIRL, WRITE A SELF-CORRECTION ESSAY.
--and being treated like a human being was how much you informed on the other girls.
If you didn't inform
YES.
you were an accessory
and you lost levels.
DON'T LOOK AT ME. YOU'RE NOT ALLOWED.
WHAT THE HELL-
I'LL REPORT YOU FOR THAT, TOO.
so EVERYONE informed.

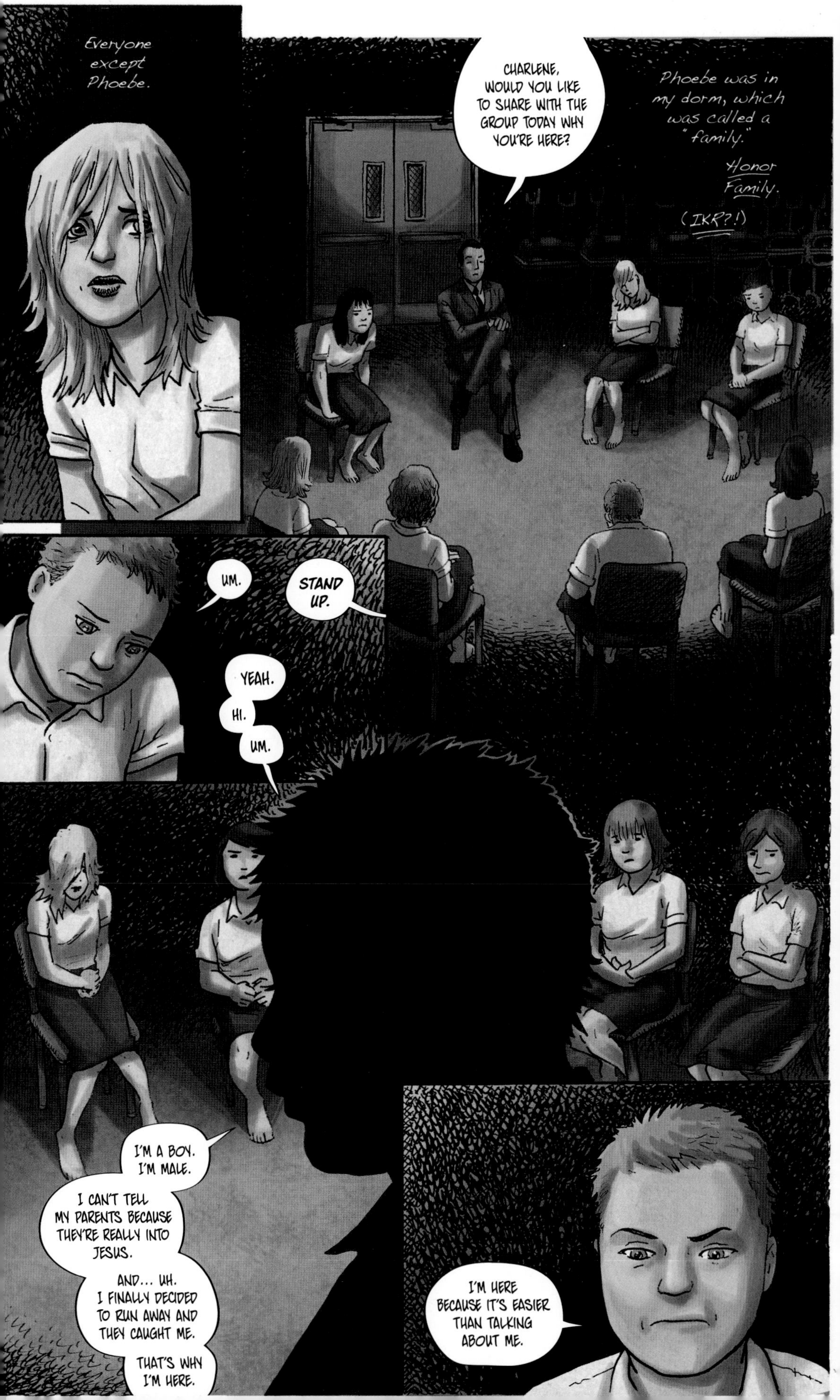
Everyone except Phoebe.
CHARLENE, WOULD YOU LIKE TO SHARE WITH THE GROUP TODAY WHY YOU'RE HERE?
Phoebe was in my dorm, which was called a "family."
Honor Family.
(IKR?!)
UM.
STAND UP.
YEAH.
HI.
UM.
I'M A BOY. I'M MALE.
I CAN'T TELL MY PARENTS BECAUSE THEY'RE REALLY INTO JESUS.
AND... UH. I FINALLY DECIDED TO RUN AWAY AND THEY CAUGHT ME.
THAT'S WHY I'M HERE.
I'M HERE BECAUSE IT'S EASIER THAN TALKING ABOUT ME.

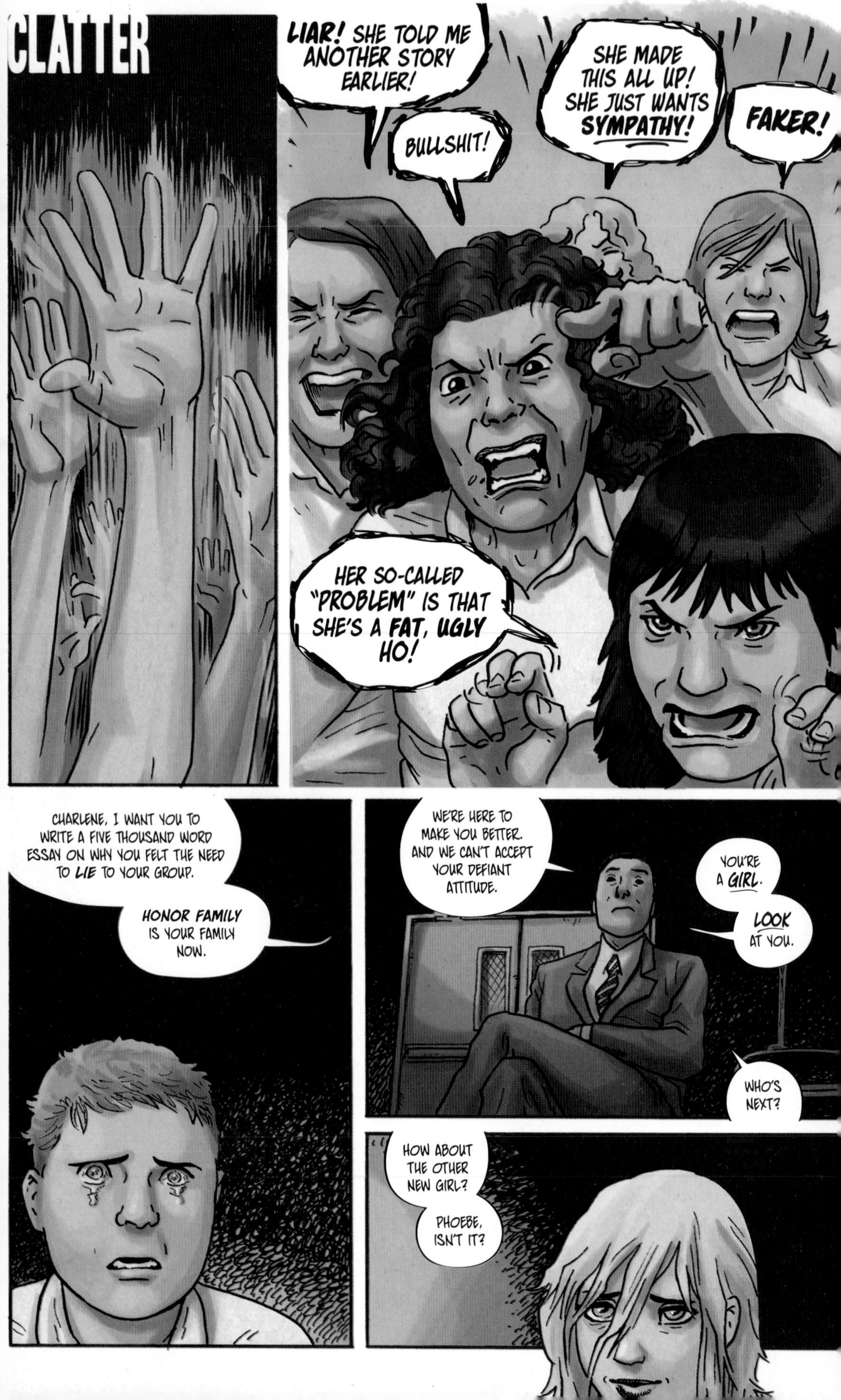

CLATTER
LIAR! SHE TOLD ME ANOTHER STORY EARLIER!
BULLSHIT!
SHE MADE THIS ALL UP! SHE JUST WANTS SYMPATHY!
FAKER!
HER SO-CALLED "PROBLEM" IS THAT SHE'S A FAT, UGLY HO!
CHARLENE, I WANT YOU TO WRITE A FIVE THOUSAND WORD ESSAY ON WHY YOU FELT THE NEED TO LIE TO YOUR GROUP.
HONOR FAMILY IS YOUR FAMILY NOW.
WE'RE HERE TO MAKE YOU BETTER. AND WE CAN'T ACCEPT YOUR DEFIANT ATTITUDE.
YOU'RE A GIRL.
LOOK AT YOU.
WHO'S NEXT?
HOW ABOUT THE OTHER NEW GIRL?
PHOEBE, ISN'T IT?

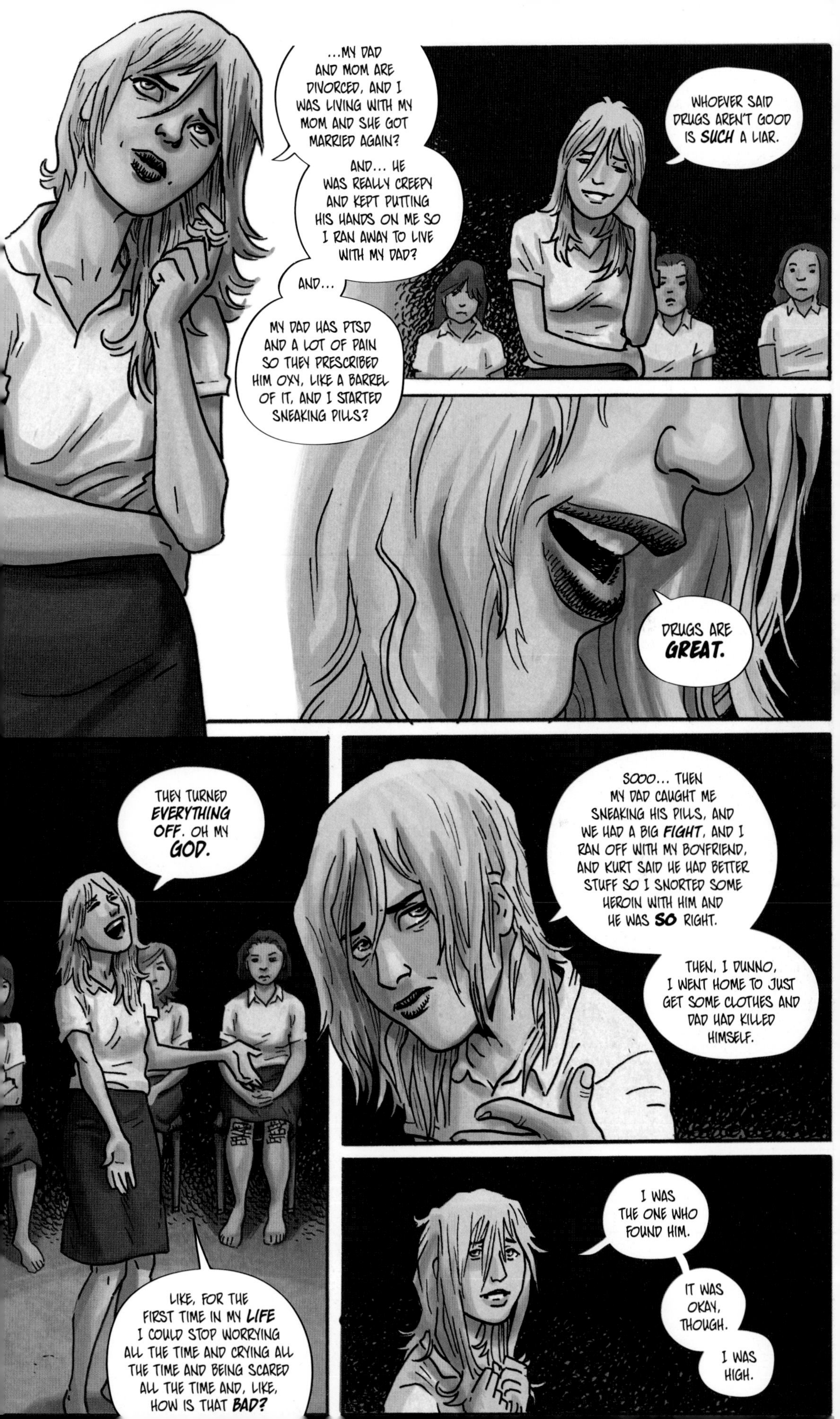
...MY DAD AND MOM ARE DIVORCED, AND I WAS LIVING WITH MY MOM AND SHE GOT MARRIED AGAIN?
AND... HE WAS REALLY CREEPY AND KEPT PUTTING HIS HANDS ON ME SO I RAN AWAY TO LIVE WITH MY DAD?
AND...
MY DAD HAS PTSD AND A LOT OF PAIN SO THEY PRESCRIBED HIM OXY, LIKE A BARREL OF IT, AND I STARTED SNEAKING PILLS?
WHOEVER SAID DRUGS AREN'T GOOD IS SUCH A LIAR.
DRUGS ARE GREAT.
THEY TURNED EVERYTHING OFF. OH MY GOD.
LIKE, FOR THE FIRST TIME IN MY LIFE I COULD STOP WORRYING ALL THE TIME AND CRYING ALL THE TIME AND BEING SCARED ALL THE TIME AND, LIKE, HOW IS THAT BAD?
SOOO... THEN MY DAD CAUGHT ME SNEAKING HIS PILLS, AND WE HAD A BIG FIGHT, AND I RAN OFF WITH MY BOYFRIEND, AND KURT SAID HE HAD BETTER STUFF SO I SNORTED SOME HEROIN WITH HIM AND HE WAS SO RIGHT.
THEN, I DUNNO, I WENT HOME TO JUST GET SOME CLOTHES AND DAD HAD KILLED HIMSELF.
I WAS THE ONE WHO FOUND HIM.
IT WAS OKAY, THOUGH.
I WAS HIGH.

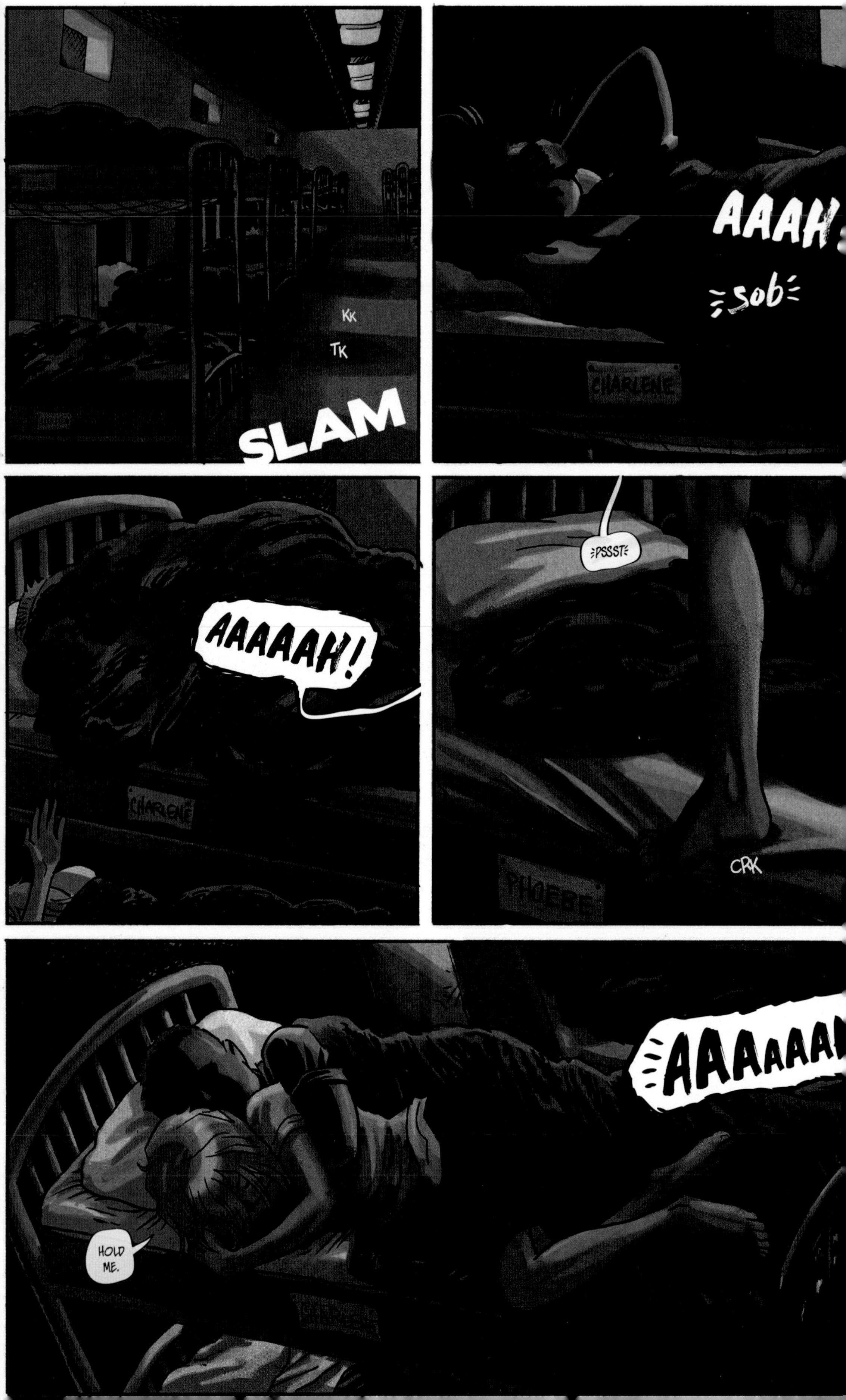

KK
TK
SLAM
AAAH!
sob
CHARLENE
AAAAAH!
CHARLENE
PSSST
CRK
PHOEBE
AAAAAA
HOLD ME.

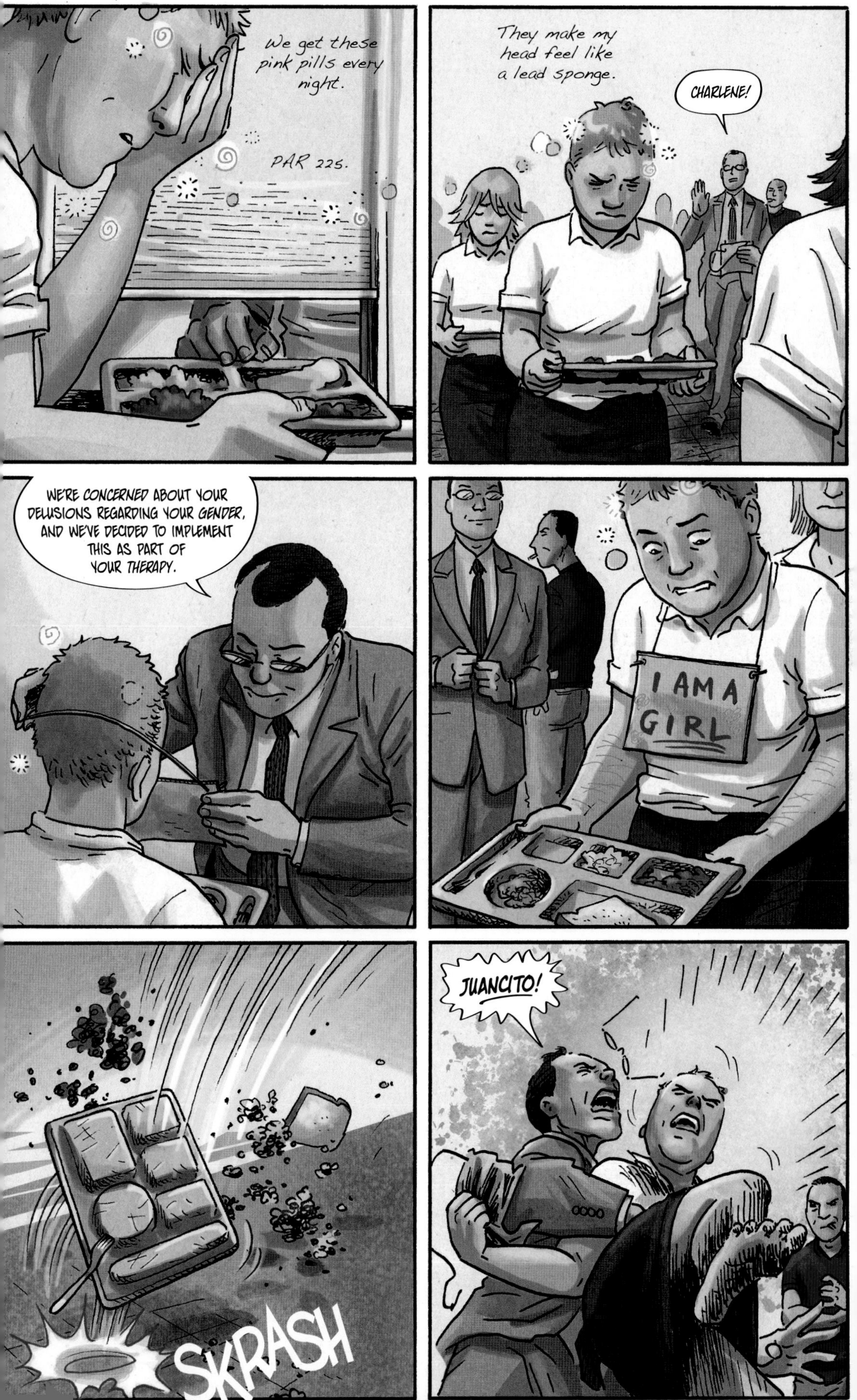
We get these pink pills every night.
PAR 225.
They make my head feel like a lead sponge.
CHARLENE!
WE'RE CONCERNED ABOUT YOUR DELUSIONS REGARDING YOUR GENDER, AND WE'VE DECIDED TO IMPLEMENT THIS AS PART OF YOUR THERAPY.
I AM A GIRL
SKRASH
JUANCITO!

YES,
LAKYNN?

ICK!

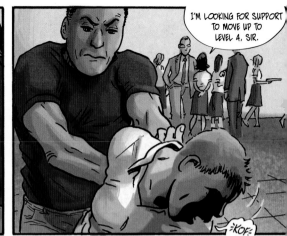

I'M LOOKING FOR SUPPORT
TO MOVE UP TO
LEVEL 4, SIR.

:KOF:

CHANK

OBSERVATION
POSITION. THAT'S
O.P., CHICA.

LIE
DOWN!

ON YOUR
FACE!

:NNF!:

fffffsssssshhhh

ffffsssshhh

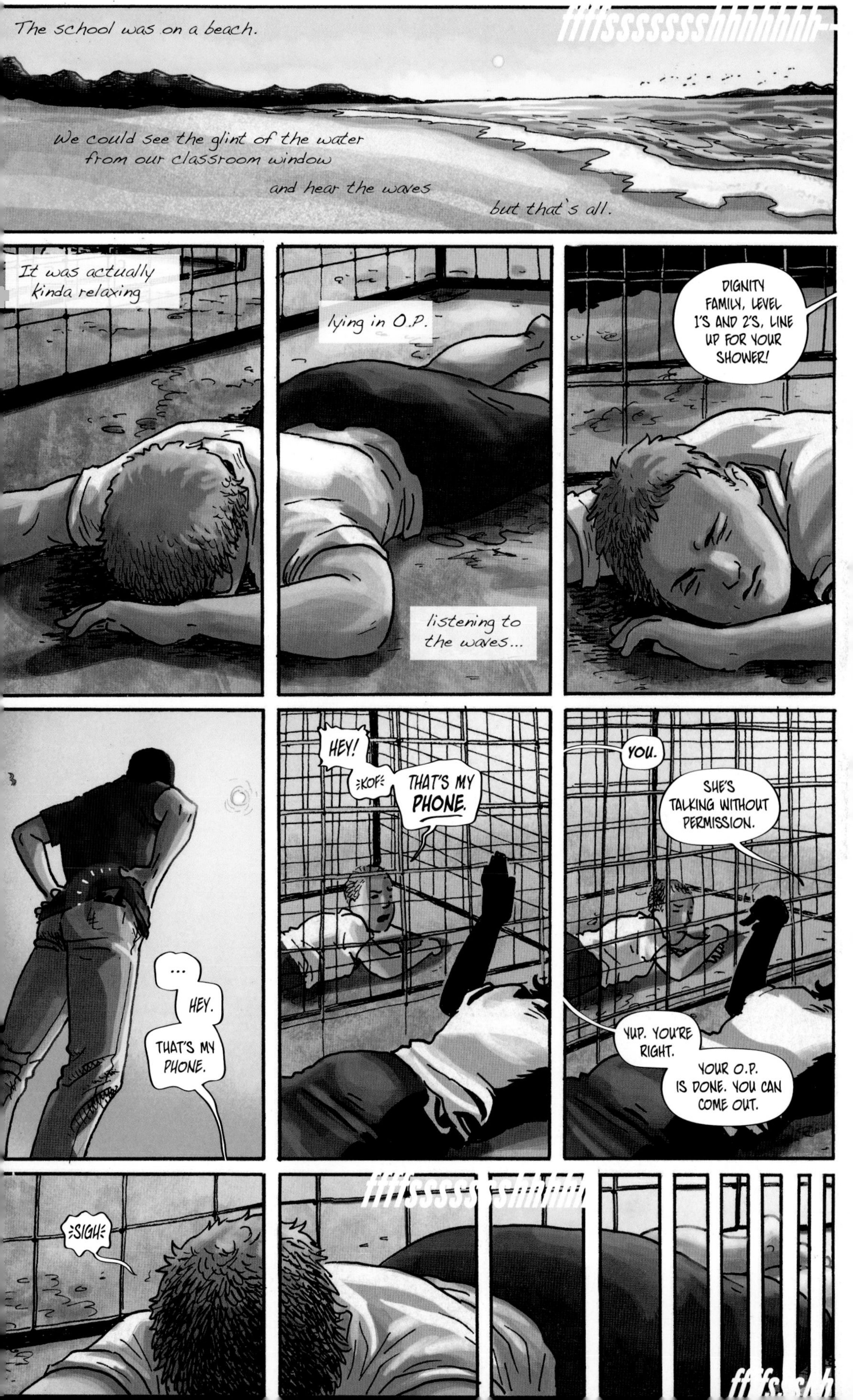
The school was on a beach.
fffsssssssshhhhhhh-
We could see the glint of the water from our classroom window
and hear the waves
but that's all.
It was actually kinda relaxing
lying in O.P.
listening to the waves...
DIGNITY FAMILY, LEVEL 1'S AND 2'S, LINE UP FOR YOUR SHOWER!
...
HEY.
THAT'S MY PHONE.
HEY!
KOF
THAT'S MY PHONE.
YOU.
SHE'S TALKING WITHOUT PERMISSION.
YUP. YOU'RE RIGHT.
YOUR O.P. IS DONE. YOU CAN COME OUT.
SIGH
fffsssssssshhhhh

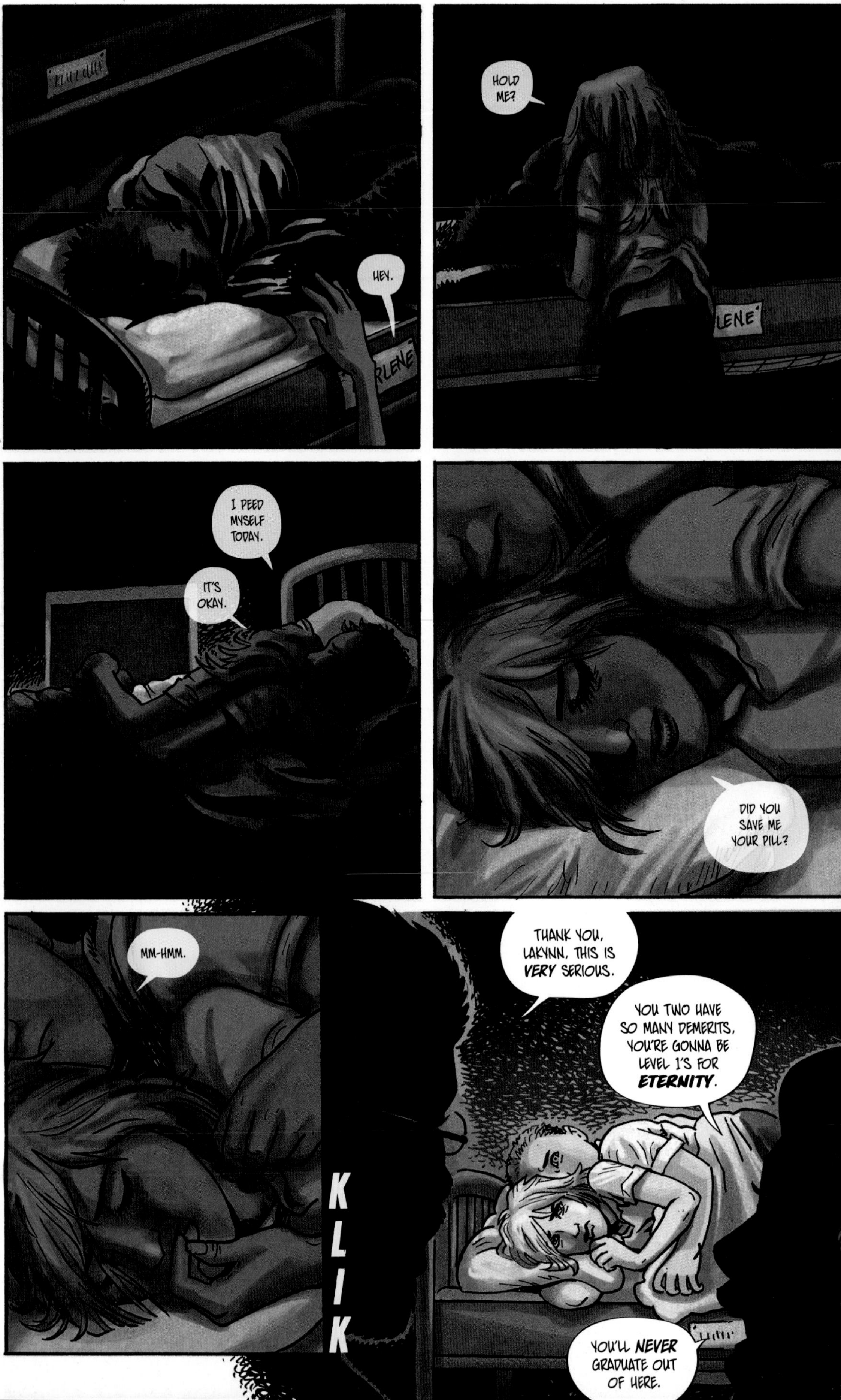
HEY.
HOLD ME?
I PEED MYSELF TODAY.
IT'S OKAY.
DID YOU SAVE ME YOUR PILL?
MM-HMM.
KLIK
THANK YOU, LAKYNN, THIS IS VERY SERIOUS.
YOU TWO HAVE SO MANY DEMERITS, YOU'RE GONNA BE LEVEL 1'S FOR ETERNITY.
YOU'LL NEVER GRADUATE OUT OF HERE.

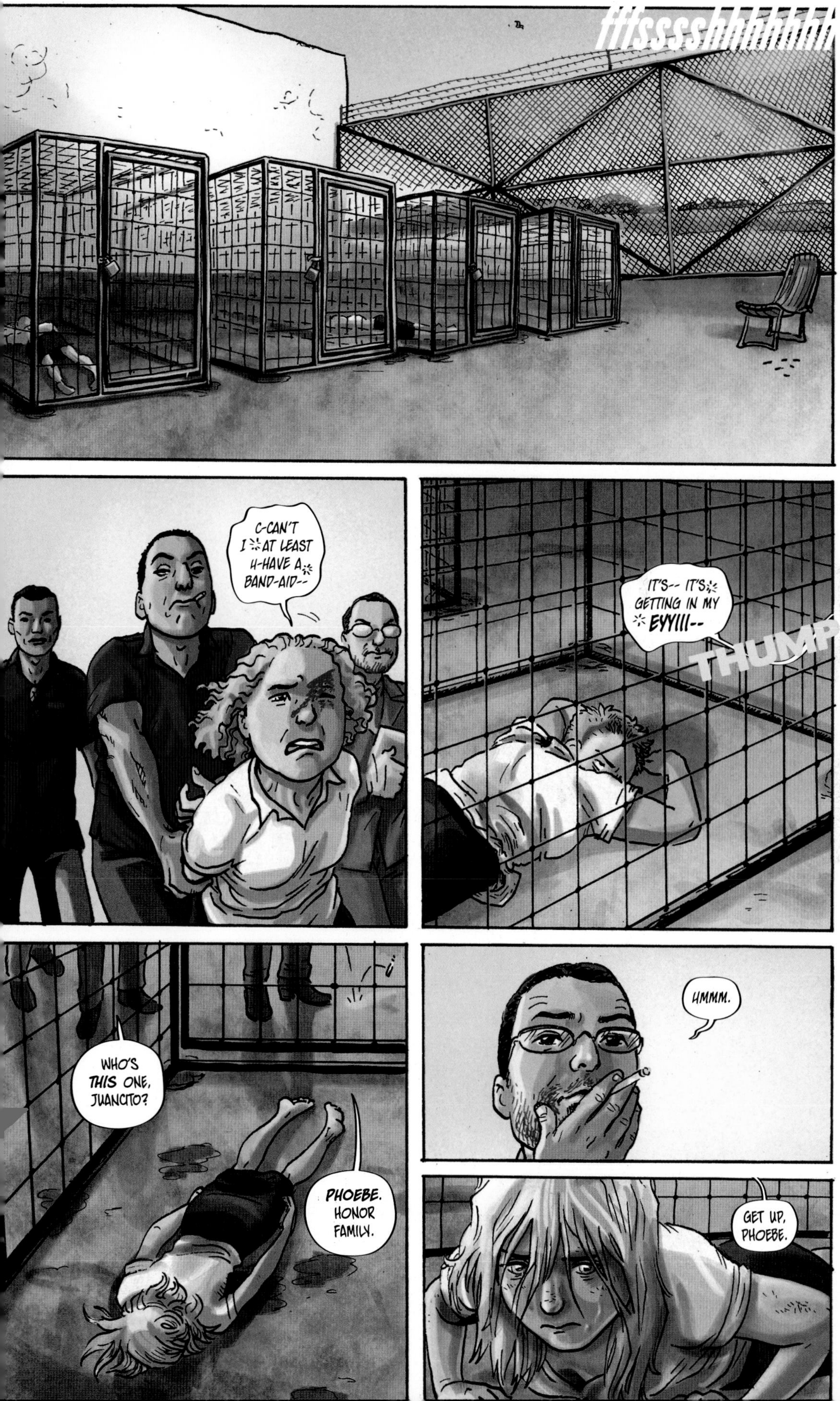
fffssssshhhhhhh
C-CAN'T I AT LEAST H-HAVE A BAND-AID--
IT'S-- IT'S GETTING IN MY EYYIII--
THUMP
WHO'S THIS ONE, JUANCITO?
PHOEBE. HONOR FAMILY.
UMMM.
GET UP, PHOEBE.

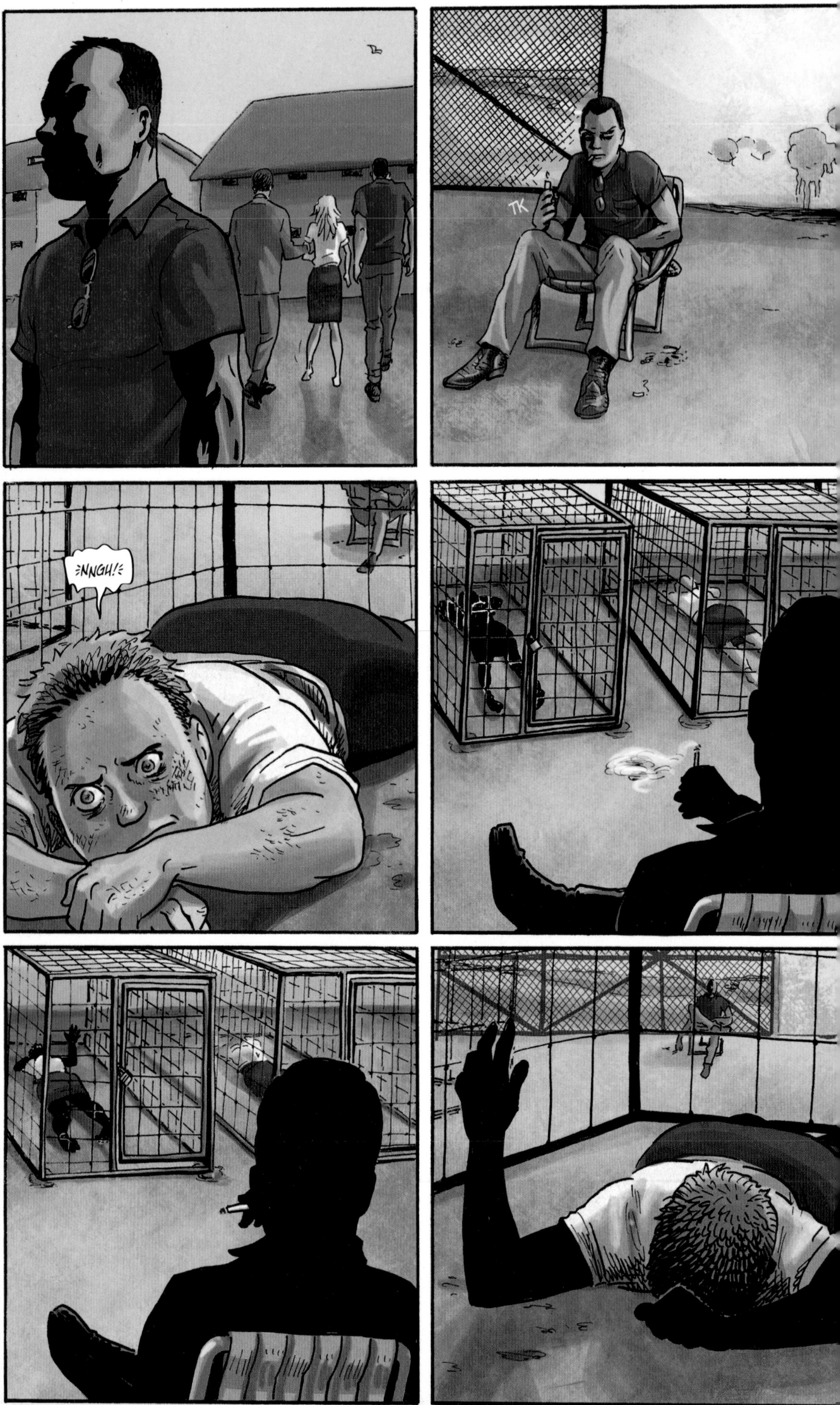
TK
NNGH!

fssssshhhhhh

HNNH.

YOU'RE DONE.

I'LL TAKE YOU BACK TO YOUR FAMILY.

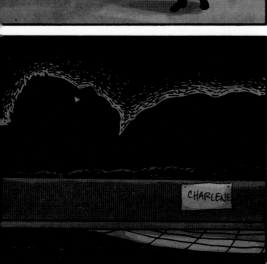

CHARLENE

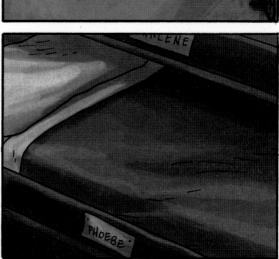

CHARLENE

PHOEBE

CROINK

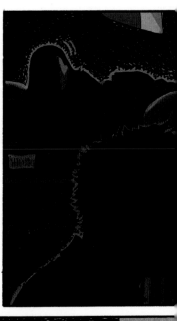

SSH!

SHUT UP, I SAID.

PAF   PAF

DO IT.

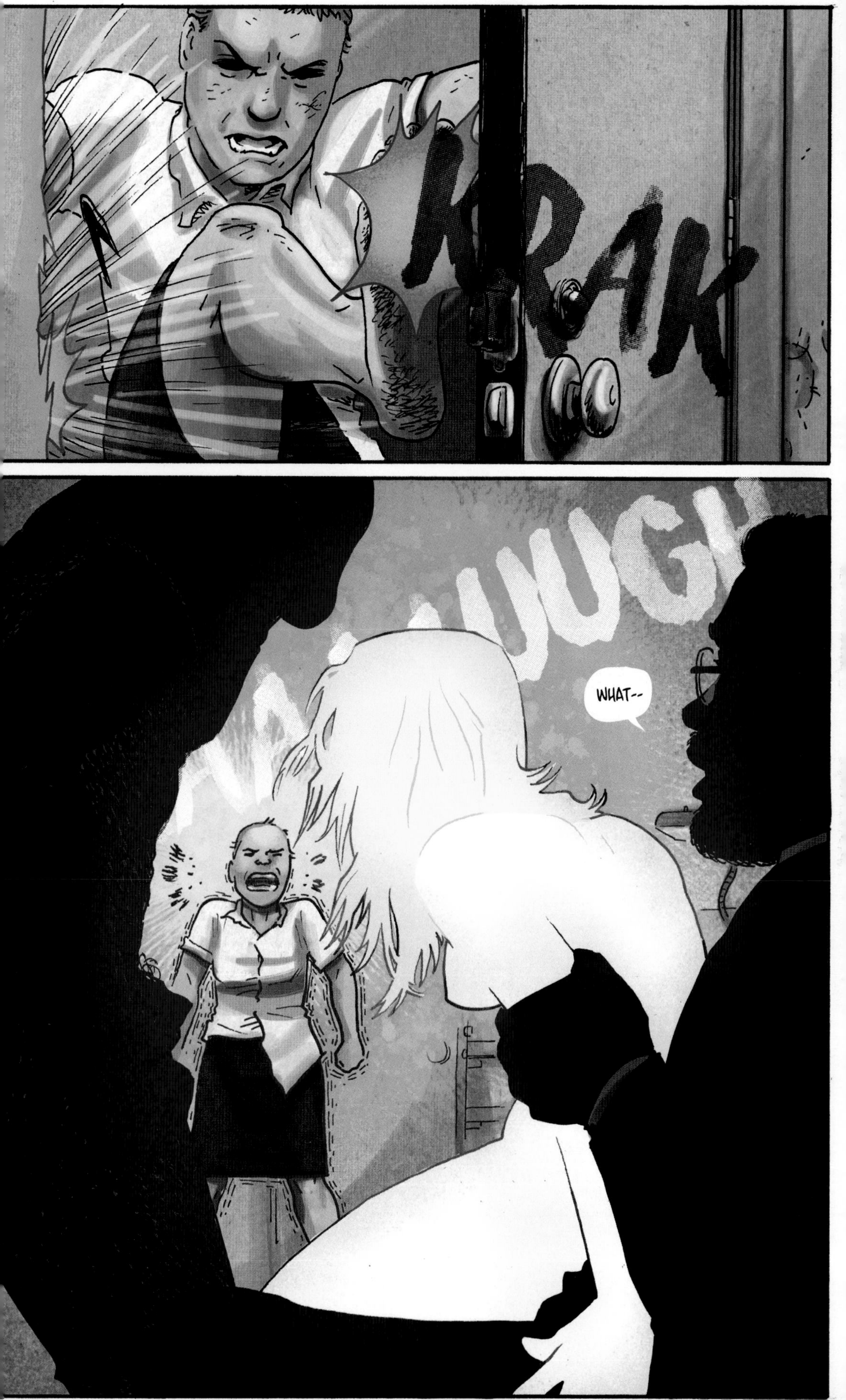
KRAK
WHAT--

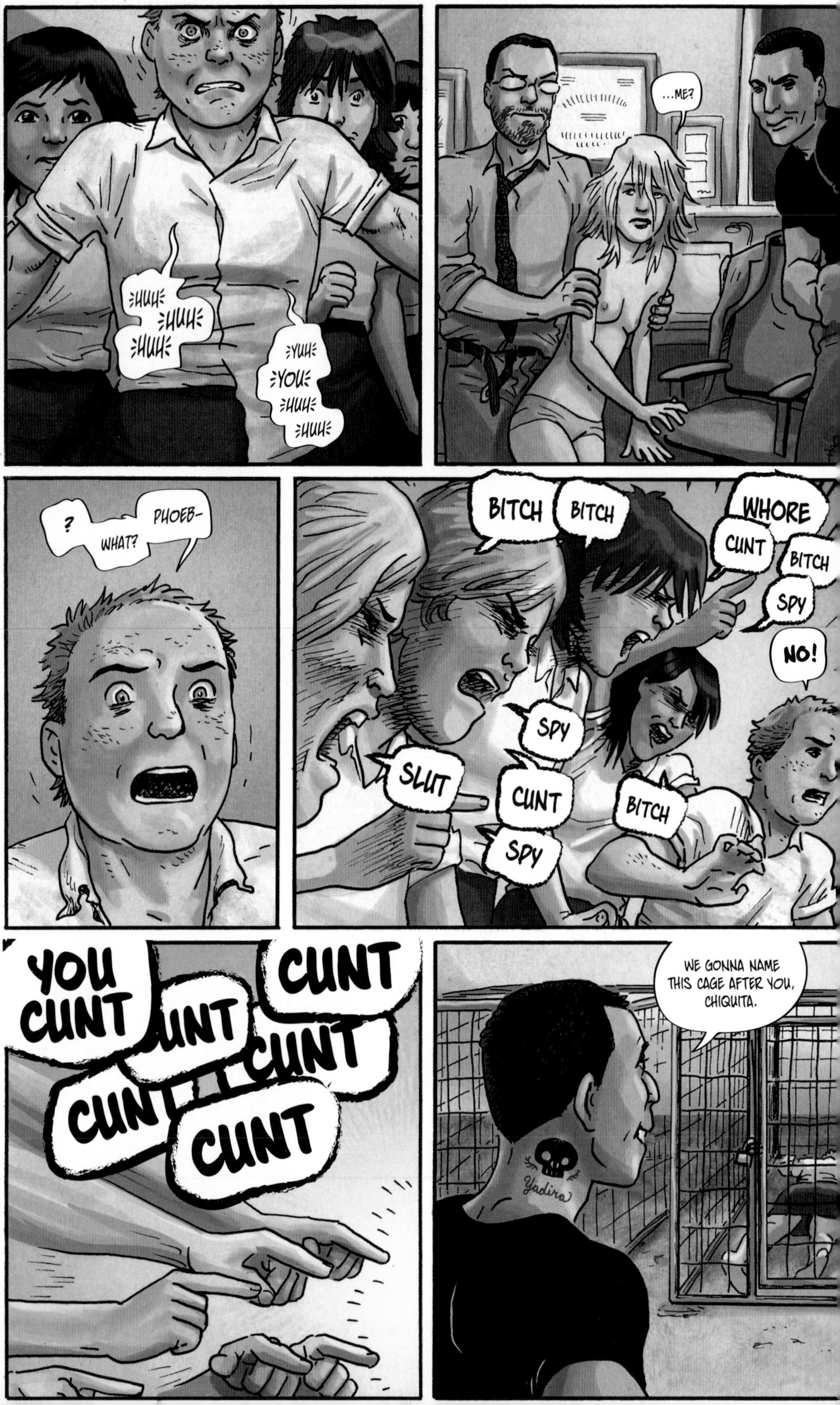
HUH
HUH
HUH
YUH
YOU
HUH
HUH
...ME?
?
WHAT?
PHOEB-
BITCH
BITCH
WHORE
CUNT
BITCH
SPY
NO!
SPY
SLUT
CUNT
BITCH
SPY
YOU CUNT
CUNT
CUNT
CUNT
CUNT
WE GONNA NAME THIS CAGE AFTER YOU, CHIQUITA.
Yadira

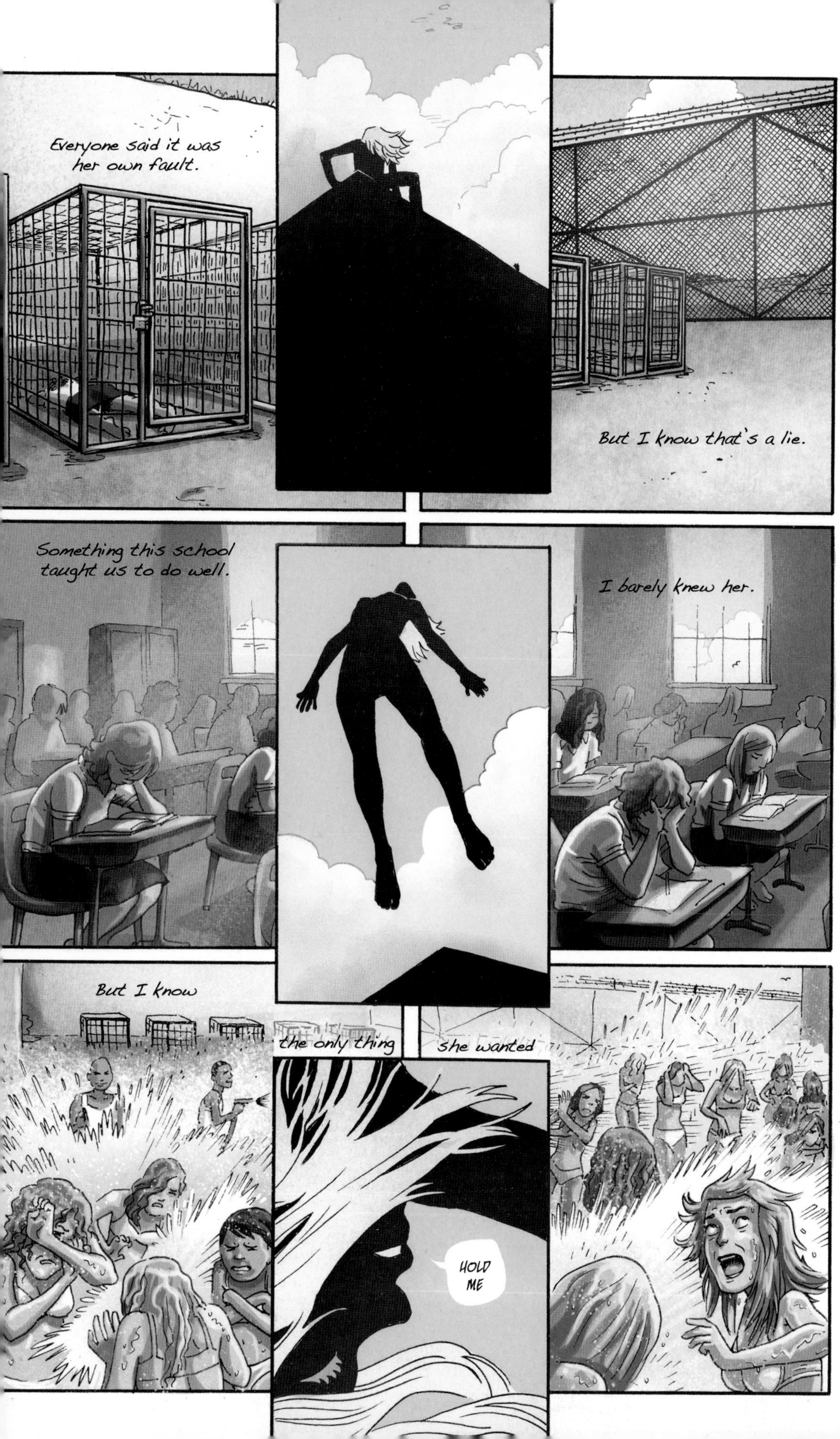
Everyone said it was her own fault.
But I know that's a lie.
Something this school taught us to do well.
I barely knew her.
But I know
the only thing
she wanted
HOLD ME

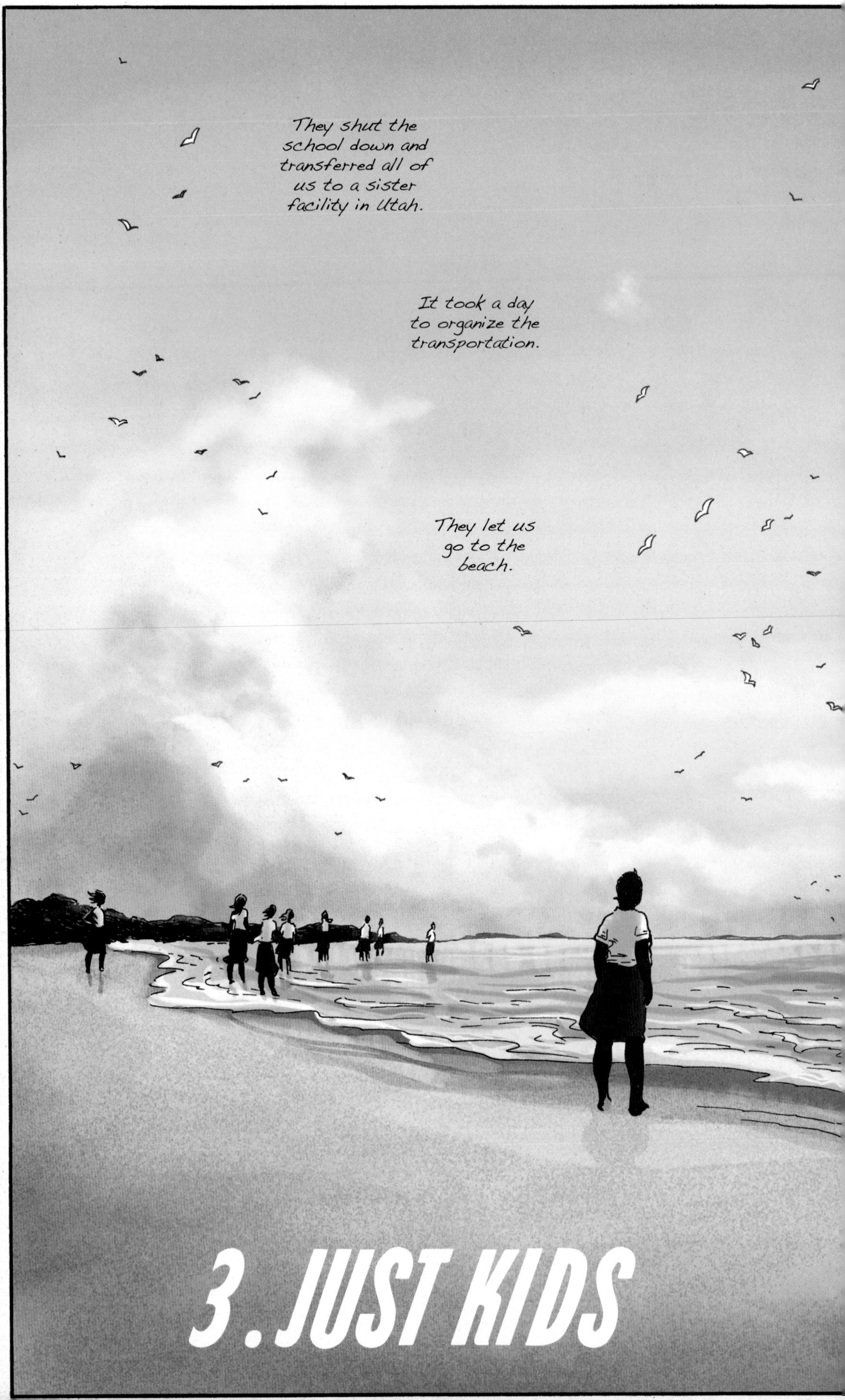
They shut the school down and transferred all of us to a sister facility in Utah.
It took a day to organize the transportation.
They let us go to the beach.
3. JUST KIDS

A Partial List of Deaths at Teen Residential Treatment Centers

Aaron Bacon
Aaron Gray
Alex Cullinane
Alex Harris
Alexie Evette Richie
Andrew McClain
Angela Miller
Angellika Arndt
Anthony Dumas
Anthony Green
Anthony Haynes
Anthony Parker
Ashley Shaddox
Bernard Reefer
Bobby Joe Randolph
Bobby Sue Thomas
Brandon Hadden
Brandon Hoffman
Brendan Blum
Brendon Ogonowski
Bryan Alexander
Candace Newmaker
Caleb Jensen
Carey Dunn
Carlos Ruiz
Carlton Thomas
Carnez Boone
Casey Collier
Cederic Napoleon
Chad Franza
Charles Collins Jr
Charles Lucas
Charles Moody Jr
Chloe Cohen
Chris Brown
Chris Campbell
Christening Garcia
Christie Scheck
Cindi Sohappy
Corey Baines
Corey Foster
Corey Murphy
Danieal Kelly
Daniel Huerta
Daniel Matthews
Danny Lewis
Darryl Thompson
David Sellers
Dawn Birnbaum
Dawnne Takeuchi
Dawn Perry
Diane Harris
Dillon Peak
Dionte Pickens
Donderey Rogers
Dustin Phelps
Earl Smith
Edith Campos
Eddie Lee
Elisa Santry
Erica Harvey
Eric Roberts
Faith Finley
Gabriel Poirier
Gareth Myatt
Garrett Halsey
Geoffrey Vorhies
Georgia Rowe
Gina Score
Gracie James
Gregory Jones
Issaih Simmons
Jamal Odum
Jamar Griffiths
James Lamb
James Richard
James Roman
James White
Jamie Young
Jason Tallman
Jeffery Bogrett
Jeffery Demetrius
Jeremy Gaulin
Jerry McLaurin
Jerry Triett
Jimmy Kanda
Joey Alteriz
John McCloskey
Johnny Lim
Jonathan Avila
Jonathan Carey
Jonathan Lenoff
Joseph Bolt
Joshua Ferarini
Joshua Sharpe
Karlye Newman
Kasey Warner
Katherine Lank
Katherine Rice
Kelly Young
Kerry Brown
Kristal Mayon-Ceniceros
Kristen Chase
Lrystal Tibbets
Kyle Young
LaKeisha Brown
Latasha Bush
Lenny Ortega

*source: residentialtreatmentcenterabuse.com

Levi Snyder
Linda Harris
Leroy Prinkley
Lorene Larhette
Lorenzo Johnson
Lyle Foodroy
Maria Medoza
Mario Cano
Mark Draheim
Mark Soares
Martin Lee Anderson
Mathew Meyers
Matthew Goodman
Matt Toppi
Michael Arnold
Michael Garcia
Michael Ibrra-Wiltsie
Michael Owens
Michelle Sutton
Natalynndria Slim
Natasha Newman
Neve Lafferty
Nicholas Contreras
Omar Paisley
Omega Leach
Orlena Parker
Paul Choy
Peter Cooper
Randy Steeles
Richard DeMaar
Robert Erwin
Roberto Reyes
Robert Rollins
Robert Zimmerman
Rocco Magliozzi
Rochelle Claybourne
Roger Eugene Benson
Roxanna Gray
Ryan Lewis
Ryan McCandless
Sakena Dorsey
Sarah Crider
Sergey Blashchishena
Shanice Nibbs
Shawn Diaz
Shawn Smith
Shinaul McGraw
Shirley Arciszewski
Stephanie Duffield
Tanner Wilson
Taylor Mangham
Thomas Mapes
Timothy Thomas
Travis Parkers
Tristan Sovern
Valerie Heron
Victoria Petersilka
Walter Brown
Wauketta Wallace
Will Futrelle
Willie Durden III
Willie Wright

Most common cause of death is restraint, followed by suicide, and forced exercise.

source: residentialtreatmentcenterabuse.com

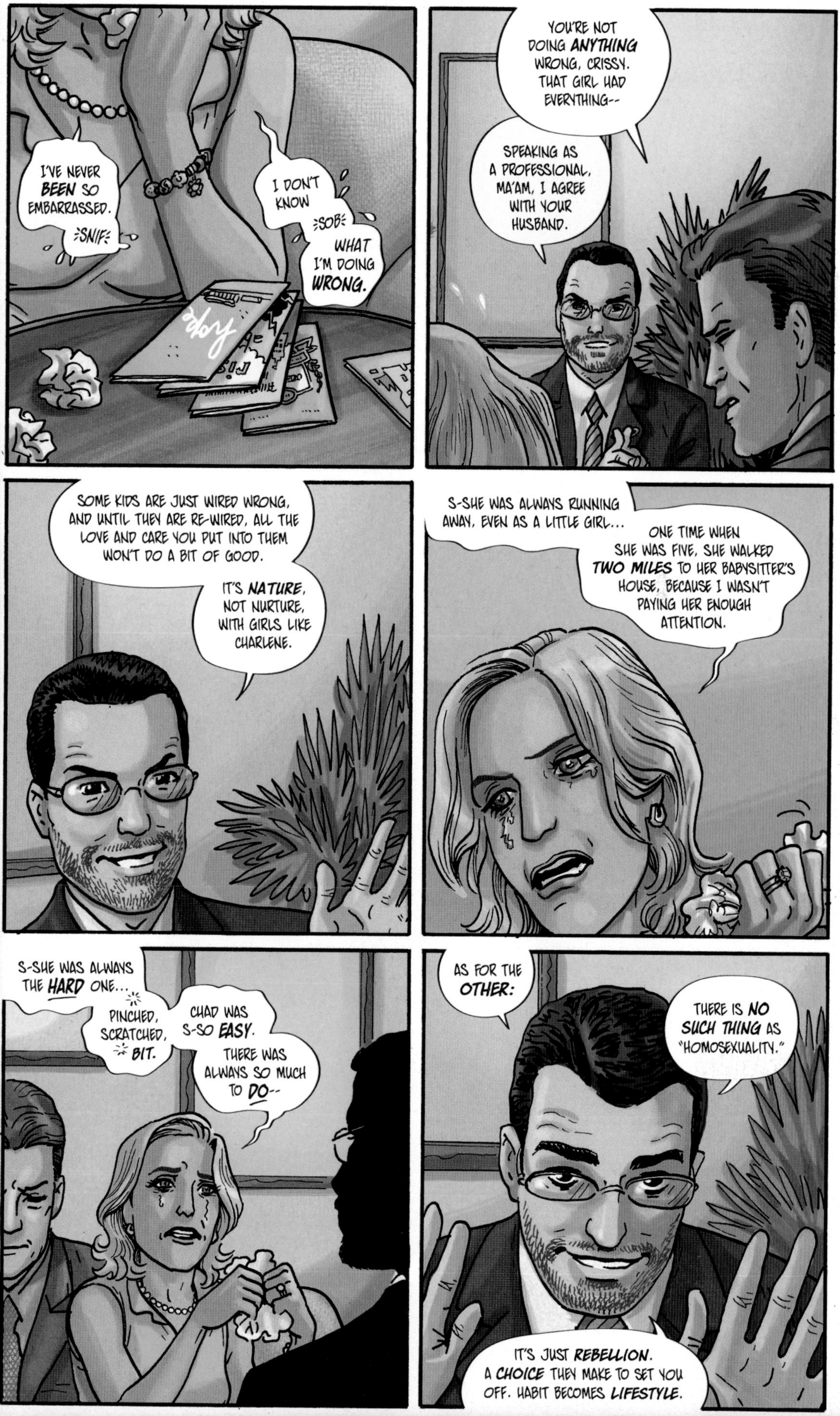
I'VE NEVER BEEN SO EMBARRASSED.
SNIF
I DON'T KNOW
SOB
WHAT I'M DOING WRONG.
YOU'RE NOT DOING ANYTHING WRONG, CRISSY. THAT GIRL HAD EVERYTHING--
SPEAKING AS A PROFESSIONAL, MA'AM, I AGREE WITH YOUR HUSBAND.
SOME KIDS ARE JUST WIRED WRONG, AND UNTIL THEY ARE RE-WIRED, ALL THE LOVE AND CARE YOU PUT INTO THEM WON'T DO A BIT OF GOOD.
IT'S NATURE, NOT NURTURE, WITH GIRLS LIKE CHARLENE.
S-SHE WAS ALWAYS RUNNING AWAY, EVEN AS A LITTLE GIRL...
ONE TIME WHEN SHE WAS FIVE, SHE WALKED TWO MILES TO HER BABYSITTER'S HOUSE, BECAUSE I WASN'T PAYING HER ENOUGH ATTENTION.
S-SHE WAS ALWAYS THE HARD ONE...
PINCHED, SCRATCHED, BIT.
CHAD WAS S-SO EASY.
THERE WAS ALWAYS SO MUCH TO DO--
AS FOR THE OTHER:
THERE IS NO SUCH THING AS "HOMOSEXUALITY."
IT'S JUST REBELLION. A CHOICE THEY MAKE TO SET YOU OFF. HABIT BECOMES LIFESTYLE.

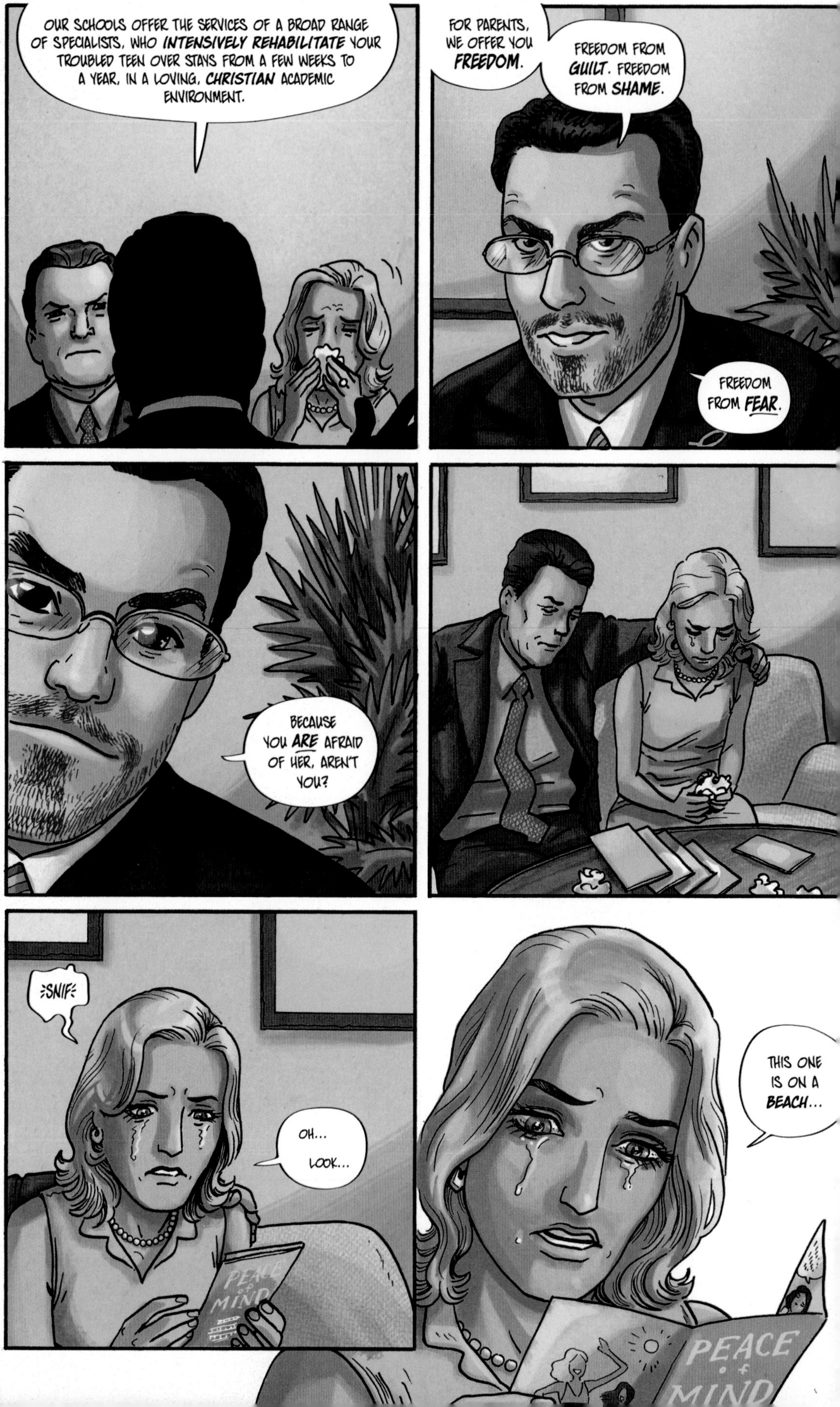
OUR SCHOOLS OFFER THE SERVICES OF A BROAD RANGE OF SPECIALISTS, WHO INTENSIVELY REHABILITATE YOUR TROUBLED TEEN OVER STAYS FROM A FEW WEEKS TO A YEAR, IN A LOVING, CHRISTIAN ACADEMIC ENVIRONMENT.
FOR PARENTS, WE OFFER YOU FREEDOM.
FREEDOM FROM GUILT. FREEDOM FROM SHAME.
FREEDOM FROM FEAR.
BECAUSE YOU ARE AFRAID OF HER, AREN'T YOU?
SNIF
OH... LOOK...
PEACE of MIND
THIS ONE IS ON A BEACH...
PEACE of MIND

PAGE 1.) 4 PANELS, FULL WIDTH

1. CHARLENE'S MOM, SMILING, EXPLAINING. SIMPLE/NO BG (THEY ARE IN C'S ROOM). C IS ABOUT TO TURN 16.

MOM: COMING OUT IS SUCH A WONDERFUL EXPERIENCE, CHARLENE.

MOM: BLOUSE + SKIRT, VERY LILY PULITZER, PEARLS (B

EVERY PROCESS BETWEEN A COMICS TEAM IS UNIQUE. *No Mercy*'s is particularly wonderful for me, because of how much input Carla and Jenn bring to the stories and how supportive everyone is of our frequent tangents into experimental ideas. In the extra material for this trade, we thought we'd take you behind the production curtain to see how the story in *No Mercy* #9 went from rough notes to penciled pages.

Most of my stories are born in nearly-illegible chickenscratch notes in a paper notebook. *No Mercy* #9 especially required a lot of research, so I had my laptop open on one side with all sorts of first-hand accounts of troubled teen schools, and my notebook open on the other. Freeform research notes about character, plot and story eventually become a detailed issue outline, with scene breakdowns, page counts, and key dialogue. These can happen all in one sitting, or stretched out over several days of going back and forth to the story and gradually hewing a path through the jungle (or, occasionally, wasteland) of ideas. I often spend a long time fretting about not wanting to do the writing, and then a fairly short time actually doing it.

By the time I've got rough scene breakdowns and page counts per scene (plus, often, key dialogue), I start transferring things over to a doc on my computer. That doc, once polished, will be what gets shared with Jenn and Carla. At that point, they bounce back to me with comments of things they liked, or questions they had. Or sometimes just a long, drawn-out howl of despair.

Carla then takes the electronic script and draws pencils. She does something that every artist (especially young artists) should do in a perfect world, which is roughs in the dialogue and SFX for placement. Carla also has free rein to change panels and improve dialogue as she sees fit. I adore Carla's lettering style. When I eventually letter the book, I never look back at my original script or notes. I go straight from Carla's pencilled dialogue, which to me has become the “official” dialogue. Not that I won't continue to tweak from there (I re-wrote an entire scene in Issue 7 at the lettering stage because I felt a character needed to be more cognizant of their actions' consequences)... but Carla's pencils are gospel.

One of the things you don't see (as we didn't have room to put in all the pencils for Issue #9) is how we often borrow from or reference other books. There are two page layouts in *No Mercy* #9 inspired by layouts Jeff Smith did in *Bone* (Phoebe's leap) and that Jaime Hernandez did in an early *Locas* (the thinner and thinner panels of Charlene in the cage). I'm constantly reading other comics and taking layout and visual storytelling inspiration from them. Writers, after all, are liars, vivisectionists, and thieves – or at least, the good ones are.

NO MERCY #9

This is a weird, special flashback issue that tackles the “troubled teen” residential treatment centre industry. It's a tough issue. I'm sorry. There will be no letter, story, or commentary from us at the back, just a list of teens that have died in or just after stays in residential treatment centres.

PAGE 1.
FOUR PANELS, all full page width. This is some sort of default for me.

PANEL 1. *Charlene's mom, Crissy, MCU, smiling, explaining. They are in Charlene's room, she is just starting sophomore year of HS/15 years old (turning 16 in the winter). Keep the bg simple here, maybe just a solid colour. Mom is wearing a blouse and skirt, and big pearls, all very Lily Pulitzer.*

CRISSY: Coming out is such a wonderful experience, Charlene.

PANEL 2. *Exterior. Superwide. The Fforde home in Scottsdale, with 3 luxury SUVs parked outside – Porsche Cayennes; a Range Rover.*

CRISSY (off panel): I made close friends that I have to this day.

CRISSY (off panel): And you meet so many cute boys.

PANEL 3. *Charlene, CU. Straight, one-length hair between chin and shoulder, held back from her face with one tragic barette. It probably has highlights. No bg. Charlene's eyes are like "there is so much I want to tell you" / deer in the headlights. She's wearing a very old, faded polo shirt with the collar up (and a little frayed). She is probably thinner than she is now.*

TITLE (OVERPRINT): 1. WHAT WE TALK ABOUT WHEN WE TALK ABOUT FAMILY

PANEL 4. *Mom again. Same framing as Panel 1.*

CRISSY: It's natural to feel nervous. But you shouldn't worry.

CRISSY (linked): Just smile and be yourself.

WE TALK ABOUT
IT'S NATURAL TO FEEL NERVOUS. BUT YOU SHOULDN'T WORRY.
FAMILY
JUST SMILE AND BE YOUR-SELF.

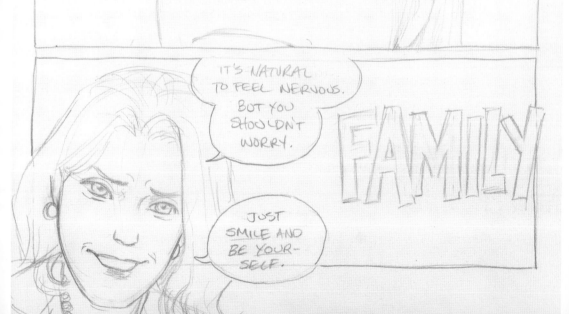

Handwritten notes (top)

P2

VIRGINAL

① 3/4 SPLASH. A PRETTY, PINK DRESS (CALF-LENGTH, BIG SKIRT - IT'S BASICALLY THE PRETTY IN PINK DRESS) HANGS ON THE BACK OF THE CLOSED DOOR. IT'S NEW. THERE ARE STILL TAGS, THE HANGAR IS A BOUTIQUE HANGAR (RALPH LAUREN, OR SUMMAT). SOME SHOES TOO - BALLET FLATS

dress is with sleeves?

MOM (OP): THE DRESS WILL DO ALL THE WORK
(AND LET THE DRESS DO ALL THE HARD WORK.)

③ 1/4. CHARLENE. SAME AS P1 PA 3 BUT NOW THE FACE TURNING AWAY FROM US, EYES SQUINTED SHUT, THE DRESS IS EVERY THING THEY ARE NOT REVULSION ...

P3 ① MOM GETTING UP. MAYBE PATTING C. ON SHOULDER M: I'LL LET YOU GET READY.

Typed text

PAGE 2.
TWO PANELS

PANEL 1. 3/4 SPLASH. *A pretty, virginal pink dress hanging on the back of the closet door. It still has tags on, and some sort of boutique hanger. Calf-length, big skirt. It's basically the Pretty in Pink dress (the original 50s one before Andie turns it into a sack) but maybe with long sleeves? Or more chiffony and puffy and frilly so it can have puffy long sleeves? It should be a really PRETTY dress, a dress that any young girl would LOVE to wear – a bit princessy, but OH SO MISJUDGED for Charlene. (Mom would definitely pick one with long sleeves because, those scars.) If we see the floor, there are shoes – probably ballet flats.*

CRISSY (off panel): The dress will do all the hard work.

PANEL 2. 1/4. *Charlene, turning away from us in CU, eyes squinted shut, that dress is everything she isn't...*

②NM9

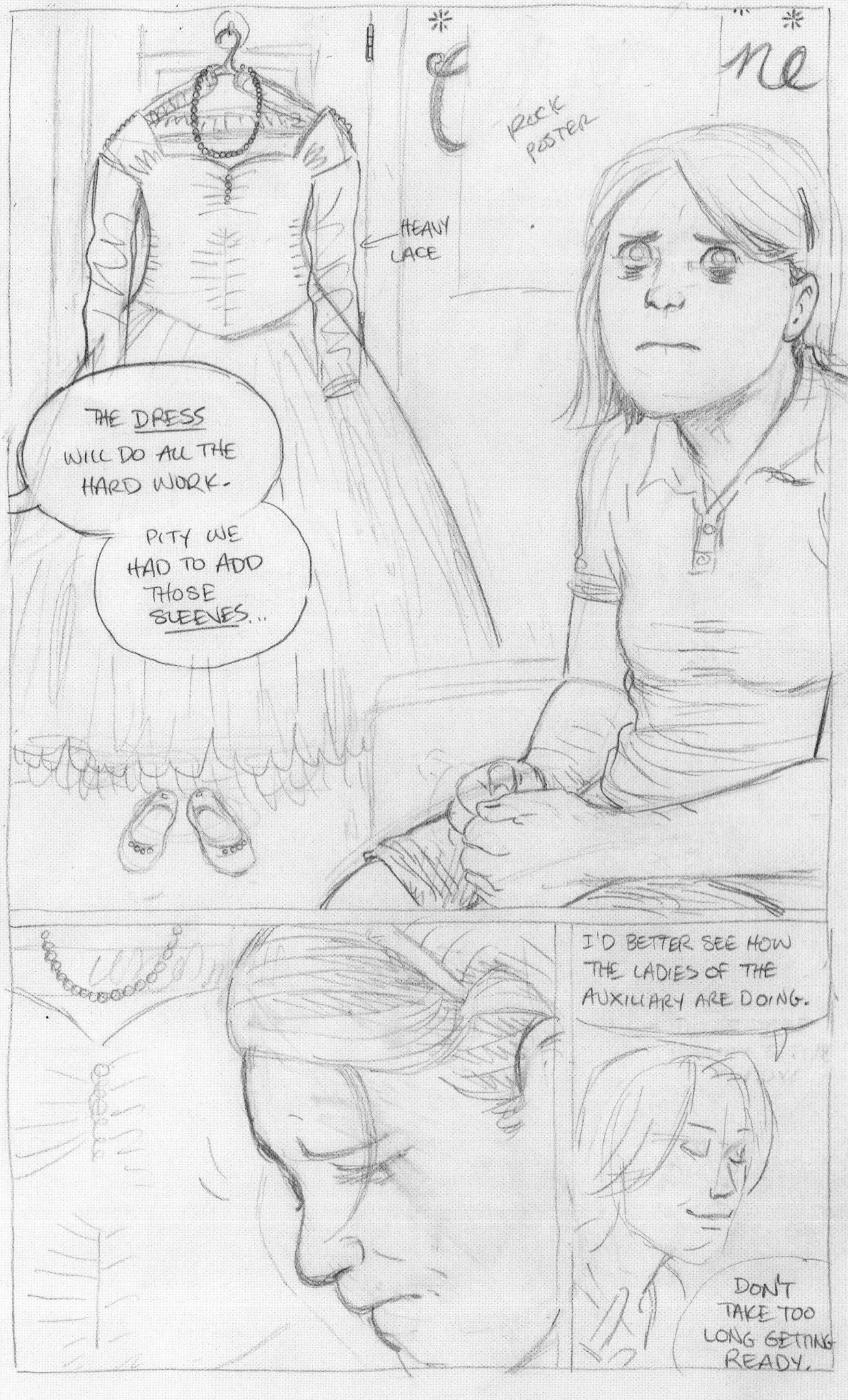
ROCK POSTER
HEAVY LACE
THE DRESS WILL DO ALL THE HARD WORK.
PITY WE HAD TO ADD THOSE SLEEVES...
I'D BETTER SEE HOW THE LADIES OF THE AUXILIARY ARE DOING.
DON'T TAKE TOO LONG GETTING READY.

REVULSION...

1 MOM GETTING UP. MAYBE PATTING C. ON SHOULD

M: I'LL LET YOU GET READY.

DEB BALL
2 THE COMMITTEE DOWNSTAIRS, ON A SECTIONAL
SOFA. CAPRI PANTS, SKIRTS. I THINK WE CRO
OUT THEIR FACES - EACH HOLD A DRINK -
LEMONADE, WINE, SHORT GLASS OR COKE.
SKINNY, PRISSY VMC WIVES. BIG RINGS,
JEWELLERY, NAILS + TOES DONE.

PAGE 3.
SIX PANELS

3 OTS CHALLENE TO MOM IN DOORWAY,
LITTLE CONSPIRATORIAL "JUST US GIRLS" SMILE
AS SHE MOM DEPARTS
MI OH, AND IF YOU NEED A TOUCH-UP JUST U

PANEL 1. *Crissy gets up. Maybe pats Charlene on the shoulder.*

CRISSY: I'd better see how the ladies of the Auxiliary are doing.

CRISSY: Don't take too long getting ready.

PANEL 2. *The Debutante Ball committee downstairs, on a sectional sofa. Capri pants, skirts. Fashionable but all a bit Stepford Wives. Big rings, bracelets. I think we crop out their faces, as this is about the sort of women they are, not about them as individuals. Nails and toes done. They each hold a drink – probably some pinkies out – lemonade, wine, a short glass of coke...*

NO DIALOGUE

PANEL 3. *OTS Charlene to Crissy in the doorway. Little conspiratorial "just us girls" smile and wink from Mom as she departs.*

CRISSY: Oh, and if you need to touch up your legs, just use Daddy's razor.

CRISSY (linked): What he doesn't know can't hurt him.

PANEL 4. *Mom goes into living room, with committee. I want to see her past a hand or two holding drink glasses but I feel that's kinda samey with 3. Big smile.*

CRISSY: She'll be right down. Butterflies!

PANEL 5. *Mom picks up an empty glass*

MOM: Now, who wants some hors d'oeuvres?

PANEL 6. *Mom calls to a maid, presumably off panel. We see the faces of at least one of the committee, who looks up and past us (to Charlene coming down the stairs), and looks horrified. (If we see more than one of them, it's just ONE committee member who looks up).*

MOM: Maria!

SHOCKED COMMITTEE MEMBER (small): Oh my god.

3NM9

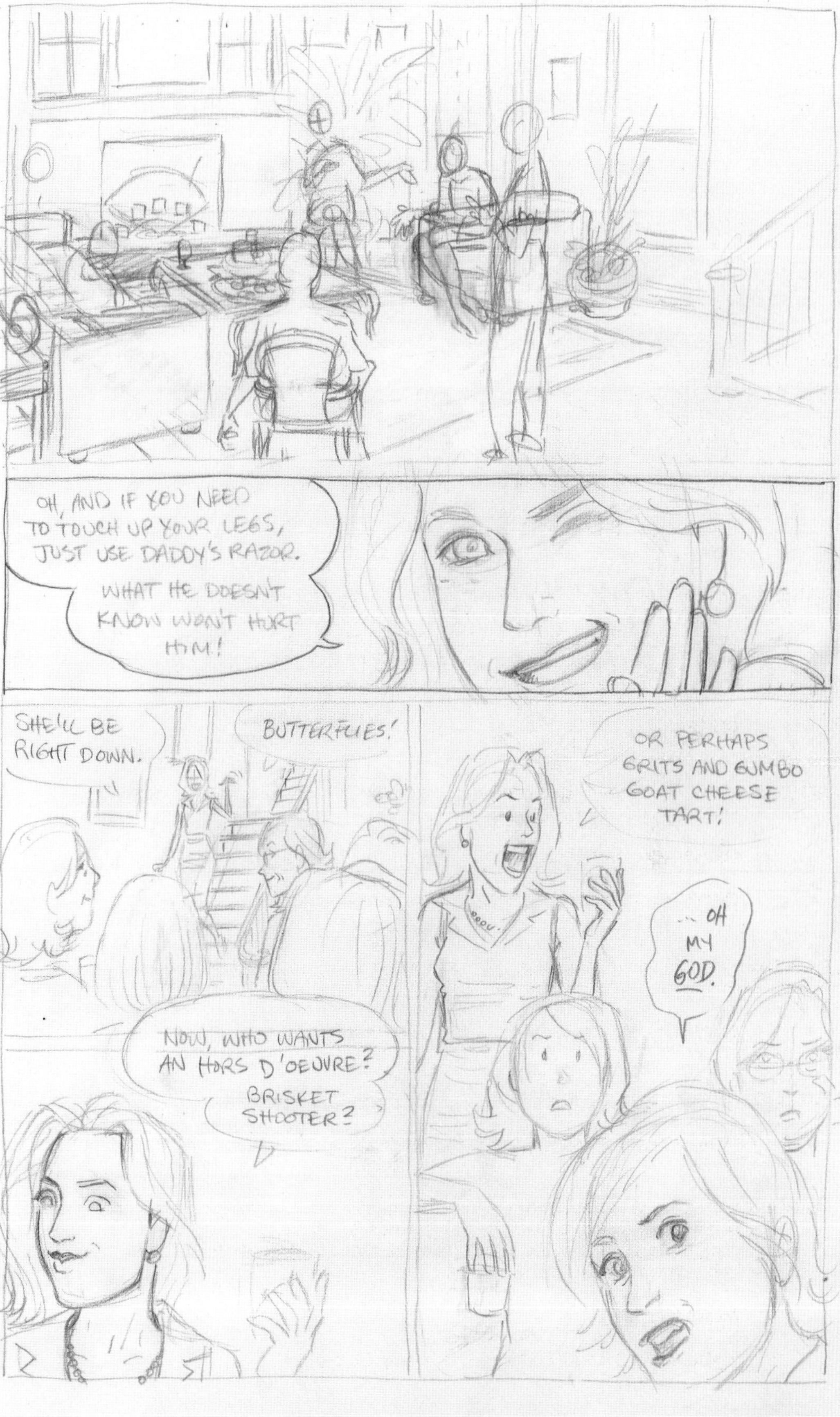

OH, AND IF YOU NEED TO TOUCH UP YOUR LEGS, JUST USE DADDY'S RAZOR.
WHAT HE DOESN'T KNOW WON'T HURT HIM!
SHE'LL BE RIGHT DOWN.
BUTTERFLIES!
NOW, WHO WANTS AN HORS D'OEUVRE?
BRISKET SHOOTER?
OR PERHAPS GRITS AND GUMBO GOAT CHEESE TART!
...OH MY GOD.

PAGE 4.
Splash.

Charlene coming down the steps in The Dress, which she has cut the sleeves off. Scars on forearms (some fresh). Her hair completely cut/shaved off but quickly and roughly, so scratched scalp and some tufts. Cold fury in her eyes. It's all a bit Leigh Bowery. She has lipstick scribbles all over her lips/face and written "Fuck you" in lipstick on the dress bodice.

CAPTION: This is how I first came to Mataguey.

CAPTION: I was almost sixteen.

WHO WANTS SOME HORS D'OEUVRES?

5 MOM CALLS TOWARD KITCHEN

MOM: MARIA!

6 COMMENTS ... MEMBER COOKS UP.

GAMBINO: OH MY GOD.

P 4

SPLASH. CHARLENE COMING DOWN THE STEPS IN THE DRESS. SCARS ON FOREARMS (SOME FRESH.) HER HAIR COMPLETELY CUT/SHAVED OFF, BUT QUICKLY + ROUGHLY, SO SCRATCHED SCALP + SOME TUFTS

COLD FURY IN HER EYES.

HAS SHE DRAWN W/ LIPSTICK ALL OVER HER FACE? "FUCK YOU" IN LIPSTICK ON DRESS?

CUT OFF SLEEVES OF DRESS TO SHOW SCARS?

CAPTION: THIS IS HOW I FIRST CAME TO MATAGUEY

I WAS ABOUT TO TURN 16, STARTING TENTH GRADE. ~~SOPHOMORE~~

LEIGH BOWERY

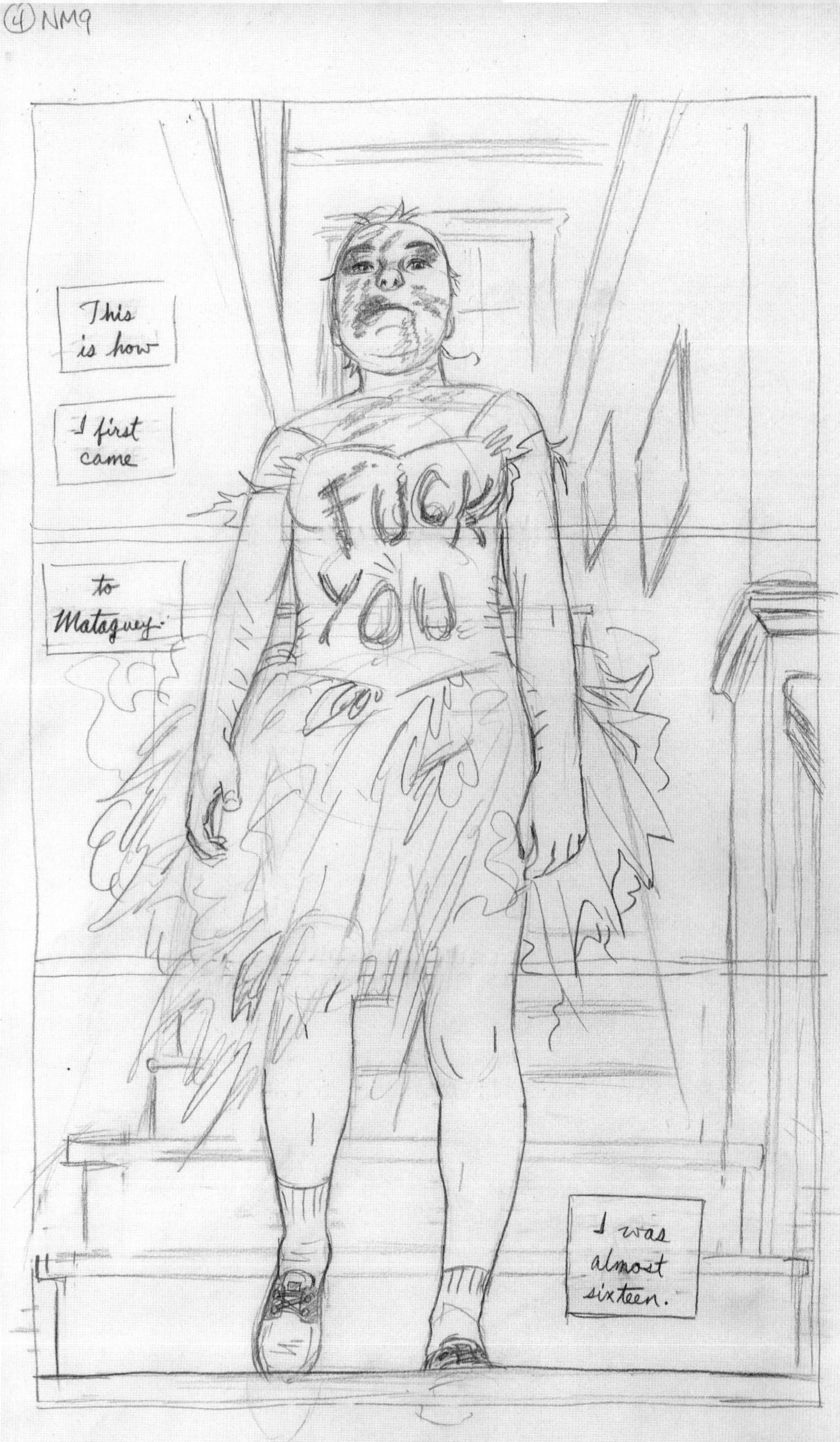

4 NM9
This is how
I first came
to Mataguey.
FUCK YOU
I was almost sixteen.

P5

1 ~~COLD LIGHT. CHARLENE PACKS~~

3AM CLOCK. (3) GREYHOUND PHX → SFO

(2) CHARLENE IN CLOTHES, IN BED

(4) CHARLENE SNEAKS DOWNSTAIRS IN DARK W/ BACKPACK

(6) (5) LIGHTS ON SUDDENLY. WHAT?

PAGE 5.
SEVEN PANELS

PANEL 1. *Night. Charlene's room. A clock reads 3am.*

NO DIALOGUE

PANEL 2. *Charlene in boys' clothes, sitting on her bed, her face illuminated by her phone. A packed backpack (full of clothes) is next to her. We need to see her phone and its case pretty clearly. The case has to be pretty memorable as we need to recognize it quickly and easily later, in somebody else's pocket. Maybe aqua blue with stars?*

S/FX: tip tip tap

PANEL 3. *Her phone screen. Shows a Greyhound e-ticket, PHX->SFO*

NO DIALOGUE

PANEL 4. *She looks out the window. Maybe seen from outside?*

CHARLENE (quietly): goodnight, moon

PANEL 5. *She picks up her backpack. I think face goes off panel at top as she is standing up.*

CHARLENE (quietly): goodnight, room.

PANEL 6. *She goes out the door.*

CHARLENE (quietly): goodnight, nothing.

PANEL 7. *She starts down the stairs. Dark house.*

NO DIALOGUE

⑤ NM9

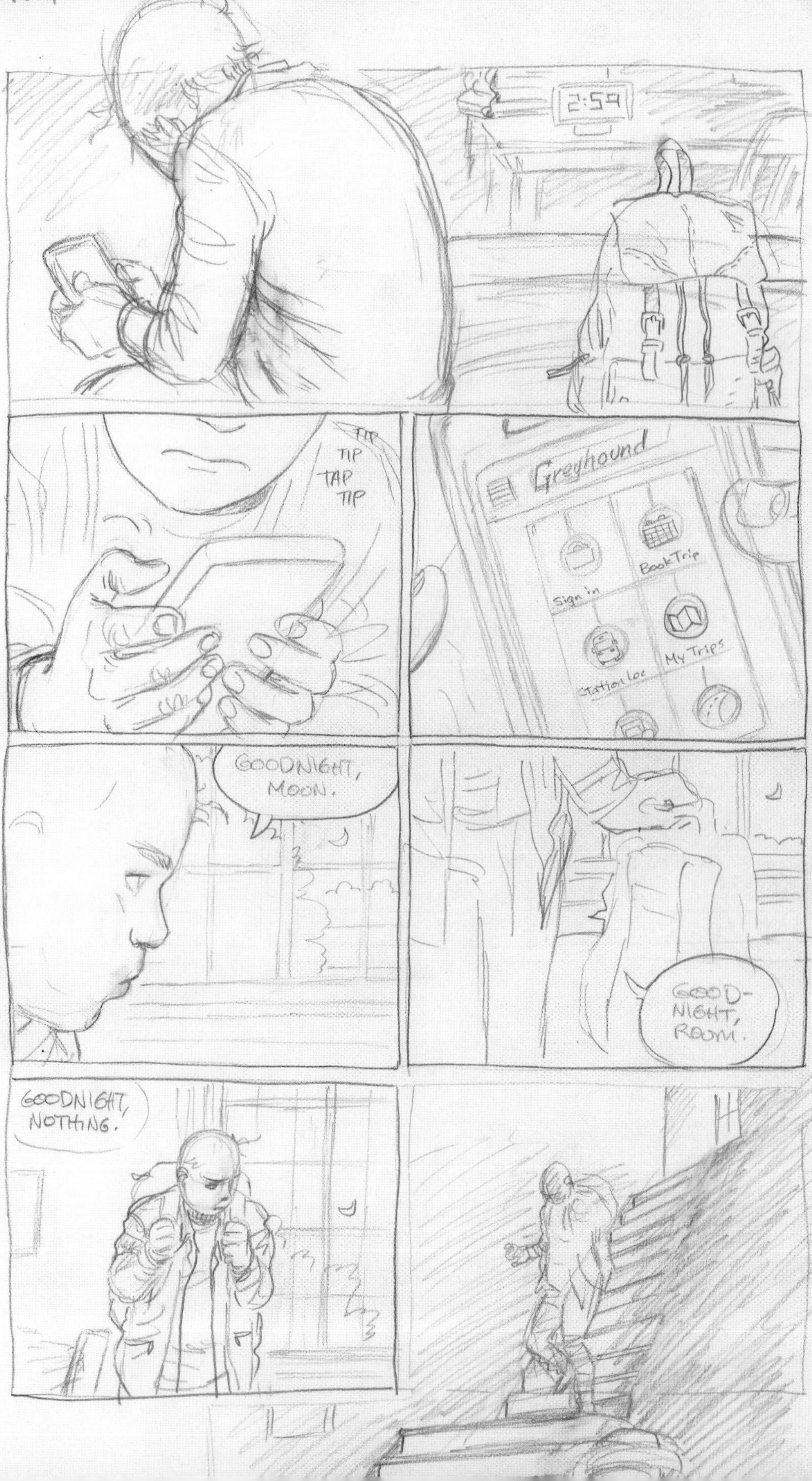
2:59
TIP
TIP
TAP
TIP
Greyhound
Sign in
Book Trip
Station loc
My Trips
GOODNIGHT, MOON.
GOOD-NIGHT, ROOM.
GOODNIGHT, NOTHING.

(6) (5) LIGHTS ON SUDDENLY. WHAT?

(6) OTS CHARLENE TO PARENTS. MOM? DAD? WHO ARE THESE PEOPLE?

2 BURLY GUYS, ONE WITH A THICK LEATHER BELT WRAPPED LOOSELY AROUND HIS HAND.

CHAD SMILING ON SOFA, ARMS FOLDED.

DAD: THESE MEN ARE TAKING YOU TO YOUR NEW SCHOOL, CHARLENE.

IT'S CALLED TRANQUILITY LODGE.

PAGE 6.
SIX PANELS

PANEL 1. *Same as Page 5 panel 7 but the lights are now BRIGHTLY on and Charlene's eyes are wide, like WHOA. Frozen. Maybe an arm up to block the light.*

NO DIALOGUE

PANEL 2. *OTS Charlene to her parents. Mom looks nervous, won't meet her eyes. Dad has arms folded. Behind them are two big guys and, in the background, Fred, the school head from Page 27. Chad is nearby, with Charlene's diary. One of the men has a thick leather strap (like a belt) wound around one hand or in one hand.*

CHARLENE: Mom? Dad?

PANEL 3. *Charlene, CU. Small. shocked.*

CHARLENE: Who are these people?

PANEL 4. *Chad with Charlene's diary. Mocks her, pretending to read from it.*

CHAD: I'm so sad, I don't want to be a debutante. I'm going to run awaaaay...

CHARLENE (off panel, shouts): GIVE ME THAT!

PANEL 5. *Over the hip of a tense Charlene (only part seen). Chrissy puts her hand on Chad to shut him up. Dad steps forwards, looks up.*

CHARLENE: Chad! Give it--

DAD (overlaps Charlene's balloon): These men are taking you to your new school, Charlene.

PANEL 6. *The men have a leather strap tight around Charlene's upper arms and chest, that one of them holds at her back. They are taking her out. She looks back at us, can't believe what is going on. The mom steps towards her. If the mom won't fit in this panel, we can put her dialogue in Panel 5.*

CHARLENE: Mom--

CRISSY: You'll like it, sweetie. There's a beach.

⑥NM9

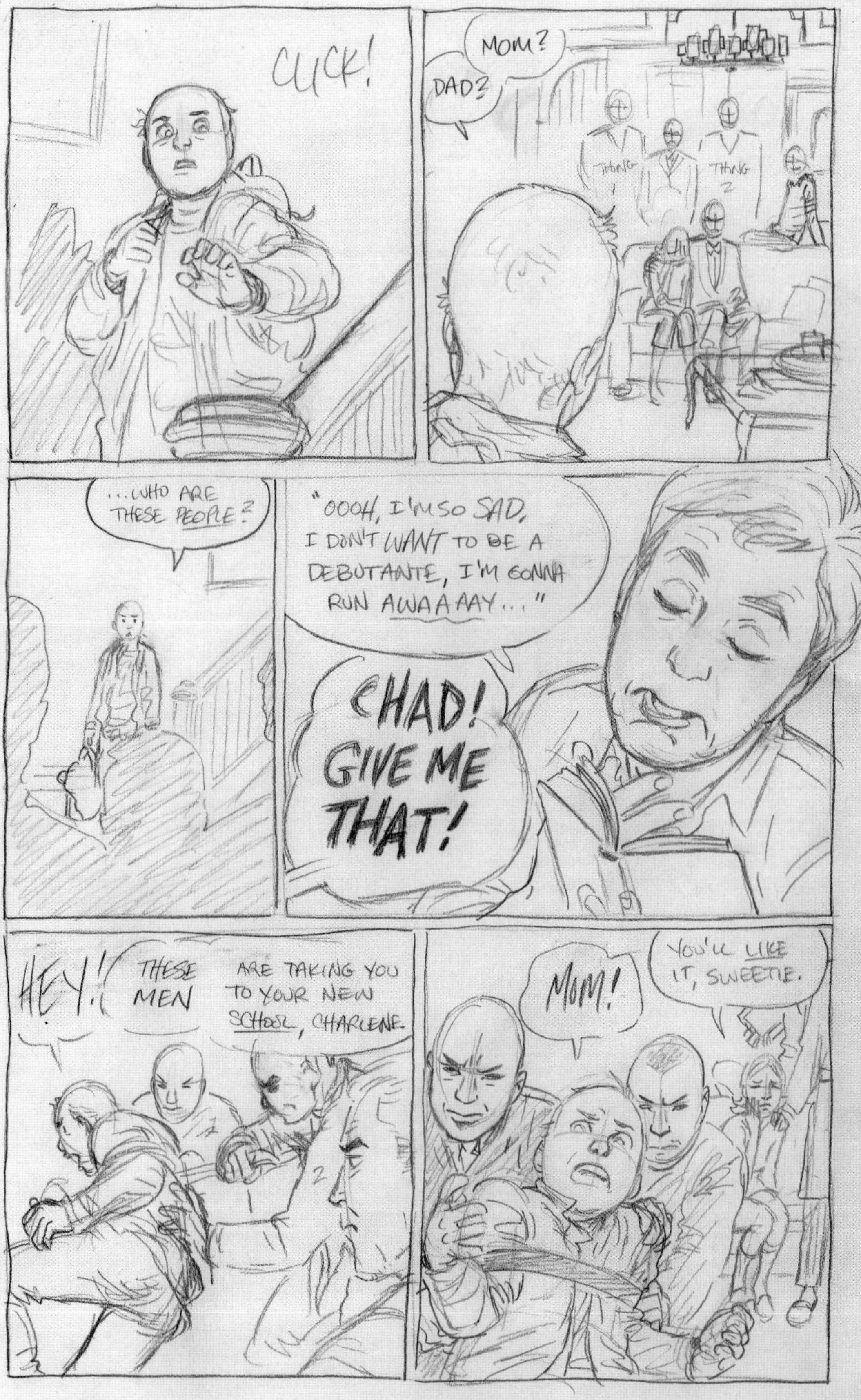
CLICK!
MOM?
DAD?
THING 1
THING 2
...WHO ARE THESE PEOPLE?
"OOOH, I'M SO SAD, I DON'T WANT TO BE A DEBUTANTE, I'M GONNA RUN AWAAAAY..."
CHAD! GIVE ME THAT!
HEY!
THESE MEN ARE TAKING YOU TO YOUR NEW SCHOOL, CHARLENE.
MOM!
YOU'LL LIKE IT, SWEETIE.

P7 Pn 1 2. LEVELS. ②(EXTERIOR of THE SCHOOL –
Low, CINDERBLOCK, UNATTRACTIVE. HIGH WALLS. GLI...
OF SEA BEYOND · CAR GOING INTO GATES– NOTHING
NEARBY.)

GIRLS UX
ALL SIZES / SHAPES.
...B in / (TATTOOS) or SCARS, LINED UP IN ...   UNIFORMS – or PRE-8...

PAGE 7.
SIX PANELS

PANEL 1. *Full width of page. Girls of all sizes and shapes, in the blue skirt/white blouse uniforms, lined up in profile, eyes down. They are outside, on cement, in front of a wall, and they are not wearing shoes.*

TITLE (overprint): 2. LEVELS

PANEL 2. *A car with Mataguey licence plates goes in the gates to the school. Low, cinderblock, unattractive. High walls. Glint of sea beyond but you clearly can't see the beach from the school, or indeed access it. Scrub; palms nearby.*

CAPTION: Twelve hours later, I arrived at Tranquility Lodge.

PANEL 3. *Charlene, in her new uniform, barefoot (we hit this next panel so can leave it out here). Looks lost, in a classroom doorway. None of the kids look at her. She doesn't have anything. Maybe a spiral-bound notebook. The classroom has windows along one side wall (important much later; we don't need to see them). The girls, all in uniform, look down at textbooks. Everything is old and doesn't match. Behind her is the guy from Page 27, aka the guy who runs the school. He has his hands on her shoulders.*

FRED: Everyone, I'd like you to meet Charlene.

CAPTION: By the way, that guy? That's Fred Mueller. He runs the school.

CAPTION: Remember him. He's important, later.

PANEL 4. *Charlene's bare feet. A couple of the higher level kids near her, sitting at their desks and not looking at her, have dirty white tennis shoes on. Maybe there is a bug or a lizard on the ground. Fred is leaving/has left.*

CAPTION: Not that it was really a school.

PANEL 5. *One girl nearby, LAKYNN, has her hand raised. Long dark hair. Wears shoes (upper level). Maybe even a necklace (a cheap bead thing).*

CAPTION: Like, a place where teachers taught math and English and stuff.

PANEL 6. *The "teacher". Looks over a trashy novel (Jackie Collins, "The Stud" or something).*

TEACHER: You.

CAPTION: It wasn't a jail either, because in jail you get a phone call and a lawyer.

(7) NM9

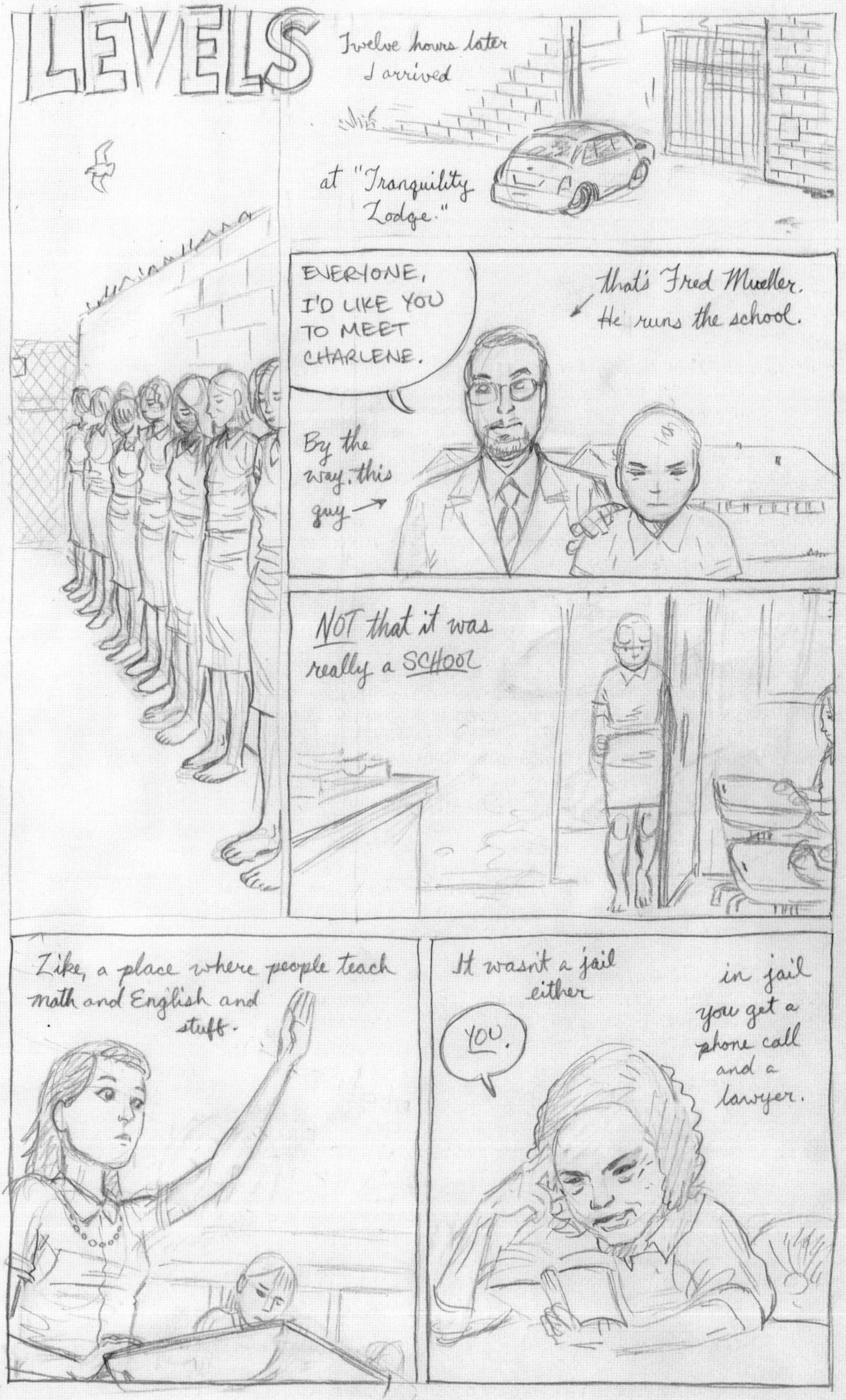
LEVELS
Twelve hours later I arrived
at "Tranquility Lodge."
EVERYONE, I'D LIKE YOU TO MEET CHARLENE.
That's Fred Mueller. He runs the school.
By the way, this guy
NOT that it was really a SCHOOL
Like, a place where people teach math and English and stuff.
It wasn't a jail either
YOU.
in jail you get a phone call and a lawyer.

P 6 COMES IN, UNIFORM. MEETS QUIZ, GETS MANUAL, FIRST SPEAKS W/O PERMISSION (FROM QUIZ)

7 GIRLS IN CLASS. EVERYONE LOOKS FWD. GIRL PEES HERSELF, C STABS. — DO CAMPAIGN 7 CHECK UPON JACKIE COLLINS NOVEL

MEETS PHOEBE COMING IN — 7?

PAGE 8.
SIX PANELS

PANEL 1. *Lakynn stands up, speaks to Charlene. Lakynns chair makes a noise as Past Charlene to Lakynn, who is Level 3 (she can wear shoes and jewellery). Maybe long straight dark hair? Lakynn is smiley but not massively energetic as everyone is doped to the gills on Haldol.*

LAKYNN: Hi, I'm Lakynn. Because it's your first day, I'm going to help you with the classroom rules.

LAYKNN (linked): You're Level 1, which is--

CHARLENE: Um, wait. How come you got to keep your shoes?

PANEL 2. *Lakynn shoots her hand up and looks forwards expectantly. Charlene looks at her, confused.*

TEACHER (off panel): Lakynn.

CAPTION: Tranquility Lodge did teach us one thing, though.

PANEL 3. *Lakynn smiles a little as she informs on Charlene. Charlene now furious.*

LAKYNN: New girl talking without permission!

CAPTION: It taught us to stab each other in the back.

PANEL 4. *Charlene is about to let fly at Lakynn, but stops herself.*

TEACHER (off panel): New girl, write a self-correction essay.

CAPTION: The difference between being treated like an animal and being treated like a human was how much you informed on the other girls.

PANEL 5. *Instead she raises her hand.*

TEACHER: Yes.

CAPTION: If you didn't inform, that made you an accessory, and you lost levels.

PANEL 6. *Charlene looks at Lakynn. Lakynn looks forwards.*

CHARLENE: What the hell--

LAKYNN: Don't look at me. You're not allowed.

LAKYNN (linked): I'll report you for that, too.

CAPTION: So everyone informed.

(8) NM9

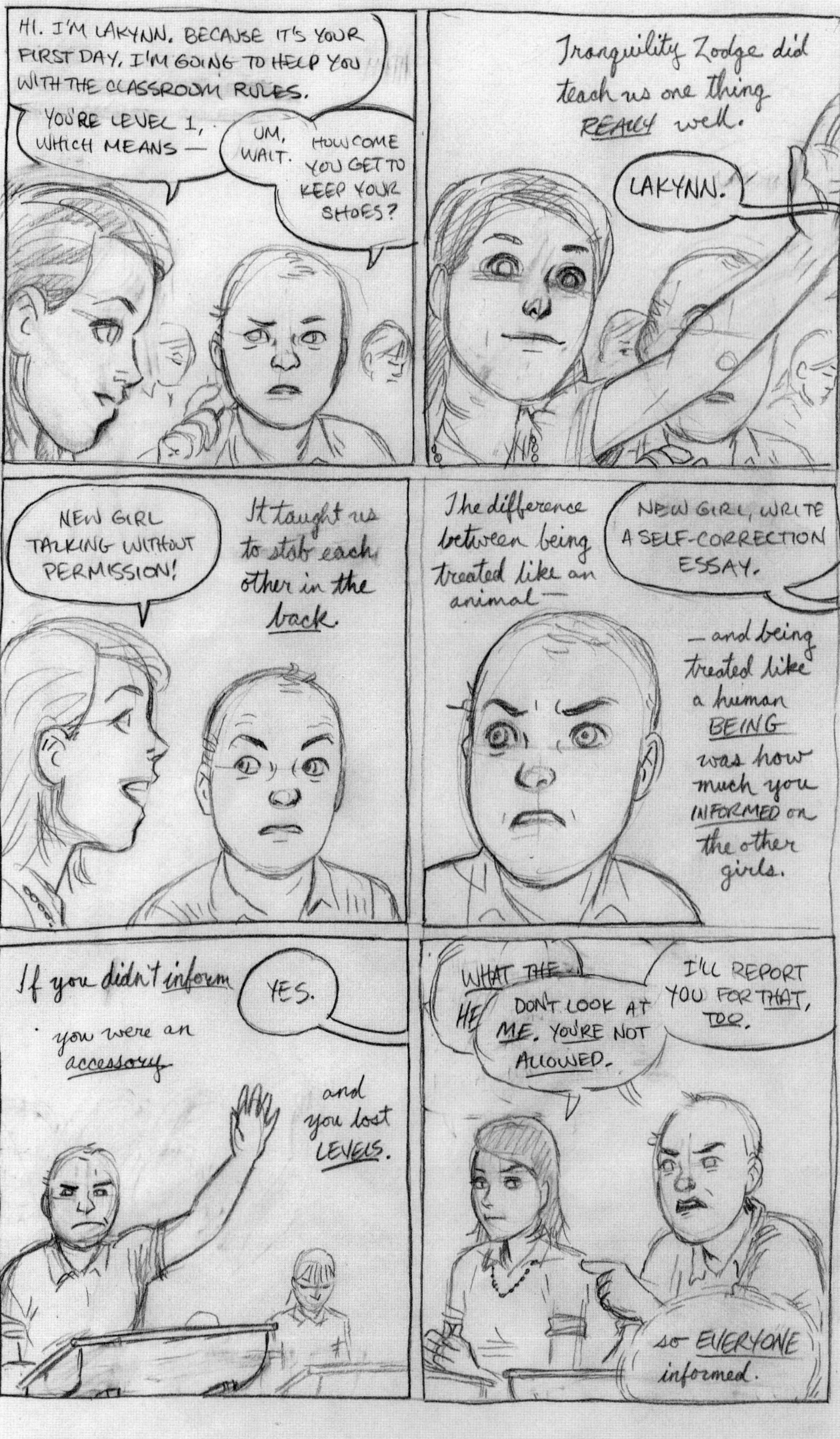

HI. I'M LAKYNN. BECAUSE IT'S YOUR FIRST DAY, I'M GOING TO HELP YOU WITH THE CLASSROOM RULES.
YOU'RE LEVEL 1, WHICH MEANS —
UM, WAIT.
HOW COME YOU GET TO KEEP YOUR SHOES?
Tranquility Lodge did teach us one thing REALLY well.
LAKYNN.
NEW GIRL TALKING WITHOUT PERMISSION!
It taught us to stab each other in the back.
The difference between being treated like an animal—
NEW GIRL, WRITE A SELF-CORRECTION ESSAY.
—and being treated like a human BEING was how much you INFORMED on the other girls.
If you didn't inform
you were an accessory
YES.
and you lost LEVELS.
WHAT THE
DON'T LOOK AT ME. YOU'RE NOT ALLOWED.
I'LL REPORT YOU FOR THAT, TOO.
so EVERYONE informed.

FAILS IS USED — PHOEBE IS SO NEEDY

REWARDS US FOR INFORMING ON EACH OTHER
DIDN'T ALLOW US TO TALK TO EACH OTHER

CHARLENE NARRATES

THE FORCE OF INFORMING ON OTHER KIDS WAS
THE DIFFERENCE BETWEEN BEING TREATED LIKE AN ANIMAL TO BEING TREATED LIKE A HUMAN.

SO EVERYONE INFORMED

DIDN'T YOU WERE AN ACCESSORY

PAGE 9.
FIVE PANELS

PANEL 1. *Phoebe in a plain wood chair. This is in a Group Therapy session. Kind of a high angle view. Maybe we see shoulders of other girls on either side. Now, a word about Phoebe. She is HOT, and a mess. Pale, slightly sallow skin; thin; pale hair almost the same hue as her skin. Hair is long, and there's a lot of it (but it's quite fine). Brown or hazel eyes. Mouth like a bruised plum. Phoebe is an addict, and will do anything for drugs. She's one of those girls that is a mix of sexy and ultra-fragile and damaged that people can become obsessed with.*

CAPTION: Everyone except Phoebe.

PANEL 2. *A teacher/therapist, in a wooden chair. The group is about 8-10 girls and the therapist. Plain room, looks like a cellar, and circle of wooden chairs.*

THERAPIST: Charlene, would you like to share with Group today why you're here?

CAPTION: Phoebe was in my dorm, which was called a "family".

CAPTION: Honor Family.

CAPTION: IKR?

PANEL 3. *Charlene looks a bit dead in the eyes, as does everyone else really. Looks down.*

CHARLENE: Um.

THERAPIST (off panel): Stand up.

PANEL 4. *Big. Rest of page. Charlene stands, talks. Maybe this is from behind Charlene, like she is in silhouette, and we see everyone else in Group silently not looking at her (they're looking ahead/down), except Phoebe.*

CHARLENE: Hi. Yeah. Um.

CHARLENE (linked: {huuh}

CHARLENE (linked): I'm a boy. I'm male. I can't tell my parents that because they're really into Jesus. And, uh, I finally decided to run away and they caught me. That's why I'm here.

PANEL 5. *Inset into 4 at bottom right? Charlene, looking down.*

CHARLENE (quietly): I'm here because it's easier than talking about me.

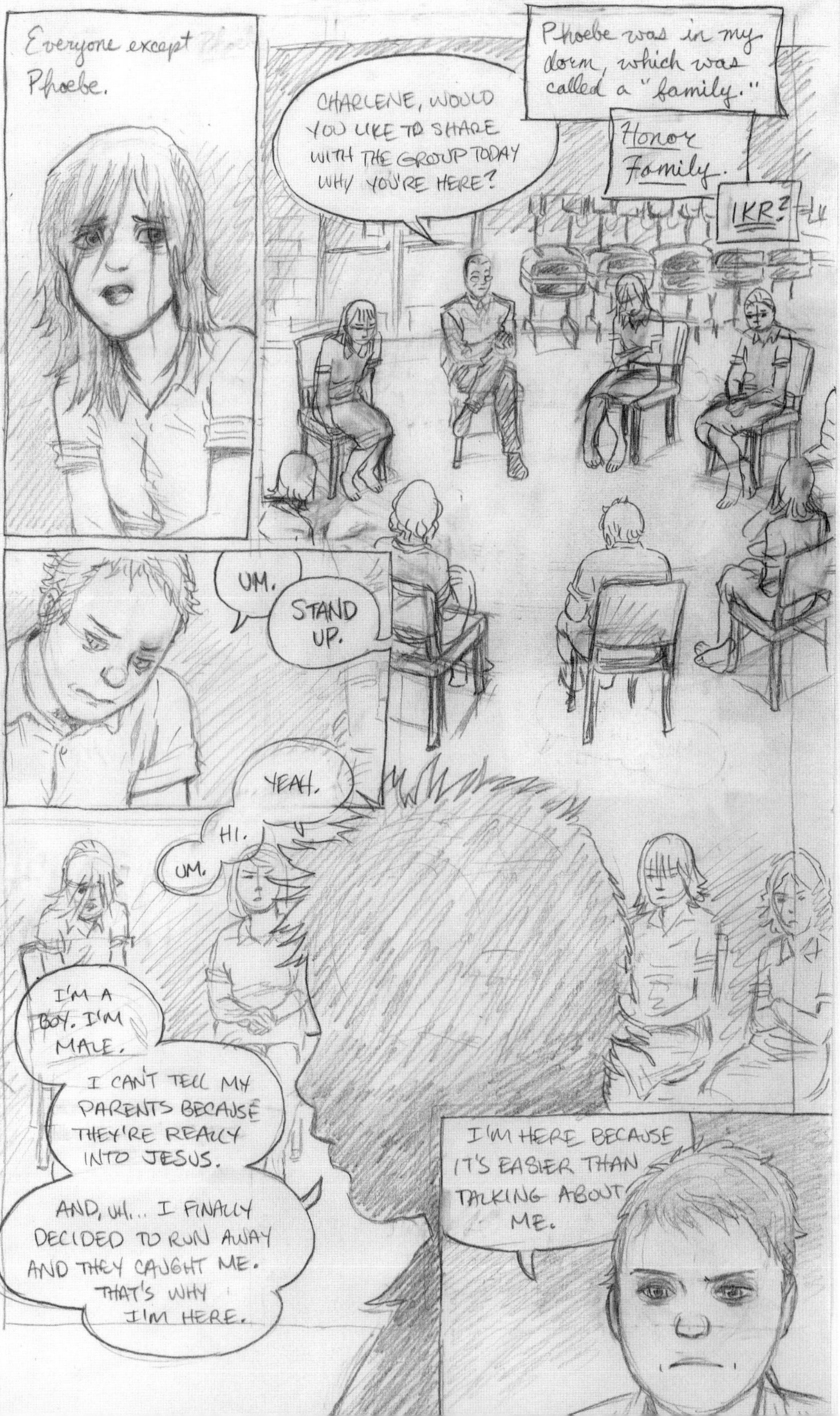
Everyone except Phoebe.
CHARLENE, WOULD YOU LIKE TO SHARE WITH THE GROUP TODAY WHY YOU'RE HERE?
Phoebe was in my dorm, which was called a "family."
Honor Family.
IKR?
UM.
STAND UP.
YEAH.
HI.
UM.
I'M A BOY. I'M MALE.
I CAN'T TELL MY PARENTS BECAUSE THEY'RE REALLY INTO JESUS.
AND, UH... I FINALLY DECIDED TO RUN AWAY AND THEY CAUGHT ME. THAT'S WHY I'M HERE.
I'M HERE BECAUSE IT'S EASIER THAN TALKING ABOUT ME.

PANEL 1. *Lots of hands in the air. (Not Phoebe's, tho)*

NO DIALOGUE

PANEL 2. *Part of the rest of the group. Phoebe is in it. Phoebe just sits there, maybe gives the tiniest thumbs-up or little smile. She looks a bit dreamy. All the other girls have their faces contorted in hate, even if it's fake hate. Phoebe is the only one who doesn't say anything.*

GIRL 1. Liar! She told me another story earlier!

GIRL 2. She made all this up! She just wants sympathy!

GIRL 3: Bullshit!

GIRL 4 (making air quotes with her fingers): Her so-called "problem" is that she's a fat ugly ho

GIRL 5: Faker!

PANEL 3. *Charlene's face, shocked. Maybe tears starting.*

THERAPIST (off panel): Charlene, I want you to write a 5,000 word essay on why you felt the need to lie to your group. Honor Family is your family now.

PANEL 4. *Therapist. Smile. Small.*

THERAPIST: We're here to make you better. And we can't accept your defiant attitude.

THERAPIST (linked): You are a girl. Look at you.

PANEL 5. *Therapist looks to the side. Also small.*

THERAPIST: Who's next?

THERAPIST (linked): How about the other new girl? Phoebe, isn't it?

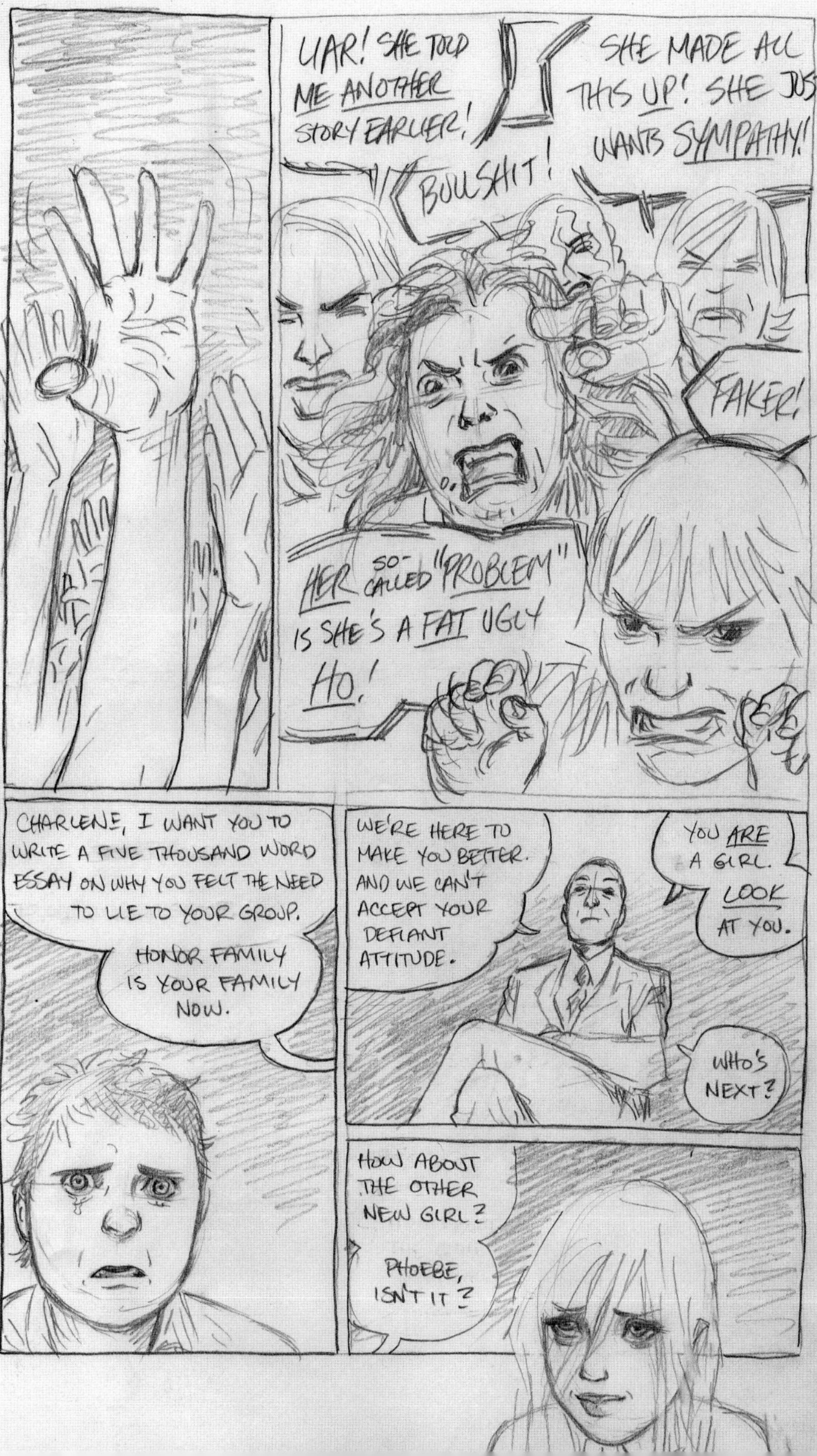
LIAR! SHE TOLD ME ANOTHER STORY EARLIER!
SHE MADE ALL THIS UP! SHE JUST WANTS SYMPATHY!
BULLSHIT!
FAKER!
HER SO-CALLED "PROBLEM" IS SHE'S A FAT UGLY HO!
CHARLENE, I WANT YOU TO WRITE A FIVE THOUSAND WORD ESSAY ON WHY YOU FELT THE NEED TO LIE TO YOUR GROUP.
HONOR FAMILY IS YOUR FAMILY NOW.
WE'RE HERE TO MAKE YOU BETTER. AND WE CAN'T ACCEPT YOUR DEFIANT ATTITUDE.
YOU ARE A GIRL. LOOK AT YOU.
WHO'S NEXT?
HOW ABOUT THE OTHER NEW GIRL?
PHOEBE, ISN'T IT?

PANEL 1. *Phoebe is standing, looking kind of up to a corner, and twirling her hair. If we can see Charlene, she is red faced, shaking, closed in on herself. Everyone else looking down.*

PHOEBE: My dad and my mom are divorced, and I was living with my mom and she got married again? And he was really creepy and kept putting his hands on me and so I ran away to live with my dad.

PANEL 2. *Phoebe, profile, looking down. There are some spots on her arms that might be old track marks, or might be mosquito bites. Maybe Charlene in bg, looking at her.*

PHOEBE: My dad has PTSD and a lot of pain and so they prescribed him Oxy, like a barrel of it, and I started sneaking pills.

PANEL 3. *Phoebe. Mostly her lips, in profile. Still very sombre.*

PHOEBE: Whoever said that drugs aren't any good is a liar.

PHOEBE (linked): Drugs are great.

PANEL 4. *She smiles. A really lovely smile.*

PHOEBE: They turned everything off. Oh my god.

PHOEBE (linked): Nothing mattered any more. Nothing hurt. Drugs are awesome.

PANEL 5. *Lots of headspace. She hugs herself. Small girl. Sorry bout all the bla-bla.*

PHOEBE: Dad caught me stealing his pills and we argued so I ran off with my boyfriend for a few days. Kurt said he had better stuff so I snorted some heroin with him. He was right. It was way better than Oxys.

PHOEBE (linked): I went home to get some more clothes and Dad had killed himself. I was the one who found him.

PANEL 6. *Very quiet Phoebe. Almost whispering. Tucking her hair behind an ear?*

PHOEBE: It was OK, though. I was high.

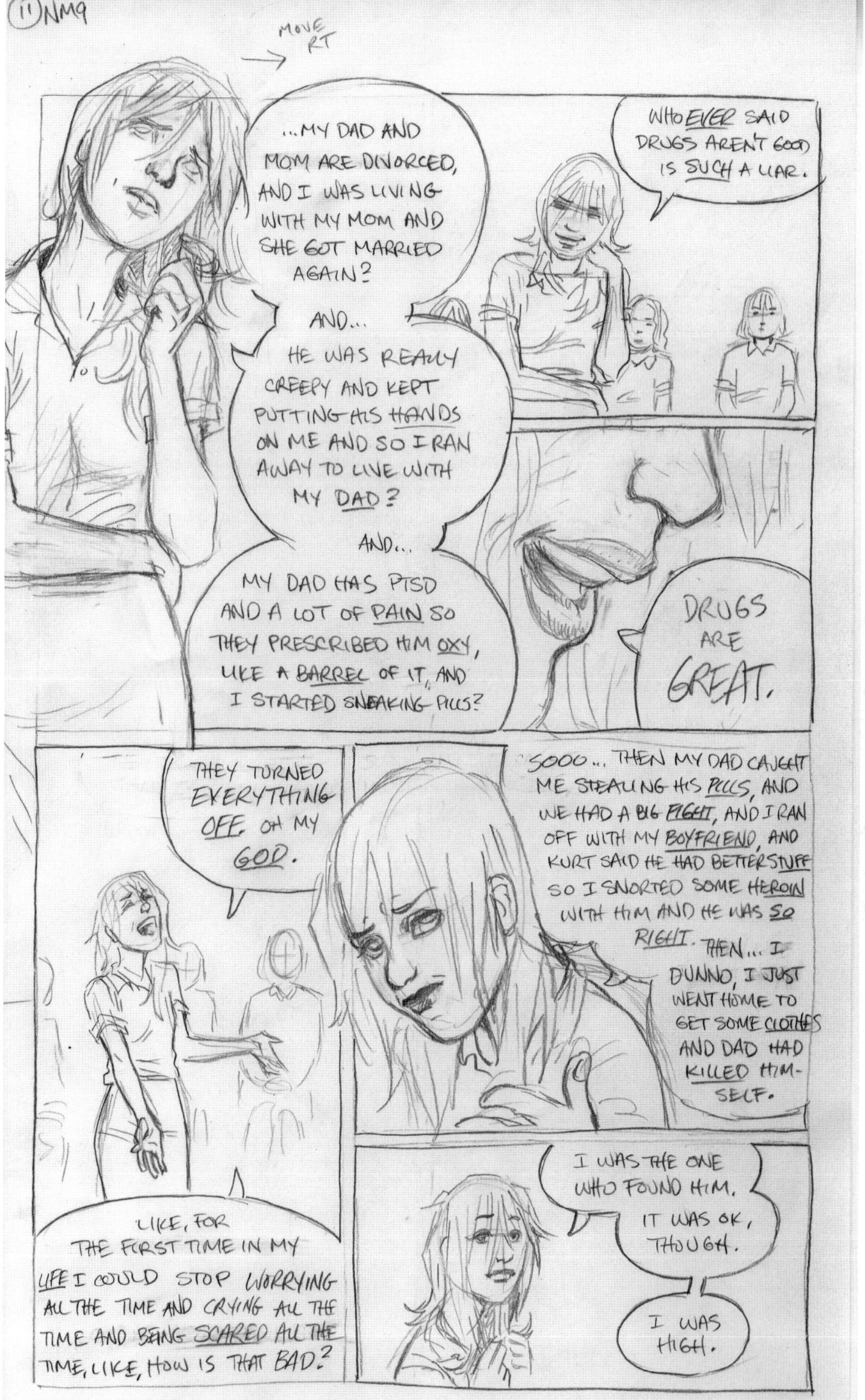

11 NM9
MOVE RT
...MY DAD AND MOM ARE DIVORCED, AND I WAS LIVING WITH MY MOM AND SHE GOT MARRIED AGAIN?
AND...
HE WAS REALLY CREEPY AND KEPT PUTTING HIS HANDS ON ME AND SO I RAN AWAY TO LIVE WITH MY DAD?
AND...
MY DAD HAS PTSD AND A LOT OF PAIN SO THEY PRESCRIBED HIM OXY, LIKE A BARREL OF IT, AND I STARTED SNEAKING PILLS?
WHO EVER SAID DRUGS AREN'T GOOD IS SUCH A LIAR.
DRUGS ARE GREAT.
THEY TURNED EVERYTHING OFF. OH MY GOD.
LIKE, FOR THE FIRST TIME IN MY LIFE I COULD STOP WORRYING ALL THE TIME AND CRYING ALL THE TIME AND BEING SCARED ALL THE TIME, LIKE, HOW IS THAT BAD?
SOOO... THEN MY DAD CAUGHT ME STEALING HIS PILLS, AND WE HAD A BIG FIGHT, AND I RAN OFF WITH MY BOYFRIEND, AND KURT SAID HE HAD BETTER STUFF SO I SNORTED SOME HEROIN WITH HIM AND HE WAS SO RIGHT. THEN... I DUNNO, I JUST WENT HOME TO GET SOME CLOTHES AND DAD HAD KILLED HIMSELF.
I WAS THE ONE WHO FOUND HIM.
IT WAS OK, THOUGH.
I WAS HIGH.

FIVE PANELS

PANEL 1. *Night. Charlene on the top bunk of a bunk bed. No windows in the bedrooms. The bunk beds are super cheap. She's not asleep. Lots of cement, hard surfaces. She's still in her clothes (they don't really get sleeping clothes). The bunks should be labelled on the edge (not at the headboard, the outer edge/ side): CHARLENE and below, PHOEBE. Probably something simple like a 3x5 card tacked into the wood. I may do all the off panel SFX in gutters, because that would be nice and tidy and conceptual.*

    S/FX (off panel): SLAM

PANEL 2. *Charlene looks worried. If we see other girls, nobody is reacting. Everyone pretends to be asleep. (We don't need to see other girls.)*

    S/FX (off panel): Aaah!

    S/FX (off panel): {sob}

PANEL 3. *Charlene puts the pillow over her head to block sound. Off panel, a hand comes in and touches her arm. (it's Phoebe's hand).*

    S/FX (off panel): AAAAAH

    PHOEBE (off panel): psst

PANEL 4. *Phoebe climbs into Charlene's bed, quietly.*

    S/FX (off panel): thump

PANEL 5. *Important, so a bit bigger. Phoebe and Charlene curl up against each other. Phoebe is always Little Spoon.*

    PHOEBE (whispers): hold me

    S/FX (off panel): AAAAAAH

(handwritten annotations)

16.

17. OP RADIO. ALL DAY. INTO NIGHT. JESS GRIFFITH + JUANCITO CHECKING OUT HONOR FAMILY... + PHOEBE

19. WOS TO GET OUT. RUNS IN ... PHOEBE NOT IN BED. RUNS OUT

FIGHT WITH ONE OF THE PROCOPTS? OUTSIDE? THE ONE WHO BROUGHT HER IN

20. KICKS DOOR OPEN

PHOEBE IN GRIFFITH'S LAP. JUANCITO

21. SHOCK FACES OF C + HONOR + EVERY ONE ELSE

RUN.

22. SPY SPY SPY SPY

NO SCREAM / THEY HADN'T HER... TAKEN 3H0 GONO

23. O.P. AGAIN. GIRLS IN CLASS STARING FORWARDS. WHISPER

FALL FROM SKY

FALLING PAST WINDOW. THEM

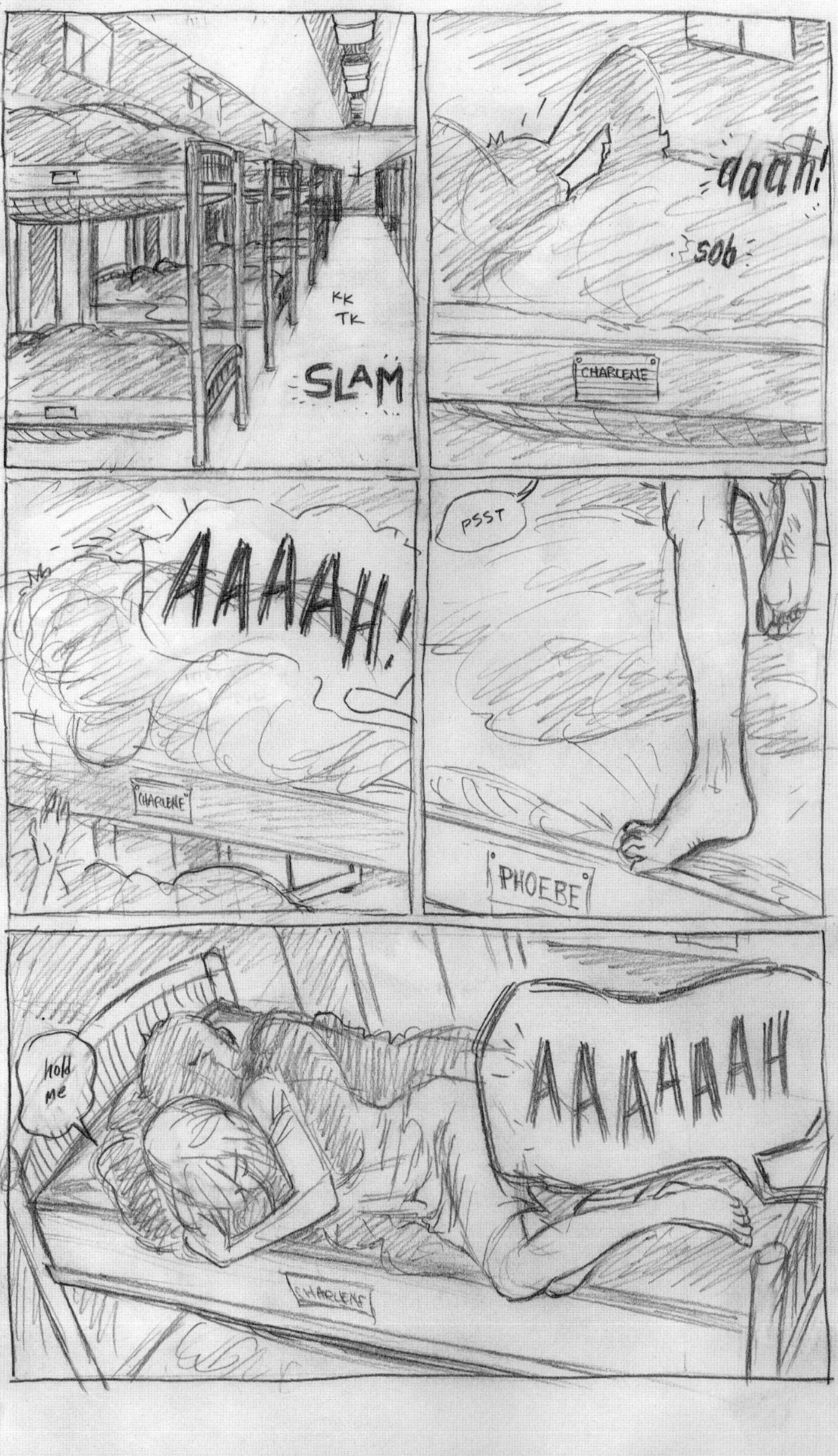
KK
TK
SLAM
aaah!
sob
CHARLENE
AAAAH!
CHARLENE
PSST
PHOEBE
hold me
AAAAAAH
CHARLENE

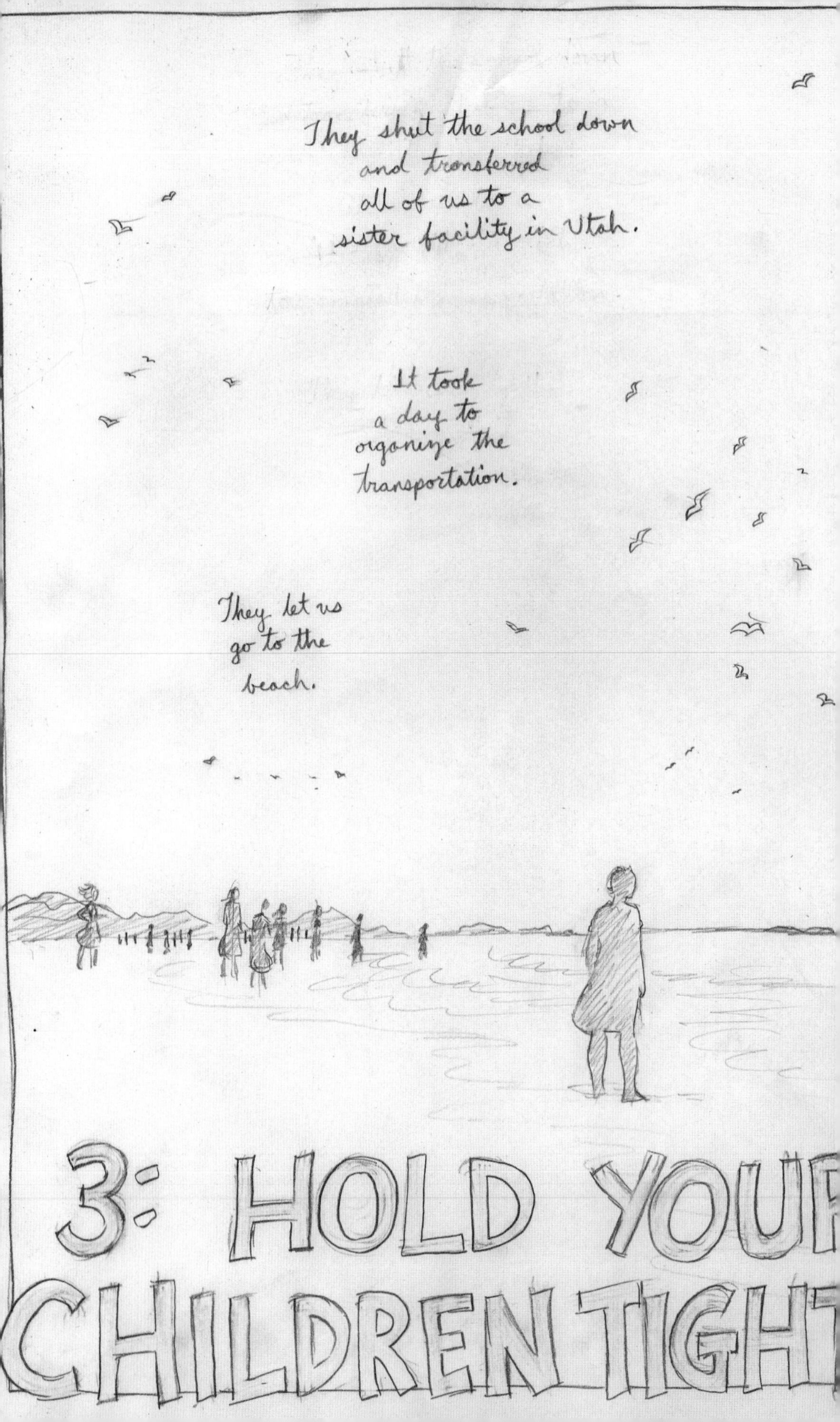
They shut the school down and transferred all of us to a sister facility in Utah.
It took a day to organize the transportation.
They let us go to the beach.
3: HOLD YOUR CHILDREN TIGHT